A Liverpool Song

Ruth Hamilton is the bestselling author of twenty-
six novels, including *Mulligan's Yard*, *The Judge's
Daughter*, *The Reading Room*, *Mersey View*, *That
Liverpool Girl* and *Lights of Liverpool*. She has
become one of the north-west of England's most
popular writers. She was born in Bolton, which is the
setting for many of her novels, and has spent most
of her life in Lancashire. She now lives in Liverpool.

Also by Ruth Hamilton

Ruth Hamilton

A Liverpool Song

PAN BOOKS

First published 2013 by Macmillan

This edition published 2013 by Pan Books
an imprint of Pan Macmillan, a division of Macmillan Publishers Limited
Pan Macmillan, 20 New Wharf Road, London N1 9RR
Basingstoke and Oxford
Associated companies throughout the world
www.panmacmillan.com

ISBN 978-1-4472-0947-8

Typeset by SetSystems Ltd, Saffron Walden, Essex
Printed and bound by CPI Group (UK) Ltd, Croydon, CR0 4YY

Visit **www.panmacmillan.com** to read more about all our books
and to buy them. You will also find features, author interviews and
news of any author events, and you can sign up for e-newsletters
so that you're always first to hear about our new releases.

This work is for two very important people for whom I hold great respect, though I seldom express it.

Diane Pearson, who discovered me (probably while digging for Roman ruins) and taught me how to edit in the good, old-fashioned way. Her input was beyond value.

Wayne Brookes of Pan Macmillan is the one who opened my wings and encouraged me to fly. I am privileged to be on the list of this multi-talented, caring and hilarious man.

Without these good friends and their publishing houses, I'd be living on disability allowance. I send both my love and boundless gratitude.

ACKNOWLEDGEMENTS

My family, God bless them. With me as mother and grand-mother, they need all the help they can get.

Billy and Gill, my stalwarts.

Carol Smith, once my agent, now a good friend and author who loves my poetry – she's biased.

Dorothy Ramsden. researcher, always supportive and ready to listen and to help.

Brendan Doherty, who should be published.

The readership – I thank you all.

I must mention my animals, since so many ask about them. Treacle (chocolate Lab) is as good as gold. Blazer (half yellow Lab and half red mastiff de Bordeaux, ie Hooch) no discernible improvements. I refused to suffer alone, so the main character in *A Liverpool Song* is endowed with Blazer's double, named Storm. Oscar, ring-necked parakeet, no comment – I can't think till he shuts up.

Ruthie

One

A ragged formation of swallows meandered in a very loose, ill-regimented fashion across the sky. Drifting from U to V to W, they looked rather like a company of soldiers who had taken the command 'at ease' rather too literally. Perhaps they'd forgotten their alphabet? Or was this yet another symptom of a world gone mad?

Andrew Sanderson continued to stare upward and decided that the birds were in two minds; climate change possibly meant that they could go or stay with impunity. 'Very much like my own situation,' he told the dashboard. 'And I went. I chose to go because the atmosphere no longer suited me. In fact, it suits very few these days.' He was supposed to feel free; he felt numb.

According to militants, the NHS was going to the dogs. Well, it could get there without any further help or argument from him. There was talk of young doctors working to rule, of mass exodus abroad, even of walkouts. Whatever was needed in order to crease the stuffed shirts in Westminster must be contrived by fitter, abler men. Andrew's time was over.

But would he understand a life without work? He removed the key from the ignition and dropped it in a pocket. 'I've got nothing to do, nowhere to go, won't someone listen to my tale of woe?' he sang in a steady baritone. 'Oh, stop feeling sorry for yourself for goodness' sake, Sanderson. You couldn't take the heat, so you walked out of the kitchen. Walk out of the kitchen, and you get no custard with your pudding. In fact, you probably don't even get the pudding, and to hell with cheese and biscuits.'

Perhaps this was the end; perhaps he would follow a path already worn flat by the passage of many who had retired, only to die within months. Did he care, did it matter? It had to matter, had to be made to matter, because there needed to be a pattern. Without a template, what remained of life could well become a total void. What might Mary have said? Oh, he knew the answer to that one, right enough. His career had taken his mind off the grief, and she would not have approved of the grieving. Her voice echoed in the chambers of his mind. *'Straighten your face, Sanderson; it takes few muscles to smile, and many to frown. You'll get wrinkled. I don't want a wrinkled husband.'*

The swallows continued to hang about, regrouping, shifting round on a skittish wind that had suddenly leapt off the Mersey. Should the half-hearted battle for leadership heat up, stragglers at the back would fail and fall. Or they might be pushed, murdered by fellows determined to press on. For a migrating bird, retirement meant death. For Andrew Sanderson, orthopaedic surgeon, it meant a gold watch, a top-of-the-range laptop computer, an OBE and uncertainty. He stared hard at the building in front of him. This house had always been big, but today it looked enormous. 'Andrew Sanderson, this is your life. So bloody well get on with it.' Without Mary, Rosewood was not a home. It was just a place where he slept and ate, where he pretended to be alive.

Twelve red roses lay on the passenger seat. At this time of year, the long-stemmed began to cost an arm and a leg ... An arm and a leg. How many limbs had he amputated in the past thirty-odd years? The children had always been the worst, yet how well most adjusted to prosthetics. Adults, on the other hand . . .

On the other hand. That poor man a few years ago, both hands severed by unguarded machinery. Andrew and a multi-disciplinary team had saved what they could, and a big toe now imitated a thumb, but adjustment? Not easy, never easy. Now came his turn to reshape his life, to learn to walk without the crutch provided by a career. Oh, there was ample money, so that wasn't the problem. Always, he'd had a timetable, a reason to go on. But the clocks wouldn't stop, and the hours they marked had to be filled somehow.

The powers had begged him to reconsider, but he'd had enough. It was as simple as that. Qualified medical and care staff were heavily outnumbered by pen-pushers – well, keyboard-clickers – while cleaning contractors had no idea when it came to thoroughness. He was well rid of all that palaver. Every week, every day, a fight for theatre space, a battle against new and stronger bacteria, germs carried home by visitors and by discharged patients to spread their malice on public transport, in houses, churches, shops. It had all become infuriating.

Elective surgeries put back and back while emergencies got rushed through. It simply didn't make sense any more. Too few doctors, too few nurses, too many administrators. Too few hospitals, theatres, theatre staff. Yes, it was as well to be away from all that. Spreadsheets, pounds and pence mattered these days; patients were just units, items on a rolling belt like those used in Sainsbury's. Five pounds of spuds, click, a dozen eggs, free range, click, a greenstick fracture, click . . .

Yet the future yawned before him, and he had no idea what to do with it. Crown green bowling, fishing, card games in the pub? Should he take up clay pigeon shooting, deer stalking, ballroom dancing? No, not his scene. His scene? Did he have one? There was surgery, there was music, there was furniture. He owned an antiquated Silver Ghost and another couple of vintage cars with which he tinkered from time to time. Voluntary labour was not his idea of fulfilment. There was work, there were hobbies, and between work and hobby stretched a chasm the size of the Grand Canyon.

Dad's voice echoed down the years. *'You'll be a gradely carpenter, son. Aye, you will that. You've got my hands.'* Oh yes. At twelve years of age and without the usual guidance of his father, Andrew had built a bookcase. After that first item, he had never looked back. The only difference was that Joseph Sanderson, now ninety-three and in a nursing home, had worked with wood. His son had specialized eventually in the treatment of human bone, and the tools had been remarkably similar.

The two areas of labour had melded one with the other after Joseph's hip replacement, and the worn bone now formed the handle of a walking stick. That bizarre item meant a great deal for both men, as it represented two lengthy and successful careers. Andrew smiled, remembering his truculent father under the influence of a drug meant to calm him before theatre. 'I want me bone back,' he had yelled at a poor nurse. 'It's mine.' Nick-nack, paddy-whack, give a dog a bone, that old man came rolling home. Dad was a character, a lovable rogue who, like fine wine, had improved with age.

'Have I done the right thing?' Andrew asked himself now. There was his other qualification, of course. Proficiency at the piano had gained him many years ago an offer of a place at the Royal School of Music, and although he had never trained as a teacher, he could now take individual pupils. Everyone knew him from recitals in

4

Liverpool, so he was respected. Music, then? Or music and classic cars?

Oh, well. Whatever, as the kids said these days. He was sixty, he was slower, he was no longer the best in his field. But one thing was certain – he would not be leaving Liverpool. This city had served him well, while he, in his turn, had given his best years to the hospitals in which he had worked. Liverpool had also introduced him to Mary, and Mary would stay in this place forever. *Why did you take her, God? Why not some damned fool instead, someone with no contribution to make? When I think of all she did, all she might have done. Don't think. Stop thinking...*

He picked up the bouquet and opened the car door. Oh no. Madam Bossy was still here, and she'd seen him. There she stood at the drawing-room window, arms akimbo, yellow duster in one hand, face like a bad knee. She'd probably watched him talking and singing to himself. The urge to drive away was strong, but it was too late. While the woman at the window was his employee, he often felt that the upper hand would always be hers.

Eva Dawson, housekeeper, cook, cleaner and general dogsbody in the house known as Rosewood, shook her head in despair. Here he came, the bloody lunatic. A patient dies of a deep vein something or other that shifts during surgery, and in his own mind it's this fellow's fault. The anaesthetist, who might have kept a closer eye on things, was carrying on regardless, but soft lad here had thrown a strop and handed in his notice. He was dafter than three Siamese cats trapped in a pillowcase. Brains? If this man was clever, God blessed those at the back who played with Plasticine, because brains seemed to restrict other areas of growth. When it came to living life to the full, Andrew Sanderson had no idea.

He entered the drawing room. 'Don't start, Eva, please,'

he said by way of greeting. This was the last day of life as both had known it. Fortunately, the house was large, but was anywhere big enough to contain the pair of them? They were both stubborn, both direct when prodded towards argument. And they had both loved Mary.

'Me?' Her eyes widened. 'I never said a bleeding word, did I? Look at the cut of you, though. Nice-looking feller, still in his prime, all that bloody learning and experience, so you go and retire at sixty. Years of wear you've got left in them hands. I mean, if you'd been a shopkeeper or something else ordinary, I might understand it, but your training cost quids. A waste, that's what it is.'

'Eva, they've had their money's worth, plus a pound or two of flesh—'

'Let me have my say for once.'

For once? She'd been known to kick off at lunch time, blow the whistle for tea, then pick up the second half from there. Left to her own devices, she added on injury time plus extra minutes on top of that, no penalties allowed. 'It's been an emotional day,' he told her. She would hand him a red card with an accompanying lecture. A small woman, she had a personality that filled a room and even spilled over into the rest of the house. She hailed from Seaforth, and she owned a husband, several offspring, a marked Scouse accent and very definite opinions on a plethora of subjects. But she was Mary's choice, so . . .

In truth, she didn't know where to start, as she had already given him the benefit of her wisdom on several occasions. The man was gorgeous. She studied him, not for the first time, and wondered whether he ever looked in a mirror properly. Grey at the temples seemed to emphasize his good looks, while excellent bone structure and a lack of loosening flesh made him a very desirable property. 'I could advertise you, I suppose,' she said. 'One previous owner, good bodywork, automatic transmission on a good day, engine in fair condition—'

'I've been round the clock a few times,' he told her. 'More mileage on me than on my 1939 MG. In fact, I've worn out three gearboxes and several handbrakes. I'm in no mood for lectures. I've heard enough of those from the young and restless at work.'

'You and your cars,' she exclaimed. 'I suppose you'll be walking oil and sawdust through, so I'll charge extra. You'll be under me feet, and God help my parquet. I'm already a slave to it without your muck.'

The aforementioned God chose this moment to deliver a flash rainstorm with accompanying *son et lumière*. Thunder rumbled, while lightning added intermittent brightness to the drama. Andrew, unimpressed by weather, watched with interest as a terrified Eva curled into an armchair. At least she had shut up. Silently, he thanked Thor, god of thunder.

He walked to the window and stared out at Liverpool's angry river. Dark grey and boiling, it leapt over fortifications built to hold it back. Years ago, houses had tumbled into the water, so concrete steps designed to prevent a repeat performance ran from Blundellsands through Brighton-le-Sands right down to Waterloo and the marina. He might have considered buying a yacht, but he'd once felt sick on a glassy-smooth boating lake, so he'd be better sticking to dry land.

'I don't like it,' the housekeeper moaned. 'Frightens the life out of me, it does.'

'I know. But it keeps you quiet, and that's fine with me.'

'You're cruel.'

'Oh, pipe down and rest your varicose veins, woman.'

She stared at his back. Straight as a die, and well over six feet in height, he had never developed a stoop. Women stared at him. She'd noticed that whenever he'd helped her out with shopping. Women in Sainsbury's almost salivated when he walked by. Every female teller in the bank smiled hopefully so that he might choose to stop at her station. He had no idea. Perhaps unawareness added to his charm, then. 'What are you going to do with the rest of your life, Doc? Play with cars and build more furniture?'

'I'm not sure.'

'Well, you'd better make your mind—' An enormous clap of thunder cut her off. She dared not look through the window, because hearing the storm was bad enough without looking at God's fury making holes in the earth. The weather was an omen; this fellow should have carried on working for at least five further years.

'Old man river isn't pleased,' he said. 'The tide's in, too. It might test our fortifications. Perhaps we should have got sandbags from somewhere to keep the water out.' That should make her forget to panic. Or at least change the focus of her fears.

Eva shot to her feet. 'A flood?' she screeched. 'That's all we need.'

He swung round and gave her his full attention. 'That would ruin your parquet, wouldn't it? Rumour has it that Blundellsands will be under water in a hundred years from now, so what's a century among friends?'

She glared at him. 'You're evil, you are.'

'That'll be why I'm cruel, then.'

He was neither evil nor cruel. Eva knew how generous he was, how kind. Many times she had arrived at work only to discover that he hadn't been home, that the meal she had left the previous day was untouched. The reason was always a patient whose progress, or lack thereof, was giving cause for concern. He didn't cope well with death, had never managed since ... 'Doc?'

8

'What?'

She swallowed hard. 'It has to stop some time, you know.'

'It will stop, Eva.'

'I suppose you're talking about the storm,' she said.

'Of course. What else?'

She hesitated, unsure of herself for once. Ten years. Ten bloody years, and he still bought roses. There was a selfishness in this one area of the man. He had lost his wife, but so had many others. For a whole decade, he had continued to mourn Mary as if she had died yesterday. She wouldn't have wanted that. Mary Collins, a nurse from the Women's, had married the best-looking, most appreciated young doctor in the city.

Their devotion to each other had been almost palpable. And Mary had died. She'd left a devastated wreck of a husband, three more or less grown-up kids who hadn't known whether they were coming or going, and a housekeeper who'd felt like running away. But Eva Dawson had remained loyal right up to this very trying day. Although she allowed him to get away with very little, she knew a good man when she saw one. And this was probably the best of men.

'The thunder will pass, Eva. There's thinner cloud on the horizon. Another few minutes, and Thor will take his mischief elsewhere.'

'She wouldn't have wanted this for her Drew, Doc. You can't even move to a more manageable house, can you? And you know better than most that the box under the garden doesn't contain her. That's just her bones now.'

'Stop,' he said. And he remembered sitting in the car telling himself that it had to matter, that he had to make use of retirement. People talked these days about closure, about moving on. For life to have value, must he leave Mary behind? Was that the next thing? Must he seal his heart against memories and hope to open it again else-where, not necessarily with another person, but perhaps with a different activity?

Eva saw that his mouth was tight. There was a point beyond which no one dared pass with Mr Andrew Sanderson, OBE. The children had known it, too. Mary and Andrew, good enough parents, had needed a lot of time to themselves, and Eva had been employed to pick up the slack. So she'd looked after the kids as well as the house. They'd been so wrapped up in each other, Drew and Mary, that their offspring had joined them at evening table only when well into their teens. 'Sorry,' she said.

'I know you have a big, generous heart, Eva,' he said. 'But she was everything to me. She's irreplaceable.'

Eva found her tongue again. 'We're all irreplaceable, only in the end we go. Nobody gets out of this lot alive, Doc. And that's proof enough that the world can manage without us. I mean, the doctors you trained will do your job now. We just have to carry on carrying on, otherwise we'd all end up like you, fixated on somebody who's not around no more. Time you pulled yourself together and got a life.'

He glared at her. 'So you imply that I should remarry? At my age?'

'I didn't say that. But sitting out there in all weathers talking to somebody long gone – that's what they call an obsession, and there's nothing magnificent about it. I see you've brought her roses again.' She stopped. His lips were beginning to clamp themselves shut once more. Mourning had been an active occupation these ten years. The man was polite, and his intentions were good enough, but he couldn't let go of a dead woman. He was wasting his own right to a decent quality of life. She felt like giving him a good kick up the bum.

An alarmingly close crack of thunder erupted right over

their heads. At the same time, a rear door crashed inward, and something brown streaked through the drawing room, out into the hall and up the stairs. 'We seem to have been invaded,' Andrew said. 'Not Vikings again, I hope. They made enough of a mess last time, all that rape and pillage.'

Eva blinked and closed her gaping mouth. She recalled her ma's behaviour during thunderstorms. 'Always keep the back door and the front door open,' Eva's mother had said. 'That way, if you get a fireball off the lightning, it'll go straight through instead of setting fire to the house.' Were fireballs brown? Did they make clacking noises as they crossed floors? And was the house about to go up in flames?

'That fast-moving article was a dog of some sort,' Andrew said.

'Was it?'

He nodded. 'I think so. Might have been a greyhound. If it was, we should back it – it shifted like . . . dare I say greased lightning?'

The look delivered by Eva at this point might have pinned a lesser man to the wall. 'Even your sense of humour is warped,' she told him. 'Well.' She folded her arms. 'You'd better try and catch it, eh? I've enough on round here without bloody dogs.'

Andrew liked dogs. He and Mary had appreciated most animals. Her horse, kept at livery near Little Crosby, was long gone, but she'd always wanted a dog or two. 'When we retire, Drew, we might consider breeding retrievers,' she used to say. Had she sent the dog? If she had, she must have slapped a first class stamp on it, since it had certainly arrived at speed. Air mail, perhaps? Or had she ordered special delivery via a courier? 'I'll get it,' he advised Eva. 'You stay where you are and enjoy the storm.'

'Don't leave me, Doc. The thunder might come back.'

So here he stood between a terrified woman and a frightened dog. 'Oh, behave yourself,' he snapped before leaving the room. What was she expecting? The Day of Judgement?

This time, he noticed his house. In recent years, it had been the place in which he had eaten and slept, but from now on it would be his base. Joseph and Andrew Sanderson, father and son, had made the curved banisters, monks' benches, doors, hardwood window-frames. The four-poster was their work, as were most timber items in the house. 'I'm a good carpenter,' he whispered to himself. But it had all been for Mary . . .

Kneeling on the floor, he peered under the bed he had shared with his wife until she had died here ten years ago. The canine cowered under Mary's side of the bed.

'Hello. I'm Andrew. What the hell are you?'

No reply was forthcoming. Andrew walked to the door. 'Eva?'

'Yes?'

'Bring some bits of meat. This poor thing's starving.'

'I can't move.'

'You bloody can, and you bloody will. Meat. Small pieces, raw or cooked, whatever you can find.'

He returned to his lowly position. 'You have to come out,' he said. 'You can't stay under here for the rest of your life. That's no way to carry on.' He was a hypocrite. The poor animal was only hiding, and Andrew was contemplating similar behaviour.

'Ruff.'

'That was nearly a bark.' Andrew stretched out an arm. 'Come on.'

The dog blinked. Life thus far had not been good, and he didn't trust these long, two-legged things. Yet he knew he must choose between safety and danger, so perhaps this one might be a genuine pack leader? How many times had he placed faith in humanity only for the breed's badness to be proved all over again?

A plastic dish arrived with another human attached to it. Eva knelt next to her employer and stared into the visitor's hungry, bright eyes. 'Here, doggy,' she said. 'Get yer dentures round this lot, eh?'

The animal edged forward, plunged his head into the bowl and inhaled its contents in seconds.

'Jesus, Mary and—' Eva didn't get as far as Joseph, because thunder rattled the air yet again. 'I'm going under the stairs,' she said when the sound rumbled away. For a woman in her mid-fifties, she certainly moved at speed.

'It's no longer overhead.' Andrew closed his mouth. She had gone. He looked at the dog. Like Oliver Twist, the intruder held the bowl as if asking for more. Unlike the Dickensian character, this one carried the empty vessel between his jaws. Slowly, he emerged, dropped the dish and licked Andrew's face with a long, hopeful tongue. Andrew, who disagreed strongly with those who promoted the idea that cleanliness was almost godliness, ignored the event; if people didn't have simple germs to fight, they would never fight even simple germs. 'I have to get my friend the vet,' he announced seriously. 'You need professional help.'

A ridiculous string of a tail twitched. The fur was soft as silk, while huge ears seemed unable to make up their minds. The bits fastened to his head appeared to want to stand up, like those of an Alsatian, but huge flaps hung down, not quite touching his face. 'You're neither one thing nor another, boy.' Yes, the dog was male, but very young. When fully grown, he would be tall enough to clear a table with that tail.

'What the hell do I know about dogs? Who sent you to me? Was she pretty, with dark hair and bright blue eyes? Did she say I'd be needing you?'

Once again, the pathetic excuse for a tail moved.

'Are you a Great Dane?'

'Ruff.'

'Quite. It is rough. The Irish Sea's on bad terms with the river, Eva's hiding from the storm, probably in a cupboard under the stairs, and I'm talking to a dog who doesn't know what he is. This is probably as good as it's going to get round here. You need younger playmates.' Andrew paused. 'Or perhaps you don't.' The poor thing looked as if he might appreciate calm and predictability. But would he respect Eva's parquet floors, or might those dinner-plate feet do damage?

'I'm going before the rain kicks off again.' Eva's dulcet tones crashed up the stairwell, seeming to hit every step in their path.

'Do you want a lift?' he called.

'No. You'd better stay with that daft bugger. It seems to like you.' A pause was followed by, 'You suit one another.' The double front doors slammed.

'Well, that's us told,' Andrew advised his companion. 'Don't go anywhere.'

He picked up the bedside phone and dialled Keith's number. Keith Morgan, a friend of long standing, was now able to stand even longer after a hip replacement performed by Andrew. 'Keith?'

'Hi, Andrew. What's up?'

'I'm up. Upstairs. Something ran into the house during the storm. Four legs, a tail, ridiculous ears.'

'Right. Is it a meow, a woof or a neigh?'

'The middle one. I think. It doesn't speak English, so it must be a foreigner. It's very hungry.'

'Any biting?'

'No, I managed to restrain myself.'

'Andy, I wish you'd start talking in a straight line. I'll be there in ten minutes.'

He sat with the dog. 'See, I don't know what to do with you.' That was a lie; he knew exactly what he was going to do. 'We should look for your owner, but you're afraid of something or other. And I think, in the daft, unexplored acres of my mind, that Mary sent you. Well, something sent you.' He placed a hand on a bony ribcage. 'Let's see what Keith says when he gets here. Follow me to the ground floor. Immediately.'

Downstairs, the animal curled himself in the inglenook as near as possible to the drawing-room wood burner. In this position he was tiny, all bones, ears and feet. Andrew studied the paws. Metatarsals seemed to stretch halfway up the leg – this was going to be an item of some size. But the worried frown, those sad eyes, the obvious hunger, meant that the whole was needy. Overgrown claws indicated that the pup had not been exercised adequately, and—

Keith entered the scene. Immediately, the dog stiffened and began to shake. 'So this is what the wind blew in,' said the vet. He held out a closed hand and waited till the pup accepted him with a wet tongue. After touching a gold-brown-reddish coat, Keith delivered the first diagnosis. 'It's roughly half French mastiff. A red one. Bordeaux. They have incredibly soft fur. The markings too, see the blaze of white down his chest? That long, thin tail also betrays his ancestry. The tail will fill out. In fact, the whole article will fill out.'

'French? That'll be why he speaks no English,' was Andrew's reply. 'What's the other half? Gestapo, German shepherd, Russian spy? Because that red was under my bed.'

'Probably half Labrador. Yes, they speak French in Canada, so you may be right. And he's been neglected. Keep him thin, but not this thin. That's if you keep him at all.' He looked over his shoulder. 'You're keeping him. Ownership's already written all over your face.' For the first time in years, Keith's friend looked almost amused and slightly relaxed. Might this new arrival provide the start of a long-awaited miracle? Animals sometimes reached the parts that remained inaccessible to humankind.

'I know. He needs me.'

It occurred to Keith that the boot was on a different foot – or paw – because Andy needed the dog. 'This fellow's five months old, I'd say. He could be five and a half months, but no more. He's probably had no inoculations, so I'll start from scratch, if you'll excuse the poor pun. In two weeks, I'll do the second jab. Keep him on your land for a month – no walkies. It's important that he stays away from other dogs, especially as he's so undernourished.'

'Anything else, your honour?'

'Feed him little and often because he's been starved. Work your way up slowly to two tins of dog food a day – this chap's still making bone and muscle.'

'Right.'

'And get the . . . get the grave fenced off. He'll ruin your garden.'

'I see.'

Keith checked the dog's general health and labelled him satisfactory. 'You're lucky,' he commented. 'He doesn't have the wrinkled nose or the drooling jowls of Hooch.'

Andrew jumped out of his chair. 'You mean . . . ? No. Not that great delinquent poor Tom Hanks was landed with?'

'The same. Underneath all the hassle and chewed clothes and ruined furniture, Hooch had a heart of gold.' The vet laughed. 'If it makes it any easier for you, think of

16

him as a Labrador. They ruin houses, too. All pups do it. He'll be company for you, Andy.'

Andrew sat down again. The film had been released in the late eighties, and he'd seen it with Mary on their very last outing together. Just months later, Mary had lost her feeble hold on life. Storm was a message, then. Not that Andrew could say any of this to Keith. People already had him down as mad because his devotion hadn't ended with Mary's death. They had no real concept of true love, because if it was true it never ended. *Oh, Mary. Why you? Why you and not me? You would have handled life so much better* . . .

'Andy?'

'What?'

'She's dead, mate.'

'You think I don't know that?'

'Still talking to her?'

Andrew nodded. 'Not every day. Not recently. Oh well, I'm retired now, so perhaps Storm will keep me busy and fit. Have you eaten?'

'No, and she'll kill me if I don't get back and do justice to her *boeuf en croûte*. She's been taking cookery classes again. Bloody murder, it is. I'd be happy enough with a ham sandwich, but oh no, if it isn't in French and difficult to pronounce, it's not proper cooking. I have developed a close affinity with guinea pigs.'

Andrew laughed. 'Would you like a French dog? It might taste good with a few spuds and a drop of gravy.'

Keith picked up his bag. 'Four Irish wolfhounds, two horses, two hormonal teenage daughters and one wife are enough, ta. See you in a couple of weeks.' He left, crossing the index and middle fingers of his left hand. Perhaps the dog would make the first crack in Andrew's emotional concrete bunker.

Andrew glanced at his canine companion. 'Just us, then. I'll leave you a bit of stew to cool. Do you need to go out?'

Storm mooched round the garden for a while, relieved himself, then walked straight towards—

Andrew stood in the doorway and stared. There was no digging, no fooling about; the dog simply sat on Mary's grave. With over half an acre to choose from, he had homed in on that one spot. This animal belonged to Mary, and his other owner wept. Eva wasn't here, so it was his party, and he'd cry if he wanted to.

That cursed inner alarm clock woke him at exactly ten minutes to seven. Time for a shower, a bite to eat, out of the house by seven thirty, look at today's list. Check theatre availability, get everything in order . . . Ah. Of course, there was no list. No, no, that wasn't true; it was just a different list, that was all. Mary had sent him a dependant, and there were things to be done.

As he surfaced, Andrew Sanderson began to realize that he was not alone. Like Tom Hanks, he was sharing his bed with a Hooch. 'We went through this last night, Storm. Didn't we discuss sleeping arrangements? *Ton lit est . . . sur le . . .* landing.' What was the French for landing? 'You'll have to learn English, dog. When in Rome and all that. Oh, by the way, do you have fleas? And I know it's only a cardboard box, but there's a nice blanket in it. You can't sleep here. That's Mary's place.'

The dog yawned. He had a set of strong, white teeth.

'You feel safe at last, don't you?'

'Ruff.'

'This isn't rough. I built and carved the bed with my dad's help, and Mary did the drapes. You're living in the lap of luxury, boy. This is a five-bedroom, four-bathroom house. That single-storey extension downstairs is an events room that runs the full depth of the building. She liked events, did a great deal for charity.' He hadn't used the events suite in over a decade. Even the formal dining room remained unloved. With a dining-kitchen, a morning room and a drawing room, Andrew had enough space. And Eva was talking about needing more help for the heavier work, but Eva was very adept at finding something to moan about.

'Shall we go downstairs, Storm?'

'Ruff.'

'Don't you know any more words? It's all getting a bit monotonous, you know. Anyway, we're going out. Not "out" out, no running, no playing. But out as in the car. The same rules apply, by the way. It's a Mercedes. We don't eat upholstery, don't scratch the doors, don't chew seatbelts. Especially in a one-year-old Merc.'

'Ruff.'

'Oh, come on. It's Weetabix or nothing, so it's Weetabix. One more ruff and I'll make you wear one. You can walk round looking mad and Shakespearean.'

A shower, a shave and a small disagreement later, both were seated in the car by nine o'clock. Storm, who had wanted to occupy the front passenger seat, was finally installed in the rear of the Merc. Andrew, nursing the suspicion that he needed a second shower, climbed into the driver's seat. 'Stay,' he ordered. 'I smell very doggy after that tussle.'

'Ruff.'

'What?'

'Arr-arr.'

'That's better. If you're going to live with me, your conversational skills need work. Though you could be a blessing after Eva's carryings-on. Half an hour with her's like a public meeting with the riot police outside at the ready. She fed you, though. She's not all bad – just half bad. Her husband's our gardener, so you'd be wise to stay on his better side, too.'

He drove to Tony Almond's, a we-have-almost-every-thing type of shop, where he bought a large dog bed, boxes of balls and toys, half a ton of dog food, collar, lead and bowls. 'What else do I need?' he asked.

'Not much,' the girl replied. 'Just your head tested. Our Alsatian ate the plastic rainwater pipes in our back yard yesterday. I see you bought a large bed. Is it a big dog?'

'It will be if I let it live.'

'Oh, and don't bother with a kennel. Get it a Wendy house. They like their own place. No chocolate – it's poison. And make sure you're the boss.'

Hmm. Chance would be a fine thing. The battle for position in the car had revealed a strong personality under all the shaking and ruffing.

When all purchases were stashed in the boot, Andrew drove to the stonemason's next door to the funeral parlour. The cross he had made to mark Mary's grave had been well cared for, treated against weather, its brass plaque always shiny clean, but, due to recently altered circumstances, she needed more protection. 'I have to make sure she stays where she is,' he told the dog. 'She may have sent you, but you're not digging her up just so you can have the last word. Well, the last ruff.'

'Ruff.'

Smiling while shaking his head, Andrew left the car. He picked out the stone, said he wanted it flat on the ground over the grave, handed over a paper on which were written the appropriate words for engraving, and gave the man his address.

'Not many people want the stone lying down these days,' Sam Grey said.

'I have my reasons.'

'And eight feet by four? Was this a big person?' He

studied the customer. 'You're that doctor who's a mister. You were in the paper, a photo at Buckingham Palace. OBE, wasn't it? And I helped our Archie bury your wife years ago in your garden – I remember now, God love her. She was tiny. Did an awful lot for cancer research.'

Andrew nodded. 'Then she died of it.'

'I'm sorry, sir. But my brother and I handle so many funerals – so very sorry.'

'The dog in the car adopted me, Mr Grey. He's confined to barracks just now because of injections against distemper and so forth. If he digs in the wrong place . . . well . . .'

Sam Grey nodded thoughtfully. 'Right. Can we get power to the grave?'

'Yes. There's electricity in the summerhouse.'

The stonemason did some mental juggling. 'Fair enough. We'll get the slab delivered later today, and I'll work on it in situ over next weekend. She was a lovely woman.' He paused for a moment. 'So was mine, but I lost her to leukaemia.'

It was Andrew's turn to express sorrow.

'I'm fine now. Remarried. I've not forgotten Mags, but Kath's a good woman. We look after each other. Step into my office and we'll do the paperwork.'

Back in the car, Andrew surveyed his companion. 'You're almost too well behaved,' he advised the pup. 'I'm just waiting for the outbreak of war.'

So that was what 'normal' people did; they put one wife in the ground and married another. He could not imagine himself wanting or needing anyone after Mary. Mary Collins, the object of many men's desire, had chosen him. Although she hadn't been his first partner in sex, she had certainly been his last. So tiny, so trusting, so affectionate and powerful. She had cajoled, begged and almost blackmailed people into parting with money for cancer research, had organized everything from jumble sales to formal balls, had raised many, many thousands in pursuit of her goal.

'And it took her, Storm.' It had been deep, widespread, difficult to diagnose in its virtually symptom-free early months. They'd trawled Denmark, Switzerland and the United States in pursuit of a cure, but nothing had worked. 'She died in my arms, overloaded with morphine. Anyway,' he dashed a tear from his cheek, 'you have toys. You will chew the toys in lieu of furniture.'

A weighty paw suddenly landed on his right shoulder and stayed there.

'Good God, how much do you know, Storm?'

'Arf.'

'Only half? Right, I'll tell you the full story later. But first, we have a dragon to face. You must remember, Eva is fair. She talks tough, but she does have a good heart. One thing's certain – neither of us will ever go hungry.'

The pup retreated to his rightful place. He was beginning to realize that there was a price to pay, and that the price was being nice. Nice was not jumping about too much inside cars and houses, but outside was OK. Somewhere at the back of Storm's mind, a horrible memory lingered. A man, a stick, bits of ripped-up stuff everywhere. The beating. Outside in the cold, no food, drinking from puddles, running, running. Lights in the sky, loud noise, waves crashing, door opening. And the man. This man. Deep inside, there was love in Storm's new person. Strength, too. He was a pack leader, a decider, one who would make life good. And Storm was here for a reason, though he'd no idea what it might be.

Eva Dawson was standing at the laundry-room window, a mobile phone clamped to her ear. 'I promise you, Joyce,

I'm not joking. Sam Grey's here with a mini tractor thingy dragging a trailer with stone on it. It's going on top of poor Mary so the dog can't start digging there.'

After a pause, she picked up the thread. 'And the doc's building a house for the dog. What? No, not a kennel. It's more the size of a kiddy's play house. Raised off the ground to keep it from getting damp. All for a stray dog. Oh, I'd better go. Talk to you later, and see you at bingo.'

Andrew entered. 'I've decided on proper foundations. I'll insulate, then run a pipe through and instal a radiator. Can't have him getting cold, can we?'

Eva's mouth snapped shut. Sometimes, it was better to say nothing. If her employer seemed to be going a different kind of mad, that might be classed as progress. He talked to the animal now. Perhaps the daft-looking bugger would help the doc stop having one-sided conversations with the deceased.

She joined him in the kitchen. 'Do you want something to eat?' she asked.

'I'll look after myself, thanks. Even my own cooking has to be an improvement on hospital food.'

'But I'm here.'

'I know you're here. I can see you here and hear you here. But I don't want to take advantage of you.'

'Ooh, there's a novelty. Months I've been asking could our Natalie come a few times a month to do some of the heavier work. She needs a few bob, being a student.'

So, it looked as if Eva had produced something that hadn't put its name down for prison. 'Studying what?'

'Medicine,' she snapped.

'In Liverpool?'

'In Liverpool. She needs work because of student loans.'

'Right. Use her and give me the bill.'

'Don't worry, I will. Now. Scrambled or poached egg on toast, bacon butty, ploughman's, salad, baked potato?'

'Bacon butty,' he replied. 'With ketchup.'

The thing Eva loved most about Doc was that he'd managed to hang on to his working-class Lancashire roots with no excuses, no pride, no inverted snobbery. He was what he was, and nothing would ever change him. What was more, she knew he'd do what he could for her Natalie. Natalie deserved the best.

Two

By 1952, Joseph Sanderson's Bespoke Furniture workshop was no longer a large shed in the back garden; he had taken a double unit under the Folds Road arches in Bolton. Three qualified carpenters and one apprentice formed his workforce, while his son Andrew always insisted on helping during long summer holidays. The lad's affinity with wood had been born in him, but so had his gift for the piano. 'Watch your hands, because your mother will kill me,' Joe often begged. 'You'll play no music with a couple of fingers missing.'

Joe was proud of his lad. How many men in this town had a son who got booked to play the piano in the Victoria Hall, who could make the most of the grain in wood, who was a front runner in most subjects at school?

1952 became the Year of the Bookcase, the summer during which young Andrew's talent became fully visible. After accepting minimal help from his father, he edged all the shelves with rosewood, then took a piece of the same to make a slight overhang for the top of the unit. With no help and no pattern to copy, he carved a Tudor rose in the centre, and vine leaves trailing outward on both sides. No one was allowed to view his work of art until it was absolutely perfect. In a corner away from everyone, he finally felt satisfied with the magnum opus, and went to fetch Dad.

Joe removed the protective sheeting, and his jaw dropped. 'Oh, my God. What size chisel did you use? Are your hands all right? There's some fine detail in yon. Are you sure you didn't hurt yourself? Your mother's going to take my guts for garters if you've nicked the skin.'

'Yes, Dad. I'm fine. No missing fingers, no blood, no bruises. I think you'll be safe.'

The older man swallowed hard. 'Eeh, son. There's folk up Chorley New Road would pay quids for that. It's grand. But you know what, our Andrew?'

The boy shook his head.

'It's not for sale. Even if we ended up with baileys at the door, we'd hide this. By God, I seldom saw finer work in me whole life.'

'Why would we get bailiffs, Dad? Aren't we doing well?'

'We're all right, son. Aye, we'll make a grand carpenter out of thee. It's an art that's dying because of machinery, but people will always want bespoke pieces. So what's the point of Bolton School and all that Latin and English literature? There's money in them hands of yours, and there's always a job for you at Sanderson's.'

While Andrew loved carpentry, it wasn't his goal. He wasn't absolutely sure of his goal, but carpentry was more like a hobby, something to help pass a few hours on a wet weekend or several days during over-long school holidays. He was a great reader, and not just of novels. Knowledge was there to be collected, and the school curriculum wasn't broad enough for him. The world excited him, but he wasn't sure which area would eventually be the one in which he would work.

'This'll all be yours one day, my son. With you having no brothers and sisters, the business will pass to you. By the time you get it, it will be worth a good few bob, because this is just a start. I have plans, son. Big plans.'

Andrew couldn't say he didn't want it, because that would hurt his father. And then there was his mother. Emily Sanderson was an excellent pianist, though she didn't practise often enough. She'd inherited a piano from a great-aunt, and this had been installed in the front parlour in their Crompton Way house. She played it occasionally, and Andrew had been drawn to it in the same way as he'd been attracted to wood. Nevertheless, although he loved to play, he was no more consumed by music than he was by carpentry. It was important, but it wasn't enough.

'She'll not let you give up the piano, though.'

Andrew grinned. Both his parents owned the knack of crawling inside his head to share thoughts. He was lucky to have such a close family.

Joe continued. 'And she'll not like you doing carpentry in case it interferes with your piano-playing.'

'I know.'

'How did you do it, though? How did you know what them dots on them lines meant? And how did you know which was left-hand music and which was right?'

'No idea, Dad. It's a bit like asking how did I know which chisel to use. It's all just part of what I am.'

Joe accepted that as an adequate explanation. With a dad up to his neck in sawdust, and a mother who used to be soaked in music, this one perfect child had been born attracted to both disciplines. When he played the piano, he became a concert pianist; when he carved, sawed and joined wood, he became a master carpenter. With Andrew, there were no half-measures; whatever he chose to do, he did it well. But he was also academically sound. 'What will you do when you leave school?' Joe asked now. 'Soldier, sailor, cabinet maker?'

'University,' was the quick answer. 'Might be a doctor. Not quite sure yet, because I'm interested in a few things.'

'A doctor? What about carpentry and music, though? Won't it be a waste of talent?'

Andrew shrugged. 'I shan't give them up. There's space to do more than one thing in a whole lifetime.'

'Your mother would be proud of a doctor. I'll be proud whatever you do.'

The praise went on for weeks, though Andrew was subjected to close scrutiny of his fingers when his mother discovered what he'd been up to. 'You've a good eye and a steady hand,' she told him. 'That's what surgeons need, you know. But surgeons have to take great and special care of their hands. And when your patients need soothing, you can play them a bit of music.'

He would never be fully sure when the idea was born, but he always felt that his mother had given him that extra clue. Such a magical family, they had always been. Childhood was idyllic until . . . until it stopped being idyllic.

Security dissipated when he found out that his father, great artisan and great dad, was not perfect. Having discovered his father's weakness, Andrew nursed it to himself for some time, as it might have killed his mother. Protecting Mother was to become his prime objective. Caring about Dad, however . . .

He found out by accident, though it would probably have come to light sooner or later. Andrew couldn't help wondering whether he might have felt better had he remained in ignorance, because the new knowledge weighed heavily on young shoulders.

Joe always tidied himself up on a Saturday night and, after a bath, a shave and a change of clothing, went out to the pub for a game of darts or dominoes. The Starkie was on Tonge Moor Road, so he usually cut through past St Augustine's and up Thicketford Road. Andrew had a friend whose family owned a corner shop there, and he was just stepping out of the domestic doorway up the street at the side when he saw Dad walking in the wrong direction.

For some seconds, he hesitated. Where was Dad going? Did he want to know, did he need to know? A strange feeling overcame him, leaving him almost breathless. In the Sanderson household, everything went like perfectly calibrated clockwork. Monday to Friday and some Saturday mornings, Dad drove to the workshop. On Saturday nights, he went to the pub. The rhythm of life was interrupted just once a year, when the family went to the seaside for two weeks, usually taking with them Stuart Abbot, Andrew's best friend from the very shop and house outside which Andrew currently stood.

Mother was a home bird. She made excellent meals, washed and ironed for everyone, kept the house sparkling clean, kept herself in the same condition, always a smile, always a pretty dress with an apron tied round her waist until she sat for the evening meal. Andrew was generally well behaved, so what was going wrong? Perhaps there was a customer nearby, though people in this area seldom bought bespoke. What should he do? It was probably nothing; Dad could be calling for a member of the darts team.

His feet made the decision. As he rounded the corner into a cul-de-sac, he saw his father disappearing into a corporation-built semi-detached. Ducking down behind a privet hedge, Andrew found a gap and stared open-mouthed through the none-too-clean front window. Greasy, ill-hung curtains gaped sufficiently to allow the boy to see into the front room. Through a film of dirt on glass, he saw Dad kissing a woman. Andrew's knees failed, and he sank to the pavement. Dad never kissed Mother.

They were polite to each other, and they talked and laughed together sometimes, but they weren't close like Stuart's parents.

Did Mother know about this betrayal? Had someone else noticed and told her, and was she the subject of gossip all over the neighbourhood? Straying husbands and women who failed to hang on to their men were served up in liberal portions alongside tea, sugar and butter at the local Co-op. Gossip was just another staple food in these parts. Oh, poor Mother. What was he supposed to do about this?

He crawled away, hoping that no one in the other houses saw him. His heart fluttered stupidly like a caged wild bird, and he felt decidedly nauseous and weak. For the first time since infancy, he feared for his family. If Dad left, what would happen to Mother? And to Andrew? At Bolton School, he mixed with the rich and the gifted, and he was one of the latter group, but would Dad continue to buy uniform and other necessities if he went to live elsewhere?

Who could Andrew talk to? Not Mother, not Dad, that much was certain. Stuart, another lad who had come good by passing his scholarship exams and the entrance exam for Bolton School was, in Andrew's opinion, completely trustworthy, but was it right to tell anyone at all about private family business?

Framing in words the fact that his dad had another woman made Dad a wicked man and Mother sub-standard in some way. A woman who did not keep her husband happy was a failure or, perhaps worse still, an object of pity. Mother was a proud woman. Surely someone else must have seen Dad going into that house? For how long had the affair gone on? And would there be a divorce?

Stuart and Andrew had known one another since starting school during the war. Mothers had to go to work, so children were enrolled in nursery class at the age of three. Nine years they had been best friends, but Andrew could not betray his parents to anyone. It was a big parcel to carry alone, yet he knew he had to bear the whole burden.

He arrived home. Later, when he thought about that evening, he could not recall the journey back to Crompton Way. Mother was seated by the fire in the living room. Her hair was pretty and fluffy and she was wearing her second-best dress. It was cornflower blue and it matched her eyes. 'Hello, love,' she said. 'I'm trying to get to grips with *War and Peace*, but I think it's beyond me.' She put down the book. 'Are you all right?'

'Yes, thank you.'

'Are you sure? You look as if you've seen a ghost. Have you been to visit Stuart?'

'Yes.' For the first time ever, he found himself tuning in to his mother's voice. She wasn't like Dad. She spoke differently, as if she'd been educated, whereas Andrew's father used old Lancashire phrasing and flattened vowels. 'Did you want to be a musician?' he asked her. 'Did you never think of taking it up professionally?'

'Sometimes,' she replied thoughtfully. 'Or a nurse. I rather liked the idea of being useful. But . . .' She sighed and gazed round the room. 'Here I am with my lovely son, so I'm quite happy, thank you.'

He wasn't convinced. 'Is one child enough?'

'Oh yes. I couldn't have any more, you see. I'm sure your father would have liked a houseful of sons, each born with a saw in his hand, but it wasn't to be. Yet we're happy enough.'

She had no idea, then. Or had she? She was clever enough to hide her feelings, controlled enough not to admit that her husband was with someone else. And if she did decide to open up, her confidences would not be awarded to a twelve-year-old boy, even if that boy was wise beyond his years. Oh, how he wished he'd never seen Dad earlier. A bubble was inflating in his chest, a new sensation that filled him till he ran to the bathroom and vomited. Hating his father wasn't easy; hiding that hatred was going to be more than difficult. And he couldn't carry on throwing up his venom, or he would finish up ... what was the word? Dehydrated, that was it.

'What's wrong, Andrew?'

He turned and looked into his mother's lovely eyes. So gentle, they were, a lighter blue and not as piercing as his and Dad's. She was unhappy. She knew. But Andrew had to pretend that he was not in on the secret, as she must not suffer more hurt.

'You've been sick,' she said, 'and you're not one for bilious attacks, are you?'

'Too many sweets pinched from Mr and Mrs Abbot's shop.' Lying was not too difficult after all. From this day, he must live a lie. At the workshop, he needed to continue to be happy and helpful; at home, he must assist his mother, play the piano, eat his meals, smile at the traitor who was his father. How could the man betray this beautiful, fragile woman? She was a natural gentlewoman who was living the wrong life. What an excellent teacher of music she might have made.

Emily's heart sank. Something was troubling her beloved Andrew, and he was her reason for living, her joy, her comfort. 'Your father's gone to the Starkie,' she said, apropos of nothing at all. 'It's Saturday. You could set all clocks and watches by that man. I always know exactly where he is.'

'Yes. He lives a very careful life, Mother.'

In a few beats of time, their hearts collided in the space between them. He longed for reassurance, wanted to run to her and share a comforting hug, but he couldn't. How might so much be said in silence? Never before had it occurred to Andrew that his mother had probably married beneath her. Apart from the aunt who had owned the piano, Mother had no relations. Or had she? Had this wonderful, adorable woman been cast out for marrying a man from a different level of society? Had she relinquished all her chances just to be with a husband who would let her down?

'Are you feeling better now, son?'

He wasn't, of course. 'Yes,' he lied.

'Come downstairs. I'll get a cold cloth for your head. Lie on the sofa, and I'll play for you.'

Her playing was untypically all over the place. Although nothing had been said, he nursed a strong suspicion that she was aware of his newly acquired knowledge. But he was unable to open a discussion on the subject, since he needed not to add to her discomfort. However, a plan took shape in the depths of his mind; he was determined to discover as much as possible about his mother's past. Somewhere, there were people – her people, therefore his people. Even if he left his mother out of the equation, he needed the information for himself, because background was important.

'Andrew?'

'Yes, Mother?'

'Do you feel better now?'

'Yes, thank you.' Deceit was about to become a way of life.

'Chopin must be spinning in his grave. I don't know what happened to my fingers. They were everywhere except where I needed them to be.'

Andrew understood fully, though he offered no reply.

'Do you feel ready for cocoa?' she asked.

'A glass of water would be better,' he replied. All he could see was a house with dirty windows, a neglected garden, a front door that howled for a coat of paint. His father had turned away from a fragrant, lovely wife, had found his own level with a slovenly person who couldn't be bothered to live a clean life.

She returned with the water. 'If anything is worrying you, talk to me.'

He shrugged lightly. 'Too many sweets and a strong dislike for geometry,' he said. 'Pythagoras and I have to reach agreement before September.' He even spoke the way she did, had taken his voice from her. While Andrew's speech was not exactly devoid of accent, it was nearer to hers than to his father's. But the lies were born in the part of him that came from Dad, because Dad was dishonest. There was no problem with Pythagoras, but he had to offer an explanation of some kind, so, like his male parent, he took the easy route.

'Just rest, then,' Emily said.

She went into the kitchen and attacked tomorrow's lamb with sprigs of rosemary. Joseph hated rosemary, so he could jolly well drown his portion in mint sauce yet again. She stabbed the meat and inserted extra pieces of the herb. *Let her have him. Let him go and live in that tacky cul-de-sac with that tacky madam. And I hope her husband finds them* in flagrante *and gives them both the hiding they deserve.*

The marriage had not been a mistake; it had produced Andrew, who was a blessing. But something had happened to Andrew this evening, and the child was frighteningly close to boiling point. *O God, please protect my boy from the truth.* He mustn't know, must never find out. Perhaps when he's older, but not yet. She shelled peas, scrubbed potatoes, put together a trifle for tomorrow's pudding. She used no jelly. Her Andrew didn't care for jelly.

It looked as if rain might be on the way. Never mind. Let Joseph get soaked on his way home. Yet she couldn't manage to hate him . . .

'Mother?'

'Yes, dear?'

'The people next door to Stuart have some kittens. May I have one?' The idea of something warm and furry suddenly appealed.

Emily stood in the doorway. 'Your father hates cats.'

'I know.' He paused for a few seconds and studied her face. 'Though he wouldn't hurt an animal, would he?'

'No. But get a queen if there is one, and I'll have it neutered. They're more sensible than toms.' *He'll be in the pub now. Tonight, he will smell of her, all cheap soap and Evening in Paris. I shall move into the small bedroom. For Andrew's sake, I'll blame Joseph's snoring. For some reason I can't fathom, today marks the end of something. He has hurt my boy – I'm almost sure of it. No one hurts my boy.*

'You've had cats before, Mother?'

'Yes, we had several on the farm.' She pulled herself together and inhaled sharply. 'When I was very young, we lived for a little while in a farmhouse.'

Farmhouse. Mother's maiden name was Beauchamp, French for beautiful field, pronounced Beecham. 'That must have been fun,' he said. Then he skimmed over the whole thing by talking about kittens while hoping that Mother would think he hadn't noticed her faux pas with its accompanying gasp. More French. False step, this time. Well, Dad was the one who had stepped out of line. Mother probably needed her family, but was, perhaps, too proud to approach them. Beauchamp spelt the French way was an unusual name . . .

While he drank his water, Andrew's mother played another nocturne. This time, she took charge of her fingers and delivered a decent enough performance. Since learning about her husband's floozy, Emily had concentrated on control of herself. Sometimes she felt a little guilty, as she had never enjoyed the physical side of marriage. After a birth so difficult that it had threatened the lives of both herself and her baby, the reason for sexual contact had been removed. Yes, she would have loved more children; no, she had no intention of leaving her son without a mother. So any fumblings involved a layer of latex, and she hated all that preparation. Did she hate Joseph? No. He was a weak and needful man, but his son had come first so far. *Dear God, let it continue thus.*

In Andrew's life since infancy, libraries had always been useful places. Inside the Central on Bolton's famous crescent he had spent many busy hours, especially in the reference section. Reading about carpentry had been as useful as his practical experience; reading about anatomy and physiology was fascinating, and many answers to homework questions were available in this quiet, peaceful place. There were times when he felt he shouldn't mind living here, because the whole world sat on shelves just waiting to be raided.

But the information he currently sought was not available within his normal spheres of exploration. In a reading room usually populated by older people, newspapers and periodicals were kept on sloping tables with wooden lips on their edges to prevent printed matter from falling to the floor. And here he found a farming magazine.

A man and a woman were pictured leaning on a wide five-bar gate. Between them, a young, prize-winning bullock rested his head. The whole photograph was pleasant and comical. But Andrew's eyes were drawn to the article underneath.

Mr and Mrs Beauchamp of Heathfield Farm with Hercules, their perfectly proportioned and amusing bullock. Hercules took first prize in the 'most promising' group,

36

*while two further firsts, for Samson and Goliath, were
awarded to the Heathfield herd's famous prize bulls.*

*Hercules, described by his owners as a beast with
humour, is pictured leaning on the gate as if listening
to gossip. Mr Beauchamp told our photographer that
Hercules loves people, though he hasn't yet managed to
eat a whole one. The Beauchamps are the fourth gen-
eration of the family to farm their vast acreage. Over
the years, they have doubled the size of their herds and
have introduced three new types of cattle.*

In a further paragraph, Andrew learned that these possible relations of his were famous for breeding prize cows,
sheep and pigs. 'We lived for a little while in a farmhouse,'
Mother had said. Days after that evening, the kitten had
been installed in the household, and Andrew had begun
his trawl through the telephone directory, though his
search had been fruitless. Not everyone had phones in
those days, and lines had not yet been extended out into
some areas of the countryside.

The people at the main desk in the library had grown
used to Andrew. He was the sort of user they appreciated;
even when he brought his friend, they conversed by
passing notes on a writing pad, thereby allowing other
reference-seekers to continue their work in peace.

George looked up. 'Hello, young man. What is it today,
then?'

Andrew grinned. 'Farming.'

The man laughed. 'It'll fill the time nicely when you're
not playing the piano or being a doctor or a carpenter.
Well, let me tell you, young Andrew, farming is more than
full-time. You need thirty hours a day in that job. What
have you got there?'

He held up the magazine. 'Just this. Can you tell me
where to buy it?'

George lowered his head and his tone. 'I can do better than that, me laddo. You can have that one. The next's due any day, and that issue's safely archived, but don't say anything. Give it here – I've an old bag somewhere.' He glanced sideways. 'And I don't mean Edith.'

Chuckling, Andrew offered his thanks, took the bag and left the building. Outside, he sat on the steps. Heathfield Farm. It wouldn't be to the south, because the area between Bolton and Manchester was mostly housing and business development. The answer lay in the building behind him, in the maps section, but he had to get home, as Mother would have the meal ready. What would she say if she knew what her son was up to? Well, she certainly approved of brains and initiative, and he was using both.

Mother no longer slept in the same room as Dad. The official reason was Joe's snoring, but Andrew wasn't fooled for one moment. He needed to find the Beauchamps, befriend them and, eventually, tell them who he was. If they were the right Beauchamps, that was. Should her marriage end, Mother might need support beyond anything her son could offer.

Now. Time to invent the next lie. He could pretend to be working on a holiday assignment on wildlife in the north-west. With his trusty steed, a bicycle bought for his birthday, together with snacks and drinks, he would be able to take off daily once he had found the farm's location. Mother would have no idea about his real intentions, and she wouldn't worry about him.

A second lie was preparing itself. He would tell the Beauchamps that he was researching husbandry with particular reference to cattle. With luck and good management, he might inveigle himself into the household. He would offer to work as a farmhand, with lunch as payment. How adept he was becoming at dishonesty. Perhaps he ought to become a journalist. They seemed to need the ability to bend the truth to achieve a headline.

He reshaped the magazine so that it fitted into his saddle-bag, and cycled home. After greeting Emily, he washed his hands at the kitchen sink and sat at the table.

'We must wait for your father.'

'Yes, of course. Where is he?'

She walked to the window and beckoned. 'Look at him,' she whispered. 'He's having the time of his life.'

Dad, who hated cats, was playing with the kitten. The animal was chasing a table-tennis ball all over the lawn, while Dad chased her. 'He's not supposed to like cats.' Childishly angry, Andrew resented the idea of Joe's taking over the care of Toodles. She was his cat, not his dad's.

'Your father's a good man, Andrew. Not perfect, but good enough. For some odd reason, Toodles' fur doesn't make him sneeze.' She paused. 'You've been missed at the workshop, by the way. The men have been asking after you.'

So the first of the next two lies was born. He'd been preparing the start of his wildlife project, he said; now, he needed to go into woods to find examples of the subject. 'We have to train ourselves in observation,' he concluded.

'Keep your distance from badgers if you see any,' she warned. 'They look sweet, but they aren't, and their anger is born in sensible fear of humans. And remember that foxes are shy, because we are their main enemy too. If they have babies, stay still and try not to let them see you.'

And there spoke a true daughter of the countryside, Andrew decided. A few months in a farmhouse? A whole childhood might be nearer the mark.

Joe brought in the cat and placed it on a fireside chair. 'This thing should run with the greyhounds. Or Bolton Wanderers could use her as goalkeeper. Hello, lad.' He went to wash his hands.

When he returned, his wife and son were discussing the etymology of the word forest. 'Some say it came from Viking invaders,' Andrew was saying, 'and it meant an area set aside so that the nobility might hunt. All very feudal. We would have been chased off as commoners.'

But Emily clung fast to the belief that it was based in Latin.

The trouble with having an educated son and a clever wife was that Joe, or Joseph as Emily insisted on calling him, often felt left out. She was now going on about the forest canopy, the lower canopy, shrub, moss and herb layers. Aye, she was betraying her origins all right.

Emily stopped. 'I read all that somewhere,' she said lamely. 'In a magazine years ago.'

'Your mother reads a lot and forgets none of it.'

Andrew munched his way through salad and ham. The magnitutde of the task he was about to undertake took the edge off his appetite and made swallowing slightly difficult. Within minutes, it became almost impossible.

'I have taken a job,' Emily announced suddenly.

Joe's cutlery clattered on his plate. 'Oh aye. What job's that, then?'

'Assistant to the almoner at Bolton Royal. It's mostly paperwork, but the almoner's office makes sure that care systems are in place for vulnerable patients leaving hospital. Just three or four days a week, I'll be working at the start. Andrew's old enough now to be left occasionally.'

Joe almost growled. 'Are you after more housekeeping? Do I not give you enough? There's plenty more if you're in need.'

She maintained her dignity. 'It isn't about money, Joseph. It's about involvement and being useful.'

'I see.' He picked up his implements. 'Education should not be wasted. I'm quoting you there, Em. So we're not enough for you, me and the boy?'

Emily, always the lady, placed her knife and fork side by side on the plate. 'If you have a sensible objection, it will be taken under consideration. As far as I am aware, no one can force me not to work. There's no law against my taking employment, but I am open to rational suggestion.'

Andrew, seated between the two, felt like a minister without portfolio. Raised not to interrupt, he simply stayed where he was, incapable of ingesting more food. This was as near as his parents had ever come to battle within his hearing. Too young to referee the bout, he had to sit through it in silent discomfort.

'I like to be the breadwinner in my own house,' Joe said, his face slightly flushed. 'You don't need a job. Anything you want, just ask and I'll get it for you.'

'I want to work.'

'So he becomes a latch-key kid?'

'No. I shall work part-time only. I'll be here when he gets in from school.'

'You've made your mind up, then?'

Emily inclined her head.

Joe left the table, walked into the hall and slammed the front door after leaving the house.

'Phew,' Andrew breathed.

'Don't worry,' she said. 'Storm in a teacup, dear. He's always at his noisiest when in the wrong. Let him tell his ... his friends about it.'

They cleared the table and washed dishes. Together, Andrew and his mother worked like a well-oiled machine, even here in the confines of a small kitchen. It occurred

41

to him that life without Dad would be a great deal better than life without Mother. If his father never came back, it wouldn't matter, because he had another—

The front door flew inward. 'You there, missus?' yelled a male voice. 'Keep your rubbish off the street, will you? We get sick of shifting trash like this.'

Emily left her son in the kitchen. On the floor in the hall, her husband was moaning and trying to get to his feet. She bent to help him.

'Leave me alone,' snapped the heap on the floor. 'I've been robbed. I've been beaten, too.'

Andrew offered to go for the police.

'No,' Joe snapped. 'He got nothing but my watch.'

Andrew backed away. There was no doubt in his mind that the probably fast-escaping visitor was the husband of the woman in the dirty house. The letter box opened, and the missing watch landed on the doormat. 'There's your watch that fell off, you cheap bastard. Even mine's better than yon, and I'm nobbut a bin man. Like I said, I'm used to shifting muck and rubbish.' The flap clattered back into position.

'Andrew, go and pack an overnight case. We shall stay at the Pack Horse tonight.'

'Why?' groaned Joe.

'Because the creature out there's angry, and he may return and burn the house down. Senseless people have a tendency to react badly.'

Joe struggled to his feet. One eye was closed, his nose was bloody, and his clothes were in tatters. 'Don't talk daft,' he snapped. 'He wouldn't dare.'

Andrew was not in a position from which he might see his mother's face, but he could picture it in his mind's eye. She would be calm, straight-lipped and steady-eyed. There'd be no nervous blinking, no outward fear, no tears.

'Andrew and I are going,' she said. 'And I strongly advise you to do the same for the sake of your own safety.'

They walked to the hotel, which was some distance away. Emily left her husband bruised and bleeding at home while she booked a twin-bed room for herself and her son. Since leaving the house, she had spoken not one word, and her son had respected the silence. But once in their room, she asked him to sit on his bed facing her.

She sat. 'You must try not to be angry with or worried about your father. He leads what I term a Saturday night life, and he meets some people who are not very pleasant. They get drunk, throw their weight about, argue over a game of dominoes or darts, and sometimes they fight. Tonight your father became a victim of misunderstanding. He may come here, or he may stay at home. I can't order him about and tell him what to do; he's a grown man.'

'We left Toodles,' Andrew said.

'Don't worry about her.'

'You said the man might come back and set fire to the house.'

'Ah, yes.' She reached across and patted her son's hand. 'I just want him to think about the people he mixes with, Andrew. If he were a little more careful, he would get less trouble.'

'Has there been other trouble, Mother?'

'Yes. Yes, I'm afraid there has.'

It was all connected to the woman with the battle-scarred front door. Mother probably knew that, but Andrew dared not say a word on the subject. Emily Sanderson courted nobody's pity.

That night, Andrew slept fitfully. Once, during a period of wakefulness, he heard his mother sobbing quietly just a few feet away. Hatred for his father deepened; had Joseph Sanderson stayed away from the filthy woman, her husband would never have come near Mother. Dad was a pig. Andrew made up his mind there and then that he would never go into a public house.

Joe Sanderson nursed his wounds, flinching slightly while cleaning torn flesh. By tomorrow, he would have a real shiner. There was no steak in the refrigerator, but ice wrapped in a tea cloth helped the eye to feel slightly less painful. She'd gone. She'd gone and she'd taken his son. 'A proper wife would've tended to me. Mind, I did tell her to bugger off, I suppose.' But try as he might, he couldn't stop loving her. He would always love Emily, but a man had needs . . .

He tried and failed to read the newspaper. Apart from his half-blindness, he was worried sick about Betsy, and he was shaking. Would the ugly, fat sod kill her? God knew he was big enough and angry enough. According to Betsy, Martin Liptrott was still 'like a little boy down there', and it had never been a real marriage. Well, Joe certainly knew how that felt, because Em was a cold fish, though it wasn't all her fault, was it? Joe couldn't stay the course. Even preparing a woman was difficult, as he got over-stimulated and . . . well, it was called premature ejaculation, and though the doc had tried to help, nothing worked.

Fortunately, neither of his women knew that he, too, was different. Emily had never expected much, so the little he had to offer had suited, as she was glad when the business was over. Betsy, a true virgin, was happy as long as he helped her attain some pleasure when he had finished. They'd been lucky so far, as no pregnancy had ensued. Most of the time, he used that thick rubber thing, but sometimes . . . He wiped his brow, flinched when he hit a sore spot. If she had a child, Marty would know for certain that any issue was a bastard.

Right. That was it; his mind was made up. The business was doing well, so he could pay cash, no mortgage necessary. The Sandersons could be living almost opposite Bolton School within weeks. Emily would be on top of her new job, as the infirmary was not far away, school would be on the doorstep, while Joe's drive to his workshop would be no more difficult than it was now. This house was about to go on the market, because he could no longer expect Emily or Betsy to accept the status quo. Hmm. The wife wasn't the only one to know a bit of Latin.

It was an end of terrace on Mornington Road, a large enough pile of Victoriana, with a back yard instead of a garden. Due to an extended kitchen, the plot at the rear was rather small, but a smart bathroom, a downstairs lavatory and a Sanderson kitchen in mint condition should appeal to Her Royal Highness.

Hidden in the wilds, Emily had married late and her family had cast her out. As they all stank of pigs, cows and horses, God alone knew how they managed to feel superior to a qualified and experienced master carpenter, though he suspected it was something to do with land. They had land to spare, acreage enough for four or five farms. It stretched in a relatively narrow swathe right across Lancashire and almost into the mountains. Relatively narrow meant several miles, of course.

They were a tough lot who had dedicated their lives to the improvement of stock, so they knew all about hard work, he had to allow them that. But they were greedy, and they had drummed into their children the concept that land should marry land. Because of Emily's undeniable beauty, they had expected a climb-up of a marriage, since she spoke well, carried herself nicely and attracted attention. However, shyness had held her back until she'd met the Sanderson chap, and it had all run downhill from there.

Educated privately, Emily was his superior in many

45

ways, but he was the one who funded their current lifestyle, who paid for uniform, school meals, piano lessons, toys, bicycles, improvements to the house, groceries, household bills, his wife's clothing. He knew that she missed open spaces, her horses, her siblings. And in spite of everything, he loved her to bits, while she respected him to a degree.

Oh God, what a mess, and all of his own making. In a way, he couldn't blame Marty Liptrott, because impotence must be a horrible thing. But.

But a man had needs, and he had needed Betsy. She was uneducated, not always clean, while her conversational skills were minimal, but she welcomed him physically, and that fact allowed him release and relief. He had never loved poor Betsy. She was a good laugh, and she made excellent chip butties, yet apart from the sex they were just good friends.

His tongue found a loose incisor in his lower jaw. Oh, wonderful. Another visit to the dentist might well result in a plate with one tooth on it. Actually, the tooth next to it wasn't exactly standing to attention. What about Betsy, though? Would she have run away to her mother's house on Ainsworth Lane? Oh, he hoped somebody was protecting her. She had brothers . . .

At last, he fell asleep. In dreams, he watched helplessly as his wife was trampled to death under the hooves of a wild horse, while Betsy was pulverized by her husband. It was all his fault; even the horse was his fault. He woke convinced that life had to change. Had it not been for the school, he would have engineered a move to Liverpool here and now, because Liverpool was recovering from a crippling war, and factory units were cheap to rent. 'All in good time,' he breathed. 'All in good time.'

*

Emily Sanderson was also deep in thought. Unbeknown to the rest of her kin, she had money. The maiden great-aunt who had always supported her, who had railed against the rest of the family, had bequeathed more than a piano to her favourite girl. The account, in Emily's name only, was supervised by an excellent adviser with the Midland Bank. She saw him quarterly, and was pleased to note that her original investment had more than doubled.

But although she had this running-away fund, she would never separate Andrew from his father unless life became unsupportable. Joseph was not a bad man. He was an excellent provider, and he took care to spend time with his son, although lately a distance had appeared to exist between the two. She and Joseph still talked, real conversations about the state of the world, politics, furniture design. Had they not been married, they might have been the very best of friends.

'Are you awake, Mother?'

'Yes, I am. You may use the bathroom first. When we're both ready, we'll go home.'

'Right.' He got out of bed.

'Andrew?'

'Yes?'

'I'll never leave him as long as he treats you well. And the move to Liverpool won't happen until you've finished school. He'll have calmed down by now, I expect. He's like a rocket – a whoosh and a bit of flame, and anger's all done. Don't worry. Life will improve, I promise you.'

On his way to the bathroom, he stopped and turned. He simply asked, 'Where are you from originally, Mother?'

She awarded him the broadest of her many smiles. 'Over the hills and far away, my darling.' She nodded. 'Yes, very far away.'

Three

Katherine Rutherford threw herself with typical careless-
ness on to her sister's sofa. She kicked off her shoes and
reached up to accept a glass of red wine. 'Helen, I am so
far beyond merely tired. Even my hair's too exhausted to
do as it's told. Why weren't we warned about the fact that
children are parasitic by nature? They're eating me up,
and I'm already too short. Daddy should have told us; he's
a doctor, so he should know about these things. He never
says nothing about nothing, does he?' Kate owned perfect
English, and came across for much of the time as an
educated woman, yet she slipped in and out of local
vernacular with no warning. It was part of her charm, and
Helen loved her for it.

'A sawbones, darling. He knows little or nothing about
humanity, and he hasn't spoken in joined-up writing since
Mummy died. Anyway, I'm the one with the newborn.
Your Philip's at school, and Rosie's in nursery. I know
you've had parents' evening tonight, but come on. You're
not stuck with the definitely-not-intellectually-stimulating
day in and day out. The most exciting part of my life is
Cassie's weigh-in. Till she pukes on my clothes or spits at
those very fierce nurses.'

They sat next to each other in a short but stony silence,
wondering and worrying about the generations above and
below them. Each had two children, plus a father named

Andrew Sanderson, an ex-surgeon so celebrated that he had been honoured by the palace. 'OBE?' Kate took an unladylike slurp of one of her brother-in-law's precious vintage reds. 'Old Bloody Egotist. Ian visited him last week, and he was more interested in some dog than in conversation with his only son. Mind, Ian can be a bit too earnest.'

Helen smiled ruefully. Her sister's behaviour was typically amusing. 'I'd better not drink any more. I don't want to make Cassie ill.'

Kate snorted. 'Get her on the bottle and take a walk on the wild side, our kid. I couldn't have managed with a succubus hanging from one of my tits for twelve hours a day. The woman next door to me has great flappy things drooping down to her waist. She's only thirty-seven, but five kids have left her looking like several hundredweight of King Edward spuds. No. I've done my bit, one of each – sorted.' She studied her elegant younger sister. Helen had inherited their father's height, while Kate, the elder by a couple of years, was tiny as their mother had been. 'You're perfect,' she grumbled.

'And you're a very pretty little doll, so shut up.' Helen sighed deeply. 'Daniel wants a son. Well, his mother does, so he does.'

Kate remained undaunted. 'Look, you have two girls, Ian has twin boys. So do a straight swap, goods returnable within twenty-eight days if customer not satisfied. If, once the warranty runs out, you find yourself lumbered with a kid you don't like, mark it up and sell it on to some Hollywood tart who wants children, but no stretch marks. Not a problem.'

Helen collapsed in a weepy heap of laughter. Kate had been impossible forever. 'Stop it, you. I'm still postnatal.' She sniffed and smiled bravely. 'They were so in love, though, weren't they?'

'Who were?'

'Mummy and Daddy.'

'They were. And we were sometimes relegated to the bottom of the division, so poor Eva looked after us while her spinster sister raised her kids. Madness all round.'

'Will you stop making me laugh, Kate? I've told you, I'm postnatal, forever near to either tears or laughter, no middle ground. And our parents always gave us good holidays. Oh, I'm so hormonal.'

Kate shrugged. 'I'm the same. I've every intention of remaining so until my kids are at least twenty. That aside, the contraceptive pill is my lifeline. I won't let Richard near me till I've done at least five re-counts of the packet, by which time he's asleep anyway. Management skills, you see. Mine are so honed that I've never had to plead a headache.' She delivered the lie slickly. Richard and she were blissfully happy.

Helen dried her eyes. Daniel's disappointment on learning that a second girl was on the way had cut her to the quick. Sarah and Cassandra were perfect little girls; why did men set so much store by reproducing creatures of their own gender? Being female hadn't held her back; she and her sister were both successful. Kate, who described herself as a go-getter running out of go and getting tired, owned an employment agency. Fortunately, she had an excellent manager, and was no longer full-time. Helen, a lecturer in modern languages, was currently on maternity leave. 'Kate?'

'What?'

'We do what Mummy and Daddy did. We have part-time nannies.'

'Yes, I suppose we do.'

'Then why ... why do we blame them?'

'Because they were occasionally too wrapped up in lurve to spend time with us. Rosie can read, you know. I made damned sure they could both read by the age of three. And I play with them, make cakes with them, talk to them whenever I'm with them. What did we get? A vague good night at bedtime, an occasional story from that tedious fairy-tale book, meals in the nursery and just each other and Eva for company. Living with an ageing Romeo and Juliet was tiresome. I'm quite determined to fall out of love with Richard for the sake of my children. It's my maternal duty.'

Helen leaned back and closed her eyes. Kate had always been strong, opinionated and amusing, while she, younger by a relatively short time, was quieter and more thoughtful. She appreciated her sister, but Kate could be rather tiring for a new mum who was breastfeeding, exhausted and unhappy because her husband needed a son. 'Kate, he wants me to have another child as soon as possible. I don't want to be pregnant again. Not yet, anyway.'

'Bloody selfish bloody men.' The older sister drained her glass. 'Look, he can't make you do anything. The law changed yonks ago. He doesn't own you – you aren't a serf. You committed the sins of giving him a beautiful daughter and a sweet new baby girl. If he wants a son, let him rut elsewhere.'

Helen shuddered. 'I adore Daniel, as you know very well, Kate. I can't share him. I couldn't bear the idea of him having special moments with another woman. That would kill me.'

Kate held her tongue for once. Daniel Pope was not all he seemed, but she wasn't prepared to break her tall little sister's heart. While in his cups, he'd tried his luck with Kate, two of her friends and even with the caterer at one event. A jeweller, he travelled in Europe and South Africa. Much of his time was spent in Amsterdam, where matchless diamonds were outnumbered only by women very happy to entertain a man, especially a wealthy one. 'Helen, get your strength back, then tell him to piss off. Two children are enough. We should replace just ourselves, because the world's already crammed and polluted.'

'I don't want to lose him, Kate.'

In Kate's opinion, the sooner Daniel buggered off, the better. Helen was stunning, even now with some of the baby-weight still lingering. She was tall, full-breasted and owned a waist that would be tiny again within weeks. Her legs were perfect, and a flawless waterfall of dark, shiny hair flowed halfway down her back. Both girls had the startling, bright blue eyes inherited from their parents, but Helen's were huge, with lashes that touched her cheeks when her eyes were closed. If Helen would just put herself back on the market, she'd be snapped up faster than goods in Harrods' New Year sale.

Kate had no illusions about herself. She was shorter, less curvaceous and nowhere near as pretty, yet she attracted men like flies round an open jam pot. Kate was a challenge, and it showed. Men liked a challenge, while she enjoyed swatting flies, so her life was fuller and easier than Helen's.

While half the male students were in love with her, Helen's head and heart were full of Daniel. She needed a new man, but she didn't even know it. 'Show him a yellow card, sweetie. Deliver a lecture on fair play, and red card him if he still refuses to be grateful for what he has. Your husband is an arrogant twit. Look at Richard. He's babysitting so that I can spend the night here. In the morning, he'll wash Philip and Rosie, feed them, dress them and take them to school and nursery. He's a bloody godsend. I really don't know how I'd manage without him.'

'I know, I know. But Daniel works so hard, always on the go, travelling, buying, looking for the best at lower prices, negotiating deals—'

'Yes, we all know how difficult life is for a millionaire,

Helen. It must be terrible; up in the air in triple-A class, champagne, pretty hostesses serving his meals. Awful. Especially for a man with no son to inherit his empire. Pope the Jeweller must go on, you see.'

'You hate him.' Helen's voice was a mere whisper.

'I didn't say that. I'm just glad I married a boring defence lawyer.' She loved her Richard wholeheartedly, but he, like everyone else including herself, was the butt of many of her jokes. 'Actually, he's not boring. He's defending a murder suspect next week. She's a very elegant woman of fifty who'd had enough of her husband's philandering. Cutting bread for toast, she was. Big house, seven acres and a lovely orchard – a wonderful life if you just glanced at her.'

'And?'

'She cut an extra slice. His throat.'

'Hell's bells.'

'Quite. So she washed the knife, washed her hands, picked up the phone and told the police what she'd done. "I made sure he was dead before I phoned you," she said. Apparently, he'd fathered several children, none with her. She couldn't have babies. Perhaps you can't carry boys? But stay away from the bread knife, sweetie.'

Helen swallowed. 'Will Richard win the case?'

'Undoubtedly. He has so many witnesses, they'll have to take a number out of a machine like they do in the haematology clinic. The judge will fall asleep due to boredom. Actually, it's a female judge, so that's a help, because she'll probably listen. Two women say they were drugged and raped, and one poor girl gave birth to a disabled child. By the time Richard's done his turn, everybody in the court will be congratulating the widow. Oh, and she's got post-traumatic stress disorder, so she's lost her sheen. She twitches a lot. Richard reckons the twitch alone will get her off.'

'Who's speaking up for the dead man?'

'Nobody. Even his family couldn't stand him. There were seven people at the funeral, and one of them was in a box. Four carried him, one was the undertaker who led the coffin in, while a vicar of some sort stood at the front. When the deceased went through the curtains into the furnace, everybody sighed with relief and went for a quick dip in beer at a nearby pub. Even the vicar took a paddle on the wild side and had half a shandy. I'd love to have been there, but I would have swelled the numbers. Anyway, I'd have applauded when he went into the fire. I wouldn't have been able to help myself.'

Cassie began to wail on the baby intercom. It was a hungry cry. Immediately, Helen jumped to her feet.

'Hang on, hang on,' Kate said. 'Do you have your milk in bottles?'

Helen nodded.

'Then leave her to me.'

'She won't accept the rubber teat yet, Kate.'

'You wanna bet? You're the adult, and she learns your rules. Start early.' She left the room and walked upstairs. After lifting the baby from her crib, she placed her on the plastic mat and changed her nappy. 'Right, kiddo. I'm in charge this time. Let's show Mummy how good we both are. Don't let me down, or I shan't let you forget it for the rest of my life.'

Downstairs, Kate took the bottle from Helen. 'Go away,' she whispered. 'Stay out of her eyeline and leave me to it. Now. Booty, booty, bootiful girl, Cassandra. This is your Aunt Katherine speaking. In the event of difficulty, an oxygen mask will drop down, so wear it. Exits are here, there and everywhere. Your lifebelt is under your seat, and we are currently cruising at a height of thirty thousand feet. What I'm not saying is that in the event of difficulty, this metal object will go into the ground like a sharply honed javelin at the Olympics, but never mind. You won't feel a thing.'

Helen, open-mouthed, stared at her sister and the baby. Cassandra Jane Pope was sucking from a bottle while her aunt talked nonsense. How did Kate manage so well? Everyone took notice of her. Babies, pensioners and all in between cooperated with her. It might have been easy to succumb to jealousy, but Helen loved the terrible, wonderful, crazy woman who was her sister. 'I love you, Katherine Mary,' she said.

'And I love you, Helen Andrea. This is one helluva smart kid. She's talking to me with her eyes. Boys are such dull, slow creatures during these early weeks. Philip was rather like a chunk of red meat, colourful, but lifeless. Rosie was born a comedienne. She never stopped smiling and making us laugh.'

'Like her mother, then.'

'Thank you. We do our best, don't we, Cassie? Don't we? Come on, it's half time.' She removed the bottle, sat the baby upright on a knee, left hand providing a second, firmer spine, right hand spread across the infant's jaw. Two belches and a gurgle later, Cassie was rewarded with the rest of her bottle.

'How do you happen to know what to do every time?'

'Study. I read. I watch, and I did a course in psychology after my degree. But I seem to know people the minute I meet them. It's not all a bed of roses, Helen. Sometimes even my heart breaks. I'll meet a decent man in his fifties, well educated and experienced, and I try to stay upbeat for his sake, because we are a recruitment shop. But I know that some smart kid with a meaningless degree will get the job. Kids come cheaper. Media studies, bloody sports science – they'll be giving honours in breathing soon. I mean, look what you have to offer – three languages, plus a bit of English, swearing included. I did politics, philosophy and economics – all relevant to my area of work.'

'Yes, it's sad.'

'Sad? The place is going to the dogs. Teachers get through on a wing, a prayer and more vodka than Russia makes. I'm lucky. Philip's teacher can spell my son's name. Will wonders ever cease?'

The phone rang. Helen picked up the nearest handset. In her opulent sandstone mansion, there were at least ten to choose from. 'Hello? Helen Pope here.' She smiled. 'Ah, Daniel Pope. I think you may be my husband.' The smile began to fade. 'What? Will you say that again? Tomorrow? Right. Right. Who was that? Who the hell was that? Goodbye.'

Kate studied her baby sister. Helen's face was an unusual shade of grey, and her breathing was wrong. 'Helen? Helen, what's the matter?' There had been no sloppy kiss delivered into the mouthpiece, no declaration of undying love, no mention of the children. Suddenly, Kate was glad she had come, because Helen was going to need her.

Helen pulled herself together and fled upstairs.

Kate followed at a slower pace with Cassie asleep in her arms. When the baby was back in her crib, Kate entered the master suite. She found her sister dry-eyed and staring at herself in the mirror. 'I'm beautiful, Kate,' she whispered. 'Even I can say that, because it's a fact, not a piece of self-praise.'

'You are, my love. You're Mummy all over again, but taller and even more of a stunner.'

'Then why?'

'No idea, Helen. Was he . . . was he with somebody?'

Helen nodded. 'A woman arrived when he was talking to me. She shouted "Hello, darling", and Daniel covered the mouthpiece, but I still heard him hissing at her. "Fuck off, you stupid bitch." My heart stopped. I couldn't breathe. It was a waking nightmare. I felt as if I might drop dead at any second.'

'I noticed.'

'Kate?'

'Yes, love?'

'Bring me the large scissors from my sewing and tapestry kit.'

'Why?'

'Just do it.'

It was on this evening in early October 2000 that Katherine Rutherford found herself on a dizzying learning curve. The sweet, biddable, loving girl named Helen was not a bottomless pit of goodness. With no expression on her face, no tears, no words, Helen cut many thousands of pounds' worth of Savile Row's finest products to pieces. Murdered silk shirts, abbreviated trousers and armless jackets were piled in a huge heap on the walk-in wardrobe floor. His underclothing was shredded, as were his socks. On top of the heap, she placed a wedding photograph, then a second picture of herself. In this black and white photograph, Helen smiled at the camera. All she wore was that smile, diamond earrings and necklace, and a pair of sky-high heels.

'Come,' she said.

Kate, now reduced to playing the part of an unquestioningly obedient servant, followed Helen into what she termed the dungeon. The first cellar room contained Daniel's photographic equipment. Cameras were smashed, and more nude studies of the photographer's wife suffered the same fate as his wardrobe. Helen cut up negatives, tore at silver umbrellas and destroyed lights. In the second, smaller room, she opened a safe and emptied it of precious gems, completed jewellery items and heaps of cash, all of which were thrown casually into a bin bag. 'This is stuff the taxman needs to know about,' she said, almost to herself. She then moved to the wine cellar, where some priceless vintages were stored.

She couldn't be bothered with a corkscrew, so she threw the more expensive wines at the walls. 'Stand back, Kate. Glass flies, and you don't want any red ruining your clothes.' By the time she was finished, the place looked like a murder scene. 'Right, that's that done. No need to bother with the whites and rosés – he doesn't like them. Now, we pack.'

'What? But where–' Kate realized that argument and suggestion would be fruitless.

'He'll be on a plane very shortly,' Helen said. 'He will understand that I haven't taken kindly to his ongoings, so he won't wait until tomorrow.' She turned and looked at her sister. 'Did you know?'

'Well, I–'

'DID YOU KNOW?'

Kate nodded.

'Why didn't you tell me?'

'Because . . . well, I didn't want to hurt you. And the messenger sometimes gets shot. Where are we going?'

'To Daddy's. It's bigger than your house, and I quite like Blundellsands.'

'There's nothing wrong with Woolton,' Kate said. 'And I'll look after you. Helen, you've a new baby and–'

'Oh, shut up. Look after me? If you'd kept me in the picture . . . Did he touch you or any of our friends?'

Kate could only nod. For the first time ever, Helen had taken the lead. 'He's a randy bastard. Sorry, babe.'

Helen looked her sister up and down as if assessing a stranger. 'You betrayed me by your silence. Now, I don't care how drunk you are. Fill your car with my stuff; the suitcases are in my dressing room. When you run out of cases, use plastic bags. Take the cases and bags to Rosewood, empty them out, then come back with the cases for the rest of it. I'll pack for the children and take them in my car. I am disgustingly sober.'

'As am I now.'

'Good. You might just survive, and you may even keep your licence. Don't forget, you'll need change for the tunnel. Sorry to have inconvenienced you by moving across the river to Neston.'

By ten o'clock, both cars were filled to bursting, though the good news was that Kate wouldn't have to return. The few bits and pieces of Helen's that were not on board were maternity wear or aged beyond revival.

They began the drive across the Wirral, a place Helen had come to love. She would miss the open fields, the farms, and Ness Gardens, a wondrous place that was the property of Liverpool University. Students came there to study botany, and Helen had often tagged along. She was leaving behind a whole way of life, but she would stick to her guns. Daniel was finished, and she intended to take him to the cleaners. His clothes, on the other hand, would need no cleaning. Oh yes, the man would have to learn to look on the bright side.

Kate unlocked her father's front door. She was accosted immediately by something that seemed to move at the speed of light.

Andrew appeared. He was rubbing his eyes, and it was plain that he'd been dozing in his armchair. 'Kate?'

She dumped the first lot of luggage in the hall. The dog returned, jumped up and almost knocked her off her feet. 'Helen won't like you,' she advised him. 'Jump up at that baby, and you'll be toast.'

Andrew remained confused. 'What's going on?' he asked.

'Helen's coming home,' was all the reply Kate offered before going for more cases and bin liners.

'Coming home?' he asked the dog. 'She has a home on the Wirral. Sorry to be the bearer of bad news, Storm, but Eva is not the only human female who speaks no sense. Come on. Let's put you somewhere safe.'

When he returned, Andrew's younger daughter was in the hall. 'Hello, Daddy. I'm afraid this is an invasion, but it can't be helped. I need four bedrooms; two for the children, one for me and one for the nanny. She had the night off, so I'll send for her tomorrow. Close your mouth, dear, there's a bus coming.'

Andrew clamped his teeth together. 'What the hell's happened?'

'He's in bed with an Amsterdam whore. Well, he was. By now, he'll be somewhere over the Channel unless the plane has crashed. One can only hope. Though it would be a pity if other passengers suffered.'

A two-year-old Sarah, still sleeping, was deposited in Andrew's arms. 'Take her upstairs, Daddy,' Kate ordered.

He complied. Where his daughters were concerned, resistance was futile. He remembered Kate dressing him down a few years ago, accusing him and Mary of near neglect, so he'd better start trying to atone for past sins. The feel of the child in his arms was lovely. Sarah was beautiful, dark-haired and perfect like her mother. And like her grandmother.

He came downstairs, lifted the carrycot and carried the baby up to her room. On the landing, he stood for a while. Sarah was only two. She probably still needed a cot. Where was it? Ah yes. He'd put it in the used-to-be airing cupboard. With his new combination boiler, he didn't need an airing cupboard to hold a tank. But he did need a cot.

Minutes later, two daughters found their father on the landing. Pieces of wood lay round him. 'Little Sarah might tumble out of bed, so . . .' He waved a hand over the dismantled cot. 'I made this, you know,' he said. 'When

Mary was expecting you, Katherine, I built this little number from scratch. Every spindle, I carved and smoothed. Dad did some of it. He was still agile back then.'

They helped him carry it into Sarah's room. As quietly as possible, they built the frame, put in the base and mattress, then folded single bed covers until they fitted. Sarah was lifted from the single bed and placed in safety. 'Thanks, Daddy,' Kate said. 'Very thoughtful of you. Cassie will manage in her carrycot for now.'

He reached out for his younger daughter. 'Come downstairs, Helen. Kate might begin unpacking while you talk to me.'

After ten minutes, his clothing was wet with her tears. The really sad thing was that he couldn't remember when he had last comforted either of his daughters. Ian had come to him for advice, but Ian was now a doctor, so their conversations had been . . . well . . . rather clinical. 'Come on, sweetheart,' he urged. 'Are you breastfeeding?'

Still sobbing, she nodded.

'Well it'll be curdled at this rate, Helen. It'll probably come out pasteurized, too.' He kissed the top of her head, wondered when he'd last done that, and what kind of a father was he, anyway? This beautiful child had inherited his height and Mary's face, Mary's body, so she was an elegant specimen, about five feet nine or ten inches tall, curvaceous, a stunning sight. Daniel Pope needed kneecapping, and Andrew would not be on hand to mend such damage, as he had resigned.

'Kate knew, Daddy,' she managed.

'She loves you, child. Kate may seem tough, but she has a big heart, and she adored you right from the beginning of your life. Don't blame her. She'll have lived for some time in a terrible quandary.'

'Yes.'

'You'll be all right here. I'll look after you, I promise.'

'Oh, Daddy.'

'I know, I know.' Poor Kate, too. Kate's beauty was in her smile, in her attitude. Four or five inches shorter than her sister, Kate projected warmth, superior intellect, generosity, and the promise of fun. Had Helen not been born, the older girl would have been judged beautiful, but she had stood for almost a whole lifetime in the shadow of utter perfection. The children had been twenty-two, twenty and eighteen when Mary had died. Had he been there for them? Had he buggery. So consumed by his own grief, so devastated, selfish, stupid, arrogant . . .

She calmed down gradually. 'I loved him so much, Daddy. Is it possible to love too much?'

'Yes. Your mother and I were guilty of that. We never really learned to communicate properly with our own children when you were little. I remember feeling terrible when I gave you both away at your weddings. The most wonderful sight until then was your mother when we married, but you outshone even her. I am so sorry.'

Helen raised her head. 'Don't worry, we got through. But you see, Daddy, had Mummy ever betrayed you, you would have hated her big-style. Daniel now has no clothes, no wine, no stash of money or jewels of dubious origin.'

'That wasn't hatred, baby. That was temper. Temper's flame is white-hot and soon burns out. Hatred comes later. It's a cold place.' He paused. 'Hey, what do you mean about the wine? I would have liked it, you wastrel.'

At last, she smiled through the tears.

'A rainbow,' he said. 'The sun shining on cloud. What a beauty you are.'

'There was no room in the cars for the wine, Daddy.'

'Ah. In that case, you could have swapped the children for wine. Daniel would have come home to a couple of screamers, and no wine to calm his nerves.'

Helen sat up. 'Now I know where Kate got her sense of humour. You're wicked, aren't you?'

'Your mother certainly thought so. I teased her mercilessly right to the ... right to the end. But she always got me back while she was younger and fit. Not straight away, because her revenge needed to be a surprise or a shock. I got into bed one night and put my whole weight on a whoopee cushion. She leapt out and sprayed the whole room with good perfume.'

But Helen was deep in thought. 'I'll never trust him again, you see. If he talked me round and got me home, I'd be on pins every time he went away. Well, I can't live like that. I'm an all-or-nothing person. So even if or when I stop being angry, his chances of getting me back are non-existent.' She sighed heavily. 'But I have my children. He'll never take them away from me. And I have sufficient money to buy my own house, but that's a secret between you, Kate and me. Ian too, when I see him.'

'Richard will help you. I know he specializes in crime, but he'll know someone who does matrimonial stuff. That's a good man with a good wife. You deserve someone more stable and reliable than Pope.'

'He'll come here,' she whispered.

'I know.'

She kissed her father's forehead. 'I must go and make peace with my sister.'

'Good idea.'

He let the dog in. 'Sit.'

Storm sat.

'More rules, sorry. You don't go near babies. They're little and kept in boxes. They smell of three things in which you take enthusiastic interest – milk, urine and faeces. All right?'

'Woof.'

'Don't scratch your ear when I'm talking to you. Sarah's the bigger one, and isn't usually in a box. Don't hurt her.'

'Woof.'

Storm's learning curve was erratic. It wasn't so much a curve as the temperature chart at the bottom of a bed containing a very sick person. A rather zigzag affair, it was, since Storm seemed to learn in fits and starts. He remained clumsy; it was hard to believe that he had just four feet, since he stumbled frequently over something invisible, and never failed to look back at whatever it wasn't.

But Storm had brought life into the house. And now there were no spare bedrooms, because– The phone rang. Andrew picked it up. 'Yes?'

'Where's my wife?'

Andrew winked at the dog. 'I haven't anybody's wife here, sorry.' He pressed the off switch and, when it rang again, answered it for a second time. 'Oh, it's you, Daniel. What? Helen? No, no, I'm sorry. I didn't recognize your voice – did you ring a few seconds ago? . . . What? Helen's with her sister as far as I know.' He paused and held the receiver away from his ear. The man was ranting like a lunatic. 'All your clothes, Daniel? I'm sorry, but that doesn't sound like my daughter . . .'

'It sounds like your other one, though.'

'Kate? No, she's all wind and water . . . She what? Oh, hang on a minute, Daniel. Kate throwing wine away? That would be like separating her from her breath.' Again he held the phone at a distance. 'No, Daniel, no. Separating my older daughter from her breath would not be a good thing. Her husband has friends in high and low places.'

Daniel moved up a gear. 'I was having a massage. Mariella calls everyone darling.'

'Yes, yes, I'm sure she does.'

'I am a faithful man, sir.'

Andrew tut-tutted into the phone. 'I hope you crossed your fingers when you told that whopper, mate. You've had a go at Kate, some friends, and a girl who was serving the food. And that was just one function. I understand this much – my Katie knows people. She has this ability to see inside, got it from her mother. Kate never liked you. Said your birth certificate was a waste of ink and paper, and you should be charged for oxygen.'

'I'll do her for slander.'

'Will you? She's married to a top barrister. Now, go to bed and leave me alone.' He switched off the phone.

Applause from the doorway made him turn. 'Stay,' he told the dog, who took no notice whatsoever and bounded over to the two girls, who bent to pet him. After all the untruths like 'Good dog', and 'Who's a lovely boy?' the girls came into the room. 'So he's looking for her?' said Kate.

'And you. He thinks you did all the damage.'

Kate shook her head. 'No, it was madam here. She was bloody magnificent.'

Andrew cleared his throat. 'Don't swear in front of Storm. He has enough bad habits as it is.'

Helen dug her sister in the ribs. 'See? I told you your warped humour's inherited. Daddy never spoke a great deal, but every sentence was a killer.' She sat on the floor. 'What have I done, Storm? What have I done?' The dog licked her face till she giggled. 'Such a soppy article you are.'

'Why the dog?' Kate asked.

'It dashed in during a thunderstorm, undernourished and afraid. It stayed. Eva wasn't best pleased, but I've never seen her best pleased. And what we have here is just seven months' worth. God knows how tall he'll be full grown. I wonder if we could get his legs shortened?'

Kate shook her head. 'The NHS won't touch it, so you'd have to go BUPA. Is Storm a member?'

'No, but I did a good job on the vet, so I play on his gratitude. What do you think? Three inches?'

Helen sighed. 'I have a dead mother, two daughters and no son, an errant soon to be ex-husband, and the father from hell.' She looked hard at him. 'She is definitely your daughter.'

Kate hooted with laughter. 'Listen who's talking. You might be slow to boil, but once you get there, you are bloody dangerous.'

'No swearing,' mouthed Andrew silently while pointing to the dog. He raised his voice to normal level. 'I have to say, Helen, that the destruction of good wine is sacrilege. But he deserved it. Right. Toast and drinking choc with squirty cream, or double brandies all round?'

They opted for toast and chocolate squirties. Helen needed her thinking head, while Kate wanted to sleep without the promise of a headache in the morning. 'Did you text Sofia?' Kate asked.

'Yes. She's going to pick up her things tomorrow and get a taxi to here. Thank goodness her English is a sight better than my Polish. She says she isn't afraid of him, but she might put 999 on speed dial. Lovely girl. She's marvellous with the children.' Tears threatened, and she blinked them away. 'Oh Kate. I am so going to miss the man I thought I had.'

'I know. But you needed to find out for yourself, love. If I'd told you during your pregnancy or just after Cassie's birth . . . unfortunately, you got the awful truth while you're still weakened anyway. Look at me, babe. I know you love your job, but get a portfolio. You should be on the front of magazines.'

'Don't talk daft; you know I'm thirty.'

'And you know you're beautiful.'

'OK, but I'm not taking my clothes off. He was my husband, so that was different.'

66

'Hmm. It certainly was. I'm glad you left the reminder next to the wedding photo.'

Helen almost laughed. 'He wanted me to be an advertisement for the shops. All a woman needs is Pope's jewellery – that sort of thing. I would have been veiled digitally, though not by him, the self-elected camera expert and purist. Well, if he uses that picture without paperwork signed by me, I'll go for the jugular.'

'Because you won't sign.'

'Spot on, Kate.'

They sat in a row on the floor, daughter, father, daughter, dog opposite and staring at them as they ate toast. They compared squirty moustaches. 'Oh look,' cried Kate. 'It's Mr Sanderson, OBE. Such a dignified man. Did you know he'd just retired?'

Helen forced herself to eat. She was feeding a baby, so the knots in her stomach had to be ignored. He was home. Tomorrow, poor Sofia had to face him on her own.

'Helen?'

'Yes, Daddy?'

'Do you want me to go and help your nanny tomorrow?'

Was he reading her mind? 'What if he hits you?'

'I shall take my guard dog. Well, guard pup.'

It was then that Helen had a fit of hysteria. She fell about laughing at the moustaches, the salivating animal, the memory of what she'd done to Daniel Pope's belongings, the idea of Daddy and Storm acting tough. Laughter became tears, tears turned to hiccups, and Storm ate what was left of her toast.

Kate jumped up and shook her sister. 'I'll slap you hard, Helen.'

She calmed down slowly, but the hiccups remained fierce.

Andrew observed. They'd probably been like this since

childhood, dependent on each other. He had worked, Mary had worked, but he had to start from now, because clocks and calendars had no reverse gears. 'When you've got your diaphragm into some kind of order, give me the address of your nanny, then text her and say I'll pick her up at about nine.'

'Are you taking the dog?' Kate asked.

The dog in question woofed.

'Shut up,' his master ordered.

Storm woofed again.

'No, he can stay here. Storm remains a work in progress, not fit for Neston. But he has a detached residence of his own in the back garden. I'll stick him in there with bones and toys. You should shop for food, Kate. Helen, lend your children to Eva. She may even smile.'

The girls went off to bed. Andrew sat with his dog. 'Four beautiful women in my life now, Stormy. No space in the house, and you and I are the only blokes. Kate will leave, but the rest will stay for a while. In your basket. Go on. See you in the morning.'

It was an icy-blue day, scarcely a cloud in the sky and a definite nip in the air. Andrew, having left chaos behind, was glad to escape in his car. Sarah was screaming because she had woken in an unfamiliar room, and Cassie had joined in to keep her sibling company. Held in the unusually tense arms of her mother, the baby was not a happy bunny.

'You're running away again,' Andrew accused himself. Eva had not yet arrived; let her take up the slack when she got here. Andrew was a man on a mission, and a man on a mission should not be held up. Kate, too, had disappeared into the bowels of Sainsbury's, where she had a list as long as an arm. She would leave this afternoon, as she had a family in Woolton, and Richard had done his fair share of late.

He found the house on Southport Road in Bootle. It was a neat semi with an apron of grass at the front, some pretty borders and an old car in the driveway. He knocked on the door.

A woman approached. He could see her through the frosted glass, and she was shouting, in a foreign language, something or other to someone or other in one of the rooms. She opened the door. 'Hello,' she said. 'You are father of Mrs Pope?'

'Yes. Andrew Sanderson.'

'My Sofia, she is not liking the man, the Mr Pope. He is saying to her things she not repeat to me, her mother. He is animal.'

Andrew offered no reply.

'I am Anya Jasinski.' She shook his hand, her expression solemn. 'My daughter Sofia, she will be here shortly. I cannot introducing you to my husband, because he die.'

'I'm sorry.'

'Yes, is bad. We come here for better life, he was builder. But heart stop very sudden, he gone. Now, I clean for job and my Sofia, she is nanny. She like very much Helen and children, but not the mister.'

'Helen left him, Mrs Jasinski. She's staying with me in Blundellsands. Does Sofia keep a lot of things in Neston?'

'No, she have little. But Helen kind and gave her some things and sewed them right for her. Altering I think is word.'

'Good. Then come with us to ease your mind.'

'This is OK I come?'

'Oh yes.'

'I get coat.'

While Anya got coat, Sofia appeared. 'Mr Sanderson?'

'Hello, Sofia. Yes, I'm Helen's dad, and you will be living

in my house for a while. Helen and the children are already there.'

'Good,' she said. 'Her husband is a pig, but I said nothing, because she was pregnant, then Cassie came. I will sit in the car.'

It occurred to Andrew that he was collecting females. He now had Kate, Helen, Sarah, Cassie, Sofia, Anya and, of course, Eva. Kate would leave today, but he and Storm would continue outnumbered. Did he mind? No, he found himself strangely content. Perhaps he might start now to become a daddy and a granddaddy.

When all three travellers were settled in the car, he realized that he had not so much a backseat driver as a backseat chatterer. Anya didn't like the tunnel. She wittered in Polish when the car entered the darkness, praised the Lord when they emerged at the other end. In fractured English, she exclaimed over everything she saw.

'She doesn't get out often,' Sofia whispered from the front passenger seat.

'This I am hear,' said the Voice.

'Her English is improving,' Sofia said.

'This I am also hear, too.'

Sofia looked over her shoulder. 'Mama, if you have also, you don't need too.'

'Am I need three and four?'

Ah, humour. Andrew managed not to grin. It was clear that he had walked in on a conversation that had gone on for months, if not years. Helen was waiting until Cassie was ready for nursery, at which point Sofia would take a course in teaching English to Polish people. She would do well. According to his daughter, Anya had arrived in England knowing just 'yes' and 'no'. Sofia was a good teacher.

They reached the 'better' side of the Wirral, and Anya

entered an ecstasy of oohs and ahs that were recognizable in any language.

Sofia opened her mobile phone and pressed a number. 'I am coming for my things,' she said tersely. 'No, I have no idea why that was done to your clothes. My mother is with me, as is Helen's father. What? No, no, she is not here. She is in the house of a friend. When I reach your house, you will not come near me, you will not touch me, you will not speak to me, or I shall tell my mother in Polish about what happened. No. It wasn't nothing. Or if it was nothing, that was because I threatened to kick you in the bollocks.'

Andrew decided that his younger companion's English was beyond the merely good.

'What means bullocks?' Anya asked.

'Young cattle,' Andrew replied.

'Ah. These I did not see in field.'

Andrew found himself wondering how many of Daniel's shrivelling testes would be needed to fill an egg cup, let alone a field. The man would be sorely diminished in the eyes of his colleagues, his fellows at the golf club, the people of Neston. The whole world loved Helen; the jewellery community adored her. She was one of those rare women who could do justice to pearls. Whenever *Lancashire* or *Cheshire Life* took photographs at functions, she was placed at the front and in the centre. Well, Daniel had certainly been careless with his greatest asset.

Thornton Hall hove into view.

'This is hotel?' asked the Voice.

'This is the Pope mansion, Mama.'

'In there could live a whole village, Sofia.'

'Yes, it's a good house, Mama, but a bad man.'

'I see.'

They rolled up the gravel drive. If the disturbed

71

chippings scratched his Merc, Andrew would be sending a bill to this creature. He switched off the engine. 'Right,' he said. 'Onward Christian soldiers, marching as to war. Come on, ladies. Let's rescue Sofia's clothes.'

Four

Andrew didn't want to move house. He was used to Crompton Way. This ring road, named after the inventor of the spinning mule, was home, and how would Toodles accept the shift to a different part of this huge town? Cats were acutely aware of their place in the world, and the achievement of that position involved a precise and complicated scientific process.

It took months for a feline to mark its borders, to learn where was safe enough to lie in sunshine, or climb a tree to a point from which it might descend with dignity and without the help of the fire brigade or screaming residents with stepladders. Cats made friends and enemies, and such contacts were vital in the delineation of territorial rights. It wasn't fair. She was just settling down, and she was only a kitten. What if she got lost? What if she tried to find her way back here and got run over by passing traffic?

'Toodles and I don't want to go,' Andrew told his mother. 'Chorley New Road isn't my idea of fun. And why move from a semi to an end of terrace? It makes no sense. I think Dad's losing his grip.'

'Darling, it will be right on top of your school and very close to my work. It makes sense for both of us. And it's by no means an unpleasant house – bigger than this one.'

'I've no wish to live near school. And there's no garden. Toodles likes a garden.'

73

'So do I, Andrew. I have plans to brighten up the yard with some colourful pieces of Victoriana. We'll have plants climbing over a mangle, flowers in dolly tubs and zinc baths – it will be fine. I've even thought of old mirrors to make the space look bigger. It *was* bigger, actually, until the kitchen was extended. But oh, yes, I have several plans. Your father's building a beautiful kitchen for us.'

He had plans, too. He wanted to locate Heathfield Farm, work in the fields, get to know the people who lived there, the lie of the land, why his mother was out of touch with her family—

'Andrew? You seem preoccupied these days. You've scarcely touched the piano. I can't remember when I last heard you practising.'

He was preoccupied. It would soon be time to return to school, and he was planning to be far too busy for school. In his opinion, the most useful parts of education bore no relation to chalk, blackboard and desiccated masters in scruffy gowns and worn-out shoes. Those men floated along corridors as if they were visitors from a distant and very different planet where knowledge grew on trees, though it could be analysed only by the precious few. And the precious few hovered on clouds of academia until brought to earth by the needs of unimportant schoolboys.

'Andrew?'

'It is definitely boring,' he pronounced. 'I learn more out here than I do in the hallowed halls of Bolton School. It's so stuffy and serious and seriously simple.'

'Only because you're far too clever for it. Learn the virtue called patience.'

'They don't teach that. It's not on the curriculum.'

Emily laughed. 'Life will teach you patience, son. It's something we collect over years like cigarette cards. It will arrive.'

Dad was a dictator. He should grow a moustache, adopt a funny walk and become the Führer, because he simply made a decision, and everyone was expected to follow his lead. 'You don't want to move, Mother. I know you'd rather stay here. Why don't we get a vote? Is there no chance of democracy setting foot inside our family?'

Emily shrugged lightly. This son of hers was too clever for his own good; he spoke like an adult, demanded to be treated as an adult. 'Your dad has his reasons, and I'm sure they're valid.'

'Because he was beaten up by that man?'

'Not just that. As I said, it's a larger house. Up a nearby side street, there's a building he can rent as a garage, and it will take even the biggest van for carrying his furniture. The house has a better kitchen and bathroom, four bedrooms, beautiful fireplaces, the sort that have been thrown away by stupid people – it's a nice place, very solid and well constructed. Another point – it's near many of his clients. Most of them live in the better houses further up Chorley New Road.'

'But this is a nice house, Mother.'

'The move is what he wants, Andrew.'

'What about what we want? Don't we count? Don't we have a say in the matter? My best friend's just round the corner.' A thought fell into his mind. Dropped from nowhere, it bounced into and out of his mouth without allowing time for processing. 'Where are your friends?' he asked. 'Over the hills and far away?' He wished he could bite it all back, especially the last bit. It had sounded like mockery, as if he were mimicking the answer she had given to him when he'd asked about her provenance. Sometimes, he went too far.

She put down the pie whose uncooked crust she had been trimming. 'Right. Sit down and I'll tell you. Not the details; the bare bones must suffice for now. I suppose you're old enough to need and deserve some degree of explanation about my past.'

He sat.

'I am from a farming family. My parents wanted me to marry someone with land, and they refused absolutely to accept your father, who was a penniless orphan. After the army, he decided to train as a carpenter, and I admired his determination. Your father does nothing by halves; it was always plain that he would excel in his chosen field. You inherited that trait, so be grateful.'

'Where did you meet?'

'Oh, it happened quite by accident. He was on a picnic with friends, and we got talking. After that, he came up to . . . to the farm regularly. Mother and Father rejected him out of hand, and I didn't want them to push me into a marriage just to gain acreage. I ran away, met my sister a few weeks later, and told her I was married. She said all but Great-aunt Celia had disowned me. And that, as they say, was that.'

'Great-aunt Celia left you the piano?'

'Yes, she left the piano to me. Now, Andrew, please be aware that I have no regrets. My marriage isn't perfect, but I feel better about it than I would have had my parents had their way. I saw myself as just another item in a dowry, as if I were being swapped for four camels, a donkey and a new tent. The whole thing was too Middle Eastern for my liking. As for my friends, they are scattered to the winds; we were educated privately, and the other girls were boarders from all over the place.'

He waited for more, but she went back to her apple pie. They hadn't loved her enough, those Beauchamps, hadn't cared about her. That realization served only to make them more fascinating. 'Are your parents still alive?' he

asked. They were his grandparents. And how could anyone on earth fail to love Mother?

'Oh, yes. My sister finds ways of getting news of births,
deaths and marriages to me. But if I seem friendless, it's
because I have led a life broken into two distinct halves.
And, you know, I need just my books, my music and you.
This little job at the infirmary will fill any gaps, so worry
not, because all will be well.'

Dad had not made an appearance on her list, but
Andrew would not mention that fact. Very carefully, he
had edged his way back into Joe's good books by returning to the workshop for the odd half-day. But he had not
yet found the time to research Heathfield Farm.

'Did you like farming?' he asked.

'Oh, I loved it. I like horses. And cows. Cows are good
people, but horses are clever and courageous. I miss
riding. And the openness of everything, that sense of huge
space. The farm's so big that there are several cottages
dotted about. My family has the main house, but farm
workers occupy smaller houses with barns and so forth,
and each house covers a certain amount of land either for
husbandry or tillage. It works well, like clockwork.'

Andrew, fascinated by his mother's sudden animation,
began to realize how much she had forfeited for Dad. Yet
she hadn't wanted to marry another landowner, hadn't
liked the idea of being part of some exchange deal. He
certainly concurred with that.

Emily read his mind yet again. 'I married late, Andrew.
I'd been forcibly introduced to every young man whose
parents owned land adjoining ours – or, since I'm no
longer a member of the family, should I say theirs? At
some point in life, disobedience with parents becomes part
and parcel of growing up, and my rebellion began when I
was approaching thirty. Like a promising filly, I had been

dragged hither and yon while the parents tried to trade me in. Had they commented on my fetlocks and my withers, I should not have been in the least way surprised. A promising brood mare is what I was for well over ten years. So here I am, and there you have it. Be a dear and shape some leaves from that bit of leftover pastry, sweetheart.'

And that was almost the end of it. Pastry leaves indicated that her soliloquy was done. Andrew made three ornamental adornments for the top of the pie. She was an excellent if rather plain cook. Emily Beauchamp was a farmer's daughter, and Andrew suspected that the recipes had been handed down for generations. His favourite was her braised steak, so tender that it dropped off the fork. 'We went mushroom picking once,' he reminded her.

'We did indeed. I remember setting off before dawn. And it rained, but we found some good, tasty crops.'

'And you knew which were poisonous and which weren't.'

'Yes.'

'That would be part and parcel of your out-of-school learning.'

'I'm sure it was, my dear.'

'That's what I mean. The really useful stuff is learned well away from teachers.'

'Your teachers will get you into a music college or a medical school. You'll need English language, Latin, maths and science. You'll also need top marks in all of them. Does the music department know you're composing, by the way?'

He'd forgotten about that. 'I should have told you. On the Thursday of the second week of term, I'm playing in the Victoria Hall. We've the choir from the girls' division, a three- or four-piece suite—'

'You mean the chamber players?'

'Yes. Then I'm playing my Overture to an Overture.'

'The being born one. Yes, I like that.'

'It's a pain. It's about pain. I'm sure being born hurts, but we don't remember. Actually, I'd better work on it. The birth scream isn't full enough.'

Emily nodded thoughtfully. 'I rather think we do remember being born. It's all tucked away in the pleats of our brain, the first warning that life isn't going to be easy. The animal in us forgets nothing, but the human deletes some unpleasant memories.'

'You're clever. You could have been anything, Mother.'

'I'm your mother, and that's enough for me.'

She was too good for Dad, yet she wasn't, because she'd made a decision and she'd stood by it. And Dad was far from stupid. He was an artist, a king in his field of work. Owning a piece signed by Joseph Sanderson was a feather in anyone's cap. Dad used to sign on the back, but he'd started to do it inside a door or under a shelf, so that his customers wouldn't end up with hernias or slipped discs when they strove to pull out a heavy article to show off its provenance.

'You should have told us weeks ago about the concert. Your father's busy inventing fitted kitchens in solid wood.'

'They already have fixed unit kitchens in America, Mother. Anyway, why should that affect the concert?'

'Because, as you know, he stays on at work designing kitchens in the evenings. He's looking for clients. It's a relatively new concept in this country, though I suppose Londoners will have taken the lead, just as they always do.'

Andrew wondered what his dad really did in the evenings, but he said nothing on the subject. 'You could come by yourself to the concert.'

'Oh no. He's incredibly proud of you. And you know I hate to be out alone, especially in the evenings. But he's been looking at someone named Poggenpohl – don't ask, I've no idea – who has a history with what he called working kitchens, time and motion, the correct way to position sinks and so forth. As long ago as the twenties the unit kitchen was in existence. More recently, fitted kitchens with worktops are being installed in America. So your father's offering custom-made superior fittings. We shall see. The first will be in our Mornington Road house. He will bring people to look at it. And I've just given you the lecture your father delivered to me.'

Andrew knew that Mother wouldn't like having a show kitchen. She was shy. When shopping, she dressed 'down' so that no one would notice her. But some men saw beyond the dowdy navy coat, the headscarf and the clompy shoes. She was beautiful. Had she not been aware of the impact she had, she would never have felt the need to dress 'down'. 'You'll be working some of the time, so let Dad show people his kitchen while you're out.'

'Good idea.' She started to set the table.

Oh well, it looked as if it had all been decided; it was a case of getting on with it and trying not to allow it to hurt too much. He sighed. It was all a part of life's rich backdrop. And he couldn't do anything about it, anyway.

Alone in the office attached to his business, Joe Sanderson was studying photographs of sensible kitchens. The basis seemed to be rooted in a triangular arrangement of sink, cooker and fridge. Even a small kitchen could be improved by the implementation of this rule, making a housewife's life easier and happier. It was all about time and motion, keeping things to hand, and work surfaces. He intended to cash in on it.

His colleagues had gone home, so he was surprised when the outer doorbell rang. No one was expected at this time of day. Customers never visited after hours, and few people came down just to take a casual look at the workshop. A burglar? Burglars didn't ring bells. Sometimes, a quality builder who wanted Sanderson shelves or cupboards installed came to place an order, but seldom out of hours. Oh well, he had better answer it, he decided.

He opened the door warily, only to find poor Betsy standing there. She'd tried to doll herself up a bit, though the result was not good. 'Hello,' he said. She looked as though she'd come out the worse for wear after going five or six rounds with a crew of Fleetwood fishwives. 'Whatever's the matter?'

Betsy pushed her way past him, which was no mean feat, as he was a well-built and powerful man. 'Oh, Joe,' she managed before bursting into tears. 'I don't know what to do.' The words were almost drowned by a river of tears. 'I'm in a right bloody mess.'

'Has he hit you? Because if he has, go to the police.'

Her head shook. 'Not yet. He's not hit me so far, but he will, I'm telling you. I have to get back soon; he's gone to his mam's for an hour because she needs a window mending.'

'Well, he bloody well hit me, lost me two teeth. Come into the office. I've a little paraffin stove, so I'll make you a cuppa.'

It took her several minutes to calm down towards sensible. Blackened eyelashes spilt their colour in twin grey tracks down her cheeks. Garish red lipstick did nothing to improve the appearance of white, albeit mascara-streaked cheeks, while bitten fingernails, also painted red, were ragged and shabby.

'What's the matter?' he asked. 'There's something up with you, I can tell.'

'This.' She placed a work-worn hand on her belly. 'This is the matter.' Her hands looked old and tired. It was clear that cleaning two pubs every morning was not a glamorous job.

Joe staggered back a couple of paces. 'This what?'

'This baby is what. He'll know it's not his, because he can't do nothing, can he? He's as limp as a dead daisy, so I'm in real bother.'

He sat down. 'Are you sure it's mine, Bet?'

The thoughtless, cruel question caused more wailing.

'I'm sorry, lass. I shouldn't have asked that. So what do you want me to do? I'll pay to get rid, but it's illegal.'

'And dangerous,' she screamed. 'I could die. For weeks I've wondered, but I've never been regular, so ... You'd be all right if I died, wouldn't you?' She picked up the sobbing from where she'd left off. After a deep, shuddering breath, she waded in again. 'I never wanted children. I don't like them, but I can't kill it. And he'll notice me getting fatter and fatter. And when he does catch on, he'll murder both of us. I can't see a way out.'

Joe swallowed. He was a strong man, because heaving about great lumps of wood made muscle, but Marty Liptrott was built like a brick outhouse. An angry bully who reacted easily and harshly to insults, he was permanently furious about his impotence. Any child born to poor Betsy could not possibly be his, and murder or serious bodily harm might well be the result when he discovered his wife's condition.

'What are we going to do?' Betsy finally said. 'I know the thing's in my body, but it took two to make it.'

'Sounds like you won't be much of a mother, Bet.'

'Well, it's not my fault. We're not all made the same way.'

Joe pondered. Bolton was a big town, but a man on the bins knew a lot of other bin men, and one of his friends would be clearing away Betsy's rubbish wherever she lived, so moving her from where she was to Halliwell or

Doffcocker was not going to provide an answer. He had to get her out of Bolton. 'I'll need a few days to think,' he said.

She dried her eyes. 'Will you look after me, Joe?'

'Course I will. But I'll not leave my wife and son. I can't leave them.' He scarcely knew why, but he worshipped Emily. She was like a goddess in his book, a lovely Greek or Roman statue that managed to move around and make wonderful meals. Even when she got uppity and on his nerves, he continued to adore her. As for Andrew – well, the lad wasn't a negotiable item, either. Andrew would go far, and Joe was ridiculously proud and almost in awe of him, too. 'You'll have to leave Bolton,' he said. 'But it must all be worked out so that Bird Brain doesn't catch on. And if he thinks I've shifted you, he'll probably cut my throat.'

'Our Elsie,' she said suddenly.

'Wasn't she the one who tackled him about how he is?'

Betsy nodded. 'Aye, she's not been let anywhere near our house since she told him I could get the marriage annulled cos he's useless.'

Joe waited. 'Well, what about her?'

Betsy shrugged. 'Moved to St Helens. They've got a pub with spare rooms. I'm welcome any time. She sends her letters next door to Mrs Bridges, and Mrs Bridges brings them to me when she knows Marty's out. Trouble is, our Elsie doesn't like kids, either.'

'But you'd be safer there. And we might find you somewhere near Elsie when the kiddy's born. Because I'll see you right, lass. From the money point of view, I mean. I'll make sure you and the kiddy have enough, believe me.'

She sighed, her breath shivering its way in and out. 'I'm scared, Joe.'

'You're not on your own. That bloody eunuch you married is madder than a box of frogs. And he has some big mates. I'm telling you now, he'll guess I've had some-thing to do with you flitting.'

'But I can't stay. I daren't stay.'

'No, you can't stay. Unless you have an abortion, and that's risky.'

They sat in silence for several minutes. Each knew that this was no small decision and that there would be no turning back once she'd left. Without risking a life-threat-ening procedure, poor Betsy would become a mother, while Andrew would have a half-sibling. It was a big thing, a damned sight bigger than fitted kitchens, Joe thought as he studied the unattractive creature with whom he had mated. 'Betsy?'

'What?'

'If you had a child, he might want to pretend it's his, then folk would think he was normal. You know what I mean.'

She knew what he meant, all right. 'Listen, you. If I tell him, there'll be no baby, no me and no Marty, because I'll be six feet under and he'll be saying ta-ra to the hangman. You'll likely be a bit dead and all.'

Joe pondered yet again. 'Right,' he began at last, 'you go to St Helens, and I'll have a word with him once you're safely out of the way.'

Her jaw dropped. 'And when he kills you? Who'll look after me and the baby then? I mean, I can't work with a kiddy, can I? I couldn't even go part-time till it's at school.'

'My will. I'll provide. And you don't think I'm daft enough to face him by myself, do you? Just remember, every man has a price. Now, if he agrees in front of my solicitor to treat the child as his own, will you come back to him?'

Betsy shivered. 'I'm not sure.'

'Well, think on it. Write to Elsie, make sure of the lie of the land. And let me know what you want to do.'

After she had left, Joe sat with his head in his hands, elbows on the table, fear in his heart. He'd needed somebody. Emily didn't like sex. She daren't risk another pregnancy, or it would kill her. Even though she was in her early forties, she might still conceive. So he'd lowered his standards and hit rock bottom with poor Betsy. She was seldom just Betsy in his thoughts; the adjective 'poor' was usually attached to her.

He remembered walking into the Starkie that night. She cleaned the saloon bar and the snug, and she'd left her purse behind earlier in the day, so she'd returned to collect it. He bought her a couple of drinks, and she was friendly enough, so he'd used her as a receptacle, and that wasn't nice. He wasn't nice. Emily knew. She never said anything, but she'd moved into the spare room and . . .

And life was a bloody mess. He would talk to Marty Liptrott only if Betsy wanted to come back. There had to be a way of persuading the great lummox that a child could be a good thing, but did Marty know that his wife was spreading the news about his impotence? She'd told her sister, but her sister was family. Oh yes. What a bloody mess this was.

The move was relatively painless. From the very beginning, Emily was happy because of a knock at the door. Surrounded by boxes and upended furniture, she climbed over all obstacles to reach her goal. And there, at the front of her new home, she met Thora Caldwell.

Thora was not a mere bundle of cellular mischief; she was a force of nature. As thin as a rake and with rusty-red hair, she breezed through life at the speed of sound. She refused to be held back by her drunken, feckless husband and four children and took an interest in everything and everyone, seldom out of place, not swayed by a different accent, better clothes, a superior three-piece suite. Thora simply belonged just about anywhere.

Her greeting was interesting. 'Hiya. I'm Thora Caldwell from next door. I've got four lads, three of them training to be hooligans, a useless husband, varicose veins, a job as an orderly down the hospital, and I could murder a cuppa. Who are you, then?'

'Emily Sanderson.'

Thora clapped her hands. 'See? I were right,' she said to nobody at all. 'It's him, isn't it? Your husband. Bespokened cupboards and stuff. Matron thought she were the dog's bollocks when she got a bespokened table and chairs. They say if you go round her house, first time, like, she makes you get down under the bloody table to look at Joseph Sanderson wrote in indelible ink on the bottom. See, let's make a path.' As she spoke, she moved boxes, righted a few chairs and marched into the kitchen.

'The kettle's on,' Emily managed to squeeze into the diatribe.

'It's all inlaid, though,' Thora continued. 'And hoctagonal. That means it's got eight sides and eight chairs. Very clever man, your husband.'

'Yes, I suppose he is.'

'No suppose about it, love. Mine can't be bothered to scratch his arse most days. I found him fast asleep on the lav the other week, with his head resting on the sink. He was supposed to be building a wall up Tonge Moor, so I booted him out, and he never came home for three days. Have you got some biscuits? Anyway, he's pulled himself together a bit, but he can't leave the booze alone. We've rent to pay, food to buy, and them lads of mine go through shoes faster than a hot knife through butter. Can I have a bourbon? I like bourbons.'

Emily felt breathless by proxy, because the woman

scarcely stopped to take in oxygen. 'Have you lived here long?' she asked while Thora dipped her bourbon into her cup and bit into it.

Thora swallowed. 'About six months. I told him. I said I wanted a decent street this time, not a midnight flit address. The number of times we've cleared off in the dark cos he wouldn't pay the rent. So I got a job and I pay the rent here, but he's supposed to tip up for the rest. Any road, I think I've found a way round it.'

'Really?'

The red-haired intruder nodded. 'I get my youngest lads in their worst clothes, drag them round to where Harry's working, and show him up. He gets a sub from the boss, I take it off him, and Bob's your uncle.'

Emily started to chuckle quietly. She'd been on nodding terms with several householders on Crompton Way, but this woman was magical. Comparing her to neighbours across town was like weighing a hurricane against a light breeze. If this was a downmarket move, it was suiting Emily already.

'Where's your lot, then?' Thora demanded to know.

'Clearing up on Crompton Way.'

For a split second, the new neighbour was stunned. 'You've left Crompton Way for here? Whose idea was that?'

'My husband's.'

Thora shook her head in disbelief. 'Ever thought about killing him?'

'So far? No.'

Both women burst into the special laughter that is the property of women alone, the helpless, boneless hysteria that reduces its emptying containers to heaps on the floor. Never in all her days had Emily felt so overpowered, yet so free. From her new position in life, she looked up and saw her husband's signature under a chair, and this caused her to shriek all over again. Her knees hurt, but it didn't matter.

Thora crawled across and joined her new neighbour. With tears streaming down her uncomely face, she pointed to Joe's name. 'I bet ... oh God, this is painful ... I bet ... I bet he thinks he's the dog's bollocks and all, eh?'

Emily managed a nod.

'But you've never felt like—'

'No. But if I did . . .' Emily failed again and descended into the shape of a comma.

'If you did?'

'Food. Poison in food.'

'Oh, no. I want to see blood,' Thora said. 'After what mine's put me through, I'd torture him and finish him off with a guillotine.'

'Do you have a guillotine?'

'No. How much are they?'

'You'd have to ask in France.'

'I'm not going there. It's full of bloody foreigners.'

When Joe and Andrew finally reached the house, they found a dignified wife and mother on the floor with a woman whose tiny frame was just a whisker away from emaciation. Andrew couldn't help himself. Seeing his mother out of control was brilliant. Her companion had removed her spectacles, which were, in her words, 'covered in compensation', and one of her eyes had floated inward as if trying to keep company with a sharp, freckled nose. Andrew burst out laughing.

This event affected the women, who were now weeping with mirth.

Whatever was in this room was a communicable disease, and Joe found himself grinning along with the rest. Worry about poor Betsy had clouded his mind for quite some time, so he scarcely knew how he was managing to laugh, but it felt good.

'Why did you move here?' Thora asked the condemned man. No, Emily mustn't poison him – he made gradely furniture.

'Most of my customers are nearby,' he replied, trying to squash a new burst of laughter. 'And Andrew's school's here, as well as Emily's place of work.'

'Then there's the kitchen.' Emily wiped her eyes. 'Bigger than the one we had on Crompton Way. Joseph's going to update it and make it into a guinea pig.'

'Clever.' Thora replaced her glasses. 'Do you pull rabbits from hats as well?' she asked Joe. 'It's all right, I know what she means by guinea pig.' She struggled to her feet. 'I'd best go and start peeling,' she said. 'The trouble with having a half-Irish husband is he eats about three pounds of spuds a day. And the lads are catching him up. Cheerio.' She was gone.

Joe looked at his wife. 'Where did she spring from?'

'Next door. Life may become rather noisy, because she has four sons and a husband who isn't always up to scratch.'

'These walls are thick,' he informed her.

'So is her husband.'

Joe wasn't used to humour from his wife; he was also having trouble adjusting to the idea of her working. 'When do you start at the infirmary?' he asked.

'A week on Monday. The house should be straight by then, unless you decide to start hacking at the kitchen.'

He wouldn't be hacking at anything; he'd be taking poor Betsy to St Helens. Probably. 'Right, let's get a shift on. Andrew, boxes marked upstairs, take upstairs. Emily, you do everything for the kitchen.'

'What are you going to do?' she asked.

'I'm directing traffic. Have you seen my bobby's helmet?'

She smiled at him. For Joe, that smile was a gold medal.

Joe drove poor Betsy to St Helens and handed her over to Elsie. Very little was said. Elsie knew nothing about the pregnancy, and Marty Liptrott was also left in the dark. After dropping off the mother-to-be at the Eagle and Child, Joe began the drive home. He was hovering on the brink of danger, and he was painfully aware of that fact.

Betsy had told her sister that Marty had gone violent. Joe, having been the recipient of one beating, knew that on this occasion Betsy was telling no lies. So. When would the second beating take place? Joseph Sanderson Ltd couldn't keep a low profile, as his products were advertised all over the town. And his name might well become mud if his dalliance with Marty's wife should be thrust into the public domain. Oh, God. Oh God, oh God, oh God. Dread filled his chest, and he began to sweat.

He parked the car, took out a handkerchief and mopped his suddenly fevered brow. Options. Were there any? Would Liptrott assume that Joe was at the back of Betsy's disappearance? How on earth could the great lump of a man be persuaded otherwise, especially since otherwise would be an outright fib? Would he search for and find Elsie, would he find out about the pregnancy, how would he react if he did? Joe's chest felt tight. He wasn't himself at all.

Suddenly, he was home. For as long as he lived – which was to be some considerable time – he would never remember the journey from St Helens to Bolton. As soon as he entered the hallway, he hit the floor. Twenty-five minutes later, Joseph Sanderson was in hospital with double lower-lobe pneumonia.

Thora arrived at the infirmary to escort Andrew home. 'Don't worry, lass,' she advised Emily. 'I'll stay with your boy. Me mam'll come and mind my lads.'

'I'd rather be here,' Andrew said.

Emily touched her beloved son's hand. 'Go and look after Toodles. I know she seems to be settling, but she needs you. Your father's a strong man. He'll come out of this, Andrew. I promise.'

So Andrew spent the evening with the ridiculously funny Thora Caldwell and her next-to-youngest son, Michael. Michael was not as rough or as loud as his brothers. In fact, his quietness was much appreciated by Andrew, who wasn't in the mood for Mrs Caldwell's wittering. His father had pneumonia in both lungs, and Michael's mother was beginning to annoy her young host.

Michael, who was strangely sensitive for a member of the Caldwell family, noticed the unease in Andrew's eyes. 'You'd best go home, Mam,' he said. 'Dad's got some Irish in, half a bottle, I think. And you know Gran can't manage him once he kicks off.'

Thora jumped to her feet and left, muttering under her breath about mad customers giving booze to Irish idiots.

Like a couple of old men relaxing, the two boys leaned back in armchairs and closed their eyes.

Michael spoke. 'Sorry about the way she carries on. Me mam, I mean. She's not had it easy, so ... anyway, I'll sleep here tonight if you want.'

'Thanks.'

The quiet was beautiful. Mrs Caldwell had chattered seamlessly about the price of cod, the perils of being married to half an Irishman – that seemed to be her best subject – pneumonia becoming treatable these days, and a woman across the way who never washed her windows or her doorstep.

Then bigger trouble arrived. Someone battered the

front door as if trying to free it from its hinges. Andrew leapt up. If it turned out to be bad news about Dad, he had to be the one to receive it. He opened the door.

'Where is he?' a huge man wanted to know. 'Left a forwarding address stuck on the window on Crompton Way. Always an eye for business, eh?'

Andrew retreated slightly. 'I'm sorry. Who are you?'

'A man looking for Sanderson, that's who. Anyway, I want to talk to the organ grinder, not the bloody monkey.' He pushed Andrew to one side and entered the house. 'Where is he?' he demanded, this time throwing the words at Michael Caldwell.

Michael said nothing.

'Where is that bastard?'

Thora entered the equation, bursting through the front door and placing her arm round Andrew's shoulders. 'Who the blood and sand are you, trying to knock my neighbours' door down?'

'Who am I?' Marty roared. 'Who am I?'

'Well, if you don't know, we can't tell you. Happen if you wore a dog collar with a disc, you could get your details carved on it.'

The invader blinked. 'Don't come the clever talk with me, missus.'

She folded her arms against a very flat chest. 'Listen, ear'ole,' she said. 'We've enough on round here without you trying to break through the front door. You can bugger off back to the stone you live under, or you can start making sense.'

This was a woman who was afraid of nothing and nobody, and Marty wasn't used to coming up against the unafraid. 'Where is Joe Sanderson?' he asked, the words spaced out as if being offered to somebody with developmental problems.

'In the bloody hospital with bloody double bloody

pneumonia,' Thora snapped. 'He came in from work today, and fell spark out on the hall floor. He's in a tent, that's what they call it. Having oxygen pushed into him cos he can't breathe proper. And that'll be why you can search this house from cellar to attic and find no sign of him except in photos.'

Marty swallowed audibly.

'If you go to the hospital and ask at the front desk, they'll confirm that my dad was admitted today,' Andrew said. 'I think I know who you are. Touch Dad again, and you'll be locked up. Now, leave my house. You weren't invited in, so you're guilty of trespass. That's marginally better than grievous bodily harm, but it's still an offence.'

Marty shuffled out.

Thora threw back her head and hooted with laughter when the front door slammed. 'Leave my house. Marginally better – that school's done a lot for you, Andrew. Though your mam talks a bit posh, doesn't she?'

Andrew sank into the chair opposite Michael's. Tears threatened, and tears shouldn't belong in the repertoire of a boy who was almost thirteen.

Michael saved his new friend. Well, he hoped that Andrew would be his friend. 'Was Dad drunk?' he asked.

'I'd say so, yes. His feet were smoking.'

Grief forgotten, Andrew blinked several times.

'Oh, not again,' Michael sighed. 'Did you light the fire, Mam?'

'No, your gran did. Said she were cold, a bit shivery. So Harry sits down with his whiskey, feet up on the fireguard, falls asleep. Your gran thought it was the sweat in his socks steaming off. Well, that's what she said, anyway. She wouldn't care if he went up in flames as long as she got the rest of us out. Some days, I feel like giving up.' She shook rust-coloured curls. 'I'll make you some toast and tea.' She went into the kitchen.

Michael and Andrew grinned at each other. 'We seem to have strange families,' said the latter.

'Then we're in the right place,' Michael answered. 'They're all a bit doolally round these parts. Your dad's bought this house, then?'

'Yes.'

'Are you rich?'

'I don't know, Mike. When the Crompton Way house sells, we'll be a bit better off. Nobody mentions anything. But I think he's using this house for a time-and-motion kitchen. If the kitchens take off, he'll move us a bit further up the road, but that's just my opinion. He wants to live in Liverpool when I leave school.'

There was a slight pause. 'Andrew?'

'What?'

'I like wood. I'd like to be a carpenter when I leave school.'

'I'll ask him.'

'Ta.'

They ate their toast while Thora chattered. After a while, Andrew began to realize that the words were fading into the background. Mrs Caldwell was just another layer of paint or wallpaper, part of his surroundings. He even drifted towards sleep . . .

Joe opened his eyes at last, and Emily was sitting there smiling at him. For a moment, he smiled back, before drifting once more towards the sleep that would mend him. She'd been there; she'd stayed with him in the hospital, and that was all that mattered.

Emily Sanderson sighed her relief, picked up her bag and walked to the door of the ward. They'd told her the penicillin seemed to be helping, and that his breathing had improved, but only slightly.

Slightly was better than nothing. And she had a son who needed her.

Martin Liptrott swept half a dozen glasses off the bar in the lounge of the Starkie public house. The landlord, who was not in the best of moods, told the drunken man that his wife was sacked, since she hadn't turned up for work that day. 'And I want a quid for that glassware,' he added. 'Coming in here and smashing my place up – do you fancy a night in the cells? It can be arranged.'

Marty blinked in an attempt to clear his vision. Betsy's boss was tilting to one side, as were several customers, some shelves and a door. And all voices seemed so far away – was he going deaf on top of everything else? 'I shall pay thee,' he cried. 'I shall pay thee what she's worth, which is nowt. She's bloody left me. I comes home from me job, and there she is – gone. Wardrobe's empty, no money in the place, no dinner – nowt at all.'

The room fell silent. Or had he really gone deaf? No, he could hear his own voice. 'Just a note saying she'd had enough, and that's that. No meal on the table, no bath run to get the stink of the bins off me. All her clothes gone except for some old bits, so I'm in a bad mood. It's very upsetting coming home to an empty place and a missing wife.'

The landlord had heard it all before over the years, and he stood his ground. 'I'm sorry, lad, but there's no need for you to take it out on us. Forget the broken glasses, but go home. I'm serving you no more, cos you're drunk as a lord. Go on. We'll see you when you've bucked up a bit, eh?'

Home? He had no home. On Thicketford Road, he noticed that the lamp posts had been breeding. Their number had doubled, and he wrestled with several on his way to the house that was no longer home. She hadn't kept it nice, but she'd fed him and washed his clothes after a fashion. Yet he couldn't be a man for her, could he? She didn't want babies, but she needed a proper husband, and he wasn't a proper husband.

'What went wrong?' he asked the post to which he clung. 'Why was I made different? And why can't I talk proper to a doctor about it?' He belched, then deposited the contents of his stomach on the pavement. He hadn't eaten, so what came up was stale beer, and it was rank.

Food. He needed food. Abbot's shop was closed, of course, and there was very little food in the house. She shopped on a day-to-day basis after work, but she hadn't been to work today. There'd be bread and cheese, he supposed. There might be spuds or an apple.

Well, she hadn't gone off with Mr Sawdust, because he was in hospital. The woman at the desk had confirmed it, so where the bloody hell had Betsy gone? She would be with a man, of course, somebody with better personal equipment and a job that didn't make him stink of rotted fish and cabbage.

He opened the door. The silence hit him like a brick in a sock; it was dense, painful and dark. 'Betsy,' he called helplessly, hopelessly. 'Betsy, come back. Don't leave me.'

Nobody wanted him. He wasn't a man, so he wasn't worth having. He sat on uncarpeted stairs, hugged himself and rocked back and forth like a child in its mother's arms. He had to eat, had to settle his stomach. Tomorrow, he'd be back on the bins, and he needed his strength.

'Why does everything happen to me?' he wondered aloud.

In the kitchen, which wasn't much bigger than a scullery, he peeled spuds at a tiny table covered in cracked oilcloth. Behind him on a gas stove the chip pan bubbled. He cut his finger, winced with pain and wiped blood on a crusty towel. It was amazing how a cut could be the last straw.

Hilda Bridges roused the neighbourhood at about eleven o'clock. The Liptrott house was in flames and, as she shared a wall with it, she, too, was threatened. When the brigade arrived, she explained about Betsy, telling them that she'd gone away and not to bother looking for her. 'He's in there, though,' she said. 'I heard him clattering about. Drunk again, I think.'

They doused the flames while their boss found the seat of the fire. It was another inebriate with yet another chip pan. He was at the top of the stairs. As the smoke cleared, the firemen saw him hanging just for a split second before the rope snapped. The body tumbled down the steps and landed in the hallway.

A fireman sought a pulse, found no sign of life. 'He's gone,' he said.

The chief checked just to be sure. 'Sometimes I hate this bloody job,' he said. 'Still, no kiddies, that's something.' He went outside to check with Hilda Bridges. 'No children, love?'

'No.' She said no more than that. The poor man was dead, and she allowed him his dignity. The details of the Liptrotts' marriage could go with him to the grave as far as she was concerned. 'Will you look at my house and make sure I'm safe, please?'

'Of course we will, love.'

Hilda put the kettle on. Tomorrow, she would write to Betsy. How did a person tell a young woman that her husband had killed himself? Hilda had been standing on the pavement, had seen him coming down the stairs, rope round his neck, eyes wide open and bulging. 'God have mercy on him,' she whispered. 'And on Betsy, too.'

Five

Daniel Pope was several miles beyond angry. In fact, he nursed the suspicion that NASA might need to track the top of his head if it blew off. Even an hour in his private basement gym followed by a hot shower and two black coffees had failed to revive him. He was literally fuming. His whole body glowed with temper, and he wouldn't have been surprised if smoke or steam had suddenly begun to emerge from bodily orifices.

The evil bitches had destroyed all his red wines, his clothes, and most of his photographic equipment. The wonderful wife had grabbed from a safe items that had been put aside for the future, had taken their daughters and had buggered off. Helen. So docile, so sweet, so like her bloody sister once the outer layer was peeled away.

All because of Mariella, who had a mouth bigger than both Mersey tunnels and the bloody Grand Canyon. Women? More trouble than cats in a bed of nettles. He wanted to scream, but no one would hear him, because his house was set in nine acres. His house. She would get none of it if divorce happened. God, he missed her. Even now, after all she'd done, he loved her. But there was something wrong with him; he couldn't leave women alone. He needed secrets; a life without subterfuge was beyond his comprehension.

What a bloody mess. The only garments he owned

were those he had packed for Amsterdam, so he needed to go out for shirts, socks and underclothes, at least. Blinking females. They were all tears and hormones and mood swings. Yet Helen had always been so quiet, so generous of heart. So confident he had been of her continuing and unconditional love, he had wandered on the wild side, convinced that she would never find out, sure that she would forgive anyway, no matter what. Somewhere, his calculations had gone very wrong. There was a limit to her tolerance, and he should have been made aware of that. She had married him under false pretences, but no law covered that area, did it?

However, the fact remained that there was one woman without whom he couldn't possibly manage, and she happened to be his wife. Aside from loving her above all else, he knew that Helen was a trophy, a living, breathing tribute to his success. Her beauty and natural elegance were a boon as far as business was concerned. At conventions and social events, she was the best possible advertisement for Pope the Jeweller. How could he attempt to explain her sudden disappearance? She'd met someone else? She'd gone to convalesce due to severe postnatal depression? Once the truth came out, as it inevitably would, he would look a fool. And that was something he knew he would never bear. 'I'm a diamond full of flaws,' he said. 'Too many carbon deposits to be useful.' Was he beginning to know himself? Was he?

Oh, wonderful – here came the troops. They should have brought pipes and drums, then he might have heard them coming. Heck, this was all he needed. Helen's father, Sofia and another female were closing the doors of Andrew's Merc. She wasn't with them. Bugger it, why had he been such a fool? He'd sacrificed his marriage for a quick fumble with another woman. Well, there'd been more than one ... But lots of men managed to win forgiveness,

99

and Helen was almost compliant in her attitude. Would she come back? How could a woman who loved him so devotedly suddenly hate him so thoroughly? And all because of a few words from the mouth of an Amsterdam whore? She should be forced to listen to him, at least.

Another car swung into the driveway. 'Oh, goody,' Daniel breathed. 'We have a quorum with a three-line whip to boot.' Kate's husband, Richard Rutherford, had arrived to complete the bench. This judgemental legal bore would think Daniel deserved everything that was coming to him. It could mean divorce, of course. Unless he managed to get to her and wear her down, she would not be coming back. Just an hour. If he could spend just an hour with her ... Someone else could do the travelling and the buying; he was willing to go so far as to promise never to leave the country again. But this wall of people would stand between him and his right to have a conversation with his spouse. It wasn't fair, because he was seriously outnumbered.

He opened the door. Sofia had brought her mother. Daniel could tell from the older woman's face that she knew he'd tried it on with her daughter. What a mess he had made of his life. Damned fool, he cursed inwardly. For a few short spells of pleasure, he had given up the most beautiful, loyal wife on earth. And she had turned – by hell, she had turned.

When the rather less than welcome visitors were all in the house, Richard spoke. 'Stay away from her.' He didn't need to name the 'her'. 'If you follow her or trouble her in any way at this stage, we'll get a court order. Should you break the terms of said order, you will find yourself in trouble. Prison could be a possibility.'

'Because of your contacts?'

'No, because of yours. Harass your wife, and I'll have you restrained like a crazy man.'

'In this hall, a small town could eat,' Anya Jasinski declared. 'One man in house this size while people sleep in streets? This not right.'

Daniel Pope looked up as if seeking guidance. All he needed now was someone of a liberal frame of mind, as he seemed to have representatives of the extreme right and extreme left here already. 'What do you want?' he asked the nanny.

Her mother looked him up and down. He could feel her opinion of him sweeping over his person.

'My clothes and personal belongings,' Sofia snapped. 'My mother will help.' The two women walked up the glamorous, curving staircase.

Even now, Daniel ran a practised eye over them. Sofia was cute, but her mother was a little firecracker, still pretty in her forties.

Richard and Andrew remained in the hall with their prey. 'I want my wife and children back,' Daniel pronounced. 'You have no right to remove them, no right to tell me what I can and cannot do where my family is concerned—'

'Helen removed herself and the children last night,' Richard said, his tone annoyingly calm. 'We had no hand in it. I was at home looking after Philip and Rosie. Our father-in-law was at his house trying to train a mad dog. Kate admits freely that she was here, and she was glad, because Helen fell apart before her eyes. You wounded her beyond measure.'

'My children,' Daniel repeated. Mad dog? Where did a mad dog fit into the recipe? Was this a time for jokes? 'Sarah and Cassie are mine.'

'Girls?' Andrew's eyebrows were raised. 'Mere females aren't good enough for you. You were already coaxing Helen into trying again for a son. The sex is in the sperm, as you probably know already. You are making female babies. Helen's eggs, like those of every woman, are gender neutral. If there is a fault, it's yours. As for your philandering – well, everyone but my daughter knew about it. Helen has limits. When she erupts, the world shakes. You made a move on Helen's sister, and Kate has spoken up about it at last.'

Richard stepped forward. 'The law is on Helen's side, you see. She is extraordinarily angry–'

'So am I. Have you any idea of the value of what was destroyed here?'

'Have you any idea of the value of your wife?' Andrew asked. 'And I'm not talking finance here. I mean her disposition, her appearance, her support, her saintly patience. You broke her. And when she snapped, you became a creature beneath contempt. She is unlikely to forgive you, because you betrayed her trust.'

Daniel shook his head in despair.

While Richard delivered a legal lecture, Andrew walked to the window. But he didn't see the formal gardens, the fountains, the obsessively neat topiary. No. He saw a large, rude man whose wife had fled, heard himself, at twelve years of age, telling the man to go away. He saw the *Bolton Evening News* with a headline that had been engraved for perpetuity in his mind, *Bolton Man Found Hanging in Burning House*, and he prayed that there would be no repeat.

But no. Daniel Pope probably loved himself above all else. Now that he knew the whole story about the Liptrotts, Andrew was only too acutely aware of Marty's reasons. But he wished he hadn't been so rude to the man who would go on to destroy himself within hours. Pope wouldn't do anything like that. While there was money to be made, he would carry on regardless.

Anya appeared on the galleried landing. 'Excusing me,'

she said. 'My Sofia, she find perfume belong to Helen, also clothes for children. These she pack. She not stealing.'

'Oh, do as you like. Empty the freezer, take my computers, my music system, my television. Because I am past caring.' He had things to do, clothes to buy, excuses to manufacture. He slammed out of the house, leaving behind him the representatives of his departed spouse. She had built a legion of guards, and she clearly intended to hide behind the structure, but he would work something out.

He started the car. Yes, that was it. Helen's father had just retired from his post as orthopaedic consultant, and Helen had gone to spend some time with him because he was depressed. That would have to suffice, as he couldn't think of anything else. He might add a bit of embroidery to the story, but he needed not to go too far. And he would find her. By God, he would.

He roared off in his car, gravel spitting upward all over the place. Helen was at her father's house. Had he been a betting man, he would have put his shirt on it. Shirts? He had none.

Eva's face was a picture coloured by a mix of emotions. She had left a man and a daft dog in the house, but now she was returning to chaos. Kate, surrounded by shopping, was in the kitchen. She kissed Eva. 'Be a dear and put that lot away for me, will you? I must help Helen with the children, then I have to get back to Woolton.' She left the room.

Eva's mouth hung open for a few seconds. She'd been about to ask for an explanation, but Kate had disappeared. Which behaviour was typical, Eva thought as she looked back down the years. The older girl had always been a torment, very swift to escape questioning, cheeky as any scally-Scouser when it came to confrontation. Helen was here? Why? And there was some very strange food in the bags; rusks, New Zealand honey, tiny bananas, some Heinz Junior meals in jars. Sarah must be here, then. Where was Doc?

She looked in the morning room. No joy. Nor was he in the drawing room. He might be upstairs, but— 'Bad pennies always return,' she said. 'He'll appear on the scene when he's least needed.'

Stupid Storm was outside, a hopeful nose pressed against glass in the outer door. He'd grown since yesterday, Eva swore he had. She'd seen Shetland ponies shorter than that cheeky mutt. Blinking paw prints all over windows and doors, giant molehills where he'd buried bones, innocence plastered all over his face. It was hard to dislike him, but she was working at it.

He woofed. Eva ignored him. Well, she attempted to.

Kate breezed back in. 'Helen wants tea and toast. I tried to push food down her before, but she was too upset. I got some SMA and a sterilizer. I think it's time Helen got Cassie off the breast. She's too upset to feed.'

'Who is?'

'Helen, of course. Turning yourself into a cow is one thing, but trying to feed a child during all this upset— Oh, sorry. You don't know, do you?'

Eva bridled. 'No, I don't know. And I haven't the faintest idea about what I don't know, because I don't know what I don't know. If you know what I mean, like.'

'She's left him.' Kate pushed the plunger on the cafetière.

'Who?'

'Helen's left the Pope.'

'I didn't know she was a Catholic. All right, all right. So she's walked out on Daniel. I like Daniel. Elton John sings it. Anyway, she knows full well he's worth a bloody fortune. A woman shouldn't leave the family home.'

'Oh, she'll get what she's due. My Richard will make sure of that. He's over in Neston now with Dad and Sofia. She's the nanny. So you'll have a full house, Eva. All five bedrooms will be in use.'

'Ooh, I am pleased.'

Kate stood back and eyed the beloved adversary. 'You haven't been pleased since the Boer War ended.'

'Cheeky monkey. I was the one what relieved Mafeking.'

'I'm sure you were.'

Eva picked up a loaf and parked it in the bread bin. 'Another woman?'

'Several.'

'Damn fool. She's gorgeous, clever, and she has the patience of a saint. I never liked him. I've seen him eyeing you up a few times, madam. And other women, too. Thinks he's God's gift.'

'Women are just toys to him, Eva. And he was so certain that he would get away with it, and sure she wouldn't leave him even if she did find out. How wrong can a man be?'

Eva took milk from the fridge and handed it to Kate. 'She'll go back to him. I've never seen a woman so much in love ... Oh, yes I have. Your mother. Your mother was daft about Doc right till the day she died. Helen's like that. She'll go back.'

Kate took the carton. 'Over my dead body, Dad's dead body, Richard's, Sofia's – she's the nanny. The thing about a love as great as Helen's is that its mirror is hatred. I think this second baby has opened my sister's eyes. Daniel wants a son, and she's sure he would have demanded that she carried on giving birth until he got his wish. Helen needs no more children. We change, Eva. We all change.'

'Do we?'

Kate shrugged. 'Except Daniel. He has no clothes to change into.'

This one hadn't altered an inch, Eva thought as she took back the milk and replaced it in the fridge. Sharp as a tack, stubborn as a mule, daft as her dad. In spite of all that, Kate was probably the most lovable kid Eva had ever known, and that included her own lot. Except for Natalie. Natalie was special. 'Why has he no clothes?'

'Helen destroyed them. She was magnificent, Eva. I've never seen anybody in that state before. Not one drop of sweat, not one hair out of place, yet she went through his stuff like wildfire.'

'Get that coffee to her before it goes cold.'

When Kate had left the kitchen, Eva perched on a stool. Helen needed to be married; she also needed her work. There were two sides to her, and each was simple, but in a very clever way. The university was her other place, and it kept her brain ticking over nicely. Home was where Helen's heart lay. She loved being a wife and mother. Rumour had it that in spite of domestic help she insisted on ironing her husband's shirts, the very shirts she had now destroyed. While the rest of the world barely tolerated Daniel, Helen had devoted herself to him. Until now.

The dog was pulling faces at her. How could a bloody dog manage that?

Andrew entered the room. In his wake were two women chattering in a strange language. 'Ah, Eva. Ladies, this is my housekeeper and good friend. Eva, meet Sofia, Helen's nanny. And this is Anya, Sofia's mother.'

They moved into English. 'I am please to meeting you,' said the elder.

'As am I,' the nanny said.

Eva eyed her competition. The girl seemed pleasant

enough, but the older woman's eyes were all over the place, as if scanning everything in the room. Big oak cupboards, click, roaming butcher's block, click, large refrigerator, beep, table and chairs, ding, dog at the door, click. 'Good kitchen,' was her delivered opinion. 'You good housekeeping, Eva. Is clean.'

Eva's feathers settled. 'He made all this,' she said, her voice raised as if talking to the hard of hearing. 'Doctor, carpenter, musician. I have looked after him for many years.'

Anya turned to Andrew. 'Clever,' she told him. 'Very clever man.'

'He made nearly all the wooden furniture, even a four-poster bed. My Natalie will be helping me soon.' She threw that into the mix in case anyone was looking for a job. 'She's my granddaughter. Her mother died, and she needs money for university.'

'You excellent woman. Family first is right. My girl here is to be teaching English to Polish peoples soon. She is teach me first. This dog is want to come in see master.'

'On your own head be it,' Eva mumbled under her breath as she opened the door.

Anya squatted down and greeted the dog in Polish. Storm ground to a halt and licked her face. She rattled on in her native tongue while the dog sat and tilted his head from side to side as if taking in every word she delivered.

'I knew he didn't speak English,' Andrew said. 'But he should be French, he's a red French mastiff cross.'

'This have happen before,' Anya said seriously. 'Chopin, he was Polish, but he go to France and is die, I think, in Paris, also in poorness, no money. Perhaps your dog is descending from Chopin dog?'

There was humour in the woman. Andrew grinned broadly. Humour was the one thing that cut like a scimitar through class, language, and any other barriers created by the human animal. I'm afraid Storm isn't musical. He does a good howl, but it's all on one note.'

'Two, sometimes,' Eva said. 'And his language is dog, just dog.'

Anya eyed the dog solemnly. 'You no speak *polsku*, then? This making me sad. And you no play for me Chopin?'

Andrew helped Anya to her feet and led her to the drawing room where the upright was housed. There was a grand piano, but that was in Mary's function suite. He put Anya in a chair, sat at the piano, tried a few notes, then played a nocturne. As the final notes died, he turned to find her wiping her eyes. 'Your language is music,' she pronounced.

'From my mother.'

'Music needs no translation, just interpetring.'

'Interpretation.'

'Thank you. Now, I play for you. I not so good, but I try.'

They changed places. She delivered a halting but note-perfect version of Beethoven's Moonlight Sonata. 'My husband, he like that one,' she said.

'Yes, it's beautiful. Do you have a piano at home?'

Anya shook her head. 'No piano since Poland.'

'Then feel free to use mine. If you want privacy, use the grand at the other side of the house. If you want help, I can give you lessons.'

'Thank you,' she said again. 'But I cannot pay.'

'I want no money.'

She stood up. 'Now, I go with Sofia and see babies.'

Had he offended her? Perhaps he shouldn't have mentioned lessons, because she needed just practice. Or the idea of charity might have been a bitter pill for her. She had the ability, so she probably needed just to take up playing again until her fingers loosened. He would talk to Sofia later, as her grasp of English was excellent.

Anya stole the baby. 'Three weeks,' she said. 'And already, fire of life in these eyes.' She looked at the mother. 'Too good for that man. My Sofia pleased you do this thing. My Sofia sensible girl. Sensible, yes, that is word.'

Helen, red-eyed and sad, offered a weak smile to Anya. 'Your daughter is a great help to me.'

'Yes.' Anya returned the smile. 'Is because she Polish. Polish women working hard from all time.'

'Verb, Mama,' said Sofia. 'Doing word.'

'Where I coming from, what I say is good.'

'You need a doing word, not a participle,' her daughter explained.

Anya's smile broadened. 'Old age come when child teaching mother.'

'You're not old, Mrs Jay,' Helen said.

'Four and three, forty-three. Sofia took me bingo for to learn say numbers, but man stupid. Why is legs eleven? Top of shop ninety? Two ducks twenty-two? And we had fat ladies, eighty-eight, which was rude, because those ladies is sit with us. Four and three is seven, no forty-three. I keep this baby, yes, take her home?'

'No, sorry.' Helen's words arrived on a whisper.

With great solemnity, Anya handed Cassie back to her mother. 'Your heart in your shoes will rise again, Elena. Soon, your eyes shine bright stars in pretty face like these in baby. He just a man. He in past. Future belong women always. Men does killing, women does making children. So future is ours. *Dzien dobry, Elena.*'

'Jean dough bree, Anya,' Helen replied.

'This was nearly right,' Anya announced as she left.

'Helen is a linguist,' Kate called.

'Good.' Anya's disembodied voice floated in from the landing. 'These, we need.'

109

'Always the last word in both languages,' Sofia told her companions. 'Where is my bedroom, please? I shall put away my things, then wash Sarah. Where is Sarah?'

'In your room waiting for you.' Kate took Sofia out to the landing.

Alone, Helen closed her eyes and nursed her infant. She missed him. Never again would he weave his magic in her bed, a magic he had distributed generously all over Europe, no doubt. She missed her house, her gardens, the swimming pool, the gym. The girls, when older, would have kept ponies and dogs. But she couldn't go back, mustn't go back.

Determinedly, she concentrated on his faults. He made fun of other people, but could never take criticism or a joke aimed at himself. He often stayed away longer than necessary, probably taking his pick of girls until he had been forced to come home or his appetite had reached saturation point. A chain like Pope's needed a helmsman, and he was at the wheel. So confident of his own importance, Daniel was.

Sarah he ignored for the most part, while Cassie was just another female child, a second disappointment. He didn't deserve a son, didn't deserve his daughters, either, because he was too engrossed in himself.

She would stay here with Dad until her mind sorted itself out. These weeks after giving birth were difficult for most women; disruption in family life could not have come at a worse time. But she had to stand on her own two feet and get on with everything. Dad and Richard would help, and she remained certain of her sister's unconditional support. 'This is the next scene, Cassandra. Or rather, the next act in our little play.'

*

Andrew drove Anya home. She chattered about the river, his beautiful home, the furniture he had made, his prowess at the piano. 'Helen tells my Sofia that you get place at Royal School. This is right, please?'

'Yes, but I decided to become a doctor. I do love music, but I preferred saving lives at the cost of limbs. Often, I saved life and limbs, and that was very satisfying. I have no regrets, Anya. Surgery, carpentry, music have all been important in my life.'

'And your wife, she was everything for you.'

'Yes, she was.'

'Me, I am same. I will not marry again. Also, I have never been asked.'

The woman was a breath of fresh air. Despite the slight break in her English, she was understandable, funny and bright. 'Anya?'

'Yes?'

'I was serious about the piano. You must come and visit your daughter, and play when you are there. Practice is all you need.'

'I thank you, good man.'

'You're welcome.'

She got out of the car and walked up the path. He missed her chatter and her cheeky wit. But he seemed to have gained a new friend, so that was good. She was a pianist, and that made everything so much better. 'Retirement isn't the end,' he told himself as he drove homeward. 'It's just the beginning of something else.'

Another person in his house was experiencing a new start, but for a far more serious and unhappy reason. Less than a month after giving birth, Helen had been forced towards something she would have preferred never to face. And he had to help her deal with it. Oh, and Storm needed him. Perhaps this time round he might be a proper

111

father, a good grandfather, and pack leader for one mad canine. He was also determined to restore Anya Jasinski's faith in her ability to play. He did have a list. Oh yes, he definitely had a list. Not all operations were surgical.

Rattling about in splendid isolation in his sandstone pile didn't suit Daniel Pope. Helen had always been there, because she was predictable; she was also bloody gorgeous and although she was safe for the moment, she would rebirth herself like Venus, and would rise from the shell of new motherhood like a splendid creation by some old master.

Daniel, like most casually unfaithful people, could scarcely tolerate the idea of any man getting close to his wife. There had been situations in which his stunning spouse had spent too long in the company of a colleague or a customer, and he had steered her away and berated her for it. Helen turned heads, and she seemed blissfully unaware of the fact, though she was, in truth, completely aware. She was beautiful, she knew it, she even said it.

A woman named Denise looked after Helen's beautiful locks every Thursday afternoon at three o'clock. Helen would not trust a new hairdresser. A creature of habit, she would cross from the mainland just to get her favourite beautician. Denise did hair, facials, manicures, pedicures and something terrible involving hot wax.

After the birth of Sarah, normal service had been resumed when the baby was about a month old, so surveillance began in mid-October. At half past two, Daniel parked himself outside a pub opposite the salon, but the first time Helen came across to the Wirral her father was with her. Andrew visited shops while his daughter was beautified, then at four o'clock he parked outside the business named Denise's Parlour, and Helen joined her dad when she'd had her spit and polish. God, what a stunner. Daniel saw only the head and shoulders, but that was enough to push him further into selfish gloom.

'I probably deserve this. She's living with her dad,' he whispered. Andrew Sanderson was a force to be reckoned with. At sixty, he retained alacrity of mind, a vocabulary that might kill an enemy from a distance of forty long strides, and the body of a much younger man. Oh yes. Andrew Sanderson OBE was a mightily clever and astute man. Daniel felt momentary hatred for his father-in-law. OBE? For inventing some kind of soldering iron that worked on minor fractures? Arrogant bastard. No, he wasn't. There was no side to him, no swank.

In the Mercedes, Andrew touched his daughter's hand. 'Don't look full on, but he's parked outside the pub. It's a new Audi, black as his heart. Give me a hug, put your eyelids at half-mast, and have a furtive peep at him over my shoulder.'

'I can do better than that, Dad. Back in five.' She left the car and sashayed towards a very expensive boutique. She had trouble with clothing unless she bought separates, since what she referred to as the north face of her body didn't comply with the southern regions. Andrew waited. The Audi waited.

Helen reappeared in a petrel-blue ball gown, extra inches of silk clutched in a hand between hip and thigh. Her cleavage said it all. Andrew raised a thumb in approval, and she went back into the shop. When she emerged empty-handed, that was par for the course, since all her dresses needed alteration. Cheaper day clothes she managed herself, but a dress of the quality she had tried on today would be left for adjustment by professionals.

She rejoined her father. 'That told him,' she said.

'Did you buy it?'

'No. He did. It cost a mere five hundred in the sale.'

'And if he stops the payment?'

'Then the contents of a certain bank vault go to the taxman.'

'Ah. Blackmail, then.'

She nodded. 'As my sister would say, abso-bloody-lutely. I have him in a vice-like grip, but he can't touch me. I know too much, and what I know, Kate knows. What Kate knows, her accountant knows. Home, James.'

Across the road, a man in a black Audi struggled with his temper. Why would she need a dress like that? She already owned a dozen or more. Where was she going? Something to do with her brother-in-law's chambers? Or was Andrew staying in touch with the medical community? Helen was an intellectual, and she would fit in well. What the hell could he do to get her back, to save her from the roving eyes and hands of people like . . . of people like him?

He swallowed painfully. He was sick of eating out, sick of badly cooked meals thrown together by himself in the kitchen at home. Home? It was a mausoleum, a vast, empty space where the echo of his own footfalls mocked him nightly, where the sight of one of her slippers made him want to weep, where photographs plagued him: *Look what you threw away, fool!*

She was gone. Again. Her father had driven her away back to the old homestead with its hand-carved banisters, home-made tables and chairs, custom-built kitchen. Eva Dawson and Nanny Jasinski would be helping with the girls, and yes, he missed them, too. They were sweet, like their mother, dark-haired, bright-eyed, pretty. Damn it, they were his daughters.

Furious now, he pursued his wife and father-in-law, keeping a safe distance between the two cars. Eva would go away in a couple of hours, but Andrew and Sofia were probably fixtures. Oh, what was the point? He found a side street and turned back. There was no sense in pursuit. He needed food. He went home.

Kate Rutherford was serving supper in the kitchen of her Woolton house. Woolton, like Blundellsands, was a district of Liverpool considered posh, as many of its residents were genuinely rich, while several lived beyond their means. This latter group was labelled by Liverpudlians as 'fur coats, no knickers', which placed them in a category worthy of mockery and deserving of swift dismissal from thought, which attitude suited everyone until it came to burglary.

'They took the DVD player, mobile phones, the TV and all Carol's jewellery.' She stabbed at her dish of lasagne before waving the cutter in the air. 'Then they drove off in her car. I want a bodyguard,' she said. 'One with muscles and a handsome face will do. Somebody a bit rough with a Scouse accent would be nice, calloused hands, a whiff of cement about his person.'

Richard, who played the foil very well, did not smile. 'I've told you before, Kate, you are not having a toy-boy or your bit of rough. If you want to play, play with me.'

She grinned at him. 'You're no fun. I'm used to you.'

'Oh, well.' Richard sighed. She was a torment, but she kept him grounded. 'I'll throw away the handcuffs. Three quid, they cost.' He wagged a finger. The new urchin-cut hair suited her temperament, as did the red T-shirt he'd had printed for her. Dressed for supper? It was a good job the kids were in bed, because black letters on the pillar-box-coloured article screamed QUEEN OF THE WHOLE FUCKING UNIVERSE, and both kids could read, thanks to this labelled queen. 'Behave yourself.'

'OK, guv.'

'I went to see Daniel this evening,' he said carefully.

'You did what?'

'Now, don't go into a strop. I did this for your sister as well. He agreed to mediation, and so must she. He'd been watching her getting her hair done and buying clothes. That is one broken man.'

'Broken?' she cried. 'He should have it broken off.'

Richard helped himself to salad. 'This needs to be done properly.'

'All right then, cut it off with a clean knife if you must be kind.'

'Kate, sit down.'

She sat. 'You are unbelievable,' she said.

'He's also agreed to therapy for sex addiction. Now, eat.'

She ate. Her faith in the man seated opposite was total. She pulled him to bits, made fun of him, even mocked him brutally on occasion, but she knew she had the best man under the sun. Kate was the heartbeat of their life, while he was the brains and the sense.

'I want you to persuade Helen to attend mediation.'

'She's not ready.'

'Exactly. Daniel knows that, too.'

'Then—'

'Then they do it when she is ready, when Cassie's a bit older. Until Helen's back to normal, we let the dogs lie. I treated him harshly at first because it was no more than he deserved, but Helen was obviously out of control when she did what she did. You must keep an eye on her till you judge the time to be right. Too many postnatal women start divorce proceedings only to regret the action later.'

Kate put down her fork. 'Listen, legal eagle. She's lucky she has no genital warts or chlamydia. Well, we hope she hasn't. When she gets her postnatal exam, she'll have to ask to be tested for HIV as well. How humiliating and frightening is that? What if her children are diseased? Had it happened to me, your new accessory would have been a knife in your back.'

'Shut up, Kate, or I won't let you handcuff me to the bed.'

She pointed to the legend printed on her chest. 'Never forget this, buster. I am the queen of this establishment and of the whole world. You are a mere consort. Are they pink?'

'What?'

'The handcuffs. Are they covered in pink fluff?'

'Of course.'

'They won't match my T-shirt.'

'You won't be wearing it.'

'Who says?'

'Me says. I bought other items, too.'

'What did you buy, what did you buy?'

'Later.'

They finished the meal in silence. While Kate stacked the dishwasher, Richard removed the cloth, dusted the table, then vacuumed the rug. Without his wig and gown, he was a thoroughly modern man. 'Alan Bennett, anyone?' he asked.

'Ooh, yes. The one where Patricia Routledge goes to jail.'

'Very well.' He went through to the snug. The children were allowed very limited TV time, so the main living rooms contained no sets. He found the disc, pushed it into the DVD player, then prepared himself.

Kate entered the dimly lit room. He was seated on a sofa, and he sported wig and gown with nothing underneath.

'What's going on now?' she asked.

'Fraud case tomorrow,' he said. 'Bloody tedious. When I

stand there wearing these clownish things, only I will know they've seen better times. Now, take off that stupid top. Let's see what's underneath.'

'Handcuffs?' she asked.

'Another time. Lock the door, come here and make a man of counsel for the defence. A defendant's future depends on you, Miss Eroginique.'

Kate awarded him her slow-to-arrive smile. 'Full body massage, sir?'

'Yes, please.'

So while Patricia Routledge played to an empty gallery, her promised audience was otherwise employed.

Helen was determined to get her figure back. With Cassie on the bottle, her mother went through all the painful binding with crêpe bandage, gentle Pilates exercises and, once her milk had gone, walking. At the top of concrete fortifications a tarmac walkway bordered a grassed area, and here she increased her pace daily.

Her fan club arrived within days, men who wanted to show off their jogging, their muscles, and their ability to outpace each other. She should have been used to it, since she had known it since puberty. Helen was beautiful, and beauty had its downside. Beauty never got its own space; it was always encroached upon.

One of the reasons for the basement gym at home was her reluctance to be stared at. Several accidents had occurred at a Neston health club because men lost concentration when they saw her. It was her boobs. They had a mind of their own and refused to take orders.

So here came the peacocks, daft men displaying not feathers but sweaty shirts clinging to six-packs, tiny shorts that revealed thigh muscles of steel, faces hard-set so as to deny their obvious interest. Little boys. No matter how old they were, no matter what position they achieved in the world of work, they remained forever children, pubescent, needy, trying to control their unbiddable bodies. As with her breasts, no binding was strong enough.

When she began the slow jogging, her stalkers suddenly lost speed. After a few days, she chose to sit on a bench while they passed. She would then stand and take off in the opposite direction, which action caused collision among the ranks on two occasions, whereupon she turned, stood still, and laughed at them.

The one thing designed to deflate a man was the laughter of womankind. Men were perfect. In mirrors, they saw not the marks of age, nor the weariness of loosening skin; oh no, they saw Adonis, Brad Pitt, Richard Gere. But she saw their desperation, the need to have, to hold and control anything that took their fancy. She imagined them using their wives but seeing different faces, hearing different voices, pretending that the poor creatures who served them were different people, in an attempt to enliven their wearying, droneish lives. Bees had it right. The guys stayed at home to do building work, while the girls got out and had the fun. Drones. How very apt.

Out of sheer bloody-mindedness, Helen abandoned the tarmac walkway and used the pavement outside her father's house and its neighbouring homes. This proved interesting. The recipients of her mockery remained where they were, on the tarmac across the green, but curtain-twitching began. So here she was, caught between the devil and the deep grey Mersey, and after catching a probably senile chap performing a lewd act in his garden, Helen abandoned the outdoors.

'What's the matter?' Andrew asked.

'Men,' she answered.

'You should be used to the inferior sex by now.'

'There was an old chap four houses down abusing himself in the garden.'

'That's Jim. Alzheimer's.'

'Right. I need some equipment. May I keep it in the function suite?'

He paused before replying. 'Of course.'

Helen hugged her dad. 'She wouldn't mind, you know. And she's not coming back, so there's no need to save all that space.'

She left the room and performed her own abuse, heaping up the agony via Daniel's borrowing power. On the internet, she ordered all the machines she might need, plus a couple she wasn't sure of. 'Let him pay,' she told herself.

Downstairs, Andrew thought about his younger daughter. She wasn't tough, wasn't complicated. All she wanted was a happy home with her children and a faithful husband. She loved her job, but she loved home more. Helen needed to be married. Alone, she was a lost sheep, or rather a lamb bleating silently in suffocating snow.

Storm was lunaticking about in the garden. 'He needs an eye test,' Andrew said. 'No spatial awareness whatsoever. How can he have a hope in hell of catching high-flying seagulls? A nice pair of specs will put him right.'

He picked up the local newspaper and studied his advertisement. *Andrew Sanderson offers piano tuition.* Very imaginative. One sentence followed by his telephone number was real poetry, what? He wouldn't charge a fortune. If he found a few competent youngsters, he would be busy and pleased.

Eva appeared. Oh, no. Andrew put down the paper. 'Yes?'

'It's ate me pot towels,' she complained.

'Tea towels?'

'Yes, them as well. If you look inside its dee-tached residence, you'll find bits of stuff all over the floor. It's took oven gloves, a loo roll and a hand towel from the downstairs bog, a tray, two forks and a spoon.'

'He's perhaps waiting for room service.'

'Well, it'll be a bloody long wait, Doc.'

He sighed. 'You handing in your notice, then?'

Eva frowned. 'No, I'm not. I promised to look after you, and I'm doing me best. But Mary said nothing about a full house and a bloody dog.' In truth, Eva had promised more than that, a great deal more, but she wasn't to tell him till he was ready. Till he was ready? At this rate, the next millennium could come, and he'd still be festering.

'Sofia cooks,' he reminded her. 'Sofia and Helen keep their rooms clean and tidy, and they do the children's rooms, so in which way are you inconvenienced? It's just the dog, isn't it? Well, Storm is not negotiable. He stays.'

'And so do I.'

'Right.

'Right.'

'Eva, what are we talking about? I sometimes think you're hovering on the brink of something, and you hide behind tea towels and oven gloves. What is this world-shattering piece of information you're withholding?'

She shook her head. 'Doc, you should see a doctor. Your imagination's running away with you. You know me – well, you should. If I have something to say, I say it. Oh, yes. Our Natalie's coming to help me later. Windows and floors.'

He nodded. 'How's she doing with her studies?'

Eva shrugged. 'She didn't faint when the corpses were wheeled in. A few of the men collapsed, and one of the girls. No, our Natalie just grabbed what she calls her cutlery and got on with it.'

'Does she want to specialize?'

'I think she'll be happy as a GP, a family doctor. She says people come first, and the local surgery's important, because the general doctor decides what's up. She's a people person.'

'Excellent. I look forward to meeting her.'

Andrew met Natalie but briefly, as he was otherwise engaged, yet she reminded him of someone, and he couldn't think who. It wasn't Eva, since Eva had adopted Natalie's deceased mother, so Andrew decided he must have caught sight of Natalie before, perhaps in town or when driving Eva home.

The rest of his family arrived that afternoon. Ian, Andrew's youngest, brought his wife and two sons. They had come to offer support to Helen, though the sombre pair of adults seemed ill-equipped to comfort anyone. Even the twin boys, Robert and Oliver, appeared old before their third birthday. Yet they were happy. Andrew amended his thoughts. Contented was nearer.

The two boys sat side by side on a sofa, each with a book, neither with a smile. They answered when addressed, were unimpressed by Storm's antics at the window, undeterred by Eva's brusqueness, soberly thankful when given milk and biscuits. Andrew had to admit to himself, and not for the first time, that his son was probably the most boring man on earth, that he had married a bore, that he had fathered a pair of budding bores. Though one could never be sure. Many people had two faces, one for outside their house, one for home.

Mary had tried to enliven her son, had taken him to the beach with the girls, to parks, to the cinema, all to no avail. Eva had taken over, as usual. 'He's just a miserable little sod,' had been Eva's oft-expressed opinion. 'More fun in Kate's little finger than in his whole bloody skeleton.'

Ian had been an avid reader. By the age of eleven, he had collected more medical knowledge than was good for him. 'We made our lives so easy at their expense,' Andrew told his dead wife. 'The girls had each other, Ian had his books, while you and I had a whale of a time. We were wrong, Mary, so wrong.'

He put Storm in his Wendy house, checked on the silent twins, and walked upstairs. Ian was droning on. 'There is counselling, of course, though its value is debatable.'

Eliza, Ian's wife, chipped in. 'I don't understand adulterers,' she said.

'Your children look well,' Ian opined.

Andrew eavesdropped from the landing. He wished Kate were here. Kate had a wonderful way of pulling the rug from beneath her plodding, dull brother. 'Exercise your face,' she often ordered. 'Smile – it costs nothing and isn't a criminal offence.'

'Will you go back to him?' Ian was asking now.

'Will you piss off?'

Andrew pushed a fist against his mouth. Kate *was* here up to a point. There was a bit of Kate in Helen, thank goodness.

'No need for that,' Ian said.

Helen's voice remained low and controlled. 'You two are about as much fun as a burning orphanage, so I'm glad you married. It's saved the sanity of two other people. You want me to feel better? Then take yourselves off to your colourless home, take your monochrome, two-dimensional children and leave me alone.'

Eliza gasped. Even from the landing, Andrew heard it. 'You're being cruel, Helen, but we understand. Such a shock must have—'

'Go away.'

'But we—'

'Go away. Go away now. I don't want you here.'

Andrew crept downstairs. The identical twins remained in place. Their slow page-turning seemed almost synchronized. Helen was only too right. Ian had manufactured a colour-free life, and it was rather too late for change. What did they do for enjoyment? Did they know the word?

He watched them drive away. Even their car was automatic.

Six

By 1956, Joe Sanderson was living in Liverpool during the week, coming home just at weekends to be with his family and to check that all remained well with the business in Bolton. Management there rested on the shoulders of a time-served carpenter with many years of experience, while Michael Caldwell had made a promising start as apprentice, so the business ran as smoothly as ever while Joe put down huge roots in Liverpool.

He had never regretted the move. The rented house in Seaforth suited his needs, just a two-up two-down with a bathroom tacked on downstairs. All his money had gone into the Dock Road business, which was thriving within a year. A catalogue brought in orders from all over the north-west, and the Sanderson empire was spreading like a forest fire in dry weather. He was already looking for bigger premises, and he expected a fleet of large vehicles to soon be carrying Sanderson kitchens to widespread parts of the country. Liverpool, still undergoing post-war regeneration, was offering cut-price rentals on business properties, while the battered docks, now renovated, continued to bring in work to the region.

He enjoyed the city once he got through the language barrier. Attuned to the slower speech of inland Lancashire with its flattened vowels and clear enunciation, he had some difficulty in keeping up with his new neighbours and employees. Scouse was rapid-fire, even guttural when it came to certain words, and the humour was swift and cutting. Jokes, especially those of the practical variety, became part and parcel of everyday life, and Joe finally began to anticipate certain events, though he seldom kept full pace with his humorous employees.

'They take some keeping up with,' he often told his wife on the phone. 'Fur is fair, and fair is fur,' he said. 'I don't know whether I'm coming or going.' But he soon found out that he was going – going up in the world, because his workforce was hard-working while managing to remain ridiculous. No one was safe; as boss, he was the victim of many jibes, but the staff worked as hard as they played, which was good enough for him. 'They put a tarantula in my snap tin, Emily. Well, it wasn't a real one, but I wasn't best pleased. There I was looking for a cheese butty, and death was staring up at me. If I ever find out who did it, I'll fight back with a bloody rattlesnake.'

Yet there was sadness, too, in his new life. Poor Betsy had remained in St Helens. Her daughter, now three years of age, was disabled. Daisy, starved of oxygen during birth, had finally started to walk, though she didn't speak. She required constant attention, and Betsy had become a brilliant mother. She focused on Daisy and only on Daisy.

When Joe travelled the few miles between Liverpool and St Helens, he was given a cup of tea, a slice of shop-bought cake and minimal attention. Daisy owned Betsy, and Joe didn't know whether to be sad or glad. That Betsy was busy was a good thing, but their child was making poor progress and was not expected to reach adulthood. It was heartbreaking. Yet in a strange way, Betsy was almost happy. She looked a wreck, but when she was with Daisy it was all clapping hands and nursery rhymes and false hope, God help her.

Sometimes the little girl was asleep when Joe arrived,

and they had the chance to talk. 'Will you stay in St Helens?' he asked one evening.

'She's used to here, Joe, used to this flat.'

'What about you, though?'

Betsy shrugged. 'It's a case of where she is, I am. But my neighbours are great, you see. I couldn't ask for better, really. They take her out in the chair, give me a couple of hours to rest or tidy the house, do a bit of washing. They even babysit so I can go and see Elsie or get to bingo a couple of times a month.' She sniffed. 'I suppose you've noticed I went clean.'

'Yes. You did it for Daisy.'

'Aye, I did. But I did it for me and all, cos after . . . you know, after he died, I realized what a sloven I'd turned into. Poor bugger had nowt to live for, no kids, no chance of kids, a wife who never cleaned up. We killed him, you know. We put that rope round his neck, Joe.'

'Yes, I am very much aware of that.'

'I may not have been much, but I was all he had. Is Daisy our punishment, though? Is she?'

'She's like she is because they should have cut her out of you. You should sue the buggers, Bets. That sweet kiddy isn't a punishment, definitely not. She's an accident, just another bloody hospital accident.'

Betsy rocked in her chair. Joe had made the rocker for her, as well as a dining table and chairs. 'Thanks for looking after us money-wise,' she said. 'And for his nice headstone. We went to see it, me and our Else. The loveliest part was that you put *father of Daisy, born after his death*. That was a lovely touch. You made a man of him, you know. I know it was a bit late, like, but I appreciate the thought.'

'Least I could do, lass. Well, I'd better get back and phone the missus, see how she's managing without the man of the house.'

Betsy nodded. 'Still no playing at bedtime?'

Joe nodded. 'Aye, nothing changes. She's not interested. I get the feeling that she'd stop in Bolton but for our Andrew. He's set his mind on Liverpool University. They have a good medical school and quite a few hospitals, so they'll both be coming when he's eighteen. She's like you; she'll follow her child just about anywhere.'

'Then she has her priorities right.'

He put some extra money on the mantelpiece. 'Get yourself a bit of something, Bets. Or a toy for the little miss. You've got my work and home numbers. Ta-ra for now.' He kissed her chastely on her forehead and left her to her sad little life.

During the drive home, he thought hard about poor Betsy. She looked so old. Daisy's birth had not resulted in adoption as expected, but had caused Betsy to become frantically vigilant. Fortunately, Augustinian nuns from a nearby hospital helped the situation for a few weeks. Although Daisy had not been born in their establishment, these good women took it upon themselves to help the new mother cope with her frail baby.

Once a routine established itself, Betsy and Daisy got on with it. But it was a monotonous life for a grown woman, and she became grey, shapeless and stooped. Joe did his best, but he was a guilty man. The suicide of Martin Liptrott sat heavily on his shoulders, as did the situation of Martin's widow. It was all Joe's fault, and Joe had stayed away from women ever since.

Then there was Emily. She remained with Andrew on Mornington Road, but she was very different. After a year or so dedicated almost exclusively to paperwork, she had done a couple of courses and was now assistant almoner at Bolton Royal. She had come out of her shell. She was prettier, livelier, happier. The job was just a vehicle; he was almost certain that Emily had met someone. A doctor?

A patient whose recovery involved visits from her? Was she capable of throwing herself wholeheartedly into a relationship? Was she?

No. Emily wasn't interested in men, wasn't interested in much. Her hobbies excluded anyone who wasn't Andrew, anything that didn't have black and white keys and pedals. Yet he felt uneasy. She walked with the spring of a twenty-five-year-old in her step, and she was wearing high-heeled shoes, perfume, Yardley's face powder, coral lipstick, jewellery. The legend on the lipstick tube read *Koral Kiss*, and that, too, made him anxious. If she'd found someone, a bloke who lasted more than a few minutes, she would know what a failure her husband was. Could he imagine Emily giving herself away in gay abandon?

The Emily he remembered had always dressed simply in order to avoid attention. She was a shy woman, afraid of her own prettiness, determinedly unadorned unless attending one of Andrew's concerts. But now, she was suddenly confident; she laughed more, talked more, was slightly less careful about the house.

He parked in a lay-by and wondered what to do. A week off? Could Liverpool manage without him? Of course it could. But did he really want to know what she was up to? 'Knowledge is power?' he mumbled. What power might he gain from finding out what Emily was doing? She knew about Betsy, though she was not privy to the whole sordid truth. As far as Emily was concerned, her husband had come home from work that day with pneumonia; she had no idea that he'd driven his lover and unborn child to St Helens. But the earlier beating from Martin Liptrott had proved his faithlessness.

A week off. He had to do it. Wondering and worrying served only to pave the road to madness, and that road grew shorter with every passing day. If he carried on, he'd end up in a straitjacket on a funny farm. Why did he care?

God, why did he have to care about Emily? And if he, the gander, had tasted sauce, why should the goose be scrutinized? Because it was different for women? Because men were wild beasts while women were angels? If women were angels, where did men find their sleeping partners?

He started the car. Perhaps he should bring Emily and Andrew to Liverpool now, let the lad do his A levels at a good school over here? That would put a stop to Emily's games. If there were any games. The O levels were almost over; Andrew was expecting top grades in all subjects. There were just two school years left, then university. Yes, they might come to Liverpool now, let their son get used to the city.

'Then I'd be house-hunting,' he said. 'I'm stupid. They can't live where I live – it's a shoebox.'

But he needed to know what his wife was up to. If she was innocent, she and Andrew could stay where they were, thus allowing Joe to concentrate fully on the business. If she was messing about . . . Joe wished he could understand himself. One thing was becoming clear – an adulterous person always suspected his partner of having the same fault. Oh, and he loved her. So that made two things.

At thirteen, Andrew Sanderson had been old enough to know that he wasn't old enough to deal with the Beauchamps of Heathfield Farm. So he'd postponed the plan, kept quiet, stayed at home, studied, done his homework. He was at a good school, the best for many a mile. Yes, it was sometimes boring, and yes, he still learned more about life while away from his alma mater, but as a means to an end, Bolton School was more than adequate. Andrew Sanderson was going to be a doctor as long as he got the grades. But in two years he would be a Liverpudlian, so it was a case of now or never.

He and his friend, Stuart Abbot, emerged from their final exam. They were on their way to Andrew's house, where his mother had left a cake for them. 'She still treats me like a child,' Andrew said. 'She's made us a celebrate-end-of-exams Victoria sponge.'

'You're lucky. You don't get sent through to serve a customer with a quarter of boiled ham when she needs a rest. I want a job this summer, something away from the shop. If I hear the ding of that till once more, I'll end up dafter than I am already. There must be something I can do to earn a few bob.'

They entered Emily's beautiful kitchen, where Andrew pondered for several seconds, filling in the gap in conversation by cake-cutting and pouring orange juice into glasses.

'This is great,' Stuart said. 'My mother would give an arm and a leg for a kitchen like this.'

Andrew chuckled. 'Then she'd need a special. Dad's doing research into kitchens for disabled people. But I'd tell your mum to hang on to her limbs if I were you. Arms and legs have their uses from time to time.'

'I suppose they do.'

It was indeed a wonderful kitchen, solid oak cupboards and drawers, a long work surface, knife blocks, new cooker and sink. 'Time, motion and geometry,' Andrew said thoughtfully. 'A triangle. Cooker, sink and fridge are pivotal. Their positioning is of prime importance. Everything's always thought out in factories, and a kitchen is a small factory, because it produces things. My dad thinks these matters through very thoroughly. Stuart?'

'What?'

Andrew swallowed. It was now or never, so it had better

be now. 'About a job for the holidays. We've exercised our minds, so how about getting some muscles? I've been thinking about farm labouring. Imagine if we go into sixth form in September all sun-tanned and strong. The girls' division will have to lock its doors to keep them in.'

Stuart grinned. 'You don't half talk some mashed potato, Andrew. They might look at you, but I've still got a metal five-bar gate across my teeth. The girls' division's already listed you as a five-star bloke. I bet I haven't even got one star with these braces. I mean, look at your height for a start. When are you going to stop growing?'

'No idea.' He could trust Stuart. He had to trust him, because two heads were better than one, and the idea of going up there on his own was not particularly attractive. 'Look, it's about my mother,' he said. 'Top secret, of course, but there's a massive farm that stretches for miles. Heathfield, it's called. It's so big that they need lots of people living in cottages all the way to the Pennines. Half a dozen or more huge farms, really, but all under one heading.'

'Right. And your mother?'

Andrew shrugged. 'She's the farmer's daughter. The main farmer. Beecham spelt the French way – Beauchamp. They kicked her out because of Dad. She was supposed to marry land, you see. When I first found out, Mother and Dad were going through a bad time, so I vowed to uncover all I could in case she needed her family.'

'Does she need them?'

'No. But I'd like to meet them, see what they're made of.'

Stuart grabbed another chunk of cake. Before biting into it, he agreed to go with his friend to try for work on the farm.

'We'll be brothers,' Andrew said. 'Stuart and Andrew Abbot.'

Stuart found this so hilarious that he breathed in a few

cake crumbs. He was standing over the sink with his friend battering him on the back when Thora came in. She took over, of course. Whatever was afoot, Thora had to be in charge. 'Your mother told me to come in and tell you she'll be late, something to do with catching up with paperwork. Or was it a meeting? Oh, I can't remember. Are you all right now?' she asked Stuart, who was probably black and blue after two beatings.

The poor lad got his breath back and sat down.

Thora turned to Andrew. 'I've two of them now,' she announced.

'Two what, Mrs Caldwell?'

'Teddy boys. I've a blue one and a green one. Kieran and Sean. Kieran's blue with bright yellow socks, and Sean's green with shocking pink socks. They look so stupid standing on corners swinging chains or combing their quiffs. I said to Harry, I said, "Have you seen the state of your two eldest?", but he just carried on watching that test card thing on the television. Did you know he sleeps through programmes but watches the test card? I'll just have a bit of your mam's cake, Andrew. She won't mind.'

There followed a brief pause while Thora gorged herself. Andrew winked at Stuart, who was not yet used to the carryings-on of the Sandersons' next door neighbours.

'So.' She brushed away a few crumbs from her flat chest. 'You've done with exams, I take it?'

'More in two years,' Andrew said. 'This is growing-up time, Mrs Caldwell. According to our masters, we've been spoon-fed so far. The gap between O level and A level is wider than the one between A level and university. So we have seven weeks to become men.'

'Well, as long as you don't become Teddy boys. I can't be doing with them there stupid suits. If you need anything, you know where I am.'

Outside, Thora sat on her garden wall and lit a Woodbine. Andrew would suffer, she thought. Emily's relationship was fast becoming an open secret, especially since her husband went to Liverpool. It was often the quiet, withdrawn ones who went off the rails. Andrew had to carry on studying, while Joe needed to stay in the dark till the affair blew over. Was it an affair, or was it something bigger? God forbid on the divorce front. That would cripple young Andrew.

For the first time in her life, Emily Sanderson was experiencing the joy of physical love. In his thirties, Dr Geoff Shaw was a decade her junior, but that didn't seem to matter to either party. While unease often weighed her down, she felt she had not betrayed her husband, but she worried about her one and only son. And might she lose her job because of the relationship?

Geoff was not particularly attractive. He wore thick-lensed glasses and was not tall, dark and handsome. In heels, she matched his height, and he was by no means a fine figure of a man, as he was slight of frame and his hair had already begun to recede, but his voice could melt her heart, while his gentle approach and brilliance of mind had taken terra firma from beneath her feet long ago. She was finally, dangerously, in love.

She lay now in his arms, her mind filled with concern about Andrew, her body satiated by this skilful lover. It had to end; she must put a stop to it. But, as she drifted towards sleep, she curled into him, unwilling to leave the smallest space between their two bodies. And she floated into a dream that would fill her nights for years to come, though its order would vary, as is the way with dreams.

'Where's Mrs Dobbs?'

Emily looked up from her typing. 'Oh. She's following

up on a patient who's being moved to the TB hospital. He needs help in understanding what's happening to him – psychological problems.'

'Right.'

She felt his eyes travelling over her face and upper body. 'May I take a message?' she asked. 'Mrs Dobbs should be back before two o'clock.'

'No, but you may take lunch with me in the canteen. One o'clock?' And he left without another word.

Emily didn't do a single tap of work after this event. She stared at the unfinished letter, blinked several times and picked up her flask and her sandwiches. Who did he think he was, coming in here and telling her where she must lunch? It was a nice day, and she intended to sit on a bench at the park side of the hospital, eat her food, drink her coffee, then return to finish the typing. The canteen food was good, but the place was noisy, filled with chattering cadets and student nurses.

But when she reached 'her' bench, he was already seated and waiting for her. 'I knew you wouldn't go to the canteen,' he told her. 'You don't appreciate being ordered about, and you like to overlook the park, don't you? Am I right on both counts?'

'Yes.'

'And when the weather's fine, you come here at exactly half past twelve. Creature of habit.'

'You've been watching me,' she accused him.

'Yes. It's become a hobby, and it's completely free of charge, I believe.'

It was his voice. It wrapped itself round her like a sheet of pure silk. What did he want? 'What do you want?' she asked.

'You. I want you.'

The sandwiches remained in their wrapping, while her coffee flask stood between them. No one had ever spoken

135

to her in such a forthright way. She stared ahead at the trees bordering Queen's Park. Her brain was on strike; she could think of no words, no response that might convey how she felt. How did she feel? She hadn't the slightest idea.

'You're Emily,' he advised her.

'I know my name, but thank you for the reminder.'

'Your husband's in kitchens and bespoke furniture, and your son's at the school up the road.'

'Yes.'

'Clever boy?'

'Yes, he is.'

'I understand that Mr Sanderson is moving to Liverpool. Spreading his wings, so to speak.'

'We shall all be in Liverpool within a few years.'

He nodded thoughtfully. 'I'm Geoff, as in Chaucer, not the American Jeff. And when you go to Liverpool, I may follow, because I am a Scouser – from West Derby. Grammar-school boy, working-class family, salt of the earth. Dad's a dock worker, and Mam works at the biscuit factory. There are hospitals in Liverpool. I'm quite prepared to play the long game.'

Emily turned to him. 'I don't play games, Dr . . .' She had forgotten his name, but he was a paediatrician.

'Shaw.'

'Dr Shaw. I'm not available.' He had beautiful hands.

'I'm a patient man.'

'I'm a determined woman.'

'Promising, then.' He chuckled quietly. 'This game is going to be challenging.' He raised a hand. 'I know, I heard you, you don't play. Well, let me put you straight, Emily. You're a dormant volcano. You are in serious need of tender, loving care. I was going to be a psychologist, but I turned left into paediatrics. You require fulfilment. I need your body. We should get together some time soon. I can promise you a satisfactory result. Enjoy your lunch.'

And he was gone.

Emily closed her gaping mouth with a snap. He wanted her? He *wanted* her? Let him want – she was a mother and just a mother. Andrew's life needed to be smooth and . . . Oh, goodness. A doctor wanted her. Lovely hands, a voice that might melt the coldest heart and, in spite of his forthright manner, a gentle, kind and humorous nature.

For the very first time, Emily reacted the way a teenager might, though she slowed down a process of which she was naively unaware. A little make-up. A tighter skirt. Button at the throat left undone, shoes with heels, a nice belt. She had her hair styled in town, got her nails manicured, enjoyed facials, bought creams and lotions that boasted the ability to make her young. And he stayed away. He was there, yet almost invisible.

The stand-off endured for almost three months. She knew when he was watching her. Even when he was behind her, she could feel his eyes travelling over her legs, her back, her hair. He watched her often. A thrill ran up her spine sometimes, rather like a shiver. Whenever she turned, he was already walking away. Even then, in the very early days, there was an inevitability attached to the situation.

In cooler weather, she ate in a little-used staffroom. And he arrived. Before walking across to where she sat, he tilted a chair under the door handle. 'What?' he asked when he turned to face her. 'I forgot the Do Not Disturb sign, so the chair's in lieu of that.'

He didn't exactly attack her. He didn't exactly do much, though he left an impression. Having separated her from sandwich and cup, he held her firmly and kissed her. And at that moment, she was defeated. It was ridiculous. She didn't know him, didn't love him, didn't . . . didn't want him?

He stepped back. 'Salmon,' he said. 'You were eating a salmon sandwich.' He smiled. He had perfect teeth. 'Your metamorphosis has been interesting to watch. Did you think I'd lost interest? You see, the chemistry comes first, and not just for men. Lust arrives before love. You dressed up for me in order to draw me in. The web is woven, my dear. Now, we need to do the rest of it. That will cure us or bind us together for always.'

'I'm married.'

'I know.'

'I will never hurt my son.'

'Right.'

'It's wrong,' she said desperately. 'There's nothing right about it.'

'That's what makes it delicious.' He returned to the door, moved the chair and left. For a split second the door reopened. 'Delicious,' he repeated quietly before closing the door again.

Emily looked at the clock on the wall. Two minutes had passed, but she felt radically altered, as if she had almost become a different person. It was silly. She was old enough to be a grandmother, for heaven's sake. Well, perhaps she would be allowed a rest from him for a few weeks? If he ran to pattern, she should get some peace for a while.

But no. His tactics changed radically. By some undisclosed method, he seemed to be tailoring several of his shifts to match hers. He rented a flat quite near to the infirmary, and he walked with her as she made her way home, but for several weeks, he didn't invite her in. When he finally did, his request arrived in terms to which she was gradually becoming inured.

'Come in,' he said abruptly. 'You're quite safe; it won't be rape. When it happens, it will be your decision.'

'Then it will be never, Geoff.'

'Hmm.' He looked her up and down. 'How do you take your tea?'

'Moderately strong, no sugar, just a splash of milk.'

'Moderation. How predictable. Come.' He held out an arm, and her feet walked past him into the doorway. She didn't remember making the decision to do his bidding; it just happened. So her legs were obeying him, while her brain remained on alert. As for her heart . . . she felt she might need surgery, so erratic was the beat.

She noticed a single bed, neatly made with hospital corners. The rest of the large room was a war zone. There was a desk in a nook near a bay window, and it was piled with papers, some of which had spilled to the floor. 'Don't tidy any of this,' he ordered. 'I get confused if anyone tries to organize me. You see a mess. Well, I know where everything is. Almost everything, anyway . . .'

Emily sat uncomfortably on the edge of an armchair while he went into the kitchen. She couldn't sit any more easily, as the seat was covered in books. The sofa was in the same condition. A pair of socks lay on the floor next to a tray overflowing with notebooks and pens. To the right of the fireplace, a tall bookcase was covered in confusion. He wasn't perfect; he was delightfully human, and so different from anyone she had met thus far.

The door from the bed-sitting room into the kitchen was to the left of the chimney breast. His head appeared. 'Come in here, please. In here, I am tidy.'

The kitchen, though very 1939, was scrupulously clean. An ancient gas cooker in blue and cream stood on bowed legs just to the left of the inner door. In spite of its antiquity, it shone. There was an inlaid table, a dresser that looked as if it had once belonged to some grandmother's grandmother, and rows of shelves supporting neatly stacked dishes and dry goods. A white porcelain sink sparkled, as did the taps.

'Very clean,' she said.

He poured the tea and offered her a biscuit. 'I haven't baked this week,' he explained.

'You bake? No, thank you, I won't have a biscuit.'

'Of course I bake. I'm a bachelor with no intention of marrying, so I cook, clean, wash, iron and shop all by myself like a good little boy.'

'I'm sorry. I didn't intend to sound critical.'

He reached across the table and took her hand. 'Marriage is for people who intend to breed. I don't want children.'

She shook her head in disbelief. 'But you love them. Everyone says you're magic with them.'

'I didn't realize I was the subject of gossip. You talk about me?' He tightened his grip slightly. 'Listen to me now. I have two much-loved brothers. Each has a child. One lost a leg to bone cancer, and the other is battling infantile leukaemia. I'm taking no chances.'

Emily swallowed. 'Geoff, I am so sorry.' She thought about Andrew and imagined ... Managed not to imagine. 'So you chose me because I'm too old to bear a child?'

His gaze did not waver. 'I had a procedure in a Swiss clinic. A vasectomy. It's been used for a couple of decades in America to stop the criminally insane reproducing, so I thought I'd join the ranks, since I'm relatively sure of my insanity, and my desire for you is probably criminal. I'm deliberately sterile, and this has nothing to do with your age. I want you, woman, and I'm prepared to wait until you want me. And I don't need you to come to me through pity because of my niece or my nephew, or because I daren't have children in case there's some weird gene ripping its way through my family. I want you to come to me in lust.'

With her free hand, Emily took a sip of tea. 'I believe I don't do lust.'

'Not yet, perhaps. But you're making progress. Presentation of self is improving, there's a sway in your hips – you're very aware of me, yes?'

He was right. She felt hypnotized. 'Don't mock me.' She claimed back her hand.

'Don't go.'

'I have things to do.'

'We have things to do.'

'Why me? Why did you choose me?'

He shrugged. 'Because I remember you from tomorrow. It's a poem I wrote. It's somewhere . . .' He waved a hand towards the chaos in the next room. 'Lonely people write, you see. No one to talk to, so they talk to paper. Don't pity me for that, either. My own company is preferable to that of most people. By the way, he's a good pianist. Your son. I went to a concert where he played Chopin. Afterwards, I took care to stay behind and congratulate him. He'll go far.'

'He'll be a doctor.'

Geoff blinked. 'With a gift like that?'

Emily nodded. 'He won't give up the piano, but he's made up his mind about what he wants. Far be it from me to attempt to dissuade him.'

'Have a biscuit. They're full of drugs to make you sleep. Then I'll get my wicked way. Go on. You won't feel a thing.'

At this point, Emily began to laugh. She was sitting in the company of a beautiful soul, and he was ridiculous. 'What's the point, then?' she achieved eventually. 'If I won't feel a thing, why . . . ?'

'As long as you're unconscious, you won't get upset, so it won't be anything untoward.'

'You have a very distinct sense of humour,' she said. He was funny, sweet, vulnerable, untidy, lovable. She dried her eyes. 'I must go. Andrew will be wondering where I am.'

'Just a moment.' He walked round the table and stood behind her, placing his hands on her shoulders. Even through clothing, his touch was deft as he massaged tension out of her upper spine. 'I do a full body treatment,' he said. 'With oils. The clothes will have to go, of course.'

His hands were not only beautiful, they were magic. 'That's wonderful,' she sighed. 'Typing makes me . . . oh, that's lovely . . . so stiff.'

'OK. Get them off.'

'Geoff . . . no.'

'I'm a doctor.' He stopped the massage, picked her up and carried her to his bed, where they lay for several minutes just kissing. 'Tell me when to stop,' he whispered.

But she couldn't. The words were there, in her head, perfectly formed and ripe for delivery, yet they seemed incapable of travelling to her lips. He unwrapped her as if she were a gift, and she clung to him, her mouth seeking his hungrily. So this was how it should have been.

'May I finish what we've started?' he asked.

'Yes.'

'Are you sure?'

'Oh, shut up, Geoff.'

Should he tell her now, wouldn't it be fairer to say the words? 'I've been lying to you, Emily. I love you.'

'I know. I'm not stupid.'

'Shall I stop?'

'Are you ready to die?' she asked. After that, not another sensible word emerged from her, though he talked softly into her ear, quiet words tailored and delivered to send her senses reeling, to reduce her to a quivering mass of brainless anticipation.

When it was over, she continued to shake. 'I had no idea,' she eventually managed to say. 'It spread all over my body. Arms, legs . . . feet. I may need to learn to walk again.'

'Told you – you've been a dormant volcano.'

'Mountains can't walk at all.'

He grinned. 'No, but they can alter the scenery. You've altered mine. I should cook for you now, a feast of moussaka, perhaps, or some bloody steak to replace the energy we expended. Come on. Let's make you decent and send you home.' And he dressed her. She hadn't been dressed by another person since she'd been four or five.

'I'm falling in love with you,' she told him.

'No, you're not. You loved me before you stepped into my parlour. Hang on, that's the wrong way round. You wove the web and I got stuck in it. We established that fact earlier. So this is all your fault.'

'Of course.'

He rolled stockings up her legs and fastened the suspenders. 'You're ready. Go and feed your son. I shall be lonely without you.'

The dream ended. It had been quite sensible this time, all in a straight line, no interruptions, no looking over her shoulder to find Mother there with a rolling pin or a pan of rising dough or a snide word and a sneer.

She had to end this affair, couldn't end it, refused to imagine a life without him, mustn't allow this situation to continue. She dressed, wrote I LOVE YOU in lipstick on the over-mantel mirror. Andrew had finished his O levels today, and she must get home.

Andrew. He had to realize that something was going on. And Joseph would be home soon for the weekend. Joseph, who had no real idea of the joy of love, the abandonment, the fun of it. Joseph, who had never covered her in condensed milk, never brushed her hair for over half an hour, never written a poem or even a note of love. This sleeping man had bathed her, dried her, powdered her body, fed her, worshipped her. She might have gone through life without any of this. Liverpool in two years. Geoff would follow. Of course he would. He had to. He mustn't. He must.

Andrew waited. He knew where she was; more to the point, he didn't blame her for being where she was. Stuart had gone, as had Mrs Caldwell from next door. There were lamb chops in the fridge. Andrew was a clever enough boy, but when it came to lamb chops he could cope only with the side salad. He was washing lettuce when his mother came in.

Right. It was time to stop messing about, time to face the music. In fact, he would have to play the music. 'Hello, Mother.'

She placed her bag on the dining-room table before joining him in the kitchen. 'Thank you for starting the salad, sweetheart.'

He turned to face her. There was no easy way of doing what he must. 'Dad phoned. He's coming home today instead of on Friday, says he needs a break from work. I asked how long he would be staying, but he was vague. I think he's suspicious.' He noticed that she had the grace to blush.

'But I didn't buy enough chops. You and he can have them, and I'll make do with an egg and some bacon.'

Andrew swallowed. 'It isn't about chops, Mother. It's about where you've been since three o'clock. Don't worry, I'm on your side, but the excuses about dealing with patients in their homes are wearing rather thin, I'm afraid.

Even the head almoner stays in more often than you do. Anyway, you have no car, so—'

'You know I've been learning to drive? I'm getting a car, Andrew. I passed the test a few weeks ago.'

'Congratulations. Let's sit down, shall we?'

They went into the dining room. 'Don't get upset, Mother. As I said before, I'm on your side. You must always believe that. I saw Dad with . . . with that woman years ago. Michael, Mrs Caldwell and I got rid of her husband when he came here to see Dad. Dad was in hospital, and you were with him. The man went home and killed himself. His wife, according to the paper, moved to St Helens to be near her sister.'

'Why didn't you—'

'We decided, Mrs Caldwell and I, that you had enough on your hands with Dad's pneumonia. Anyway, to cut a lengthy story short, when Michael took up his apprenticeship he found out from other people at Sanderson's that Dad didn't work that day. All the men remember it clearly, since it was the day he went into hospital. It's likely that he took the woman to St Helens. Because of Dad and her, the man committed suicide. I didn't help, of course, because I was harsh and rude.'

Emily took her son's hand. 'Darling, you aren't to blame.'

'I know, but I was a factor, as was Mrs Caldwell.'

'No. You did as you thought best.'

'Neither are you to blame, Mother. I know you have separate rooms and that you started to sleep away from him because of the woman. Snoring is the official line, of course. But I'm not stupid.'

She squeezed his fingers.

'So I'm not going to tell anyone what I know.'

'Thank you.'

What did he know? 'What do you know, Andrew?'

'I know you've found someone to love, someone who loves you back. I know you've been with him today, because your hair's wrong and you look ... well, you look younger. I also know you're happy.'

Emily expelled a long sigh containing an improbable mixture of relief and fear. 'Thank you, son.'

'You must go and make yourself look more like somebody who's been making dinner. He'll be here shortly. But your secret is completely safe with me. Oh, the other thing is that Mrs Caldwell sometimes asks where you are. There's a knowing look on her face, if you see what I mean. Remember, she works at the infirmary. It may be time for the big break I used to dread. I want you to allow me to come with you. I'd try not to be in the way.' There, he had managed to say all of it.

'I would never, ever leave you, Andrew. And you'd never be in the way.'

'I hope not. And he seems to be a decent chap.'

It occurred to Emily that this was probably the strangest conversation she'd had in her life. He was so adult, far more sensible than she seemed to be. 'He came to a concert at the school,' she said.

'Yes. And one in town. He spoke to me about my piano-playing and I told him I'd inherited the gift from my mother. It was an interesting moment. Nothing was said, yet everything came across. He's special, Mother. I mean, I love my dad, but I know you need something else. I'm not a child any more. And your marriage has been dead for years. I just want to see you happy. Go on. Calm down and sort your hair. I'll set the table.'

Emily went away to dress herself in something dull. She would explain herself to Geoff tomorrow. Who else knew or suspected? Someone must have seen them walking into the Chorley New Road flat; the affair had lasted so long that only a miracle could have allowed it to pass unnoticed. Perhaps this was the time to make a change?

The front door opened, and her heart sank. Living with Joseph at weekends was difficult enough, while the idea of an extended stay appalled her. She was fast becoming the sort of woman she'd always despised, libidinous, immoral and adulterous.

Muted voices crept up the stairs. He and Andrew were having one of their rare conversations. She didn't want to go down, but a meal required preparation, so things had to appear normal. Normal? When had this marriage been normal?

Emily descended the stairs, found her husband and son in the dining room. She greeted the former with a customary peck on the cheek. 'Sorry I'm a little late. I'll make a start now.' She went into the kitchen. Her heart was in overdrive again, but for no pleasant reason. Looking at Joseph wasn't easy. She'd managed for some time, but she was now acutely aware of the fact that Andrew knew, that her neighbour suspected . . . Oh, goodness, she had been careless.

As she prepared potatoes and chops, it occurred to her that she didn't know what Geoff wanted. He seldom encouraged discussion about practicalities. Perhaps her status as a married woman suited him, so if she left Joseph, what then? With a sickening thud, she realized that she was probably a toy, a plaything that even put itself away at night. He didn't want to live with her, certainly wouldn't like the idea of living with her son as well.

'Emily?'

Love? Geoff's kind of love suited his requirements and catered for nothing beyond his own needs. He would run a mile if she suggested moving in with him.

'Emily?'

'You're miles away,' Joe said. 'You need a plaster on that.'

She looked down. Her finger was bleeding, but she hadn't felt a thing, because she was swallowed up by a far bigger pain.

Seven

'It's going to be chaos on toast, just you mark my words,' Eva promised after depositing shopping in the kitchen. 'I've never seen anything like it in me life, even in Manchester, and that's saying something. It's every man for himself down Duke Street, loads of folk cutting through and shoving me out of the way. Worse than the bloody Liverpool and Everton derby, it is. It's a wonder I didn't get crushed underfoot. What's happened to manners? That's what I'd like to know. Now me corns have got corns. And me worst bunion got trod on every five minutes. I wouldn't care, but nobody even bothers to say they're sorry.'

Andrew groaned inwardly. When had Eva last apologized? She was away. She'd be on her high horse now till she fell off, or until the poor beast lost the will to carry on living under the weight of Eva's angst. Oh no, there was more. She sucked in her cheeks the way she did before going for goal in the next chukka. If he'd owned armour, he might well have girded his loins at this point.

'Have you done your shopping for presents, Doc? Three quarters of an hour I stood yesterday, just waiting to pay in Marks and Spencer's. Are you having that big table out in the function suite? Because you'll have all the kiddies as well, you know. Five of them, anyway. Cassie's a bit young for sprouts.'

He opened his mouth to speak, but she motored on regardless. 'Whatever possessed you to open up that barn of a place? Talk about the feeding of the five bloody thousand – have you got loaves and fishes? And you'd best find us a removal van for the turkey. Williamson Square was packed full with some carol festival and brass bands, I was tripping over Salvation Army folk all the way down Dale Street, and the cafes and bars was fit to bust, so no chance of a cuppa . . .'

Her voice faded as she left the room, but her head returned briefly by itself. 'Lewis's was life-or-death. Two women fighting over one cardigan, a drunk asleep on the floor in his own pee, then management trying to drag him out through the crowd. I'm telling you – hell on gas mark nine.' Her head followed the rest of her royal righteousness into the kitchen. 'Bloody Christmas,' she yelled.

'Par for the course,' Andrew murmured. 'Full of festive spirit as per usual, tidings of comfort and joy.'

She was always throwing questions, though she seldom waited for answers. Anyway, none of what was about to happen had been his idea. The function suite had been thrown open by his daughters, and he'd been caught in the crossfire. For the main Christmas meal, just about everybody was coming. Here. To Rosewood, his house, his sanctuary.

They called in every year at Christmas, but he'd never fed a multitude before. Six grandchildren would be present for a start, and they would be in the company of five adults, one of whom was the most boring, judgemental man on earth. 'My son, my son. However did you manage to become such a bloody bore? I must have a word with you, try to work out what makes you tick.' Or did he tock . . . ?

Andrew had loved his parents, and he continued to love Dad to this day. Ian was distant, cold and apparently lacking in humour, yet his patients doted on him, as he was a 'root cause' man. He would spend hours finding treatment for an ingrown toenail, and he'd broken down many a pen-pusher in his search for new and expensive treatments for his flock. He had his uses; even civil servants feared him. But Andrew longed to see him enjoying life.

'We were wrong, Mary,' he whispered. 'We should have spent more time with him.' He thought about Mother and the love of her life, Dr Geoff Shaw, recalled the torment she had suffered due to ethics and conscience. Like her son, Emily Sanderson had loved completely, exclusively and dotingly. But she had always included Andrew in her life, had even consulted the then sixteen-year-old when certain decisions needed to be made.

'Come on, Storm. Let's get away for half an hour.' Helen had taken over the dining room and seldom imposed on her father, but Eva permeated the whole house like gas from a burst main. Natalie joined her twice a week to do floors and windows, but Natalie was not intrusive. While her adoptive grandmother spread herself all over the place, the girl concentrated on her job, asking only to borrow some of Andrew's medical books for her course. She was a sweet, hard-working girl; very quiet, too. Natalie shared no blood with Eva, and that fact certainly showed.

He walked with his dog across the green to the beach. Storm, whose devotion to Andrew was now total, needed no lead. He walked when Andrew walked, stopped when his master stopped. Until they reached the Mersey's shore, at which point the dog regressed towards absolute lunacy. A latter-day Canute, he fought the river, snarled and barked at it, got thoroughly wet, and delivered a great deal of flotsam to Andrew's feet.

A huge length of seaweed was the first of today's offerings. 'Thanks,' Andrew said. 'You are definitely bipolar if not schizophrenic. Good as gold in the house, though *she'll* never admit it, then stark raving bonkers out here. I wonder what Daisy would make of you?' Daisy, Andrew's half-sister, was in a St Helens care home. Dad had looked after her since Betsy Liptrott's sudden death, and Andrew had taken on the duty, as he held power of attorney over Joe's estate. Not that Joe was mentally impaired; the old man had simply had enough. At ninety-three, he had every right to demand some peace.

The dog carried on trying to rule the waves like an unfrocked Britannia. Storm was almost the best thing that had happened to Andrew this year, though he had to admit that his daughters were wonderful, as were their children. But Ian? If anyone in the country had the ability to wet-blanket Christmas, this was the man. Eva came a close second, he supposed.

He snuggled into the collar of his sheepskin coat. Perhaps Storm should have a coat. A tall, long and leggy creature, he seemed to have very little body fat. But no. Storm in a coat would become Storm in a wet coat, and that wasn't a good idea. It was cold. He needed to go home, but Eva might pounce again. He was fed up with being her buffer. In the manner of a loaded goods train at the end of the line, she threw herself at him daily. But he couldn't fire her. In her strange way, she was loyal; she was also Mary's choice.

'Dad?'

He turned. Helen was cupping her mouth with her hands, was shouting, then beckoning him home. So he collected his dog and a bough of a tree to which the animal seemed to have sworn undying affection. 'Leave it,' he ordered. 'We're needed elsewhere. It'll still be here if we come back this afternoon. And Eva wouldn't like it on her parquet. You should know by now that you mustn't even breathe on her floors.'

Storm dropped his precious burden and switched to obedient mode. It was time to babysit, and he was very good at his job. Had any stranger ever dared to approach Storm's girls, he would have gone for the throat. He was a special dog, and he knew it.

Helen welcomed her father and his dog into the dining room. 'I'm going for food,' she said. 'And Daniel will be coming on Christmas Day, though not for lunch. He wants to see the girls, and it would be subhuman of me to refuse. After all, they're his children, too.'

'Oh, what a shame. May I refuse to let him in? It's my house, after all.'

'Behave yourself, Daddy. Anyway, we have invited Anya.' She nodded. 'You two seem to get on well together, and it'll be nice for Sofia to have her mother here. But I warn you – no Eva.'

'No Eva,' he agreed readily. 'She has her own family. So you and Kate are cooking?'

'Yes.'

'Right. Stick indigestion tablets on your list, will you? Kaolin and morphine, too. And who's sleeping where, pray?'

'Worry not, darling Daddy. No one will be poisoned, though I'm sure we could make an exception for Eva, should she put in an unscheduled appearance. We have camp beds, sleeping bags, prams and cots. You're sleeping on the drawing-room sofa, Kate and Rich will have your gorgeous four-poster, and I am already catered for. Ian won't drink, so they'll go home after the meal, please God.'

Andrew lowered his head thoughtfully. 'Your mother and I could have been better parents. You and Katie had each other, but he was a Lone Ranger.'

'Oh, stop it. Look what he married. Eliza's about as

cheerful as a funeral tea on a wet Monday, and those two little boys need teaching how to play. Not everything's your fault.' She kissed him and left.

Not everything's your fault. Andrew heard his mother saying those very words to his dad. Oh God. Life repeated itself so often . . .

For the first time within living memory, Emily Sanderson threw caution to the winds. Her husband, who had quite possibly come home to spy on her, was asleep in an armchair, while her son had gone off somewhere with Stuart Abbot. She was in a panic. Emily wasn't used to panic, and had no idea of how to deal with it. Did Geoff love her? Was it just sex? If she . . . should she . . . would he . . . might they . . . Uncaring about who saw her and fired up by a rush of adrenaline, she dashed as quickly as possible down the main road. It was the wrong thing to do. She had to do it. She had to do the wrong thing.

There was nothing pretty about her this evening, as she had changed into housewife mode. For Geoff, she always dressed carefully, because he loved unwrapping what he called his treasure, his gift from above, his prize. This evening, she was no prize. She ran round the back and pushed the gate wide. His flat was on the ground floor, and she knocked on the window against whose sill his wobbly desk was propped.

A huge key turned in the aged lock, and the heavy kitchen door groaned inward. 'Emily? What's the matter? Did you forget your keys to the front?'

With the flat of her hand, she pushed him inside and followed. 'Joseph's home. For several days. Andrew knows.' She took several seconds to catch her breath. Was she being stupid? Well yes, she was, but she couldn't seem to control herself. Was the wrong thing sometimes the right thing to do?

'Slow down, slow down. Of course Andrew knows his father's home. Unless the poor lad's gone deaf and blind. Whatever's up with you? I'm thinking words like phenobarbitone here, or would an aspirin do? Whisky? A double gin?'

She sat down on the sofa, which was almost clear for a change. 'I can't carry on any more, Geoff. It's all right for you, no family, no ties. But you don't really want me, do you? You just picked someone married so that you'd be safe. You get your fun, then I go home, and that's that. It's so easy for you, isn't it?'

He stood in front of the fire, one hand scratching his head. 'What the fu— What the fun and games are you going on about, darling?'

'You should have finished that word. You whisper it into my ear often enough when we're ... in bed.'

'Or on the floor,' he said with mock solemnity. 'Or across the table, in the bath, on a chair ...' He noted her fierce expression and stopped talking.

'Do you love me?'

'Of course I do, you stupid girl.'

'I am not a girl and I am not stupid.'

'Right.'

'Sit.'

He sat in the armchair. In view of the mood she was in, he did as he was told, but maintained a safe distance. If she burned any hotter, there'd be smoke coming out of her ears and steam pouring from her nostrils. 'Start again,' he said. Stephenson had invented the railway locomotive, but he needn't have bothered, because a human one sat here tonight. She could shift ten goods trucks unaided with the power she was producing.

She closed her eyes. 'God give me strength.'

'Amen. So that's the prayer meeting over with. Did you choose the hymns? "All Things Bright and Beautiful" springs to mind.'

Emily glared at the man she loved. 'Andrew knows about us.'

After a few seconds, Geoff answered. 'He won't betray you.'

'My neighbour knows. Well, I suspect she does. And if Thora knows, half the infirmary might be in the picture, because she works there. You can't tell with Thora, because her mouth's sometimes bigger than her brain.'

'Ah.'

'Ah? Is that it? Is that your summary?'

'I'll make some tea. Just sit there, calm down, and shut up before we get a case of spontaneous human combustion. I must remember to buy a fire extinguisher.'

He didn't care. She sat, hands clasped in her lap, knowing that he didn't care. *Come to me in lust,* and *I need your body* – it all came rushing back to her. What could she do? Where could she go? She needed to think. It wasn't eight o'clock, so the park gates would still be open. Sitting here was not an option. He'd also said the words *I love you.* Was this man a liar?

While he clattered about with kettle and cups, she left by his main door, went through the communal hall and out on to the road again. But she didn't go home. Instead, she passed the roller-skating rink and ran down a side street to the park. He didn't want her, not really. She couldn't live without him, yet she must, for Andrew's sake. Suicide was not to be considered, because Andrew was precious. But without Geoff, life would not be worth living.

'Emily?'

God, he was quick. The trouble with a younger man

lay in the fact that he was too agile by far. 'Go away. You don't want me.'

He sat next to her. 'You're talking rubbish. Come on, tell me what you mean. Tell me what you want.'

Emily swallowed pride and temper, as she could ill afford either luxury. 'I want to live with you, eat and sleep with you, care for you. But I want my son, too.'

He sat back and thought for a few moments. 'And you thought I didn't care? Darling, don't you see – I couldn't ever ask for that? How could I expect you to walk out of your life just for me? It's always been clear that Andrew is your number one priority, and rightly so. What have I to offer? I'm not ambitious, I own no property, I'm still supporting my parents. Come here, woman.'

She leaned into him and allowed him to hold her.

'Emily?'

'What?'

'Your son's at an excellent school. I think he'll do better if he stays where he is for the next two years. But, if you insist, we could move to Liverpool before term starts and stick him in Liverpool College or Merchant Taylors'. However, he needs his dad. Joseph is almost like a brother to you, and you can tolerate him, I'm sure. We should live near him so that Andrew sees both his parents.'

Relief flooded her body. It was so powerful that it made her weep. How had she managed to doubt Geoff? 'You'd have to find another job.'

'I can do that. But if any of this is to happen, I have two conditions.'

'What is this?' Emily managed. 'The Treaty of Versailles?'

'Shut up.'

She shut up.

'I need one messy room, and no one must tidy it.'

157

'Very well.'

'And we talk to your husband. Together. If we're moving on in this relationship, we have to come clean.'

'Now? Do you mean right now?'

'Of course not. Tomorrow. You look like a boiled shrimp. Come with me, and I'll damp you down with cold water.'

They stood up.

She allowed herself to be led from the park like a child clinging to her father's hand. Sometimes, one did as one was told.

Andrew had always known that his Katie had made a good choice in Richard Rutherford. Outwardly, the man looked every inch the barrister, stern of face, square of jaw, tall, dark and brooding. But Richard was a wicked man. He was in charge of crackers, and Andrew found himself wondering whether his ultra-clever son-in-law might have introduced dynamite to the mix, since Richard seldom delivered what was expected.

'We should pull these now,' Richard announced almost too casually while the dinner was still cooking. 'I have another lot for later.'

There were just eight crackers in the box. He distributed them to Helen, Kate, Andrew, Ian, Eliza, Sofia and Anya. 'You must have two,' he explained to Anya. 'Because I am in charge.'

'God help us,' Kate whispered.

While his seven adult victims pulled their crackers, Richard donned wig and gown. 'This is a serious business,' he warned. 'Anyone who fails to obey the rules goes to jail. Kate knows how I treat prisoners.'

'He's harsh,' she admitted. 'I've been on bathrooms, kitchen and utility for three months, no time off for good behaviour. I have the marks of this man's whip on my back. Dressed up in that stupid lot, he does some terrible things.'

Richard glared at his wife. 'Any further disturbance in court from you, madam, and you'll be thrown out with the turkey bones.'

'Promises, always promises, Rich.'

'You above all should know I deliver.'

Andrew felt wetness in his eyes. They were so in love, so unafraid of letting it show. *Oh, Mary, Mary. I'll come out and talk to you later.*

'Excusing me,' Anya said. 'What is this to be? And why I have two?'

'You're musical, aren't you?'

'Well, yes—'

'Then shut up and do as you're told.'

It was bedlam. Children sat and laughed; even Ian's twin boys began to giggle. Everyone but Anya had one plastic whistle. Richard owned the baton and would act as conductor of the Rosewood Symphony Orchestra. 'Arrange yourself in order of the tonic sol-fa,' he ordered.

Anya bridled. 'But I am being two times, and there is me only one person.'

'Oh, sort yourselves out.' When they were in order, he pinned to each victim the name of his or her note. 'When I point, you blow. Anya, when I point to your left, that is low doh. Your right is high doh.'

Anya muttered under her breath and in Polish. High doh, low doh? All she knew about dough was that it made bread and pies. Polish people did not use dough for music. The English, she declared inwardly yet again, were very strange.

They ruined 'Jingle Bells', 'The First Noel', 'Rudolph the Red-nosed Reindeer' and 'Silent Night'. Richard fired Eliza and Ian, as they were laughing too much and saved no

159

breath for blowing. 'Give me your children,' he ordered, winking at Andrew. Laughter from those two? It was a Christmas miracle. Robert and Oliver tried their best, but Storm took the gold medal.

Something lupine in his ancestry came to the fore. A primeval howl emerged from deep in his throat, following which impressive event he began to yodel. His music was far superior to the din currently being delivered by his humans. But when the whistles stopped sounding, so did Storm. He looked at the sad specimens before him. They were rubbish, so he scratched an ear, mostly for want of a more interesting occupation.

'The dog you should train for opera,' Anya said.

'That animal is the best judge ever,' declared Richard while wiping his eyes with a handkerchief. 'And he says you should all go down for life. But there will be no parole, especially for you, Mrs Rutherford.'

Andrew stepped out of the room. Ian laughing? From a long way back in time, he heard Geoff Shaw saying, 'Andrew needs you, Joseph. A boy needs his father.' Oh yes. 'What goes around comes around,' he whispered. Ian had needed his dad—

'Woof.'

'Glad you agree, boy. So very glad.'

Emily was terrified. She walked with her lover for the world to see from the bottom of the main road all the way to the family house. Joseph, who had been working at the Bolton factory today, had agreed to come home early.

'He won't kill us,' Geoff reminded her. 'And in view of his own past behaviour, he must admit that we are being honest, at least.'

'He'll be angry,' she said. 'Angry and upset. He isn't here yet, or the small van would be parked outside.'

For the first time, Geoff Shaw entered his lover's house. When he reached the kitchen, he let out a low whistle. 'He knows what he's doing in one area of his life, then. I suppose a gift like his has to be paid for, and he's paid by being unable to keep you happy. Lack of staying power ruined everything for the poor chap, yet he got to concentrate on this area of genius. Magnificent.' He turned to look at her. 'You're blushing.'

'Well, I didn't need to tell you that. It's his business, his secret, and I should have kept it to myself.'

'Perhaps. But I got to wake Sleeping Beauty, didn't I? So by my calculations, I owe the man a great deal.'

'Yes. Stop now. I hear the van.'

Joe entered the dining room from the hall, while the other two came in from the kitchen. His pace slowed. What the hell was going on now?

Emily sat at the table. The two men joined her.

'Well? What's all this, then? Is the bloke in need of a kitchen?'

Andrew, knowing that eavesdroppers seldom heard anything beneficial, nevertheless maintained his position on the landing.

'This is Geoff. Geoff, this is Joseph, my husband.'

'And?' There was an edge to Joe's tone.

'I love her,' Geoff declared, 'and she's daft enough to love me.'

Emily bit her lower lip.

A silence followed. 'Sorry to be so slow, but where's this leading?' Joe asked eventually. He ached. He loved her, too, but he wasn't man enough, was he? And she was leaving him. Life without her would be like an ugly vase with no flowers in it.

Emily cleared her throat nervously. 'We wanted everything out in the open, Joseph. Honesty's important. We need to be together, but there's Andrew to consider. So, if we all move to Liverpool, Andrew will have both parents. Geoff's from Liverpool. His family's still there.'

'How cosy. What do the French call it? Ménage à trois?'

Geoff answered that one. 'Two houses within walking distance of each other. That way, Andrew can choose where he eats and where he sleeps.'

'So, you've had it all worked out behind my back?'

Geoff remained patient. 'No, we've had it all worked out since last night, then we came to you today, because neither of us likes subterfuge.'

Joe nodded. 'So how long have you been carrying on, Emily?'

There was yet another pause before she delivered her answer. 'Not quite a year. Since last summer, but it was months before we . . . before anything happened.'

Joe scraped back his chair and went to fetch a glass of water. In the kitchen he had created, he took a tumbler from a cupboard and held it in a hand that shook as water hit the glass. The man in the dining room had satisfied her. She'd bucked up no end in the area of fashion, was a great deal more confident than she had been, and he now knew why. He'd already suspected anyway, so why the pain? Because he bloody well adored her. Because he would always worship her.

He returned to the table. 'Right. What happens now?' he asked.

'That's up to Andrew. If he wants to stay at his school, we just continue as we are until he goes to university. He's expressed a preference for Liverpool, and even if he gets his own flat, he'll know where we are. Or we could go now if he doesn't mind, and he could do his A levels at another school. Though Geoff thinks he'd be better staying here with people he knows.'

Geoff watched while the man's face darkened.

Joe's lip curled. 'Oh, Geoff thinks, does he? Geoff knows

all about what's best for my son, then? How nice. How bloody sweet.' A thought struck home. 'Does Andrew know what's going on?'

'I'm afraid he does,' Geoff replied.

'I was speaking to my wife, thank you.'

'Yes,' Emily whispered. 'He's always known about everything, Joseph. Since he was thirteen.'

'What?'

'He saw you. With her. He never said much, but he knew when the man caught up with you that there was trouble. And the day she disappeared, the day you took her to St Helens – yes, I read the newspaper and guessed the rest – her husband came here, probably to do you further damage. You were in the infirmary. Andrew and Thora sent him away with a flea in his ear, and he hanged himself. The house was burnt, as you know. So don't get nasty, Joseph. You were never truthful with me. At least I'm trying to be decent.'

Joe inhaled very deeply. 'Andrew knew?'

'He didn't say much at first, yet I could tell he knew the score. But remember, we're just human beings. Not everything is your fault. And I love Geoff with all my heart. This isn't easy for any of us.'

The man of the house stared at his glass of water for several seconds. 'If we're all coming clean, you may as well know that Andrew has a sister. Well, a half-sister. Betsy never wanted kids, but Daisy came along. She's handicapped. Never said a word so far, but she loves being read to, likes music and teddies. Three, and all she wants is soft toys. She's registered as Marty Liptrott's child, but she's mine. That poor bugger was impotent.'

Emily placed a hand on her husband's arm. 'I'm sorry, Joseph.'

Geoff spoke. 'Andrew needs you, too, Joseph. A boy needs his father. Perhaps he should meet his sister one day.'

Emily agreed. 'He deserves the whole truth.'

Joe nodded. 'I've grown fond of the lass. But she's not expected to live till adulthood. See, in a funny way, she's perfect because of her disability. Daisy can do no wrong. She's a little angel with blonde curls and a sweet face. But her brain's buggered.' He twisted the glass. 'She never cries, never laughs.' He wanted to cry, though.

Geoff, who had seen more than enough damaged children, offered no comment. This poor man had lived long enough with his secrets.

'So, are you going home with him?' Joe asked.

'No, I'm staying here with Andrew. Also with my best friend, Joseph Sanderson. You've always been good to me. You're a brilliant dad, teaching him carpentry and listening to him when he wants to talk. I don't want to lose you, either. There's no hatred, and there never was. Carry on being my friend, please.'

Joe, almost in tears, nodded. She was right. She was always bloody right. But he couldn't lose her. She was his best friend and, compared to him, she was so honest. Betsy and Daisy, hidden away like dirty secrets – Emily was prepared to speak the truth, at least.

Geoff stood up. Although these two were hardly man and wife, they still shared intimate moments during which he remained an intruder. 'Bye, Emily,' he said. 'See you at work.' He didn't kiss her. Whatever happened between her and him was private, as was her time with the father of her son. He pitied Joe, yet respected him too well to allow that to show. Joe Sanderson would work himself to the bone and all the way to millionairedom. And, like Geoff, he loved her.

Forty-four years later, Andrew remembered the day well. There'd been a fly on the landing. Nothing dramatic, not a bluebottle, just a common housefly with absolutely no brain. A newly spun web stretched across a corner of the oriel bay, a luxury afforded to the house as it was end-of-terrace. In truth, it was a rather splendid house: built-in wardrobes, magnificent fitted kitchen, all wooden furniture built by the man downstairs. In fact, Dad had been talking about going into upholstery . . .

The man downstairs was Andrew's father, while the second fellow was Mother's beloved. This was all so weird. He wished he'd gone out, but he'd realized that something was afoot and wanted to be an ear witness, and he couldn't very well walk out in the middle of everything. That fly on the window needed a map and binoculars.

Dr Shaw seemed a decent enough bloke, straight, honest and protective of Mother. But Dad was hurt. There was something missing in his voice, as if he'd suddenly lost weight through illness. Mother was going to walk out on Dad. No, she wasn't; they were leaving the decision to Andrew. 'I'm just a kid,' he mouthed silently.

Then he heard about his half-sister, child of that dirty woman from the cul-de-sac behind Stuart's house and shop. The little girl was disabled. Poor Dad had kept that to himself until now. She was lovable, since she was never naughty, because she didn't know how to be naughty. It was so sad. Sadder still for the stupid housefly, now tangled in the web of a skilled predator. The fly suddenly seemed to be an omen of some kind, though Andrew didn't believe in omens.

Mother's lover left the house. Dad was sobbing like a child. 'If you knew how much I love you . . .'

Andrew couldn't bear any more. They were busy, so he took the opportunity to escape just as the spider returned to claim its prize. Dad was still crying, while Mother made sounds that were meant to be comforting.

He caught up easily with Dr Shaw. 'I heard it all,' Andrew said. 'And I'd rather my mother didn't know that.'

Geoff stopped walking. 'All right. Would you like to come to my flat?'

For answer, just a nod was offered.

'Bit of a mess,' the visitor remarked once inside Geoff's place.

'Oh, it's really quite tidy. Your mother says this room's like the inside of my head – chaotic.'

'Is she right?'

'No, she isn't. As a doctor, I live the careful life. This is my rebellion.'

'Aren't you rather old to be a rebel?'

Geoff laughed heartily. 'Not all rebels wear drainpipe trousers and long jackets. Some of us are born rebellious. I hated school, church and Mrs Armistead. She was self-elected queen of our street. If your windows weren't clean, she'd tell you. If your curtains needed a wash, she'd send you a note. If you weren't a churchgoing family, she'd send the vicar or, worse still, the vicar's wife, thin as a rake, all in black. The weapon in her hand was the Bible.'

Andrew thought about that. 'What if you were Jewish?'

'No idea. Judaism would be a bit exotic for Mrs Armistead. She couldn't manage even Roman Catholics. As for gypsies and beggars, she chased them with her clothes prop.'

Andrew sat. 'Will you look after Mother? He's always looked after her, you see. And he's pretty rich.'

It occurred to Geoff that he was being interviewed. Usually, the woman's father did the vetting, but this wasn't a usual situation. 'I'll do my damnedest. So will your dad, because they'll always be close in their own way.'

'It's weird, isn't it?'

'Yes, I suppose it must be from your point of view. All I

can tell you is that I fell in love, and she eventually felt the same. It took a while, Andrew. Your mother's a woman of principle. But I chipped away till I got through the ice.'

'You've made her happy. Now, what do I call you?'

'Not Dad. You've got a decent father in full working order.'

'Geoff, then?'

'It's my name. Yes, Geoff will do.'

There followed a short pause for thought. 'Geoff?'

'What?'

'My sister.'

'Oh. Right. The sister you don't know about because you weren't eavesdropping.'

'Bugger.'

Geoff agreed. 'Double bugger. You're best off admitting to being in the house and overhearing by accident. Then there's the other matter. School.'

Andrew had the answer to that one. 'Moving now while schools are closed for summer would be mad. As for renting or buying and selling houses in the space of a few weeks – more madness. Then you have to find a job. It would all be too much of a panic.'

'So we stay.'

'Yes.'

Most kids of Andrew's age would be rampaging about and inflicting damage on innocent furniture, yet this lad was as cool as a frozen cucumber. 'This must be hurting you,' Geoff said.

'It is. But, you see, I hated Dad for a long time. I was about thirteen, but I'm into my seventeenth year now. Things change. Dad and I are OK at last, but Mother's really important to me. Of course, I'd prefer it if they stayed together, only that wouldn't make her happy, would it? The way I look at it is that one of them will be happy.' He looked directly into his companion's face. 'My life hasn't begun yet – the part where I make my own choices. But I tell you now, hurt her and I'll kill you. And I mean that.'

Because the threat had been made without anger, Geoff understood only too well that it was meant. 'She and the job are my world, Andrew.'

The younger man blinked. 'It's vital that she stays steady. She'll be comforting him now, and they'll be crying. However life turned out for them, it was theirs. It's all they know. The other thing is that we both almost died the day I was born. I know she's over forty, but if she does . . . you know what I mean. We could lose her.'

'Yes, I know all that. It won't happen.'

'Promise?'

'On a stack of Mrs Armistead's Bibles. And more to the point, on the lives of two women I adore – my mother and yours.'

With that, Andrew had to be satisfied.

He walked home slowly. In two years, he would be miles away, probably cutting up corpses from a Liverpool morgue. It was time to find his grandparents; he needed to see what they were made of.

'Well, I have to admit, Mary, we had fun. Our son fell to bits, because no way could he cope with Richard. We had a symphony orchestra – what a bloody mess. The dog you sent wiped us all out. He has a good baritone, though he goes a bit flat now and again. I must send for the tuner. He can do both pianos and the mutt.'

'Dad?'

He straightened and turned. It was Ian. 'Hello, son.'

'Still talking to her?'

'Of course. By the way, your Eliza wears the same

168

perfume. Mary used Estee Lauder, too. What's going on in there?'

'Richard's going on. He made the second set of crackers himself. He used newspaper and wrote our names in lurid orange on each one. A very amusing man.'

'He made you laugh.' Andrew cleared his throat. 'It was good to see you laughing, Ian. You're such a serious family, you, Eliza and the boys.'

The younger man raised his eyebrows. 'Not always, I can assure you.'

Andrew stumbled on. 'Your mother and I were rather selfish, you see. Wrapped up in each other. We should have given more time to our children.'

Ian shrugged. 'I never felt deprived in the least way. This is how I am, Father. The boys are the same, and my wife's studious. But we have fun. We swim, play chess and bridge. Then there's the sky-diving. The children are very young, but they're eager to join in when they're older.'

'Your marriage is happy?'

'Very. Look, too much emphasis is placed on parental guilt. You gave us a good life, excellent holidays, you did your best, and we were well provided for.' He blushed. 'I'm proud of you. Look at the number of lives you saved among bacterial meningitis sufferers. Look how many supposedly necrotized limbs you rescued. Then there was your famous bone putty. They don't give out OBEs like dolly mixtures. My patients ask after you. Eliza has a scrapbook that holds every newspaper and *Lancet* article about you or written by you. We're quiet people. My sons are quiet people. That's all there is to it.'

'Thank you.'

'What for?'

'For telling me we weren't to blame, Mary and I.'

'We are all what we are, Father. But our lifespan will be somewhat abbreviated if we don't get inside and pull Richard's crackers.'

They walked towards the house.

'Sky-diving?'

'Yes, Father. Sky-diving. There are books and covers, you see. Never judge one by the other. Daniel Pope's all cover and no substance. By comparison, you, Helen, Kate, Richard, Eliza and I are a full set of encyclopaedias.' They stopped at the door. 'Find another wife, Dad.'

'On which page did you find that, Ian?'

'It's on the bookmark. Do it.'

The crackers were wonderful; well, their contents were wonderful. Richard explained the women's gifts. 'One, I got them at cost – please don't ask where. For all I know, they may be the ill-gotten gains of one of my rather less than innocent clients. In my game, it's silly to ask too many questions. Two, I get to touch other women. My ball and chain here doesn't allow me to touch other women.' He fastened delicate gold chains round the neck of every female. Even Sofia and Anya were included. From each chain, a small pearl hung.

While stroking Sofia's neck, he spoke to his wife. 'She has wonderful skin, Kate. You can put your own jewellery on. I can strangle you whenever I please.'

Andrew hid a smile. This was a magnificent marriage. He watched his family and was suddenly relieved and glad that they were here. Perhaps he wouldn't become a dog-walking recluse after all?

The men had silver cufflinks decorated only by a large hallmark celebrating the millennium. 'I'm already wearing mine,' Richard announced, displaying the proof.

For the children, there was a bran tub. Ian and Eliza's twin boys distributed gifts, thereby proving that they could read names. Storm received a huge bone, which item he dragged happily all through the house. Already, Andrew could hear Eva: 'Who's done this to me parquet?' Perhaps he should carpet the whole house.

In the midst of merriment, Daniel Pope arrived. As he entered the largest room in the house, a heavy silence fell. Even Helen's baby became still in her carrycot. One by one, people began to leave the room. As his wife followed the rest, Daniel tried to stop her, but she avoided him. 'Your little girls are over there,' she told him. 'You're here to visit them, no one else.' She ushered her siblings' children out into the hall, leaving him behind with two daughters he had neither wanted nor needed.

Ian waited for her. 'Come on, Helen. He's not worth a single tear. I'd have loved a daughter, and we may well try again, but we take what we're given, don't we?'

Eliza joined her husband. 'All right, Helen? Eva left a Christmas cake, and your father's been voted in to be taster. If he gets out alive, we'll all have some. He's already doing the I-am-choking-to-death bit.'

The party didn't pick up after that. Daniel's head appeared briefly while he announced his intention to leave. He had spent barely ten minutes with his daughters. As he walked down the gravel path, he seemed hunched, older and defeated.

'You going to do that mediation thing, Helen?' Kate asked her sister.

'Yes, I suppose so.'

Kate glared. 'You're mad.'

It was in that moment that Richard showed his colours. 'Kate? Leave it. Every marriage deserves a chance, and no two marriages are alike. What happens next between Helen and Daniel is their business.'

Andrew was watching Anya. She understood more

English than she cared to admit. And she was a very pleasant woman . . .

Andrew and Stuart Abbot, supposedly brothers, were worn out. A merciless sun glared into their eyes as they followed a path that meandered across about half of Lancashire, east to west, turned north for a mile, west again, south, back to west and the dazzling rays – it was crazy. 'This is like a maze without bushes,' Andrew announced. 'Why couldn't they get land in a straighter line?'

'This is not doable,' Stuart complained, leaning bike and self against a five-barred gate. 'The only way we could manage is if we camped up here.' He took a handkerchief and mopped his forehead. 'I wouldn't care, but we don't even look like brothers. That's the long and the short of it, and I'm the short by a good four inches.'

'How many heaths have we seen so far?' Andrew asked. He was fast becoming tired of the word *heath*.

Stuart pulled a notebook from his pocket. 'Clover Heath, Heathlands, Orchard Heath, Forest Heath, Oak Tree Heath, Heathdale, Heathmoor – all one word, the last two, like Heathlands. Bloody hell, Andy. How much further? They must own half of England. My legs are too short for all this cycling.'

'My fault, sorry. I should have got a more detailed map. The next has to be theirs.'

'You said that miles ago.'

'I know. But my mother has a stake in all this. It was her birthright.'

Stuart disagreed. 'They can disinherit her, you know. It's not against the law. She can fight it, but only after they're dead. Let's sit down. I've had enough.'

They drank tepid lemonade and licked melted chocolate from its wrappings. While there was a pause in conversation, Andrew decided to come clean with his lifelong friend. He took a deep breath. 'Things are awkward at home, Stu. Mother's taken up with a doctor at the infirmary. In two years, we're all supposed to go to Liverpool.'

'No!'

'Yes. Not sure I should be camping up here while Dad's at home. He won't hurt her, but I feel I should be there, because he's upset, she's upset – even the cat's depressed.'

Stuart studied his friend of thirteen years. 'What about you?'

'Me? I'm the only sane one. Dad's biggest base is in Liverpool, so he has to be there. But Mother and her doctor? I don't want my mother following me to university. Nor do I want to be keeping an eye on her. Dad will get me a flat, I hope, so I'll gain my independence gradually. But Geoff – he's the doctor – has ailing parents in Liverpool. Dad, Mother and Geoff intend to get two houses close to each other so that I'll have both my parents to hand. Am I sixteen, or am I twelve?'

Stuart nodded to indicate empathy. 'Every morning when I'm leaving for school, my mother shouts, "Have you cleaned them teeth? Costing us a bloody fortune, they are, so make sure and look after them." It's like a daily prayer. I get the same at bedtime. The braces come off in a few weeks.'

Near-silence enjoyed a few seconds. Then Andrew asked, 'Can you hear that?'

'What?'

'Running water.'

Both listened intently. 'I can,' Stuart said. 'Come on.'

They abandoned their bikes and threw themselves happily and fully clothed into a stream so cold that it deprived them of breath. 'Beautiful,' Andrew yelled when his lungs recovered from shock. 'We'll stay cool in wet clothes.'

Wet through, they returned to their bikes and sat for a while on a small, grassy hillock. 'Nice up here,' Stuart said.

'You're right. It's also my mother's. Well, part of it is. They got all this land and the properties by marrying land. My mother married a person. OK, it turned out wrong, but she refused to sell herself for acreage. So they cut her off.'

'And you want to work for them?'

Andrew considered the question. 'No, I don't.'

'Then why the fish and chips with peas are we here?'

'I'm not sure.' But very suddenly, he was sure. 'Right. Stay here if you like, and I'll come back when I've done what needs to be done.'

'Which is what?'

'Not sure yet. But I'm getting there.'

Eight

'So I open up and I say to him, I say, "Who do you think you are knocking on my door in the middle of me washing?" And he just stands there with his mouth gaping like the Mersey Tunnel. I felt like telling him he'd be catching flies in his gob, but I decided not to bother.'

Andrew closed his eyes. The Harbinger of Doom was behind him once more, and he did his best to ignore it while writing cheques to pay household bills. She was getting worse. Or was it just because he saw more of her now, after retirement? Did people mellow with age? Perhaps normal people did; Eva showed no sign of improvement. Was she an alien? If she'd been an alien, she would have been taken to a leader, wouldn't she? Who was leader? Probably an American Republican, but who cared? Whatever, she was still here in the house of an ex-sawbones who deserved better.

'So he tells me he's from Jehovah, so I say he'd best get back there sharpish, cos we've enough idiots of our own without bloody foreigners invading. That's when he gets a bit more confused, like. Anyway, two others land up next to him, and he says one's his wife and the other's his daughter, and they're witnesses. I asks, like, are they for the prosecution or the defence, and he frowns. No sense of humour at all, face like a smacked arse.'

Andrew put down his pen and turned to look at her.

Mary, I know you loved her, but she's driving me daft. 'Get to the point, Eva. By the time I pay this gas bill, we'll be into the next quarter.'

'Ooh,' Eva breathed. 'Who rattled the bars of your cage? And there I was, thinking you'd passed away at your desk. Where was I?'

'Standing at the front door surrounded by laundry.'

'Eh?'

'You said you were in the middle of your washing.'

'And you do that deliberate, don't you? Twisting words. You know what I mean. Sometimes you're a bit too clever, Doc.'

He nodded and folded his arms. 'Get on with it before I *do* lose the will to live and take an overdose of something or other.'

'Oh. Right. So then, our Natalie comes to the door. You know what a nice, quiet girl our Natalie is. So she excuses herself, all polite, like, and talks to these people from Jehovah. "We are all blood donors in this house," she tells them. "And I am training to be a doctor. Transfusions will always be vital in the saving of lives. If your daughter ever needs blood, I do hope you'll think again." And she drags me in and shuts the door right in their faces. I mean, they were ugly to start with, but my brass doorknocker wouldn't do any favours to a nose that got too near. Yes, she's got class, has my Natalie.'

Andrew tutted. 'People in this country are free to adopt any faith they choose. We are also allowed to disagree with them, but I always think it best to thank them and tell them I'm not interested.'

Eva narrowed her eyes. 'Remember our Lucy? We adopted her years ago? Your Mary found people who recommended us.'

'Yes, I remember. Very sad.'

'Thirty-six, she would have been now. You know she

bled to death when our Natalie was born on the floor in our back kitchen. We kept Natalie. She's got strong opinions when it comes to blood, and I understand why. Nat's a donor. So she gets a bit mad with people who try to persuade other people not to give their blood.'

'Ah. Now I certainly stand corrected.'

'Thank you. She's never nasty, Doc, cos it's not in her nature. She just gets her point across. That's why I think she'll make a really good doctor, cos she always sticks to her guns till somebody puts her right. She's a good learner, our Nat, always ready to listen.' Eva turned to walk away, changed her mind and doubled back. 'Is your Helen going to that meditation thing about staying married to Diamonds are Forever?'

'Mediation, Eva. Not meditation.'

'Whatever, she wants her head looking at. Well, is she going? Cos I'm telling you now, he could charm a blind bird out of a tree, that one. He'll promise her the earth, and he'll give her nothing but headaches and more children than she wants.'

'I tend to agree with you there, Eva.'

'So what are you going to do about it, eh? Sit there cogitating over your gas bill and the *Times* crossword?'

'I'm doing nothing about anything. I stopped trying to interfere with other people's business years ago, because it got me in more trouble than enough. The messenger can be shot, you know. It gets positively Shakespearean if you start picking up handkerchiefs.'

'You what?'

'Sorry, Eva. Just a reference to the Moor of Venice.'

She glared at him. 'They've got no moors in Venice. It's all water. Moors is foothills near mountains; I remember that from school.'

Andrew turned away and paid the gas company. Where Eva was concerned, Othello was of no interest whatsoever.

'Doc?'

Oh, God. 'What?'

'Shall I do some coffee?'

'Yes, please. Black, strong, and served with a large slice of silence.'

'OK, boss.'

The price of electricity had gone up once more. And Helen was out again. Was there another man ... ?

After three sessions of mediation, Helen felt almost sure that she could never go back to Daniel. Perhaps the time she'd enjoyed away from him was a factor; another distinct possibility was that she saw him out of context. In their area of the Wirral, he'd been completely at home, and not just in the house. Everyone knew him. He got the best seats in restaurants, was a member of Rotary, while invitations to house parties had always arrived thick and fast, especially at Christmas and New Year. He was in a pickle. Refusal of such invitations had to involve lying, since his wife was popular, and rumours of her departure would be circling by now like buzzards over carrion.

She stared at the curtains while Daniel and the counsellor droned on. The curtains were horrible, yellow with pinkish-brown flowers dripping down their lengths. That these malignant drapes should hang at a beautiful Georgian window offended Helen's sense of order and good taste.

Order. She looked at the desk. Mr Purcell's work area spoke volumes about obsessive compulsive *dis*order. A green blotter sat dead centre. To its right, four sharpened pencils lay together in a row, identical quadruplets placed in perfect sequence, all points facing the door, all exactly the same length. To the left of the blotter squatted the phone and a very overweight green Buddha. The carpet was pinkish-brown. Mr Purcell's chair was brown. Clients' seats were brown. The walls were covered in framed diplomas. The frames were brown. And Helen was browned off.

Oh. They were both staring at her expectantly.

'You see?' Daniel cried. 'She doesn't care enough to listen.'

She looked at him hard and long. 'You like it here, don't you, Daniel?'

'It's OK.'

'Of course it is.' In Liverpool, Daniel was on foreign soil. For him, this was a good thing, as he didn't want to wash dirty linen on his own side of the Mersey. For Helen, too, this was a good thing, because she saw him here more clearly for what he was, a moaning mother's boy. He was, indeed, his mother's creation, his mother's monster. According to Beatrice Pope, her 'boy' was perfect. She had raised him to believe he was a messiah of the jewellery business, a prodigy who, at the age of five, could pick out the finest diamond, the rarest emerald, the best Ceylon sapphire.

At this third session, Helen decided to speak her mind thoroughly. 'I shan't be coming again,' she advised the counsellor. 'There's no point. Yes, I have a young baby, and no, I am not suffering from depression.' She fixed her gaze on Daniel. 'Nor do I have any of the sexually transmitted disorders you might have distributed so freely. I simply prefer not to be married to you. Go back to Mummy and her four-course breakfasts. But watch your cholesterol. I told you often enough that her doting could have damaged you irreparably. Only here, in this setting, have I realized how deep her damage really did go.'

Daniel blinked. 'You never liked my mother.'

'True. Though she improved greatly with age, which you haven't. She taught you to believe that you were God, and you never learned any better. Really, you would have made an excellent Victorian, because you think women are here simply to do your bidding. Whores know their place, but I don't accept what you perceive as my position. You'll be hearing from my solicitor.'

The counsellor stood up. 'Please, all I ask—'

'All you ask is sixty quid an hour,' Helen said, no malice in her tone. 'So sit down and be quiet while I use up the time that's left.' She returned her attention to Daniel. 'Tell Mummy that nasty Helen refuses to hang round until a son puts in an appearance. If you need a son, look elsewhere – you're good at that. I want half the value of the house, together with something from the business – I put my hours in listening to dirty old men with eyes halfway down my cleavage.'

This was Kate-speak. Helen's sister had primed the bomb, lit the fuse and stood back while his life went up in flames. 'I love you,' he said desperately.

'You love you, Daniel. Buy a small pocket mirror and look at your beloved whenever you feel the urge.'

'You're getting nothing from the business.' His eyes narrowed.

She nodded. 'Yes, that sounds like your kind of love. However, certain items from a certain safe in a cellar . . .' She shrugged, neglecting to finish the sentence. Quietly, she sang about the taxman having taken all someone's money on a fine day. 'And a hundred pounds a week for each child. No negotiations, or I'll finish that bloody song and finish you as well.'

'Shut up, you daft cow.' He jumped up and left the room.

Helen stayed where she was. 'So, away he runs, Mummy's boy. She'll comfort him later with egg and chips followed by vanilla ice cream with hot chocolate sauce. Yes, she'll regress him to the age of nine by providing the menu he loved then. As for me, I require escorting to my car. He has a very low threshold of self-control. His mother's fault, you see.'

As they walked through the building and out to Helen's car, the counsellor apologized profusely for failing to improve matters.

'Don't worry,' Helen said. 'Not your fault. It's my problem, because I refused to see what everyone else noticed years ago. What concerns me most is the thought of him getting into a permanent strop and ignoring our daughters. He sulks, unfortunately. Sarah shows signs of missing her daddy, though Cassie's still a baby. He's quite capable of just walking away.'

'And you don't mind?'

'Not for myself, but for the girls. I have a supportive, decent family. My dad's the kindest man. He let us turn his dining room into a living room, and he plays with the children, so they have a man in their life. But they also have a dad and they have a right to their dad.' She shook his hand. 'Thank you for being there. You gave me the opportunity to see straight through a man I used to adore. Oh, and change those curtains, for goodness' sake, because they belong in a skip, not in a beautiful Georgian window. And stop being so bloody tidy.'

She drove off.

Halfway up Rimrose Road, she noticed that Daniel was following her, so she parked illegally, used the central locking system and phoned her father. Daniel remained where he was, about thirty yards away. The stand-off endured until Andrew appeared in his Rolls-Royce. There were times that begged for a bit of swank, and this was one of them. He turned the ancient but pristine Silver Ghost and purred into position in front of his daughter.

Daniel Pope's tyres screamed as he wasted rubber in a dangerous U-turn that caused many horns to sound.

'Oh well, he'd better stay alive,' Helen mumbled. Though she might do better as his widow? No. She shivered. Wishing someone dead was wrong, even when he was a total pillock. A very rich total pillock, he was. All the same, death was a stride too far.

'You all right, love?' Andrew asked when they reached Rosewood. 'We can get an injunction.'

'Yes, and thanks for coming, Daddy, but no injunction. If he makes any trouble, we'll resort to the law. He was in a fairly bad temper because I knocked this mediation lark on the head. It's just a waste of time and money. I didn't realize how typecast I'd allowed myself to become. Freedom is beyond value.'

They entered the house. 'We're all right to talk,' he said. 'The News of the World has gone home. Today's lesson was on the subject of Jehovah's Witnesses and blood transfusions. I swear I'd get rid of her except for your mother.' He wiped his brow. Sometimes, Eva wore him out.

Helen patted his arm. 'Mummy's dead. You have to live your life for yourself now. Which is what I plan to do. I've . . . I've met someone.'

'Oh?' He pretended to be surprised.

'My new solicitor. He's single, thirty-ish, thinks I'm beautiful and wants to take me out for lunch in the near future.'

'Oh, Helen. Did you never hear about on the rebound?'

'Yes. Floyd Cramer recorded it. You and Mum used to play it.'

'You know what I mean, madam.'

'Yes. I also know it's just lunch with a very nice man. And he doesn't merely leer at me – he listens. Baby talk gets a bit tedious, Daddy. All these dedicated Mumsy types who say they enjoy the company of infants are either liars or thick. Another day of Humpty-flaming-Dumpty, and I'll throw myself off the wall, and to hell with the king's horses and the king's men. Anyway, I'll be back at work soon enough, and Sofia's starting a foundation course to become a translator. She needs to move on, because she's bright.'

'Ah. So what about the children? You know I'm devoted to them, but—'

'But. Anya will take the job.'

'Right. Will she live here?'

'To begin with. When everything's sorted out, I'll buy a house near Kate and Rich. Then you'll get a bit of peace, just you, Eva, and that poor dead woman in the back garden.' She made a sound that was remarkably akin to a growl. 'Protracted mourning isn't grief. It's self-pity.'

As he walked his dog hurriedly in the face of an incoming tide, Andrew heard his daughter's words. Self-pity, not love. Was she right? He also wondered about the value of peace and quiet. At this precise moment, there was no chance of it, as Storm had taken serious umbrage at Mighty Mersey's renewed vigour. The dog's attempts to prevent the inevitable were hilarious and clumsy, but at least the tide was moving in the right direction, and he'd be washed ashore if he went too far. 'It doesn't listen, Storm,' he shouted. 'It's fastened to the Irish Sea and won't sue for divorce.'

Peace and quiet? Was that what Andrew really wanted or needed? Apart from Eva, who was something of a mixed bag, his retirement might have been lonely. Instead, he had gained a household teeming with life, and although a move began to seem attractive whenever the baby had a screaming fit, he often liked the house being busy. Was he mentally ill?

Then there was Mary. He couldn't take her with him, couldn't leave her here alone. A new householder wouldn't want a grave in his garden, would certainly neglect it. The flat stone might well be used as a stand for plant pots or statues or a water feature. And this was not love, it was indulgence of self. Was Helen right? She'd become a clever and capable young woman, and he was an old enough fool. A soggy dog joined him. 'Woof.'

'Ah. Here comes the aforementioned water feature. The Dripping Dog by Henry Moore, huh?'

'Woof woof.'

'It's OK, Storm. We walk up the steps.' Another few metres, and the tide would be fully in. The vagaries of man and Mersey were items Andrew had come to terms with long ago. Forty-two years, he'd lived in Liverpool. He could scarcely recall the undulating moors he'd missed so badly four decades earlier. *They've got no moors in Venice.* What a card she was. Perhaps he should commit Eva to paper, let the world take a look at her.

But one aspect of the moors he would never forget. Heathfield Farm and the Beauchamps. That particular chapter he would always remember. It had once been etched deep inside him, in a cold place reserved for the worthless, the inhumane and the downright evil. Eva visited that place occasionally, though she had not yet become a resident and probably never would. She was in the pending tray; but the Beauchamps had sat in the refrigerated area for several years during Andrew's teens. And he had been wrong. Again. His cold storage now contained several inadequate doctors, Daniel Pope, and ministers who had systematically hacked away at the NHS. Beauchamps were forgivable and had long been forgiven.

He remembered that boiling hot day when he had dragged poor Stuart halfway to nowhere and back. He would never forget any of it.

*

He found the main farm. It was a remarkable building, reminiscent of a medium-sized stately home: sweeping driveways, white columns upholding an exterior open porch, striped lawns, a fountain, the word *HEATHFIELD* curled into tall, wrought iron gates. Window surrounds and lintels were hewn from stone, and all windows were patterned in stained glass. This was true opulence. It would do as a setting for a film populated by mustachioed airmen and hopeful products of girls' Swiss finishing schools.

Andrew's heart hurt. Mother had been raised here on a diet of duty heavily laced with emotional blackmail. With her education geared towards the genteel arts, she had been propelled in the direction of wealthy, land-owning families. By 'selling' their children through generations, the Beauchamps had acquired a portfolio of properties that stretched from here to the feet of the Pennine Chain.

With steam beginning to rise from his water-drenched clothes, Andrew returned to his friend. All previously planned strategies were dismissed; neither boy would work for the farmers, as Andrew had decided to meet them as an equal. That would mean a week or more of study, but he was equal to it. Oh yes, he intended to be ready for them.

He hailed Stuart with a wave. 'We're going home,' he called.

'Thank God for that – I'm like a poached egg in these wet things.' It was clear that Stuart Abbot was not amused.

The ride back was slow and almost silent. Fortunately, it was largely downhill, and Andrew got the chance to think. He needed that time; he also needed to be less damp when presenting himself at their door. A bit of reading, and he would talk like an expert on cattle. Work for them? Oh, no. They were his target, his goal, his holiday prep. 'Build them up, then drop them like worthless stones,' he mused aloud. He was tall. He had no acne, and he was beginning to produce stronger facial hair. The fly in the oriel bay came to mind. 'I'm the spider,' he said.

'Talking to yourself again, Sanderson?'

'I am. This way, I'm sure of an intelligent and handsome audience.'

'Andy?'

'What?'

'Drop dead.'

'Not today, Stu. Things to do. Yes, several things to do.'

After the fateful third session of mediation, Daniel Pope was seething with temper. He wanted the contents of that safe back. First, they were valuable; second, they were dangerous. The problem was that Helen thought things out carefully, and his ill-gotten gains, now her ill-gotten property, might not be at Rosewood. The stuff could be in a bank vault somewhere.

On the other hand, Andrew was a millionaire, or would be when his old man died, because Sanderson's Bespoke Furniture was worth a bomb, while Sanderson's Intelligent Kitchens PLC was the size of an active volcano, so Father-in-law possibly had a safe in the house. However, even if the stuff was there, its container would be impenetrable, since Andrew Sanderson bought nothing but the best . . .

Oh, sod it. He booked himself in at the Adelphi, as he hadn't the energy to drive home. The house would have to be sold, because he could no longer live on the Wirral, where every man and his dog knew that Helen had walked out with both children, one of them still just a few months old.

He sat in the hotel's largest bar, nursed a double cognac and stared gloomily at the table. Life in the vibrant city of

Liverpool continued outside, but he had hit a full stop. There were clubs, eateries by the score, women a-plenty, but he suddenly seemed not to care. He didn't feel like dancing, talking or watching surgically deformed females removing clothes or sliding down poles. A light had gone out, and its name was Helen Pope.

Women. He'd had more than his fair share over the years, but being married had been part of the fun. He'd been getting away with something forbidden. Childhood had been the same, because a vigilant, doting mother had made disobedience inevitable. Lying had become part and parcel of everyday life, since he had been forbidden to do even normal things like swimming, playing football or straying beyond certain local boundaries. As a consequence, he had done all the aforementioned plus several other activities of which Mother would certainly not have approved.

He took another sip of brandy. Helen was probably right; Mother had made him deceitful. Sex addiction therapy had failed, due to the fact that he was judged clear of the disease. The therapist had been cruelly blunt. 'You're just selfish,' she had said. 'You don't want to stop, so you carry on.' Another bloody woman, a bluestocking rejected by society and pushed into a position where she could judge the afflicted.

He was sick of women, yet he wanted his wife back. 'Why?' he asked the brandy globe. The answer lay not in the bottom of a glass, but deep within himself. Life without her was going to be terrible. She was well known and loved in the business, particularly among the northern chain of six huge shops. Jewellery looked wonderful on her, though her beauty drew the eye away from smaller items, so she had always arrived at functions in huge pieces whose prices looked like telephone numbers.

He drained the glass. A blonde at the bar was giving

him the eye, but he wasn't interested in her. She nudged her friend, then showed Daniel three fingers, thereby indicating that they were willing to make a threesome, but he remained unmoved. The bartender, however, was moved. He shifted them out to where they belonged, on the street. 'Sorry, sir,' he mouthed. 'We do our best, but they still wander in.'

'No problem.' No problem? Of course there was a bloody problem. It sat a few miles up the coast in its father's house. He remembered how she'd looked in the Rodney Street consulting room, animated, alive and magnificently angry. The idea of a fight was stimulating. Even now, he knew that if he managed to get to her while she was alone, she would allow him to make love to her. Allow? She'd be glad of it. That sweet, quiet girl was dynamite in bed, and . . . and she'd get picked up by someone else unless he staked his claim soon. The thought of her with another man was excruciating.

Upstairs in his en suite, he lay in a frothy bath and tried to plan. Sofia had every Wednesday afternoon off. She visited her mother's house, and returned to her job late on Wednesday night, or early on Thursday morning. When lecturing at the university, Helen shaped her working week round Sofia's comings and goings. Wednesday was the day, then, as Wednesday was also Eva's day off. But he had to get rid of his father-in-law. Not easy, but by no means impossible. There had to be a way of arranging something.

By the time he was dry, powdered and lying on the bed, Daniel's plan was complete. He would need to be clever and prepared for all eventualities, but he knew that Andrew had his daughter's best interests at heart, so surely he would come to discuss those interests? 'Once he's driven away from the house, I get in,' he advised the ceiling. 'He won't be back for well over an hour, so that will give me plenty of time to talk her round.' He would dominate her. She had always enjoyed games.

Satisfied by his own cleverness, Daniel Pope fell asleep, and for the first time since Helen's abandonment of him, he stayed asleep for the whole night.

Andrew had raided his piggy bank, his Bolton Savings Bank account, Dad's old suit pockets and the bases of upholstered furniture. The cost of a taxi from town to the back of beyond was considerable, as was the price of an elegant briefcase, but he needed to look the part. Fortunately, he had a good suit that was usually saved for concerts, weddings and funerals, so he dug that out and borrowed one of Dad's ties. He still looked young, but older than sixteen. 'No shaving,' he ordered his reflection. 'A bit of shadow adds a couple of years.'

Mother was at work, while Dad had returned to base in Liverpool. Andrew was going for his mother's pound of flesh; for the first time ever, he had discovered the place just south of his stomach where feelings could be put in cold storage, which facility allowed him to fear little or nothing. This was his day, and he would grab it with determination, a leather briefcase and a non-existent farm at the other side of the Pennines.

As expected, their greed made them gullible. Invited into one of several reception rooms radiating from an octagonal hall, the sixth-former turned bereaved business-man sat with his grandparents at a long conference-style table. They had stony faces; meeting their eyes wasn't easy. Briefly, he caught sight of his mother's features in a much older female face, but the moment didn't last. Emily Sanderson was pretty; her mother was not.

'My parents died,' he explained sadly. 'In an accident abroad. They were in Greece looking at different types of fowl with a view to cross-breeding, and there was a bad crash on a poor road. We buried them a few weeks ago. So I'm stuck with hundreds of acres I don't want, some prize-worthy pigs – Tamworths, I believe – then beef cattle, dairy cattle, orchards, vegetable fields, livery stables, farmhouse and farm cottages. We've two shepherds who live up in the hills, thousands of sheep, and, well – I want to be a doctor. Farming has never appealed to me and, as the only child, I inherit the lot.'

Irene and Alan Beauchamp were very concerned about this unfortunate young man. His farm was currently in the hands of caretakers, but the eventual sale would be effected by a firm of solicitors. Andrew spoke again. 'There's no point in telephoning, as I'm not there any more, and the caretakers know little about my plans. In fact, I'm off to London in the morning to do some voluntary work in a teaching hospital for a few days. But you might want to go and look at Crawford Farm. Here's the address.'

'Thank you.' Alan Beauchamp's face was a picture of wonderment. 'Why us?' he asked.

'My parents noticed you in several farming publications. You care for your beasts.'

'Oh, we do, we do,' exclaimed Irene.

'Almost as if they're family,' Andrew continued. 'And family is of paramount importance, yes?' He left a pause. 'I'll come back next week with my lawyer. It's time the Houses of Lancaster and York came together at last. The Pennines are no real barrier. Your empire will bestride those mountains, and rightly so. As do goats. We sell goats' milk for people allergic to cows' milk. Oh, and we make cheeses and butter.'

'How much are you asking?' This from Alan, whose eyes had narrowed considerably in hungry anticipation.

'Awaiting valuation,' was Andrew's swift response.

'With the funeral and so forth, I've been extremely busy. But I'm here because my parents admired you.' He stood up. 'I shall be back next week, but please visit the farm in the meantime. You shall have first refusal. Unless your offer is ridiculously low, I shan't advertise the business elsewhere. Feel free to order your own valuation.' He looked at his watch. 'Must dash. Darned car broke down, and I've a taxi cab waiting. Good day.'

His cold place failed him for a while, and he was shaking when he left, but he walked carefully and remained as steady as possible. They were going on a wild goose chase, while he was going to Stuart's for a brown ale, after which interval of enjoyment he would return home and dress normally.

Revenge? Was this revenge? Mother didn't even know about it.

He tried, and failed, to imagine her reaction. She was not a vengeful person, yet she had rebelled against the wishes of her parents, had refused to comply with their demands. Assuming that they'd put her on the marriage market at the age of eighteen, it was clear to Andrew that she'd held out for at least a decade, as she hadn't married until she reached her very late twenties.

Mother was forty-five and still beautiful. She had given up on her marriage, and now planned a future with a doctor more than ten years her junior. Of a normally placid disposition, she would probably hit the roof if she discovered what her beloved son was up to. Revenge by proxy was probably a bad idea, yet the exuberance of youth had forced him to act.

His grandparents had never known him; from this day, they would never forget him. Because he intended to wipe the floor with the pair of them.

*

191

Unfortunately for Daniel Pope, Andrew Sanderson was very much on the ball when it came to fooling people. Having sent his own grandparents up hill and down dale years ago, he was several strides ahead when the phone call came. He was supposed to go across the river to Neston, where he and his ridiculously stupid son-in-law might discuss, as 'reasonable fellows', the divorce settlement. Helen had stopped listening. Helen was making unreasonable demands. Helen was far too emotional to negotiate.

Helen would be alone in the house, wouldn't she? So Andrew changed that fact, by putting the babies in the back of the Merc, each little girl fastened in safely, and leaving the passenger seat for his daughter. Her friend Barbara would be pleased to see her and the children, so all areas were covered.

Andrew was almost certain that Daniel would be on his way. When he arrived, he would get a sizeable shock. If the man had spoken the truth, which was unlikely, Andrew would arrive on time at the Neston house. He backed the car out and drove off in the wrong direction.

'The tunnel's that way, Daddy,' Helen said.

'Yes, but I thought we'd have a drive through Little Crosby. Such a lovely spring day shouldn't be wasted.' He hadn't told her about his suspicions. She had enough to worry about without learning this particular truth. If it was a truth. Either way, it didn't matter. She and her children would be safe, and that was good enough for Andrew.

'Where will you go while I'm at Barbara's?' she asked.

'To the cliffs. I haven't been there in a while. Should have brought Storm, but the car's full.'

'Go, go, go,' shouted Sarah from the back seat.

'Women,' Andrew sighed. 'Surrounded by them.'

'Go, go, go.'

'You heard her,' Helen said sternly. 'Get driving, Jeeves.'
'Jeeves' got driving.

Same suit, same briefcase, same taxi, different tie, different attitude. He was going in for the kill, yet he felt as strong as a newborn kitten. Andrew Sanderson, aged sixteen years and eight months, was on his way to a situation he had created, with no way of predicting the outcome. Would the Beauchamps have a lawyer in tow? Would Andrew be prosecuted for something or other? Telling lies, impersonating the son of a non-existent farmer, wasting time, costing them money for a survey on land and a house that simply weren't there?

He was a great deal more nervous than he had expected to be, though he knew he had to finish what he'd started. The I'm-in-charge confidence of the previous week seemed to have evaporated. They were older and more experienced in the ways of the world. They owned massive tracts of land, and they hadn't come this far without a degree of intelligence. They were breeders of prize cattle and pigs; they lived in a house that almost defied description.

He must think about Mother, who had been unwilling to become a champion cow prepared to mate with a champion, land-owning bull. These people were utterly devoid of normal human emotion, a pair who knew about cost, but not about value. 'Oh, God,' he breathed softly.

'You all right?' the driver asked.

'I'll let you know if I get out alive.'

The driver grinned into his mirror. 'They're not exactly popular, from what I've heard. They'd sack their workers as soon as look at them, and they pay minimum wages. Who are you to them?'

'Nobody. Like everyone else, I'm nobody.'

'Aye, well, good luck with whatever it is. I'll keep my fingers crossed for you.'

Daniel was very pleased with himself. The Mercedes wasn't in the driveway, but Helen's car was. The plan seemed to have worked. Eva and Sofia would be elsewhere, so all was well in the world of Mr Daniel Pope, who wore a four carat diamond tiepin that was a perfect twin to his wife's four carat engagement ring. Diamonds were forever, and these two fine specimens would be reunited within days – perhaps within hours.

God, he missed her. He'd never realized how badly he needed her, and he was determined never to stray again. With his heart pounding in his ears, he walked to the door and pulled the bell. Andrew was a purist where original features were concerned. The bell was a manual thing that actually jangled, as did servants' bells in the kitchen. Servants? All Andrew had was the dragon and her rather beautiful granddaughter, and the—

And the door opened. Daniel's mouth opened, too, and he snapped it shut, biting his tongue in the process. 'Where's Helen?' he managed, trying to ignore soreness and the taste of blood.

'Gone,' snapped Kate. She took hold of his tie, closing her fingers over the four carats he treasured so dearly.

'Hang on,' he yelled as she dragged him inside.

Oh, no. Eva, Sofia and Anya stood in a row behind Kate. Each wore an angry expression, and all arms were folded. Kate returned to the door in order to prevent the prey's escape. 'What do you want?' she asked.

'To see my wife and children,' he snapped.

'I see. So that's why you arranged to meet my father, is it? He's gone to Neston, but he made sure that we'd be here and Helen wouldn't.'

He opened his mouth, but no words emerged. So Andrew had seen through his ploy, and here Daniel stood, four viragos facing him. 'I was desperate,' he said at last. 'I haven't seen my children for ages, so what do you expect?'

Richard entered from the kitchen. Under Andrew's orders, he and the four women had hidden in the summerhouse until Helen had left, while their car was parked up the road near the coastguard station. 'One more trick from you, Pope, and you'll be served with an injunction. Defy that, and there'll be court and press. I'll be happy to sink you and your chain of rubbishy shops.'

Daniel blinked. Rubbishy? Pope's catered for all pockets, and what was wrong with that? 'Look, there seems to have been a misunderstanding,' he babbled nervously. 'I thought I was supposed to come here, but . . .' The sentence died of exhaustion.

'You will never be invited here,' Eva snapped. 'You can't fool Doc, because he's had your measure since you first turned up. This young woman here – Sofia – should have kicked you where it hurts, but she's too bloody polite and was too scared of losing her job.'

Anya Jasinski stepped forward. 'Swinia,' she said coldly.

'My mother says you are a pig,' Sofia translated helpfully.

Anya nodded. 'Pigs is better. They give good bacon and leather from skin. You bad man, no use for nothing.'

'Proceedings have begun,' Richard said. 'Helen has seen a solicitor, so any harassment from you will serve only to make matters worse. She's happy. Some women don't realize how unhappy they were until they put down the millstone. It's over. We'll look after Helen and her children from now on.'

'I demand access,' the intruder said.

'You'll have supervised access to the daughters you didn't want, but no access to Helen. She's settling well, and she mustn't be disturbed by you. The whole family's behind her.'

'She's still my wife,' Daniel shouted.

Kate looked at the ceiling as if seeking inspiration.

Richard shook his head. 'If one partner says the music's finished, that's the end of the dance. Feel free to tango alone, or pick a different partner. Let's face it, you've plenty to choose from.'

Daniel swallowed painfully. He was losing his trophy wife, the best display unit in the Pope empire. Not only did she look the part, Helen could hold a conversation at any level. She never patronized, never made anyone feel inferior, seldom allowed pompous bigots to talk over her head. Helen was clever, talented and amazingly beautiful. 'Will you tell her I'm having therapy?' he begged. He wasn't, but he'd shown willing, hadn't he?

Kate answered. 'Your solicitor will tell her solicitor. Any communication must be in writing between the two lawyers. She's so happy now, Daniel.'

'Good for her.'

Kate agreed. 'Your Amsterdam whore did Helen a favour, because she was blinded by love for you. We saw through you, but she lived in hope. Yes, she's clever and yes, she was stupid where you were concerned. But she knows now what you are. At last, the fog in her mind has lifted. So leave her alone, or my Richard will make sure you're dealt with. OK?'

Daniel pushed Kate out of the way and escaped. The company listened as his car roared off angrily. 'He must keep Dunlop or Michelin going,' Richard said. 'Right. Eva, Anya, Sofia, I'll take you home. I'll come back for you, poppet.' He kissed his wife on her forehead. 'Won't be long.'

'Now, that's a marriage,' Eva said. 'You let your man make his own mind up as long as he does as he's told.'

Even Anya understood. 'Eva, this is true. Always say he has good idea, but idea was yours.'

Richard almost growled. 'Ah, but there are double bluffs, you know. I let her think I'm being led by the nose, but barristers are good at fooling people. I know how to turn her on, off or set to medium heat. Simmering is fine, but I keep a bucket of cold water handy in case she overheats. It's a delicate balance. Ouch!' He rubbed his head, took a notebook and pen from a pocket. 'March 2001,' he said slowly. 'Hit again on head with blunt object.' He scribbled. 'Anything to say in your defence?'

'It's a cushion,' Kate cried.

He continued to write. 'It's a cushion with a brick inside. Come along, ladies.'

They left. Kate sat with the 'lethal' weapon clutched to her chest. Why hadn't poor Helen been lucky? Why couldn't everyone have a Richard? It just wasn't fair. 'My sister is the sweetest girl. She needs a Richard. Where do I find one?' Helen needed to be married. In spite of her beauty and talent, she was an ordinary girl who wanted the ordinary life. 'Hmm,' mused Kate. 'Perhaps not a Richard, then.' Rich was not ordinary. He was adventurous, imaginative, and very naughty.

Meanwhile, Daniel drove with unusual care towards the tunnel entrance. He needed more points on his licence like he needed an extra hole in his skull. She was divorcing him. In the past, whenever there'd been a disagreement, he had won her over with ease, but no one was allowing him a chance this time. There had to be a way. She would be returning to work sooner or later. Her dad couldn't take care of her all the time.

When he reached the house, he found her solicitor's letter lying in the mail box on the inside of the front door. Irretrievable breakdown. Adultery with persons unknown.

Unreasonable demands, blah, blah, blah. So, it was unreasonable to want a son? She couldn't prove adultery, and the marriage had broken down due to the intervention of her family.

Shoot. There was nothing in the fridge. Beans on toast again, then. There were plenty of restaurants in the Neston area, but he didn't want the glances, the whispers when people noticed Helen's absence. He had to sell up and move. She wanted half of everything. Well, she already had the whole of one item – his heart. He'd been a bastard, yet he'd never stopped loving her. He had to get her back. Without Helen, he might as well be dead.

By the time Andrew reached the gate of Heathfield, his resolve had deserted him. He had done wrong, and he had done wrong deliberately. He couldn't have cared less about them traipsing about looking for a farm that wasn't there, because they deserved to be put out, so why was he trembling now? It was about his mother, a woman he respected and adored, and these creatures had treated her abominably. 'Be strong,' he whispered.

He didn't need to knock, because the door flew inward as he entered the open porch. 'What the bloody hell do you think you're doing?' snarled Alan Beauchamp. 'We were back and forth all over villages round Huddersfield – people thought we were mad.' His eyes bulged in his head, their whites wearing a tracery of thready capillaries.

'Perhaps you are,' Andrew surprised himself by saying. 'And we usually get what we deserve, anyway.' He had to hold it together, must hide the inner turmoil.

'Cheeky bugger – get in here.' He was dragged into the octagonal hall with its black-and-white chequered floor. For a man in his early seventies, Alan Beauchamp retained a great deal of brute strength.

His wife waited inside, her cheeks reddened by temper and time spent out in all weathers. 'Take him in there,' she ordered. 'Till we get to the bottom of this.' She followed her husband into the room they had used a week earlier.

Andrew found himself seated at the conference-style table once more. His grandfather stood in front of an enormous marble fireplace, while his grandmother hovered near a window. She fingered a curtain, and seemed to be expecting somebody. She'd probably sent for the police or a lawyer.

'Well?' screamed the male half of the marriage. 'What do you think you're playing at? No Crawfords, no land, no beasts. We asked everywhere before we realized you were playing some sort of trick on us. We missed two cattle fairs because of you.'

Andrew, suddenly calm, waited for silence. 'There was a mix-up of some kind,' he said calmly. 'Codicils and so forth. The farm disappeared in a puff of smoke to all intents and purposes. It was a bribe so that a rich landowner would marry a cousin.' He paused and looked at their faces. It was clear that they didn't realize what he was talking about. 'The Crawford land was absorbed into bigger acreage. Some of these landowning families sell their daughters to people with land. Their daughters are like cattle. Can you imagine disinheriting someone who refused to marry for land?'

Irene Beauchamp's hand fell away from the curtain. 'What are you talking about, you young fool?' Slowly, she approached the table.

'I'm talking about you,' Andrew replied before turning to the man near the fireplace. 'And about you.'

A clock chimed in the hallway. 'Who the devil are you?' Alan Beauchamp asked.

'I am my mother's son.'

'And?'

'And you are my mother's parents. Therefore, you are my grandparents.'

'Emily,' breathed Irene, staggering slightly before grabbing the back of a chair. 'Did she put you up to this?'

'She most certainly did not. Neither did my father. Joseph Sanderson is a manufacturer of bespoke furniture and kitchens. They are separating, though they remain close friends. Mother married the first man who wasn't a farmer. She held out against you for so long that she probably married in a hurry. Her next husband will be a surgical consultant.' Well, it was nearly the truth. 'And I am at a good school, hoping to go to Liverpool University to train as a doctor.'

They both joined him at the table. 'How is she?' asked Irene.

'Well, thank you. Though she had a bad time when I was born.'

Alan cleared his throat. His eyes were redder now, and suspiciously wet. 'You're a grand-looking lad. But you shouldn't have done what you did.'

Andrew looked into the eyes of an old man he was determined to hate. 'I knew you cared about land above anything else, including your children. I watched the greed in your faces when I talked about Yorkshire. And yes, I was paying you back on behalf of my mother, who's just about the best person I know.' He stood up.

'Won't you stay?' Irene asked.

'No. No, I won't stay.'

'But when will you come again?'

'I will never come again.' He left the room, strode across the hall and went out through the front door.

They followed him. He heard them calling, asking his name, but he quickened his pace.

The driver leapt out and opened a rear door. 'The local

bobby's on his way up from over yonder on his bike. Get in here, lad.'

The car rolled away quickly. Andrew turned just once and saw Irene Beauchamp weeping in the arms of her husband. Oh well, it was too late now, wasn't it? Let her cry all she liked, because misery was what they both deserved.

Nine

Andrew Sanderson answered his mobile phone. He had an inkling about who the caller might be, even before she almost deafened him. As her voice rattled his brain, he found himself thinking of New Year's Eve when, at midnight, every ship in dock sounded its foghorn to mark the occasion. If she didn't rein herself in, he was in danger of losing an eardrum.

'Doc? Doc, are you there? Can you hear me? Only there's not much of a signal here, what with all the traffic and whatnot. And it's gone a bit windy through the alleyways. I nearly got blown under a bus before.'

'Ah, Eva.' She was bellowing beautifully today. According to her, the satellite moved about a lot, and she lost signal if the moon or a tree or an asteroid got in the way. Even a double-decker bus was not to be trusted. As for the microwave in his kitchen . . .

'You there?' she screamed again. 'That was a motorbike going past.'

'I'm here.' Or the problem might be caused by a lot of cloud, a storm, even a hurricane in America. Aeroplanes got blamed, too, as did anything launched from the United States. According to Eva, space was getting filled with junk, and this affected her reception something shocking. 'Me satellite's wandered off again,' she yelled. 'Are you receiving me?'

Andrew couldn't help grinning. 'I think Hobart in Tasmania's receiving you loud and clear, Eva.'

'Are they? See, they should get these bloody satellites sorted out, Doc. I only need to reach the Wirral. I'm just on me way to the Co-op. Do you think I should phone Richard Branson when I get home and complain about being diverted to Tasmania? Where is Tasmania, anyway? Manchester?' That was another thing. She blamed Manchester for a lot of stuff.

The trouble with Eva was that a person could never tell if she was serious or taking the Michael out of him. 'Eva, I've told you – it's a phone mast, so forget the satellite for a while.'

'But the phone mast gets the signal off a satellite and bounces it.'

He gave up. 'So what happened?' he asked. 'Was I right, or was I right?'

'Don't start the clever talk about always being right,' she replied. 'But yes, he arrived not long after you'd gone, and you should have seen his face when Kate answered the door. His chin dropped that much it nearly landed on the parquet. You know what she's like if it's anything to do with her little sister. She had a big cob on, I can tell you. I swear if she'd owned a gun, she would have shot him there and then. Oh yes, she'd a real cob on, fit to burst, she was.'

'Right.' A cob was a bad mood that showed in the face. 'She gave him short shrift, then, did she?'

'You what? No, she never gave him nothing; she dragged him in with his tie. He was wearing that pin with all the chains and safety locks on, so he wasn't pleased. Demanded to see his wife, then Richard came in and told him what was what.'

'What is what, Eva?'

'What is what is that Helen's started proceedings. Then

Danny Boy was asking for his children and saying he was mixed up and thought he was meeting you at Rosewood. Bloody lies. Anya called him a pig in Polish, then decided he wasn't a pig, because pigs are some use, and he's none at all. I like Anya. She might talk funny, but she's all right. I thought she was going to spit at him for messing with her Sofia.'

'I see.'

'He ran away in the end, Doc, flew out of there like a fox with a pack of hounds up its arse.'

'Some wisdom in him, then. I wouldn't like to face Katie with a cob on. Thanks for being there, and thanks for letting me know.'

After saying goodbye to his difficult, lovable old retainer, Andrew continued his leisurely walk along a path above the White Cliffs of Wirral. He had named them when he'd first visited the area with Mary, way back in the mists of time. Was there a mist? Not really.

He could see her now as clearly as ever, dark tresses bouncing as she ran barefoot as a gypsy through greenery, heard the shriek when she stepped on a small, sharp stone. Eyes dark blue like his, but so much prettier, livelier. He'd dressed her foot with a clean handkerchief, had fallen in love with an ankle, a shin, a knee, a woman. She wasn't his first, but she was the only one he'd loved. Everything else had been physical, just for release of whatever built up in a young man during periods of celibacy.

He enjoyed a mental picture of her on horseback. She'd loved Percy. A small woman, so a small horse, and from a distance she'd looked like a teenager. After her death, Percy had been donated to a riding school for handicapped children. He'd been happy, because he loved the company of other horses. Andrew had visited him a few times, but he'd stopped going because Percy had always looked past him for Mary.

Sometimes, at home, he imagined her voice calling melodically down the stairs. That voice, like its owner, had been more than pretty. She sang, played the piano, threw enormous parties for cancer charities and for deprived children. But now, Andrew heard only his younger daughter's words. *Protracted mourning is not grief; it is self-pity.* Was that true?

What was he supposed to do? Should he take the usual retirement cruise, get trapped on a floating prison with company he had not chosen and could not avoid? No, he was too much of a snob. No way did he want to spend weeks trapped in the company of plump, self-satisfied men with fat wives and fat wallets. He'd been offered a free cruise if he would give a few recitals on board. He could have a stateroom, all meals included, a place at the captain's table. He shuddered. He'd rather jump now, throw himself off the cliff and end up in bits at the bottom.

So. He liked music and carpentry. There was a function suite with a grand piano, and he already had pupils, one of whom showed promise. In fact, Anya Jasinski displayed a genius of sorts, though at first she had been mercurial and not always in the right mood. Yet as time passed she was finally beginning to take the piano slightly more seriously. Furthermore, she had an excellent mezzo-soprano voice, and he was beginning to wonder about a small choir. People liked singing. Singing lifted the soul.

Carpentry. He had all the tools he needed; he also had all the furniture he needed. No, he wouldn't take that up again. 'I've sawn through too many bones in the past,' he mumbled to himself. A choir, then? A choir backed up by the piano, perhaps a cello, a violin and a viola? Or what about his cars? He pondered for a few moments. There was a possibility that he might become one boring old fart among many boring old farts, and too many farts made a stink.

Jesus, this retirement lark was hard going – it took up far too much thinking time. He didn't want to be idle, didn't fancy working himself into the grave, hated the possibility of becoming flabby and useless. And he was skirting something central, something he already knew. Not since Mary . . . no, no, no! *Let it through, old chap. You like her. You don't know what she's rattling on about half the time, but she appeals to you. Keep Anya as a friend, at least. Learn a bit of Polish, take her for a drink, go to the cinema with her. It's no big deal. IT'S NO BIG DEAL!*

He smiled. Shouting at himself internally was ridiculous. He was ridiculous, ambling along the Wirral coast wondering about cruises, carpentry, music, cars and Anya. Anya. Mary would have liked Anya. She was different, a character, a musician, a singer. Her daughter was a lovely girl, too. Oh well.

His watch advised him that there was more time to fill, and he made a sudden decision. Divorce was such a final thing. Mother and Dad never got divorced. Mother stayed faithful to Geoff, yet they never married, and they both looked after Dad in their way. Eventually, Dad and Mother had been forced to look after Geoff. He shivered.

Andrew didn't like Daniel Pope, but who was qualified to be judge? Life wasn't fair. It carried no guarantees, so it didn't have to be fair. For now, Helen needed her space. But Pope was a human being and, with two hours to kill, Andrew was going to talk to him. There was a sudden need to lift Daniel out of cold storage and hear his side, time to find out what made him tick. Mother had always said that there was good and bad in everybody. Though for many years she had drawn some lines where her parents were concerned.

*

206

They found Andrew when he was in the lower sixth. He was on his way out with Stuart at the end of the school day when he saw the car. It was parked on Chorley New Road, and two people stood by it on the pavement. Andrew gulped. 'Grandparents dead ahead,' he said, the words forced between tightening lips. 'You'd better leave me to it.' Embarrassed and determined to hide his shame, he approached the couple.

Stuart peeled off in the direction of town, leaving Andrew to face the music alone. 'What do you want?' was his greeting. His cheeks were warm, and he hoped he wasn't blushing too brightly.

'To see you,' replied Irene Beauchamp.

'And your mother,' her husband added.

Andrew dropped his case of books on their car bonnet. 'She doesn't know I came to visit you,' he said. 'And she wouldn't be pleased if she found out. How did you find me?'

'Phoned a few schools,' Alan said. 'You're something special according to your headmaster. He said the Royal College of Music's after you, but you're not taking the place. Still stuck on being a doctor.'

Andrew made no reply.

'You're our grandson,' Irene said.

'And my mother's your daughter, but you wanted to sell her on, so she'll have nothing to do with you, and neither shall I. You should have treated her better, and you know it.'

Irene sniffed and patted her eyes with a handkerchief.

'We'll keep coming till we see her.' Alan nodded vigorously. 'We'll not give up, I'm telling you. We did wrong. But we want to make good, see she's all right, make provision.'

'You don't need to see her to do that. Just alter your

will or whatever, but stay away from my mother. Anyway, she's at work for a while yet.'

'What does she do?' Irene asked.

'I'm not discussing her with you.' He'd done enough damage already. 'Go away, please.' He picked up his bag and ran towards town. They turned the car and followed him. Weaving in and out of narrow streets and back alleys, he still failed to shake them off. Whenever he returned to a main road, there they were, sitting, waiting.

He finally lost them when he crossed Trinity Street pedestrian bridge. Breathing heavily, he went into the train station and hid in the men's lavatories. His grandparents, last seen stuck in a car outside St Patrick's, wouldn't seek him here. But he'd better tell Mother, because everyone was findable. Dad still had the works off Folds Road, Mother worked at the infirmary, and the grandparents were far from stupid.

He shouldn't have done it. He should have left well alone. But now he needed to prepare his mother for the inevitable. The trouble was that Mother wouldn't blow her top and tell him off. She'd be sad. Making her sad was something he hated, because he couldn't bear her disappointment. Failing her was what he dreaded most in life. She was too precious for all this, and had she wanted or needed her parents she was perfectly capable of dealing with the matter herself.

So, he had to tell her. Like a Catholic preparing for confession, he lined up his sins and rehearsed the delivery silently. Dear God, she didn't deserve any of it. She was blissfully happy these days, and an amazingly civilized relationship was developing slowly between Dad and Geoff, since they seemed to get along so well. Dad had learned a great deal from his relationship with Betsy and from the birth of Daisy, and his anger seemed to have dissipated. Who could dislike Geoff, anyway? And who could possibly dislike Mother?

He walked home slowly. Boys were supposed to walk reluctantly to school; for once, Andrew trudged reluctantly the other way. From time to time, he looked over his shoulder to see if he could spot a certain car, but there was no sign of it. Yet they would be back. There was a stubbornness in them, a quality he seemed to have inherited. Oh yes, they would most certainly come back.

Daniel opened the door of Thornton Hall, surprised beyond measure to find his father-in-law standing on the top step. 'Erm . . .' He couldn't put his tongue across a single sensible word. Andrew had this effect sometimes. He was a highly respected surgeon, an OBE, and a decent man. And Daniel had tried to fool him.

Andrew pushed dithering Daniel aside and walked into the house. 'You'll be rattling round here like a pea on a drum, I expect,' he said by way of greeting. 'Rather like I was until Helen and the children arrived with Sofia.' He looked the householder up and down. 'I know what happened earlier, Daniel. And you must have realized that I set it up. She doesn't want to see you.'

'I gathered that.'

'To be fair, I must tell you that she didn't know anything about my arrangement. Richard and company were hiding in the summerhouse, so Helen had no idea. But never try to kid a kidder, because you'll fail. I've been devious in my time.' He thought about his grandparents and the dance he had led them. Yes, his planning skills had improved greatly with age.

Daniel shrugged and found his tongue. 'You were right not to trust me, I suppose. You see, I need to talk to her.

All this with solicitors – it becomes Chinese whispers after a while. Once the words hit paper, they take on a life of their own and make everything so much worse. She loves me. And, despite all rumours to the contrary, I love her. Come through and sit down, please.'

Andrew followed his son-in-law.

They settled in the opulent drawing room. 'So you want to talk her round?' Andrew asked. 'Then you can lead her back to square one, with her on Merseyside and you fornicating your way across the world?'

'Something like that, but without the women. Someone else can do the travelling.'

'Wrong answer, Daniel. She needs to trust you without having to become your jailer. Even if you did stay in the country, there's little to prevent you doing the same thing here, and her suspicions can't be eradicated just because you stop using aeroplanes.' He paused. 'I understand the need to sow oats – I did it myself in my late teens and early twenties. But once I'd met Mary, that was all in the past. If you loved Helen, you wouldn't need other women.'

'We aren't all the same, Andrew.'

'In some respects we are all different, I suppose. But you adore your mother, and I worshipped mine – we have that in common. When we were young, we respected the women in our families, so when did your attitude change?'

Daniel nodded thoughtfully. 'Tell me, did your mum try to keep you locked up? Did she attempt to control your every move?'

'Never. But, you see, she was an unusual woman. In a time when changing partners was a disgrace, she led a somewhat bohemian existence. I've always regarded her as a quiet trailblazer. She lived with the man she loved, and cared for the man she'd married.'

'Well, mine did try to stop me having a life outside her reach, so I learned escape techniques, how to lie, how to be evasive. My development seems to have been arrested at that point. I still have the need to get away with things. There was stuff I couldn't even mention at home. Like when I needed a support for sports at school – I made my own. The thing is, I was so repressed that I couldn't walk into a sports shop and buy what I wanted. Nor could I ask my parents. If people kissed on the TV, it was "Turn that rubbish off", so I was raised knowing that sex was taboo and was something I had to find secretly.'

'And you're being treated as a sex addict?'

'No. It's deeper and more complicated than that, but the counsellor didn't see it. I didn't tell her much. She was another judgemental type, and I couldn't talk to her. I do love your daughter, but the teenager in me never grew up and still needs his conquests. Not now. As a single man, I have no one to hide from, no challenges. I am now totally celibate.'

Andrew stood up and began to pace up and down, hands joined behind his back. The man was being unexpectedly honest. 'Helen and Kate often say you're your mother's monster. I suppose there's more than a whisper of truth in that.'

Daniel shrugged. 'I'm also an adult. Whatever my mother is or was, I should be able to control my stupid urges. I brought this all on myself, Andrew. If my mother has ruined my life, am I a man?'

'Oh yes, yes, of course you are.' He stopped pacing. 'My stepfather almost became a psychologist, then he got the irresistible urge to treat children, hence his segue into paediatrics. But he could have analysed you, I'm sure.' He stopped pacing. 'Would you like me to find someone who might help you?'

'I can't talk to women.'

'Fair enough. Leave it with me, but please stay away from Helen in the meantime. Richard has many friends in

211

the law game, and Kate will do just about anything for her sister. Oh, and stay away from your mother, too. The cotton wool she wrapped you in was toxic. I'll go now. I have to pick up Helen and the girls.'

At that moment, his phone vibrated and gave out the text sound. He opened the message. COME AND GET ME NOW, PLEASE. HELEN. 'She's had enough. Look, I'll phone you.' He dashed into the hall.

'What's the matter?' Daniel asked. 'Is there anything I can do?'

'Yes. Eat some protein and vegetable matter. You look like Dracula waiting for nightfall. And don't give up hope.' He jumped into his car and drove off.

Within minutes, he was at Barbara's house, where he found Helen, Sarah and Cassie in the driveway, the latter swaddled in a shawl in her mother's arms. 'Whatever's the matter?' he asked.

'Don't ask, Daddy. Just get us home.'

In the car, Andrew waited for his daughter to speak. He noticed that her knuckles were white, as was her face. Like the man he had left minutes earlier, she looked as if she needed a few square meals. 'I thought she was my friend,' she whispered. 'All she wanted was gossip about me and Daniel. It took her a few hours to get round to it, but I felt I was in the dock.'

'Oh dear. Why didn't you send for me earlier?'

'I had to get to the bathroom with my phone. In the end, I asked her would she like me to affirm, as I wouldn't swear on a Bible before giving evidence. Then there was all the stuff about her not knowing what I meant by that, and about the whole of Neston being concerned for me and the children. Oh, how I wish Kate had been there. She's my backbone.'

'You have your own backbone, sweetie. You're a remarkable woman, a linguist, a beauty, a great mother.

Close your eyes and have a rest. Sofia will be back, and when she's fed and washed the children you, she and I will have the goulash I prepared yesterday. Everything will be fine, I promise.'

He couldn't tell her yet that he'd spoken to Daniel. All he could do was drive through life in the dark like everyone else. He was picking up handkerchiefs again, but they didn't have moors in Venice. Oh, Eva. Unforgettable, unforgivable, yet so lovable . . .

The official offer from the Royal School of Music arrived, and Andrew discussed it with his parents. Dad still came home at the weekends, so life continued in a vein with which all were familiar. 'You're not going, then?' Joe asked. 'What I mean is, you did so well at the audition, might you regret turning this down? You do have the edge, son, because you compose for the piano as well as playing like a concert pianist.'

Andrew shook his head sadly. 'If I could do both medicine and music, I would. But the offer's in from Liverpool, too, depending on my exam results, of course. And medicine's what I want for a career. Mother, I'll never give up music; Dad, I'll always do bits of carpentry, but I want to be a doctor. I think I've always wanted that, can't remember not wanting it.'

Dad awarded his son an encouraging wink before going off to check on the Folds Road factory, leaving Andrew with the opportunity to talk to his mother.

He didn't know where to start. Unused to being tongue-tied, he ran upstairs to check on his notes. There was no way of dressing up what he had to say, yet he dreaded the hurt he might cause. After many false starts while making his notes, he had reached the conclusion that he must just say it. Like a diabetic injecting insulin, he needed to be quick, because quick was kinder. Poor Mother. She deserved a better son, one who wouldn't run about looking for the family she'd rejected.

When he came downstairs, Thora had planted herself yet again in a dining-room chair. She was talking about everybody in the street, especially 'her at number thirty-one' who was letting the side down by failing to clean windows. 'They say the last time she bothered, King George had just died, so that's 1952. February, I think.'

Mother simply nodded; she didn't like gossip, but her neighbour was always full of it.

'Seems she got a shock when the windows were clean. She could see out. With her never leaving the house for years, she forgot there were other people in the street.' Thora dipped a custard cream in her tea. 'It's her husband I feel sorry for. Shift work, then all the shopping on top, so it's not fair on the poor man. She needs a kick up the Khyber, I think.'

'It's agoraphobia,' Emily said.

'Aggra-what? Aggravating, that's what I call it.'

'She's frightened, Thora.'

'What of? What's to be afeared of round these parts?'

'Nothing. You know that, and I know that. But when you're talking to your mother while she's making sandwiches in the scullery, and the scullery and your mother get sliced off by a German bomb, you're allowed to go strange, especially when you have your own injuries to endure.'

Thora's jaw dropped. It wasn't a pretty sight, as she'd switched from custard creams to bourbons, so the inside of her mouth was colourful. 'How do you know all that, Emily?'

'Because I spoke to her husband, and he took me across to meet her. She keeps a lovely house and yes, she knows about the windows. Kitty, her name is. Her daughter's coming to clean the windows and to put up thick lace curtains, so don't condemn her, Thora.'

Andrew watched while Thora seemed to shrivel physically. She didn't enjoy being proved wrong. She stood up. 'Well, I suppose you've no room to talk, anyway. You do understand you could both lose your jobs, eh?'

After a pause, Emily said. 'Yes.'

'And your husband still in the picture?'

Emily continued to dust the mantelpiece. 'Don't threaten me. I'd be quite happy to have you charged with slander, and with blackmail. People who have little to do often spend time pulling others to pieces. At least I'm not poor Kitty. At least you finally found the courage to talk to my face rather than behind my back. Go home, Thora. Go home now. In spite of rumour to the contrary, I do have my limits. When my temper does finally go, you'll need to be in another country, because I'll see you in court unless you make a run for it.'

When Thora had slammed her way out of the house, Emily sank into a chair. 'Oh, Andrew.'

'Yes, it's a mess. If you tell people the truth, you're condemned. If you tell lies, you're condemned, and you're still guilty if you say nothing.' He couldn't recount it all now, could he? She was already upset, so if he started talking about his grandparents, her parents, that would be a full carton of salt in her wounds. 'Why did you marry Dad?' Well, he'd managed that, at least.

'I thought it was love.'

'But it wasn't?'

'Not the sort that lasts, no.'

'You were running from your father.'

'And my mother. She was as bad.'

Right. He remembered the insulin injections. Perhaps now *was* the time; all the pain in one day. And she'd be prepared if they turned up. 'Mother?'

'Yes, dear?'

He sighed. 'I stepped out of line in a very big way.'

She gazed at him steadily. 'In school?'

'No, in real life.' He sat down opposite her, then he told her about seeing Dad with Betsy, about worrying and wondering what would happen if Dad deserted his real family. 'So I got this idea. I saw them in a farming magazine and, because I knew their name was unusual, went about the business of finding out where they were.'

'Oh, Andrew.' Her knuckles whitened as she tightened her grip on the yellow duster. 'Well?'

'I decided to go and work for them during the holidays, then decided not to. But I did meet them not very long ago. I played a terrible trick on them, sent them over the Pennines to look for a farm that was not only imaginary, but also up for sale.'

'I see. What happened?'

He shrugged. 'They were angry about having been sent on a wild goose chase, but I faced them. I told them who I am.'

'Oh, Andrew,' she repeated.

He looked into her eyes and saw the disappointment he had dreaded. 'They found me at school. And they want to see you, too. They intend to put things right. She was snivelling into her hanky, and he just looked distressed. They'll find you. They followed me all through town to see if I'd lead them home. Now, I'm always watching for them.'

Emily rose to her feet. 'Leave them to me, darling.'

'Mother?'

'Yes?'

'It's worse. I went too far by a long chalk. I told them you'd rushed into marriage to avoid being sold by them.' He literally hung his head and stared at the floor. 'They know about Geoff. I told them your second husband's a paediatric consultant.'

'Whoops,' she exclaimed. 'Joseph and I won't get a divorce unless he wants to remarry. Geoff and I don't need marriage. We're joined in a way that doesn't require a blessing from society. Right. I'll deal with this. I'll drive up in my pretty little Austin and talk to them.'

Andrew swallowed. She was so brave; she might have been talking about a jaunt to the seaside. 'Aren't you afraid?'

'Of course not. And thank you for telling me. That took courage. I wish you hadn't done it, but I've no intention of allowing regrets to pave my life. Forget all about it.'

Of course, he never would.

'What do you mean by different? And why do I always have to sit at the tap end?' It was awkward. When he washed his wife's hair, he needed to be a contortionist to get the telephone shower off the bath taps.

Kate threw a soggy sponge at her beloved. 'I don't know what I mean by different. If I knew what I meant by different, I'd say it. Stop interfering with me while I'm thinking. Keep your toes to yourself, or I can't concentrate.' He was a naughty boy. Kate continued delighted to have such a wicked husband.

'If I had you in court, I'd break you in ten seconds, Kate Rutherford.'

'You couldn't have me in court. No bench is wide enough.'

Richard thought about that. 'The judge's bench is quite wide. We could use that. As long as the judge doesn't need it. I suppose he could give an opinion about our performance. Or should we leave it to the jury? After all, this is the mother of democracy.'

'Popcorn,' she said, her head nodding vigorously. 'Like popcorn.'

'Popcorn? Where the hell did that come from?'

'Maize, I think. If you pop your corn and have it plain—'

'You sound like a chiropodist.'

'Shut up. Plain popcorn is ordinary, right? You need something to give it flavour. My father has a plain popcorn voice. He was all maple-syrupy this time.'

Richard studied his wet wife. She was a miniature version of her younger sister, small, delicate, rather like a porcelain figurine but with spiky hair. 'You're making me hungry,' he warned. 'And not for food.'

'Shut up,' she repeated. 'Oh, I've ordered a new bath, an enormous roll-top with claw feet and the taps in the middle of one of the long sides, so you won't have to moan about being stabbed by hot and cold. Cast iron, rescued antique, so we may need the foundations reinforced to take the weight of bath plus water plus you plus little me. But we'll have the best en suite in Woolton.'

'You were telling me about your father.'

'Oh, him. Yes. He was talking about Daniel, said he'd visited him, and he was kind of *sotto voce*, all sympathy and concern. Doesn't want Daniel to top himself, says he needs help.' She turned round and sat between her husband's knees. He was her hairdresser, though she never let him play with scissors, since scissors were for grown-ups.

He twisted round, took the telephone shower from the taps, clicked the lever and shampooed her mop of dark hair. When she was clean and rinsed, he performed his famous Indian head massage with conditioner before rinsing again. 'You only want me as a slave,' he complained. 'You purr like a cat when I massage your head.'

'Of course you're my slave. And don't forget, cats have claws, too. That was lovely, thank you. You'll get your reward shortly, serf.'

Wrapped in bathrobes, they crept downstairs for a nightcap. 'So,' he said. 'What's going on?'

'I think Dad's trying to mend fences.'

'Helen will still get impaled, my love. Daniel won't change his spots.'

'I think Daddy rather thinks he can, with help. Something to do with a mental and emotional divorce from his ma.'

'Oh. Drinking chocolate, darling? I need a clear head for tomorrow, so booze is a no-no.'

'Yes, sure.'

Richard turned in the kitchen doorway. 'It's not one of those Oedipus things, is it?'

'Sort of. But without the sex. Dad reckons that Daniel's mother did a great deal of damage to her one and only child. Whether or not it's reversible remains to be seen.'

'Quite.'

Kate followed her man into the kitchen. 'Shall I warn Helen?'

'No.'

'Why not?'

'She has to find her own way. I know mediation failed, but perhaps something else might help.' He looked at his little wife. 'I'm so lucky, Kate.' He was lucky. He had the best wife, the best kids, the greatest job.

'You will be lucky. Once the taps are in the middle.'

She had forgotten how beautiful it was up here on the moors. Gentler than Yorkshire, Lancashire's land was pleated decorously, stitched together by hedge and stone wall. Here and there, farmhouses and cottages stained the air with threads of smoke rising from chimneys. Cows grazed, while two horses held a conversation in their paddock. 'Magic,' she whispered. She could breathe here. In her heart, the country girl would abide forever.

Emily parked her favourite possession, a little Austin with what she termed a happy face. She stood in the lane and gazed at a scene Constable would have loved. She remembered being taught to milk a cow, to drive a tractor, to help at the birthing of a calf. Raised to be a gentleman farmer's wife, Emily had also been trained in gentler arts like the piano, cooking, embroidery and dressmaking. Her parents had invested in her, but she had failed to comply with their wishes. Running to Joe had been wrong, but if she hadn't run she would never have had her wonderful son, would never have met Geoff.

Back in the car, Emily drove towards Heathfield. All the trees she remembered were bigger, a lot older. Wild black-berry bushes thrived in hedgerows, and there were seven or eight rescued donkeys in Mrs Dean's large paddock. One of Father's famous bulls gave her a lugubrious glance as she drove past him. Father's bulls were famous all over the country. He had a way with male cattle, a method of keeping them calm until breeding times.

A large but rather garish house stood where the farm-house had existed since 1832. That beautiful, century-plus place with its crooked chimneys and sash windows had been replaced by a monstrosity that would not have been out of place in Hollywood. This was the Beauchamps showing the world how wealthy and successful they were; here sat their daughter thinking how stupid they had become.

She paused just fractionally before marching up the drive and knocking on the door. There was no room for fear; her main emotion was cold fury because they had chased her son through town. Andrew came first, just as he always had and always would.

Irene pulled wide the door. Her face seemed to drain of

blood, and she clutched the handle, her mouth opening but refusing to deliver words. Emily pushed past her mother into the octagonal hall. Eight walls, eight doors, eight rooms. No. One wall held a fireplace. 'Where is he?' she asked.

Irene cleared her throat. 'He's . . . er . . . he's through there, in the kitchen.'

It was a reasonable facsimile of a proper farmhouse kitchen, huge central table, pine dressers against walls, copper pans hanging from a rack. 'No need to get up,' Emily said. 'We already know each other only too well.'

'Emily,' he breathed. 'How are you?'

'Not quite as well as I was before I knew you'd been hounding my son all over the place. Of course, I must apologize for his behaviour, because he shouldn't have tricked you.'

'He's a clever young man,' Alan replied. His wife placed herself in the seat next to his. Both seemed smaller than they had been. 'Going to be a doctor,' he said.

'Yes.' Emily stared hard at her parents. 'He won't need to marry land, because he'll make his own way in the world, as did I. It wasn't easy, and I didn't always get it right, but an adult should have the privilege of learning through his or her own mistakes. I'm here to advise you to leave us alone.'

'But we only wanted to—'

'To interfere?' Emily cut sharply through her father's words.

'To give you this.' He opened a drawer in the table. 'It's a parcel of land.'

'Is it?' She felt deflated, almost disadvantaged. They were being nice. Emily had not expected nice.

Irene chipped in. 'One of the earliest ones. We renamed it New Moon, because you loved that book, *Emily of New Moon*, didn't you? And we had the old house rebuilt there, because we knew you all loved it. Not quite the same, but nearly the same.'

Emily's heart lurched. 'What do I want with a farm? We won't be living anywhere near here.' Confusion governed her. Gratitude was something she hadn't catered for and didn't want to feel.

Alan shrugged. 'Cottagers will take care of the house when you're not there. It'll always be kept nice, and your parcel will be tended. This is the deeds. Use it for holidays. Or give it to your lad, let him have it.'

Emily felt flummoxed. She should take it and sell it on, thereby creating a gap in the flow of their land, but such behaviour would be petty. And she noticed how old they were and how frail her mother looked. Underneath the weather-coloured surface, there was pallor, and she had lost a considerable amount of weight. Her jawline was loose, while the neck was stringy. They had built the old house again. For her. She felt terrible.

'Take it, Emily,' Irene begged. 'Put tenants in, or use it for peace and quiet at weekends. All we ask is to see our grandson, and I don't mean every week. A couple of times a year would be grand.'

Emily nodded, walked the length of the table and picked up the envelope. It was sealed with wax. 'Thank you,' she said rather stiffly.

'We are sorry, you know,' Alan said.

'Yes, I'm sure you are. But I'm not sorry I held out against you. No adult in her late twenties should be expected to do her parents' bidding. Andrew knows what happened, which is why he did that terrible thing. I knew nothing of his behaviour until a few days ago when he warned me that you were looking for me. So.' She placed a piece of paper on the table and scribbled with a pencil. 'There's my current address and telephone number. You know where I am now.'

'Andrew's a lovely name,' Irene said. 'Do you have a photograph?'

'I'll send you some. I promise.'

'Thank you.'

She left them sitting there, but felt guilty immediately. After a few seconds of consideration, she went back and opened the kitchen door. 'Tea on Sunday? Four o'clock – the address is there. I'll give you the photos then. I'm sorry I was rude.'

'All right. Thank you.' This from her father, because her mother was sobbing heavily.

As she drove homeward, Emily thought about justifiable anger and retribution. Neglect of the elderly was always a crime; she saw it often enough in the course of her work as assistant almoner. Other family members were nearby, but that was no excuse for her behaviour. Old people needed variety and new company. They could take a look at Joseph's kitchen.

And she would see the old farmhouse again.

'How was she?' Joe Sanderson sat by the window in his Southport nursing home. As ever, his first question was about his disabled daughter.

'Just the same,' Andrew replied. 'It's all soft toys and cartoons on TV.' He always visited Daisy in St Helens before coming to see Dad. Now forty-seven, Andrew's half-sister had not been expected to reach maturity. 'And how are you?'

'Still old, still here, still missing Emily.'

Andrew sat opposite his father. 'You're dafter than I am.' Mother's ashes sat on a shelf in a splendid pot. The most amazing thing about Dad was that he'd mixed Geoff's ashes with Emily's. Andrew's instructions were to buy a bigger pot and put Joe in with the other two when the time came.

'How did you do it, Dad? How did you manage to stay in love with Mother while she was living with Geoff?'

'We looked after each other, lad. And when poor Geoff died, we clung together like brother and sister. I know it all seemed mad, but it worked. If it works, don't knock it.'

Andrew nodded. 'Our houses are both consulting rooms now,' he said. 'But you can bet your bottom dollar that they've kept the kitchens.' Sanderson's products managed to be timeless, always in vogue.

'Nay, some folk are having unfitted kitchens now, Andrew.' He closed his eyes. 'There's something you don't know, son. I might as well tell you now, because I've nowt left to lose except my life. I couldn't satisfy a woman. There. I've managed to tell my son at last.'

Andrew paused for several seconds. 'Oh Dad, I'm sorry.'

'It's all right. Remember how your mam kept Geoff's ashes in that big trinket box I made for her? She couldn't let go. So when she died, God love her, I kept them together. He was a good lad, you know.'

'Yes.'

'So you know what to do with me?'

Andrew shivered. 'Listen. You're hanging about till you get your telegram.'

'I'm tired.' As if to prove the statement, he fell asleep. He was always doing that. It was almost as if death claimed a little more of Joe's time every day. Hands that had worked hard for well over half a century rested on his stomach. Near-transparent skin allowed veinous maps to show, while fingers whose dexterity and accuracy had been famous were now twisted, their joints swollen and deformed.

'Oh, Dad.' Andrew blinked back the tears. He, too, closed his eyes. And he saw those two splendid houses on Rodney Street, both near the Mount Pleasant end, one diagonally opposite the other. He'd had a top floor flat in each house, and his parents used to joke about him dirtying one, then moving into the other until that, too, became disordered and unclean.

Dad had blamed Geoff. 'It's you, you great lummox, you with your Do Not Tidy room.' The two men had often gone for a pint together, painted and decorated together, eaten in each other's houses. Although Mother and Geoff could not have existed apart, Joe had become part of the recipe. Andrew had never been deprived of a father, while Geoff had become a great friend who helped during exams and in various areas of study. Having two dads had been great.

And Joseph Sanderson had outlived both his wife and her lover.

'Wake up, Andrew.'

He opened his eyes. 'I wasn't asleep. I was just thinking about our Rodney Street days.'

'Grand times, we had. Remember going to see Ken Dodd? I was in pain through laughing.'

'Oh yes, I remember. You got loud hiccups and Ken Dodd made you stand up, told you you should never have swallowed that hand grenade. Then he pretended to ask management whether the theatre should be cleared.'

'Nearest I ever came to causing a riot, that was. Eeh, we had some times. New Moon, eh? You and me fishing and helping with rescued donkeys – I remember all of that. But not yesterday or this morning. I never know whether it's Tuesday or breakfast time.'

'Normal at your age, Dad.'

They stared hard at each other. 'But it wasn't normal for poor Geoff, eh, Andrew?'

'No, it wasn't.'

'We looked after him, though.'

'Yes, we did our best, Dad.'

'Your poor mother.'

225

'I know.'

'Fine man, fine brain. Come here, son. Hold my hand.'

So Andrew Sanderson was awarded the rare privilege of being there when his father died. Weary eyelids fluttered, breaths rasped over worn airways, while the old man smiled. 'Hello, Em,' were his last happy words. Then life left him on a soft, easy sigh, and the hand Andrew held was suddenly heavy.

Staff found him there half an hour later when they brought Joe's pills. Until then, Andrew hadn't realized that he was weeping. Very gently, they separated him from the cooling corpse and sat him in an easy chair. They said the usual things like, 'It was his time' and 'He didn't suffer'.

Andrew dried his eyes. He picked up the remains of Mother and Geoff. 'Thank you for looking after him,' he said. Outside, a warm breeze fanned in from the sea. Everything looked washed and bright from recent rain. And Dad was dead. How could birds sing at a time like this? There was a poem about a similar moment, W. H. Auden, he believed.

Life has to go on. That was another saying. Well, of course bloody life had to bloody go on. He packed Mother and Geoff in a car rug before fastening their seatbelt. The lid was taped on, anyway, so there'd be no spillage. Outside the home, he sat in his car and looked up at Dad's window. The curtains were closed. They would be washing him now, tying closed his mouth, preparing him for the next step. 'I'll get Grey's,' he said, referring to the company that had taken care of Mary.

But before phoning the funeral director, he rang Stuart Abbot, his friend of fifty-seven years. 'Joe's dead, Stu. My dad. He just died. I'm outside the nursing home now.'

'You going back to your house?' Stuart asked.

'Yes.'

'I'll be there soon. I'm sorry, Andy.'

'So am I, Stuart.'

He was a sixty-year-old orphan. After driving home, he did everything in order. He called Grey's, Dad's doctor, Daisy's nursing home, Kate and Ian. When the children were upstairs with Sofia, he told Helen. Then he sat in a window and watched the water and the sky on this day, the last Dad had ever seen.

And when he'd gone through a thousand memories and dozens of emotions, a thought finally struck. He was a multi-millionaire, and he would give away every penny if he could just have them all back. Yes, all of them. Mother, Dad, Geoff, the Beauchamps. And Mary.

But life had to go on. And the phone was ringing again.

Ten

Every single day started with a discussion . . . well, a heated exchange, or even a row, between Eva and Andrew. Like morning prayers in better-organized households, this was the rule, the law at Rosewood. A small complication like a funeral did little to encourage Eva to hang fire, and she was in fine form today, as she was dealing with frozen flaky pastry shells. 'How many of these volley venties do we want?' she asked. 'And Anya's arrived just now with a load of Polish sausages. Oh, that dog of yours has gone and ate some of the skirting board in the lav. And me feather duster's gone missing, too. I'm sick of buying towels. Bloody animal's not right in the head.'

Andrew eyed his friend/enemy. 'Eva, none of that is important, especially today. Just throw the food in the function room and let them all fight among themselves. By the way, they're vols au vent. And the dog's name is Storm, and he is not negotiable. He's a family member.'

'Oo-er.' She folded her arms. Eva with folded arms bore a strong resemblance to a miniature Sherman tank. 'Your dad was a very well thought of bloke all over this country, so he deserves a good send-off. Half the bloody kitchens round these posh parts are Sanderson jobs. He done a butcher's block for a woman down Burbo Bank, and it's going strong after thirty years or more. It's a bit dented, like, but—'

'Eva?'

'What?'

'Shut up. This is my poor old father's funeral, so I want no chewed skirting boards or ruined feather dusters in the mix. And if you leave your books on the piano, I'll get Stuart to sign them later, I promise. Now, go away and try to behave yourself for a change. Any change would be greatly appreciated.' She needed surgery to sew her mouth closed for a few hours, yet her heart was in the right place. She probably thought she was taking his mind off the loss of his dad.

Her body disappeared, but the voice didn't. 'Stuart Abbot's coming,' she screamed at poor Anya in the kitchen. Eva was clearly of the opinion that the deaf and the foreign needed shouting at. 'He writes them wonderful mystery stories what have been on the telly. Supposed to be for young folk, but I've always stayed young. My favourite's *Fingal's Folly*. He's going to sign books for me later. I've got every one of them.'

Anya joined Andrew. 'She shouts at me,' she said, her head shaking sadly. 'As if I am child who will not listen. Sometimes, she is make me anger.'

'I know. It's because you're Polish.'

'Polish is not being deaf or daft,' Anya said. She was picking up English very quickly. 'How you feeling today, Andrew?'

'Better, thank you. Not wonderful, but glad I was with him at the end. He knew he was going, because he asked me to hold his hand. Oh, I did want him to get to his century, though. But he was tired. I think he made up his mind that the time was right. He seemed happy enough. Almost smiling, he was, like a child preparing to go on holiday.'

'And he saw his wife as he went?'

Andrew shrugged his shoulders. 'I don't know. I don't

know what I believe, Anya. But his last words were a greeting for Mother, and he spoke quite clearly. Hey, hey, don't cry. Don't set me off. I have to talk about him at the crematorium.' She was lovely. She looked beautiful in black, neat little figure, pretty face, beautiful smile. When she wasn't weeping, that was.

'Daniel is coming today?' She dried her eyes.

'Yes. Dad was great-grandfather to the children. Not to worry. Daniel's treatment, whatever it is, seems to have calmed him down considerably. We must be grateful for small mercies and just do our best with things as they are.'

But Eva wasn't calm. She rushed in, her face like the thunder she feared so much. 'He's had it away with one of Anya's sausages. I was slicing it for topping pizzas – kiddies and your daughters and Sofia love pizza – and I'm cutting one end while he's eating the other. I let go, and he buggered off with it. By the way, he's chewed the toothbrush I use for cleaning round the taps. And he hates me.'

Andrew coughed.

Anya shook her head sadly. 'He is naughty, Eva.'

'He's a dog with discerning taste,' Andrew told his disgruntled housekeeper. 'Just for once, can we have a day without your moaning? It's like living with an audio version of the *News of the World*.'

Eva left in a hurry. There were times when Doc's face wore a look fit to freeze a woman on the spot, and it was best to make a swift exit rather than hanging about like Lot's wife. No, he wouldn't sack her. She was Mary's choice, and he still kept Mary close in his heart. And in the back garden.

'Do not mind her,' Anya advised. She slipped her right hand into his left.

He inhaled sharply. This small, friendly touch travelled

up his arm like an electric shock. *Oh, Mary, Mary.* The little Polish woman sought only to comfort him, yet for the first time in ten years, he wanted more than comfort. And on this day, too. *Are you here, Dad? Are you making this happen?* Did he really want this woman? Did he want any woman after all these years of drought?

A flurry of arrivals put the brakes on Andrew's train of thought. He switched to automatic for the greetings, and his hand forgot to tingle as soon as it made contact with ordinary mortals. Daniel was here. Without a word to his wife, or a glance in her direction, he picked up his daughters and carried them away into the dining room. All the children were to stay here with Sofia and a friend, as they were judged too young for funerals.

Andrew peeped round the door. His disreputable son-in-law was playing with his older daughter while cuddling the baby. It was clear that Daniel was avoiding close encounters with Helen; perhaps this was part of his treatment. A small glimmer of hope warmed Andrew's heart. *Never mind me, Dad. Concentrate on Daniel, Helen and these little girls. If there's a power beyond, try to help my daughter and her family.* What was he doing? He was supposed to have travelled beyond agnosticism towards atheism. And he didn't like Daniel Pope. Daniel Pope was not good enough for Helen. Yet . . . Yet there was a funeral to be got through.

Sam Grey, the stonemason who had made Mary's dog-proof cover in the garden, stood outside the front of the house. He wore black clothes, including a frock coat and stovepipe hat. In his right, black-gloved hand, he carried a staff much taller than he was. His brother Archie sat at the wheel of the hearse, while several black cars followed.

The coffin looked too small for Dad. Joseph Sanderson's only son stood briefly by the hearse and studied its contents. The casket was covered in white lilies; this was a

perfect copy of Mother's final transport. *Goodbye, Dad.
Thanks for everything you were, everything I wish I could be.*

Andrew and his three offspring occupied the main car.
When Sam began his slow, stately march, the sombre
cavalcade crept along behind him until the hearse reached
the coastguard station at the end of the road. After a short
full stop during which Sam joined his brother in the
hearse, the procession set off in the direction of Thornton
Crematorium.

All were unprepared for what they found at their destination. His employees were there. People from Sanderson's
in Reading, Birmingham, Devizes, Liverpool, Bolton, Leeds
and Durham lined the final couple of hundred yards.
Among them were customers who had become friends,
some in wheelchairs, since Joe had catered for special
needs.

Andrew clung to Kate and Helen. He mustn't cry,
couldn't cry.

Six of Joe's managers lifted their boss and carried him
inside. When family mourners were seated, the rest
flooded in until there was standing room only. The music
played was Acker Bilk's 'Stranger on the Shore'. Andrew
found himself thinking that if there was a shore, Dad
wouldn't be a stranger, because Mother and Betsy would
be there to greet him.

A vicar paid lip service. He was there only to appease
believers, since Joe and Andrew had always nursed reser-
vations about the hereafter. Wasn't one life enough without enduring eternity?

Then it was Andrew's turn. He looked at a sea of faces
and decided to concentrate on his children. Someone was
sobbing quietly, but he didn't need to wonder who,
because any sound coming from Eva was immediately
recognizable. She was hurting. She and Dad had been
great friends.

'I come to pay tribute to a person of great talent, greater humour, and the greatest heart. I am fortunate, since this unique and splendid man was my father. Joseph Sanderson began his work in a large shed at the bottom of a back garden. Some of his tools were borrowed, and I remember him buying up a set of cottage doors to reshape into furniture. He taught me the little I know about carpentry, and I always blamed him for my foray into orthopaedics. The tools and the rules are similar.

'He and my mother led an unusual life in a time when prejudice was rampant, because they had the sense and the ability to follow their own path without reference to mainstream atlases. Although they became almost brother and sister, their affection and respect for each other never wavered.

'By the time we came to Liverpool, Dad had founded the first Sanderson's Intelligent Kitchens factory on the Dock Road. He built good, solid kitchens, and continued at the same time with bespoke furniture for any room in any house. Chelsea, Kensington, Knightsbridge, Burnley, Blackpool and Liverpool – all these places and many more boast samples of Joseph's pieces or kitchens, often both. I thank his workforce and his customers for taking the trouble to come here today. Your positions are safe, and the company is now yours. He thought of everything and everyone, and his trust in all of you was absolute.

'Joseph loved young people. One of the men who carried him just now is Michael Caldwell, taken on as apprentice in the mid-fifties, now managing director of the Birmingham branch. As a teacher, my dad was painstaking and kind, always managing to bring out the best in every new recruit.

'In his personal life, too, he was loving and giving. He and my stepfather remained the best of friends until Geoff's untimely and cruel demise, after which Joseph and Emily continued close until my mother, too, lost her life.

'I'm sixty now, yet I still feel like an orphan adrift on a sea whose currents I don't trust, because Dad was my rudder and my anchor. He was magic.

'But time and tide wait for no man, and I must now take up the position of head of the Sanderson clan, the grandfather, the elder. Would that I owned half the wisdom and strength of my father. With respect, gratitude and much love, I bid him farewell on his last journey. We all miss you, Joseph.'

As the coffin moved away, Debussy's 'Clair de Lune' was played. Blue velvet drapes closed, and Andrew stood, a clenched fist covering his mouth. Mother's music. Emily of New Moon, her music, Moonlight. Oh, Mother. Oh, Dad. Ian stepped forward and led him away. 'Come on with me. It's over now. We'll look after you.'

Andrew had not expected to be hit so hard. Wasn't he used to death? The grandparents, Geoff, Mother, Mary, now Dad? Did anyone ever become inured to the knowledge that he or she would never see a loved one again? It was the finality of it, the stomach-churning void left behind when a much-loved family member shuffled off the coil.

His hand was shaken so many times that he felt it might drop off. Eva caught up with him. She had clearly continued weeping. 'You've not to worry about your dad's workers,' she told him. 'They've fetched food or ordered it to be delivered. He'd be happy to see them, Doc.'

'Yes, he would. Now, get in your car and let's go home. I hate these places.'

Once back at the house, he found Stuart buried beneath the weight of fans, but there was no sign of Daniel. Eventually, he came upon Helen with Kate and

Richard. 'Where's Daniel?' he asked. 'I've looked everywhere.'

'Gone,' Kate replied. 'Disappeared. He must know what's good for him.'

Andrew studied his older daughter. 'There's some of my mother in you, madam. She was a wonderful woman, but had I not been foolish enough to intervene, she would have turned her back on her parents – my maternal grandparents – for the rest of their lives. Stop being so judgemental. Daniel Pope has buggered up his life, but don't crow about it. He is going through treatment designed to wipe his own mother out of his mind, so have some bloody charity, woman.'

When Andrew walked away, Kate shut her gaping mouth. 'Hell's bells,' she declared after a couple of seconds. 'What's got into him?'

Helen stared down into her glass. 'He's lost his dad. It's a day for truth, perhaps.' She raised her head. 'You do crow, Kate. Everyone from the postman to the mayor knows you have a wonderful marriage, and you use that like salt in my wounds. You were so happy when I left Daniel, so loud about my destructive behaviour–'

'He was cheating on you, Helen.'

'Yes, and you rejoiced–'

'Because we already knew or suspected.'

Richard chipped in. 'Stop this, both of you. Kate, I've told you already, keep your nose out of it. Helen has her own way to make. Excuse me.' He left the two sisters together.

'Oh, Helen. If that's how I've carried on, forgive me. You and I have been the Forever Sisters since long before we had men in our lives. Remember? When we pinched a razor and cut our fingers and mixed the blood?'

Helen smiled. 'And Daddy threw a maddy, so he was

Maddy Daddy? I remember. But the most awful thing just now is that I've come full circle and I want Daniel back. And I daren't have him back because of what you and others might say. I tried. I went to lunch a few times with Paul – that solicitor – but he wasn't Daniel. Nobody is Daniel.'

Kate understood that up to a point. Without Richard, she'd be lost. 'You know what, Helen?'

'What?'

'No, you'll think I'm daft.'

'I already know you're daft. What? What?'

'I think Granddad's here. I can feel him drifting about.'

'See a doctor, Kate.'

Kate nodded. 'OK. Speaking of doctors, our brother seems to have cheered up a bit lately. Did you know he goes sky-diving? Eliza, too?'

'No!'

'Dad told me. They're off to Somerset soon on an archaeological dig, then they're taking up potholing.'

Helen giggled nervously. 'Whatever floats their boat, I suppose.'

'They have one of those, too. It's moored at the marina down the road.' Kate took a mouthful of wine. 'Helen, do what you have to do, but not yet. Ian and Dad have had their heads together on this one, so make no mistake, Daniel is working hard to get you back.'

A single tear crawled down the younger sister's cheek. 'He won't look at me, let alone talk to me.'

'Then that must be a part of what he has to do. Look, you know me and my mouth – even I can't keep up with it. Whatever happens, Rich and I will support you. And him, too. If he can drag himself out of the pit, we'll be there.'

Outside, Richard caught up with the escaping Daniel near the coastguard station. All cars were parked at the erosion car park in order to leave room for the cortège. 'Wait.' He bent over, hands on knees as he reclaimed the oxygen he had been forced to use. 'By heck, lad, you can't half shift.'

Daniel agreed. 'I'm a teenager. I've been regressed.'

'Are you . . . are you taking the urine?' Richard continued to fight for breath.

'Yes,' was the answer. 'But they're trying to help me recapture my youth for myself rather than for my parents. Mother and Father stole it, apparently. No point in going to the police, because the case against them is cold by now. I haven't been to work for three weeks. Oh, and I mustn't talk to Helen.'

'We gathered that. Am I allowed to tell you that she loves you?'

'No.' Daniel actually laughed.

Richard straightened.

'That's better,' Daniel said. 'You looked like a question mark.'

'All right, then, she hates you. Just do what you have to do, then come and get her. The thing about both these Sanderson women is that they stick to their guns and their men.'

'I don't deserve her.'

'Then wait till you do. I'd better get back and tell her you're all right.' He turned.

'Richard?'

'What?'

'Thanks.'

'Oh, bugger off, Daniel. Make me run a half-marathon again, and I'll sue you for personal injury.' He looked his brother-in-law up and down. 'Also, Kate's enough for me. Looking after two of them is more than I can manage. And Andrew might just want his house back.'

But at that moment, Andrew, staring through his

237

bedroom window at the Mersey, was thinking quite the opposite. He'd got used to Helen and the little ones, used to Sofia and Anya – he was even dangerously close to tolerating Eva. If Helen returned to the Wirral, Sofia would accompany her, while Anya, who was going to take her daughter's place during the translators' course, would also be in Neston. He was going to be lonely.

His bedroom door flew inward, and Stuart entered. 'Bloody hell,' he said. 'If I get any more people asking me about books and plays, I'll go bonkers. How are you doing, anyway?'

'I'm so-so. It's your own fault for getting so famous. Where's Colin?'

'Oh, he's at war with Germany. Something about a contract and the wrong date or the wrong quantity – I'm not sure. I'll be glad when he gets back, because the phone never stops.'

'You writing?'

'Trying to. It's difficult when he's not there clinking about with cups and tutting because I haven't eaten. I seem to need the interruptions, but only from him. The phone calls drive me spare.' He sat down. 'Joe was ninety-three, Andy.'

'I know. I can count. And I'm still not over Mary.'

'Ten years, Andy.'

'I just told you I can count. You've been with Colin for well over three decades, so use your imagination. You're the bloody writer. If he died—'

'Don't.'

'See? And we're all different. Look at my mother and dad. They lived the oddest life, but they lived it to the full. It's the to-the-full bit, Stu. I'd forgotten what it was like till Helen and the babes arrived. When they go . . . It's a big house. It's Mary's house.'

'Move, sunshine.'

'She's in the garden.'

'Yes, she's in a coffin inside a supposedly everything-proof container. Take her with you and plant her elsewhere.'

They sat in silence. After a friendship that had lasted well over half a century, they needed few words. Although there were forty miles between them, each knew the other was always there for him. Stuart had agonized alongside Andrew when Geoff had arrived on the scene, and Andrew had propped up his best 'mucker' when he'd come out to his parents as gay. Good days, bad days, all had been shared by these two since nursery class.

'We're having a surrogate wedding,' Stuart said suddenly. 'Will you be my best man?'

'Only if you'll let me tell the audience about Gloria Tattersall's knickers.'

'Not on your nelly.'

'It wasn't Nelly. It was Gloria.'

'And who bloody dared me?'

Andrew shrugged. 'It was you who pinched them off the washing line, and you who fastened them half mast above the girls' division. God, that poor Gloria was so fat. Everybody knew they were hers.'

Stuart sniffed. 'One mention, and you're dead, Andy.'

'Dead's not a good word today. So many dead, and now my poor old dad. He never lost his marbles, you know. Bit of a problem with short-term memory, but nothing spectacular.' His voice broke.

And they sat together on Andrew's four-poster, two little boys who were no longer little, two men aged sixty who had never completely grown up. When Andrew broke down, it was Stuart who comforted him, the same Stuart who had spat in a hanky to clean his friend's grazed knee, the same Stuart who had shared wartime rationed sweets, then toys and secrets. What they enjoyed transcended and almost obliterated all else. This close bond of true friendship, tempered and shaped under dark skies and to the accompaniment of sirens, was unbreakable.

Then the dog came in and stole the moment.

'What the Carter's Little Liver Pills . . . ?' Stuart's jaw dropped.

Keith, Andrew's veterinary friend, chased the animal out. 'Sorry, Andy,' he said. 'Sorry, Stuart, he's half French, you see. Stubborn bugger, thinks rules don't apply to him. He's eaten at least twelve sausage rolls. And he likes beer.' He followed Storm, who was clearly on a drunken rampage.

Alone again, the two men stared through the window.

'Andy?'

'What?'

'Have we ever had a normal life?'

'No. You were all quarters of corned beef and would you save a small Hovis for tomorrow, and I ended up with three parents. School was unreal. Now there's Storm, mad as a frog in a box. Then there was Gloria Tattersall and her—'

'Shut up. You going to be our best man? For Colin, too? But without knickers?'

'You know I will. She became a model, you know. Gloria lost all that weight and went very Jean Shrimpton, married a chap from Honiton. He was in antiques.' Andrew sighed. 'She'll be an antique by now. We're all bloody antiquated.'

'Speak for yourself. Colin and I keep ourselves young.'

'How?'

'We soak ourselves in marinade every Saturday after line-dancing. Old meat comes up tender if you marinate it.'

'The meat might, but doesn't it shrivel your veg?'

And they were schoolboys again, laughing at their own

crudity, digging each other in the ribs and roaring for no good reason.

Andrew dried his eyes. 'We must have another weekend at New Moon some time soon.'

'Move back there,' Stuart suggested. 'We only rent it. I can soon find somewhere to live.'

Andrew shook his head. 'No. There's something about Liverpool. It welcomes you with open arms no matter who or what you are. Then, after a few years, it absorbs you into its system. The friendly arms assume a vice-like grip, and you can't leave. They're special people, a breed apart, kind yet tough, humorous but empathetic. I love town. I could sit on a Williamson Square bench for a week without getting bored. I'd be cold, rained on and covered in pigeon shit, but I'd never get fed up.'

'Takes all sorts, I suppose.'

'Thank goodness. If we were all the same, what a bore.'

People were beginning to leave. Andrew, already aware of his antisocial self-indulgence, went down to say goodbye. He paid particular attention to all who had travelled to be at Dad's funeral, men and women who, alongside their workforce, now owned the company. He clung to Michael, son of the family next door in Mornington Road, the lad who had begged for an apprenticeship and had risen through the ranks. 'Keep his name,' Andrew pleaded.

'Don't worry. We will. He'll be missed.'

Helen, Sofia and Anya were upstairs putting weary children to bed. From the kitchen, Eva's dulcet tones delivered a plethora of swear words while she filled the dishwasher. An inebriated Storm stretched out on the hearthrug, while Stuart rested in a fireside chair opposite Andrew's. 'This dog's an alcoholic,' he said gravely. 'Do they have Alcoholics Unanimous for dogs?'

'Wouldn't work. He's half French.'

241

'Ah. That's a big problem, though my French is excellent.' He scrutinized his host for a few seconds. 'So, Andy, I've known you all my life, and I can read you like a book as long as you're not in Swahili. Who is she?'

'Be quiet.'

'Ah. The mother rather than the daughter, yes?'

'The one in the kitchen can hear the quietest whisper. And it's nothing,' Andrew mouthed.

'You're different.'

Eva arrived. 'Whisperers have a lot to hide,' she announced.

'And eavesdroppers hear nothing good,' Andrew snapped. Who was he to talk? He'd done his share of listening on the stairs in Mornington Road . . . 'Go home,' he said. 'You've had a long day.'

'I'm doing me pots.'

'They'll keep.'

She noted the facial expression and went to get her coat. One of these days, she might find herself out of work, and she didn't like that idea. With just her husband, her sister, and granddaughter Natalie at home, she didn't fancy being idle, especially when her man was out doing gardens and Natalie was at college. And she'd promised Mary that she'd look after him, hadn't she? Oh well, she knew when she wasn't wanted.

The front door closed. 'The mother, then?' Stuart asked. 'Little foreign woman, black lace dress, fitted jacket?'

'She's a pianist. Hadn't touched the keys since leaving Poland. She practises here.'

'Right. And?'

'And nothing.'

'Liar. I've seen how you manage not to look at her. More to the point, I've noticed how she looks at you. She's smitten.'

'You don't half talk some carrot and turnip, Stuart.'

242

'And you got that saying from my mother.'

'Is it carrying a copyright?'

'No, but you pinched it.' He glanced down. 'Can dogs die of alcohol poisoning?'

Andrew shrugged. 'We can but hope.'

Stuart stood up. 'Right, I'm off. I'll let you know when we set the date, and you'll let me know when you've–'

'Bog off, Stuart.'

Stuart bogged off.

As soon as he was alone, Andrew got down on his hands and knees. 'Storm? Storm? Don't leave me.'

The dog opened an eye. 'Brrruff,' he managed before continuing his beer-fuelled dream.

Storm's master returned to his chair. Dad's ashes would be cooling now, and he must keep his promise. So, after a short rest, he brought water for a potentially dehydrating animal, then went out to his workshop. The casket he had made needed a lid, and he began the task of carving into that lid three initials; there was G for Geoff, the first to die, then E for Emily and finally a J for Joseph. The last letter passed through the other two, as if welding the whole together.

When the hinges and lock were fitted, he inserted the lining of strengthened ceramic. As he finished his task, birds began to sing, while a rosy glow announced the sun's imminent advent. He could do no more. Never again would he read aloud from a newspaper to allow Dad's eyes to rest, nor would he carry in a hip flask a small amount of whisky so that Joe might have a secret swig between meals.

As for Mother – well, he hadn't seen her in years, had he? That sweet, gentle soul had reappeared in Helen, who had her limits. Just as Mother had faced her family, Helen had punished her husband. Kate, too, had inherited Mother's stubbornness, while Ian displayed Emily's quiet,

243

pensive side. And they had all been gifted with her loyalty. Ian was a surprise. He had found the help for Daniel Pope; he had organized the sessions.

Oh well, at least life was never dull, though it might become so once Helen and the littlies were gone. Eva would be here in a couple of hours. He made a notice, Do Not Disturb, and stuck it on his bedroom door. The dog had survived the night, and Eva would feed him.

Time for bed.

In 1958, Andrew Sanderson received a definite offer from the University of Liverpool's Faculty of Medicine, a thousand pounds from his grandfather, medical books from his mother's lover, and a car from Dad. He passed his driving test before his eighteenth birthday, grew to six feet and two inches, lost his virginity and learned that his best friend was different.

Stuart Abbot accepted a place at Durham to read French. During the long summer holidays, he began to shut himself away in his room above the shop for hours on end. When asked what the hell he was up to, he muttered darkly about Fingal Fergusson, characters not behaving themselves, writer's cramp, a sticky typewriter and an inability to read his own notes.

'You're writing what?' Andrew asked.

'I don't know. I'm coasting like a car with no gears coming down a mountain road at three hundred miles an hour.'

'Put the bloody brakes on,' Andrew suggested.

'I can't. I'm not in charge – he is.'

'Who is?'

'Fingal sodding Fergusson.'

Andrew drained his glass. They were sitting on the

pavement outside the Man and Scythe, and Stuart was decidedly pale. Locking himself away with Fingal Wotsisname was clearly doing no good. He was eating rubbish, getting no exercise, and was obviously being pushed along towards insanity by some kind of brainstorm. 'I thought you wanted to teach French.'

'I can be a writer at the same time.'

'Really? Seven age groups, seven different levels, Racine and Corneille in the sixth form – thank goodness I never had to work them out – where's the spare time? Can you wrestle with thirty essays on Guy de Maupassant and still have time to write?'

'How the hell do I know? According to experts, nobody under thirty has anything to write about, but I do.'

So Andrew sat while his friend tried to delineate the character who was stealing his final summer before university. Fingal was an accidental hero. Like the prince in a fairy tale, he always happened to be where he was needed, and his natural ineptitude was very appealing and totally invisible to those he rescued.

'So it's comedy?'

'Not quite. He's funny in a way, but clever underneath. He lacks confidence, yet the ladies love him.'

'Ah. Will you let me read some?'

Stuart thought about that. 'Not yet. It's like asking to taste a pie before it's cooked. Fergus is shy. I'll have to dress him up a bit.'

'You've gone mad, haven't you, Stu? You've finally cracked.'

'Something else. I don't want a girlfriend. I'm queer.'

'You're drunk. Come on, let's get you home.'

Later, back in Mornington Road, Andrew thought long and hard about Stuart. He didn't mix. He'd never been out on a date with a girl, always finding an excuse if Andrew

245

found a pair of females ready for a night out. But he didn't chase boys, either. So how did he know he was homosexual, and would he end up in trouble?

Geoff peered round the door. 'Have you packed anything yet? We go in just over a week. Andrew? What's the matter?'

The most amazing thing had continued. Dad and Geoff got along better every day. They both loved Mother, yet managed not to hate each other. Miracles did happen.

'Andrew?'

'How does a person know he's queer?'

Geoff closed the door. 'You're not homosexual, Andrew.'

'Not me. It's Stuart.'

'Bloody hell. Mind, he's not one for the girls, is he? Whereas I'm damned sure you already have notches on your gun . . . but I thought he was, perhaps, just a bit slow in developing.'

'And he's writing, Geoff.'

'That doesn't mean a thing. All kinds of people write. What's he writing? The Ballad of Strangeways Jail?'

'That is *not* funny.'

'No. Sorry. Has he told you directly? There are all sorts of campaigns going on, but it could be years before the law changes.'

Andrew gazed at the wall. 'He's in a bit of a state. I shouldn't move to Liverpool yet, because he needs me. And no, he hasn't got his eye on me, but he's my best friend. I don't care what he is, and I'm more worried about the writing thing, anyway. It's running away with him, like a tiger that's got him by the throat.'

'Most good writers are mad,' Geoff said. 'Seems to be a prerequisite. Look, you have to pack. Your mother's getting irritable, and your father's starting to grunt a bit. I'll go. I'm on cutlery. She reckons I can't break that. Little does she know . . . And don't worry. In my experience of this kind of thing, people are what they are and none the worse for it. If Stuart's going to write, he's going to write. If he prefers men, he prefers men. The agonies he'll go through are imposed by a so-called civilization that condemns out of hand. I'll have to go before I get condemned by your mother. I've discovered the hard way that she can be quite fierce.'

Andrew ignored the packing yet again. He drove through town back to Thicketford Road and knocked on the side door. Mrs Abbot opened it. 'Come in, lad. Happen you can get him out of his room. He's not sleeping. Says he thinks he won't have time for university because the cart's driving the horse. We're flummoxed, me and his dad.'

'So am I, Mrs Abbot. He's brilliant at languages, and he's always wanted to teach. Shall I go up?'

She nodded vigorously. 'Tell him we're going to break the door down. And that flaming typewriter's keeping us awake at night.'

Andrew went up three stairs at a time. 'Open the door, Stuart, or it comes down. Your mother's sending for the fire brigade.'

The door opened. Stuart stood back, a letter in his hand. He thrust it at his best friend. 'They say I've found a niche market. Teenagers and young twenties. I don't know what to do.'

Andrew took the sheet of paper. 'Open the curtains and the window, Stu. This place is like the black hole of Calcutta.'

When there was sufficient light, Andrew read the letter. It was from a Wardour Street agency, a very big one that represented writers, directors, musicians and actors. 'Bloody hell.'

Stuart sank onto his writing chair. 'What the heck

should I do, Andy? If I miss this chance, I'll never forgive myself. If I don't go to Durham and fail as a writer, what then?'

'This woman's got you interviews with three publishing houses. But I'll tell you what I'd do. OK?'

Stuart nodded.

'Well, I'd come clean with Durham if I got an offer from a publisher. So I'd go to London, see all these people, then make a decision. Your choices aren't yet clear cut, are they? You don't do anything at all unless or until you have a firm offer backed by money.'

'Right. Then what?'

'Beg Durham for a postponement. Tell them you're being published, and the editing and so forth means you need a year. A choice between two definites would have to be made, whereas a choice between one definite and one possible is actually impossible.'

'I wish I had your brains, Andy.'

'And I wish I had your talent for writing. Anyway, get washed and come home with me. I have to pack, and you're elected to help. No arguments.'

So Andrew was packed and ready to go by tea time.

Five civilized people sat and ate together. They discussed the two Rodney Street houses they had bought, talked about Andrew's two second-floor flats, Stuart's book and his chances with three publishers, the cost of the removals men and their vans, Andrew's future as a doctor.

Stuart seemed happy enough, Andrew mused as he bit into Mother's apple pie. Perhaps the unconventional household suited him, since it probably conveyed the notion of acceptability. Andrew experienced a need to protect Stuart, just as he might have looked after a brother, but they were going their separate ways, and nothing could be done about that.

He drove his friend home. It was the end of something,

the beginning of something else. Stuart's something else *had* to be OK.

'I'll see you before you go to Liverpool, then?'

'Of course. I'm coming to London with you. You're not grown-up enough to be allowed out on your own in the big bad city. I might let you go to meetings by yourself, but someone will have to make sure you're wearing matching shoes and carrying a clean handkerchief.'

'Thanks, Andy.'

Andrew drove back to a house that would soon cease to be home. He supposed that his true address was New Moon, as the property had been signed over to him. The grandparents and Mother were fine now, and weekend visits would continue even over the greater distance.

An idea dropped into his head. If Stuart took a contract with a publisher, he could move to the farm and write there. The parcel was used by farmers, so the land wanted no minding. But Stuart did. He needed to work on his books and to take time to think about himself and his future. If he carried on living with his parents, they'd be complaining about the typing, his absences from table, his unwillingness to help in the shop.

Up in the countryside, he could take walks between chapters, start looking after himself and work without interruptions. But first, they had to do the London thing and see what came of it. Andrew didn't know what to hope for. Making a living from teaching was safe; survival through writing was a less dependable prospect. Whatever, he intended to do his best for Stuart. That, after all, was what friendship was about.

Daniel Pope opened his front door. 'Ah, do come in.' Ian Sanderson had turned up trumps for his brother-in-law, while Andrew had done his share. The latter remained in touch by phone, keeping Daniel informed of the children's progress, and twice each month he brought the children to visit their daddy. 'Good to see you, Ian. Go through, I'm in the kitchen.'

Ian stepped inside. As with his own patients, he hung on like a bulldog where Daniel was concerned. This outwardly quiet, thoughtful and humourless doctor was amazingly thorough. His personal pledge was to improve life wherever he could, and that philosophy embraced all comers, even those who weren't his legal responsibility.

Daniel was cooking an omelette. 'Would you like one?' he asked.

'Yes, please.' He perched on a stool. 'I smell paint,' he remarked.

'I've taken more leave,' Daniel said. 'So I'm doing the place up a bit. If Helen and the children come back, it will be ready for them. If they don't come back, it will be ready for sale. Decorating's quite therapeutic, I find.'

They tucked into omelettes and side salads. Ian found himself quite impressed by his sister's errant husband. Therapy had been holistic, and had included psychotherapy, group discussions, counselling, hypnotherapy and physical exertion, all of which the man had endured without complaint. In fact, Daniel had emerged with muscles, a more relaxed attitude and a determination to get better involved with life away from work. 'When am I jumping?' he asked now.

'Tomorrow.'

Daniel gulped. 'Blood and guts,' he said quietly.

Ian's mouth twitched. 'You'll need the guts, but with luck and no gale-force wind, there'll be very little blood.'

'My omelette's doing back-flips.' Daniel placed a hand on his stomach before glaring at his new friend. 'There's a bit of Kate in you, Ian. You might be quieter than she is – thank goodness – but I sense mischief.'

'This, unfortunately, is the truth, as my wife would attest if asked.'

'Tomorrow, though. Couldn't you have given me a bit more warning?'

'No.'

'Why not?'

'Because your stomach would have had more time to react, and hospitals are too busy to deal with a galloping ulcer. Look, you won't be doing a jump. You were told that in the training sessions. A trainer will jump with you strapped to him. All decision-making will be out of your hands.'

'Bugger.'

'Quite. I felt the same on my first drop, thought I was going to wet myself. But Eliza was there on her first time, and I had to keep my dignity. When the chute opened and we went higher again, I started to enjoy it. Now, I prefer the freefall, but it all takes time. You'll be fine, I promise.'

'I know what you're doing, Ian.'

'Good. I'm glad somebody does, because I've no idea.'

'You're helping me to hand control to somebody who isn't my mother. In a few weeks, I'll be depending on just me. Eventually, my wife and children may come to depend on me, too. And the grandson Mother wants doesn't have to appear. If she carries on tugging at the reins, I tell her to bog the hell off. I've already told her what she's done, but I don't want to break her heart completely. She knows she has to back off.'

'Good, good. There's no point making her more unhappy than she needs to be. If you want Helen back, though, you must concentrate on her if and when she does return. I know she's my sister, but I have to say she's a work of art. It's not just the physical perfection – she's a good person.'

'Yes.' Daniel grinned. 'She's excellent with scissors and red wine.'

Ian smiled too. 'We all have our breaking point. Kate cracks up easily. Helen's slower to boil, but more dangerous when she does.'

'And you?'

'I jump out of aeroplanes, mess about in potholes and dig up bits of Roman pottery. My job helps. Winning the slightest concession from the health service is a huge kick. I fight quietly but concede rarely.' He stood up. 'Thanks for the food, and we'll pick you up at seven in the morning.'

Daniel swallowed audibly. 'I go early to my doom.'

'Well, you could always play golf and get hit on the temple by one of those vicious little balls. There are many ways to die. The hardest thing is to live properly. See you tomorrow.'

And he was gone.

Daniel felt horribly alone. The house was so big, so empty. Helen had always held things together, because she was very much the home-maker. Were she here now, she'd be filling the dishwasher, tidying the kitchen, preparing the baby for bed, all with just one pair of hands.

And tomorrow, he was to jump from a plane . . .

Eleven

'He never listened to me when he was a kid. No matter how loud I shouted, no matter what I tried to bribe him with – no joy. He wasn't what you'd call naughty; more like he just couldn't be bothered because none of us was good enough. Acted like royalty, that lad of yours.' Eva's right foot was tapping. She was working her way towards a momentous declaration, no doubt. 'Used to get on me bloody wick, he did. It was like talking to a brick wall or me husband or that flaming daft dog of yours. I gave up at the finish.'

Andrew groaned quietly under his breath. Why wouldn't she give up now before he exploded? 'Ian never listened to anybody, as well you know, Eva. He was the same with everyone. As far as I was concerned, he needed a good talking to about manners. Mary thought he was deaf, wondered if he needed an operation on his tympanic membranes.'

'We had one of them, but the wheel fell off,' Eva responded smartly. 'Anyway, it's one thing him and Eliza chucking theirselves out of a plane's back passage, but Daniel might be suicidal. It's all wrong. Ian never listened to nobody, but he goes and tells Daniel Pope what to do. Oh, yes, he can dish it out, all right. I mean, I don't like Pope, only he shouldn't be spread like strawberry jam all over some field somewhere. It's not good.'

'He won't be spread like jam of any flavour, Eva. And he isn't jumping. He'll be fastened to somebody else who *is* jumping. It's part of his therapy, making him trust somebody other than his ma before getting him to trust himself.'

Eva rattled a new feather duster along the mantelpiece. 'If they said getting in a pool of sharks was therapy, would he have done that?'

'Getting in a pool of sharks would not be therapy, though I'm sure the sharks would buck up no end and enjoy it.' Andrew was approaching the hem of his patience. The woman seemed to get a bee in her bonnet at every conceivable opportunity, and he had to suffer the consequences. 'Freefalling is supposed to be an exhilarating experience.'

'So's a Siberian wind across Scunthorpe, but I'd rather stay away from it, thanks. The world is going mad, especially this flaming family.' With reverence, she dusted the chest Andrew had made for the ashes of his parents and his stepfather. 'You done a good job here, Doc. All three of them back together. I loved your dad. It was a bit of a rum do, your mam and the other feller, but Joe made the best he could of it. What a wonderful character, eh? You were a great man, Joe Sanderson,' she told the container. 'You were loved and treasured, me old mate.'

The head of the household folded his newspaper and collected Storm from the utility room. To this day, Andrew didn't like anyone criticizing Mother. She'd been special. What she and Geoff had shared had been particularly special. 'Come on, lad,' he said to his dog, 'before I strangle her. My hands are itching to get round her throat. She goes too far by a mile or more. Why do we put up with her?'

Storm, taller than ever and thicker-set, followed his master through the side gate and across to the green. He was a proud, obedient dog, a special dog with a master who cared for him, so he was on his best behaviour till he reached the sand, where he met a friend, and all good intentions disappeared instantly into the ether. Storm loved women, and was particularly fond of this one. Anya was seated at the bottom of the concrete steps, a blanket folded beneath her. The animal performed his usual Stormy greeting, face-licking, paw-offering, plus a few soft, throaty woofs, his tail wagging furiously.

Anya laughed, pushed the fool away, stood and spread her blanket. 'Sit with me,' she told Andrew. 'You, dog, go and play. I love you, but you cheeky. Talk to the water.'

Storm ran to the river. It was on the ebb, but he was determined to keep up with it.

'One of these days, he'll turn up in Belfast,' Andrew said. He was so aware of her, too aware. Was it because, like Mary, she was small? Or was he finally managing to feel truly lonely? For some odd reason, the little Polish woman reached his soul. She was warm and friendly, yet unsure, because she was in a foreign country with different customs and a language that followed no dependable pattern.

'I visit Sofia in house,' she said. 'Helen not happy. Sofia thinks Helen wants go back to Daniel. If she does, Sofia comes home. I not let her go near that man. My Sofia needs be safe.'

Andrew understood, and yet . . . 'Helen won't allow anything to happen to Sofia, Anya. And Daniel has changed. He's worked so hard to change, because he wants his family back.'

'Sofia is my family. I know about family. My daughter, she is everything for me.'

'Yes, she is.'

'So she stay with me. We manage.'

He didn't want to lose her, didn't want Helen to lose

Sofia. 'There's a good chance that Helen will take both of you if she goes, and I shall supervise by visiting twice a week. Please don't desert us, Anya. Don't leave us when we're all just getting to know you.'

She hoped he didn't notice her sharp intake of breath. Sometimes, she got the idea that he rather liked her; on other occasions, he seemed not to care. He was still missing his wife, and Anya sympathized with that. Although Jan had been dead for fewer years, she knew that what had happened to Andrew could easily have happened to her. She was in a foreign country, was learning a terrible language, so she might well have hung on to her husband's memory as some kind of comfort. The difference was that she was a woman, and women were stronger. Oh, yes. She was a woman, and she wanted to take care of this lovely man. Why would he look at her? The wife, Mary, had been beautiful like Helen.

'We shall see,' she replied. 'But the man Daniel I do not like.'

Andrew watched his dog trying to turn the tide. Storm didn't appreciate the Mersey when it was coming, but hated it more when it was going. Fortunately, the dog stayed in shallow water and, thus far, had met no sinking sand. 'Daniel has been through rigorous treatments,' he said quietly. 'An overprotective and domineering mother made him what he was. When they managed to reach back into his youth, the life he lived was so inhibiting, so bad for him.'

'I am not bad and overprotecting,' she replied.

'She's your child, Anya, yet she is not. Sofia is a young woman now, and needs to make her own way in the world. To keep them, we must let go.'

'So it is wrong I say don't go back to Neston, to him and that great big house?'

'It's what we Brits call a grey area. The decision should

256

be hers. Helen is helping with Sofia's education, firstly with the translators' course, then later the qualification for teaching English as a foreign language. Sofia has much to lose.'

'If he touch her, I kill him, and this I promise.'

'If he touches her, there'll be a queue of people wanting to kill him. And you'll all be standing behind me.' He paused. 'He's jumping out of an aeroplane somewhere in Staffordshire today.'

Anya's head whipped sideways. 'Why?'

'Part of his treatment. As a child, he had to do everything in secret, or his mother would start a row. Cheating on Helen was an extension of that. Now, he's literally taking his life and putting it into the hands of a free-faller. So far, Daniel has been a naughty boy. He's now becoming a man. Anya, there is a parachute.'

'*Powodzenia.*'

'What?'

'Good luck he will need.'

'We all need that. We wake every day and jump into life hoping our parachute will open. And there's no map, Anya. We arrive as babies in the world with no instructions and no manufacturer's guarantee. Each day's a blank page, and we make our own roads with no idea of what we'll meet. Nobody's a perfect cartographer.'

'Is meaning?'

'Map-maker. When we wake, we're never truly sure of how the day will be. And much of the time, our activities are in the hands of other people who—'

'Who have no map.'

'Exactly.'

'We make map when we can.'

'Yes.'

She loved the way he talked and listened, because he never seemed to mind stopping to explain. This silly language had virtually no rules. Hole and whole, sew, so and sow, not and knot, through and threw, no and know, new and knew, all the same, all different. 'Thank you for explain, Andrew. Many peoples angry when I not understand, but my Polish language easier. English not easy for learn, not for me.'

'English is difficult because we stole words from all over the world. Come on, let's go home and get something warm to drink. I just hope Eva's stopped complaining, because she's hovering on the brink of my hit list.'

'Hit list is?'

He drew a finger across his throat.

'Ah, yes. I am understand. Eva is noisy lady, good in heart.'

A soggy Storm joined them as they made their way up the steps, across the green and round to the back of the house. Andrew explained that the dog was not allowed near Eva's parquet.

'Floor is Eva's, baby Cassie is Eva's, you are Eva's.' She laughed.

'We let her think these things, but we know the truth. Eva collects articles and people. She's bossy and controlling but, as you say, kind underneath all that. It's her way, it's how she was raised.' Why was he defending the dragon?

Anya went into the downstairs bathroom. While washing her hands, she looked at herself in the mirror. 'You don't know everything, lovely man.' Eva had made a friend of Anya. They went to bingo together where, to use a phrase of Eva's, Anya made 'a right pig's ear of keeping up', and Eva had endowed Anya with a piece of knowledge that was onerous. 'I wish she had not told me about this thing and those peoples.'

She dried her hands and tidied her hair. 'I think he likes me. I hope he likes me.' Anya Jasinski told herself that she was being silly. Perhaps Andrew had many friends and didn't want a lover or a wife. Perhaps Eva's information about . . . about the other business was mistaken. No. There was something there, something unusual.

She sighed. Did he know deep down, had he noticed? Or would it all come as a shock? Why did life have to be so difficult, so complicated?

With an unsteady hand, she reapplied lipstick. No, he didn't know what Eva knew. Had he realized, things would have been different. And he was definitely unaware, because Mary had made sure of that. Mary had loved him enough to guard him from a huge truth. He was easy to love.

With the healthy and unappeasable hunger of youth, Andrew gobbled up Liverpool like a large sponge collecting water. It was alive, vivid, buzzing with street hawkers, flower-sellers, amazing shops. People talked to him. He heard other languages among sailors whose transport was in dock, got his earliest helping of the local dialect and accent, and his first glimpse of the river. Crowds milled about, groups chatted, women called to each other across busy roads. Two things hit him on Dale Street; laughter, and the guttural delivery of words ending in 'ck'. Was that caused by the proximity of Wales, which was just a few miles down the road?

Newspaper sellers shouted out headlines, a policeman chased a man with a suitcase that possibly contained contraband, or perhaps the chap had no licence – at any rate, his case opened and scattered contents everywhere. Andrew's first Liverpudlian purchase comprised two yellow ducks for his bath, which he had bought from the chap who was now on the run. 'Quack, quack,' he said quietly before continuing his walk.

The route to the university was easy, but he needed to see so much more. He found the famous Pier Head, the Liver Buildings, doubled back and hit the shops again. Oh, Mother was going to love this. Department stores, specialist shops, the smell of fresh-ground coffee, bacon flitches hanging from beams, a busker playing a banjo and singing, instrument and voice both sadly out of tune.

He discovered a huge bookstore that sold the medical tomes he needed, some second-hand, traded in by student doctors who had moved onward and upward. This was a wonderful place. But he had to leave it, needed to go back and help Dad, who was setting up home on his own. Having memorized the names of streets, he began the walk towards his new homes.

There was a plot on, and Dad was at the back of it. So huge were the two pre-Victorian houses that both had superfluous reception rooms. These were to be beautifully decorated and filled with Sanderson's bespoke pieces, which were timeless. The step into upholstery had been taken, so anyone who expressed interest could visit as guests these fully Sanderson-furnished unofficial showrooms and order any pieces that took their fancy, including sofas and easy chairs.

Dad was a clever man. Of late, Andrew had come to realize just how gifted and sensible his father was. Joe had accepted a situation he couldn't change, and had shaped it to serve his purposes. Furthermore, he had started to go for a pint with Geoff, thereby accepting him into the fold. So Andrew had two fathers and two flats on two top floors. Compared to most students, he was wealthy.

He found Mount Pleasant and made his way back to Rodney Street. Even on moving-in day, he judged the city to be the right place for him. Yes, he could be happy here.

*

Ian, acting totally out of character, had visited all the members of his troubled family. Over dinner, he explained himself to Kate and Richard. 'Neutrality does not mean ceasing to care,' he said. 'But in this situation, we're depending completely on sense rather than on emotion. Yes, Eliza and I took him out, but only after consultation with his mentors. I have to say he's doing brilliantly.'

Kate expressed the opinion that Daniel Pope was a bloody good actor. 'With a mother like his, he's had to develop to RADA standard,' she said. She kept to herself the fact that she had difficulty in imagining her brother to be even slightly emotional.

Ian agreed. 'Yes, he's an actor, but all this is for Helen, too,' he said. 'She needs him, but needs him to be different. She still loves him, Kate. Love seems to be one of the things we can't ever explain thoroughly.'

Kate closed her gaping mouth with a snap. Love? What did little brother know about love?

Richard rescued his shocked wife. 'But can you change somebody who's so radically affected?' he asked. 'Is it possible to turn him through a full circle and expect to alter him along the way? I must say I've sometimes seen changes in criminals, though. Occasionally, when an old lag says he's going straight, he means it.'

Ian nodded. 'No one can change anybody. What we can do is furnish him with the tools to change himself. But with my sister and two nieces involved, I decided an effort should be made get the necessary implements for Daniel. If Helen goes back to him, he'll need to toe the line, and he must be able to draw his own line. She won't give him another chance, I'm sure of that. The poor woman's had enough, so something needs to be done for her.'

When Ian had left, Richard and Kate stared at each other across the table. Minus Eliza, Kate's brother always wore his professional hat. In fact, most of his hats were similar, but the man had turned out to be almost human-oid. 'There's gold in them there hills,' Kate said finally. 'He actually cares about Helen. He loves his family, Rich.'

'Dishes, then upstairs,' ordered the man of the house. 'I've new briefs from Hadleigh's to read.' He cleared and vacuumed before going up.

Kate took her time before checking on the children, then she sauntered into their en suite. Richard appeared in the doorway. As ever, he was beautifully prepared for the occasion. 'Shall we continue our conversation?' he mumbled through a green plastic tube.

Kate looked at him and sank to her knees, so powerful was her laughter. 'What the hell are you doing?' she asked. No man could possibly look attractive in this gear. He wore flippers, armbands made for a child which just fitted his wrists, goggles and snorkel. Apart from these items, he was stark naked.

He removed the snorkel. 'That's not a bath; it's a bloody swimming pool. Mummy said I have to be safe. She warned me about people like you who would lead me astray.'

'You sound like Daniel Pope.'

'Shut up and get your rubber ring. I don't want to be pumping water out of your lungs – I've better things to do.'

There could never, ever be another man like this clown. She'd seen him at work, the mouthy barrister who fought like a tiger for his clients. He was serious, beautifully spoken and handsome in his wig. So elegant in court, he acted like an escapee here, in the privacy offered by their master suite.

'It is rather large, isn't it?' he said. 'I'm talking about the bath, dear.' He shook his head sadly and blessed himself like a Catholic.

'I must have got my measurements wrong,' she said.

'You did. You could have been taller.'

'Complaining again?'

He nodded. 'Where's the diving board?'

'Oh, use the windowsill. And note, the taps are in the centre of the long side.' She shook her head. 'Use the bloody windowsill,' she repeated.

He thought about that. 'The trajectory's wrong. See, according to Einstein, there's no relativity between a windowsill and a diving board. Then think about Darwin. We crawled out of the water billions of years ago. Nostradamus said—'

'Richard, get in the bath.'

He got in the bath, still muttering about Galileo, Archimedes and the brides in the bath murders. 'If you pull my feet now, I drown.'

'Don't tempt me, Mr Rutherford.'

'Ditto. Are you getting in or what?'

'What,' she replied, and entered the shower cubicle. While she showered, she watched the madman she had married. He was playing underwater, breathing through his snorkel and splashing furiously. In almost everyone, a small piece of the child was preserved. Richard's mother had not tethered him, so the child in him was joyful and funny. Whereas Daniel Pope . . .

He joined her and washed her hair, as that was his job. 'Richard?'

'Yes, my love?'

'I wonder how Daniel felt about that sky-dive. Old Beatrice would be furious if she knew, and that's the problem, isn't it? Just the hair, sweetheart. I've done all my other bits.'

He muttered a few words including 'spoilsport'. 'It seems she is the problem, yes. Though if he hurts Helen again, I shall let you loose on him. That, as I know to my cost, is a fate worse than death.'

They dried off and went to bed. Richard picked up his book.

Once again, his wife was reduced to helpless laughter. Because of the new bath, her beloved's reading material was *Deep-Sea Diving for Beginners*. Kate picked up *She's Getting Away with Murder*, and then they were both laughing. She was the first to stop. Why couldn't Helen have this? 'If my marriage became sane, I'd need locking up, Rich.'

'Don't worry, pet lamb. I've got your name down for a lovely private home. The first wrinkle, and you're out of here. We've some stunning girls working at Liverpool Crown Court. A young solicitor brought her briefs to me the other day, and I put her name on the waiting list.'

'Did you give her back the briefs?'

'No. I'll wear them at work. Secretly, under my silly stuff.'

With the lights out, they drifted towards sleep.

'Richard?'

'What now?'

'Daniel. Is he going to come good? Does the marriage stand a chance?'

'People never cease to surprise me, Kate. Strangely, I do believe he's serious. And I know she needs him. All we must do is stay out of it unless someone needs us. Your brother's done a tremendous amount while managing to remain away from Daniel for the most part.'

'Biggest surprise of all. My brother acting human? Incredible. Turn on your other side, because I don't want you snoring in my ear. I never expected Ian to come here, though. He laughed once.'

'Twice. You were grinding coffee beans in the kitchen. But he is right, Kate. He provided the materials, but the only direct contribution he made was the sky-diving. A very wise man, your brother.'

She tried to imagine her grim-faced brother sky-diving, potholing or making love. 'I suppose the world needs people like Ian.'

Richard snored. Oh well. Perhaps if she gave him her briefs . . .

Emily Sanderson had never expected such joy and satisfaction. It was as if the whole world had been handed to her on a golden platter, since she had her son, her lover and the man who had become her best friend all in the one place. Her one regret continued to reside in the fact that she had wed in haste to escape the prospect of marrying for land. Joseph had been her victim just as she had been a victim. None of it had been his fault. He was an excellent man.

Having made her peace with Thora Caldwell, she and Joseph had placed the Mornington Road house in her hands. Thora would let it, take a small fee, make sure the place was looked after, and deposit the remaining money in Joe's account. Aunt Celia's legacy had bought both Rodney Street houses, leaving Joseph free to plough everything into Sanderson's Intelligent Kitchens and its older brother, Sanderson's Bespoke Furniture. Andrew was settled, so everything was well in Emily's little world.

Until now, Liverpool had been no more than a city on the Mersey, while Rodney Street had been the place where Stuart Abbot, Andrew's friend, had come to have his teeth straightened. Beyond that, Emily had known nothing about the place. After a few weeks, she knew plenty. There was a quality to life here that was almost indescribable, and it had to reside in its populace, since they had created and developed the city. It was cosmopolitan to a degree, because people from all over the world came and went in ships, while there was a sizeable Irish community. It was, she supposed, fun.

Toodles loved it, so that was another hurdle cleared. She made a friend of next door's kitty, and was settled within days. The butter applied to her paws had not been needed, and she had simply distributed it throughout the house, but Geoff had cleaned it up. He was a treasure. His chaos room on the first floor was reinstated, so he was content, as was Joseph.

Emily went to work for her husband. She took charge of orders, the books, the design and printing of brochures, postal advertising, newspaper advertising, and dealing with customers. She enjoyed every minute, especially her time spent front of house, because workers had a habit of coming out of the workshops for 'smokos', the term they used for a cigarette break. Wood was a material that burned easily, so they were not allowed to light up in the back.

It was here that she got her first closer encounters with the indigenous. 'Right. Soft Lad's your first husband then, queen?' 'Soft Lad' was the boss.

'Yes.'

'And you've got a new one what works down the children's ozzy?'

Ozzy was hospital. 'That's right.'

'And you work for your first old feller and he's your best mate, like?'

'Indeed.'

A head was scratched. 'You Woollies are weird. Split-ups round here mean fights in the streets, windows broke, chairs wellied all over the place, black eyes, priests running for their lives, her mother and his mother rolling about in the middle of the road with handfuls of each other's hair.' The same head was shaken. 'World War Three in these parts, divorce.'

'We're not divorced.' Strangely, she didn't care any more. These folk seemed to accept just about everything. 'Geoff and I live over the brush.'

'And across the road from Soft Lad.'

'Why do you call Joseph Soft Lad?'

The man shrugged. 'He's the boss. I've heard bosses called worse.'

'But you like him, all of you.'

'We do. He's as bad. Sent an apprentice out for a bucket of elbow grease and a tin of yellow and green striped paint.'

'No!'

'Oh, yes. Then he went in our back room one day and pinched all our dinners what we'd brought from home. Sawdust sarnies, he put there in our boxes. He buggered off and brought us all fish and chips, but we were looking for him, and we carry dangerous tools, missus.'

Missus burst out laughing. The 'war' between management and shop floor had to be maintained, no matter how good the relationship. It was historical, rooted in the days when men had queued for dock work, when the Mersey Docks and Harbour Board had been blamed for everything from scarlet fever to world war and late-running buses.

Joseph's head entered the room. 'Oi, Juster,' he shouted. 'Get back in here.'

Juster saluted and went to do Soft Lad's bidding.

The latter joined Emily.

'Juster?'

Joseph nodded. 'It's always "just a minute" or "just a sec", so we call him Juster.'

'Then you have Neely.'

'Yes, Neely finished, Neely home time. Ghost's the moaner – red-haired chap – Harpic's clean round the bend, Jigsaw falls to bits when something's wrong, Rattler's teeth don't fit, and Donor's very pale, as if he gives blood every other day.'

'And you're Soft Lad.'

He grinned broadly and nodded. 'In Liverpool, soft is daft. And I must be daft for hiring this shower.'

'Well, I think they're wonderful.'

'So do I, Em. I've always enjoyed work, as well you know, but there's fun here. And in spite of the larking about, they're meticulous. Mad dogs, though, the bloody lot of them are. Now. We have to have a meeting, me, you and Rattler. Orders are coming in at a rate of knots. We need more transport, more fitters, bigger premises again. And some of the lads will have to move on. We are going nationwide, Emily. I want training premises and thirty hours in every day.'

So Joseph was on his way. All Emily wanted was for the three men in her life to be fulfilled and happy. She wished Joseph could meet some nice, gentle woman, but she realized that his confidence in that area of life was seriously corroded. Now that she understood the true joy of physical love, she had difficulty in hiding her pity for Joseph, but he was a proud man, and she mustn't let her feelings show.

She drove homeward, deliberately avoiding the shops. If she went anywhere near George Henry Lee's again, she'd spend a week's wages in five minutes. She'd spotted some lovely linens and towels . . . 'Oh stop it, Emily. You've the life of Riley as it is.'

Andrew was in when she got home. 'How did it go?' she asked. On his second day at college, he had met his first corpse.

'Fine,' he answered. 'Well, I was fine, but some poor devils hit the floor, while a couple vomited. Not the girls, though. One had to go out for a bit of air, but she dragged herself back in and got down to it. It's rather like carving a giant Sunday joint.'

'Andrew!'

'Well, you asked.'

'Was your body male or female?'

'Female.'

268

'Ah.'

'Mother, I'm no innocent. I've seen the female form, though in a warmer state, I'm glad to say. And you can kill that blush, because there are no innocents in this house.'

The front door opened. 'Coo-ee.'

'Saved by the grandparents,' Andrew muttered before going to greet them.

Irene was in a state of excitement that approached hysteria. 'Oh, what a wonderful house. Georgian, isn't it? But wait till you see what we've got you, Andrew. It was the best we could find. Emily? You there, love?' She walked up the large hall to greet her rediscovered daughter.

Alan entered with a massive box. 'Your skeleton,' he said. 'We got you a good one.' He lowered his tone. 'Park it somewhere visible. And you have to name it. Apparently, naming your skeleton is part and parcel of being a medical student. Then watch your mother's face when she claps eyes on it.'

In the morning room, Andrew placed George carefully on his stand. He was a fine figure of a man, though somewhat lacking in the flesh and skin department. 'A Georgian house, so you're George. Let me get you something to wear, poor chap.' When a coat was draped across shoulders and a hat topped the skull, a hyper-innocent Andrew entered the kitchen. 'Shall we have tea through here?' he asked.

Mother's face defied description when she entered the morning room. Morning rooms were meant to be small, but this one was big enough for ballroom dancing. She clasped her chest. 'Very nice,' she said. 'Just what we need to go with our tea and scones.'

'I tried,' said her son, his voice trimmed with sadness. 'But he wouldn't stop dieting. George, meet my mother.'

'If you were younger,' Emily said.

'I know. Smacked bottom and up to bed with no supper.' He picked up a plate. 'Cake, anyone? Whatever you leave, George can have. He needs the calories.'

Emily sank into a chair. Because of this precious boy, she had her parents back. Andrew owned a country house and a skeleton named George. Geoff would be home soon. Joseph was doing what he did best, and was contented with his life. All was bliss in her hemisphere. She crossed the room and shook George's hand gently and with great seriousness. 'Welcome home, George. We'll get you better, so not to worry.'

Daniel Pope knew he was a changed man, though he was still discovering himself. He was enjoying the teenage years that had been denied to him, he supposed. It was rather like peeling off wallpaper in a neglected house where there was always another layer underneath. Somewhere behind all the Anaglypta and woodchip and layers of emulsion paint, a hormonal teenager waited to be found, released and allowed to grow.

He spent a fair amount of time talking to himself in a mirror. What he saw was a handsome man who was two-dimensional, as flat as the surface that reflected him. He also saw someone whose self-interest was constructive, because he needed to find out exactly who he was. Everyone had been right – his mother had done damage. Although unprepared to lay all the blame at the feet of Beatrice Pope, he was tracing many of his problems back to their source, and he was finding Ma in every picture, sometimes at the edge or in the background, but always there. Always there, always right, always interfering, questioning, probing.

It was almost time to face her. She had never liked

Helen, but Helen's quiet strength had precluded open warfare. Ma was jealous. Ma wanted to be the only woman in Daniel's life. She continued to play an active part in the business, and these weeks he had taken away from work had given Daniel time to think. And what he thought wasn't pretty.

Yet he didn't want to hurt her. 'You have to tell her, old fruit,' he advised the figure in the mirror. 'Because you damaged Helen, and Ma was at the back of all of it.' And Ma couldn't conceal her joy about Helen's desertion of him. 'Come home, son. I'll look after you.' She was to blame.

Or was she? Surely, when a person grew to adulthood, he should accept responsibility for all choices and misdeeds? But regression, a process of which he had been unaware, had borne fruit, and the harvest was audible on discs. Under hypnosis, he had let it all out. Strapped to another man, he had screamed it out on his way back to earth. Oh, that had been brilliant, and he could scarcely wait for his first solo jump. Fastened to a trainer was exciting, but he needed to be alone – that would be symbolic of his final break from Ma.

'I won't stop talking to Ma,' he advised his reflection, 'but she will know her place in the scheme of things.' Then, he would have to face Helen. Helen, like many even-tempered and controlled people, had limited patience. It took a lot to shift her but, once moved, she was a virago. He grinned, though the smile didn't light up his eyes. The photographs on top of his ruined clothes had needed no accompanying note, as they still screamed *Look what you lost, you damned fool.*

But he hadn't lost, not quite, not yet. Staying away from her had been part of the plan, and he saw his children when Andrew drove them across. Andrew, Ian and even Richard had been his backbone during the time it had taken for him to form vertebrae of his own. As for those who had listened, the professionals – they could not be faulted. 'Do you think of me, Helen? Do you?'

She, her sister and her brother had not been restricted throughout development, though Eva wasn't an easy vehicle to pass. If anything, they had suffered a degree of genteel neglect, since their parents had been so tied up in each other. But Kate, the fiery one, the gentle-till-pushed-too-far Helen, and Ian, the studious boy, had all come through relatively unscathed, while he had been so badly affected by a doting mother that he had been emotionally crippled. He could never keep company with 'rough' boys, was forbidden to go swimming without an adult family member, was not allowed to enjoy camping, fishing, roller-skating, cycling. He'd been imprisoned by his own mother.

So, he had to shape a distance between himself and his parents. If Helen came back, the statutory trips to Chester, where his parents lived, would be cut down. Visits to Neston by Ma and Pa must also be limited. Helen needed space, as did he, yet grandparents deserved to see grandchildren, and vice versa. Many lines must be drawn, then. And this time, the pen would be in Daniel's hand.

He was getting stronger. Everyone knew that he and Helen were having a trial separation. What they said behind his back no longer mattered.

While living in her father's house, Helen changed. She adopted and adapted her older sister's method with men, which was to swat them like flies by going for their vulnerable spot, otherwise known as the ego. Thus freed, she dressed as she liked, went where she wanted to go, and developed a range of dirty looks to be delivered to

272

roofers, builders, painters and any other wolf-whistlers. She was a free woman, and they could bog off.

Her sister joined her once a week for lunch, and they went round all the bars in turn, giving marks out of ten for a subject entitled the Most Imaginative Use of the Baked Potato in North Liverpool. So far, Barry's Bar was winning, while Louie's Tavern trailed behind with limp lettuce and some terribly depressed tomatoes with a rancid blue-cheese sauce.

'We shall send the league table in to the local press,' Kate said after their escape from Louie's. 'And I'm posting this to a laboratory for testing.' She unfolded a paper napkin inside which a cherry tomato did its best to look normal. 'Naw,' she said. 'Can't be bothered.' She dumped her parcel in a bin.

'Kate?'

'Yes, Helen?'

'I think Anya's fallen for Dad.'

Kate shrugged. 'He's gorgeous. OK, he's our father, and we don't notice, but he is very handsome. And, I think, very aware of Anya. She's different, she's vulnerable, and she's pleasant.'

'I may be getting in the way, though.'

'Rubbish. What will be will be, Helen-babe. Now, let's get you back to Dad's, because I need to be elsewhere. Richard's training for deep-sea diving.'

'You serious?'

'Oh yes. Everybody seems to be taking up hobbies. Your fellow, if he is yours, is jumping out of aeroplanes, while mine's leaping into water. Strangely, it started in the en suite with some goggles and a green plastic snorkel. Yes, he's a worry. I don't know whether to get a psychiatrist or a vet. I watch him doing his job, and I wonder whether people know he's not fit to be out on his own.'

'Oh, Kate, you're so lucky.'

Kate put an arm across her sister's back. 'Sorry. I don't mean to rub salt in. I've told you I love you and I want you happy—'

A wolf whistle from a window cleaner stopped Kate in her tracks. She knew she was pretty; she also knew that the whistle had been for her sister, who was film star-ish.

'Listen, Mr Soap and Water, you couldn't afford her. And you've missed a bit. Get in the corners, you lazy sod.'

In North Liverpool, this was not the behaviour expected by residents, and some passers-by stopped and stared.

'She's married to a millionaire, so why would she look at you?'

Helen dragged Kate away. 'Stop showing me up. I can deal with this myself.' She looked at the whistler. 'Sorry about that, sir. Oh, pull your jeans up. These people can see the crack of your arse.' The words, delivered in clipped, educated tones, caused a ripple of laughter among spectators, but Helen took her sister's arm and walked on. 'Can you imagine the old me doing that?'

'Oh, God. I've turned my little sister into a delinquent.'

They continued a constitutional designed to walk off a baked potato. 'How would you feel if Dad married again?' Helen asked.

'Not sure. I want him happy. This grieving for our mother bit has gone on too long for my liking. He doesn't talk to the grave still, does he?'

Helen wasn't sure. The flowers got changed, though she hadn't noticed him standing there for any length of time. 'He and Anya have a place, bottom of the erosion steps. She takes a car rug, and he sometimes takes a flask. They drink out of the same cup.'

'Hell's bells.' Kate giggled. 'I hope Polish isn't contagious. If he catches it, we'll be flummoxed.'

'I like her,' Helen said.

Kate agreed. 'And he prefers small women – Eva's the exception, of course. Because he's getting ratty with her. Remember how he was a father as well as a husband to our mother?'

'He's a wonderful person, Kate.'

'He is. He most certainly is. Come on, let's give Sofia her well-earned break.'

Andrew loved his time at college. He worked hard and played hard, though not as hard as some when it came to the playing bit. As time passed, the medical school's population diminished due to the disappearance of people who failed examinations, missed deadlines for written work, didn't turn up at hospital placements, or simply gave up because the course was beyond them.

Andrew applied himself as best he could in all disciplines, though what remained with him was the moment he'd opened that box and lifted out George. George was a miracle of engineering. The human skeleton amazed Andrew, as did the structures that fastened bone to muscle, bone to bone, hand to arm, foot to leg. Da Vinci had expressed his interest in the human form, had examined bones, had doubtless been cursed for so doing. Bone mattered. Without strong infrastructure, bodies failed. They lost movement and protection for vital organs; for Andrew, bones were not quite everything, but their strength was vital.

He had his share of enjoyment, particularly when it came to women. They all but fell at his feet, especially when the world drifted into the 1960s. Although oral contraception was not universally available, many female medics managed to get hold of supplies, and sexual freedom became a much appreciated facility during the new decade. So he sowed his wild oats, managing by fair means or foul not to become romantically involved, and was much talked about among liberated women of the age. He was a good lay, and he wanted to be no more than that. If a woman became affectionate, he moved on. Was he cruel? He suspected that he was.

Then he saw her. She was among a throng of girls queuing excitedly at the Cavern Club. Tiny, beautifully formed, perfect facial bone structure, dark hair as shiny as the polished casing of his baby grand in Rodney Street, she wrapped herself round his heart in that first moment.

When she raised a hand to her beautiful hair, the rhythm of his heart altered noticeably. It was her left hand, and the ring finger boasted a sapphire flanked by two small diamonds. She wasn't chattering and yelping alongside the other females. Like him, she had probably come to see what all the fuss was about. But the maniacs by whom she was surrounded were not music lovers; they were stupid, hormonal females here just to worship at the feet of four ordinary lads whose music would not be heard because of these screaming idiots.

He turned to walk away, but something made his feet still. She was looking at him. The mass hysteria continued while she held his gaze for what must have been a second, no more. Then the seething, screaming dollop of semi-human frogspawn oozed forward, and she was flattened against the wall.

He fought his way through the senseless flock, picked her up and carried her across Mathew Street. 'Are you hurt?' he asked.

'Just my pride.'

Blue eyes exactly the same shade as his own blinked back tears of shock. 'I was frightened,' she said.

'I'm not surprised. How brutally insane is that behaviour? Do you like the Beatles?'

'They're OK.'

'Well, they won't be OK for long after they've been flattened by those stupid people. Shall we get a drink somewhere?'

In the cafe, he noticed that she was still shaking. 'I'm Andrew Sanderson,' he told her. 'Trainee doctor.'

'Mary Collins, nurse at the Women's.'

She had flawless skin, incredibly long and dense eyelashes, good legs, a tiny waist and breasts that begged for no support. While carrying her, he'd noticed her braless state. 'Can I tempt you to a night out? Dinner, theatre, cinema?'

'I'm engaged.'

'I see. You're fettered.'

The chin came up defiantly. 'Not exactly. I choose to be faithful.' She crossed her fingers when she told the lie. She was nearly faithful. Most of the time.

'And dinner with me would be an act of infidelity?'

She smiled. 'I think it might well be just that, Andrew.'

And she left. But her smile remained, rather like the Cheshire cat's. It was emblazoned across his eyelids, engraved on their inner surface. 'Well, Casanova,' he mumbled as he stepped outside. 'You met your Waterloo.'

He wasn't alone – she, too, had felt something, known something. When was he scheduled for gynaecology? A stint at the Women's might just help. She was afraid of him. And he had to admit, albeit only to himself, that he, too, was overawed. He'd met his wife today. No matter what it took, with the possible exception of murder, he would lay claim to her, and woe betide any mere human who stood in his path.

Twelve

According to her housemates in Sefton Park, Mary Collins had a cob on. She was spending a lot of time in her own room, wasn't eating much, refused many invitations, and was generally out of sorts. And she remained in this state of suspended animation till the leaflet came.

When the leaflet came, everything changed in the blink of an eyelash. She suddenly had to have a new dress, VO5 shampoo, a lipstick from Boots the Chemist, a pair of shoes that added a few inches to her abbreviated personage, and a book about Grieg, plus a record of some of his music.

In her absence, the other girls pored over the leaflet. It advertised Sanderson's Intelligent Kitchens, Sanderson's Bespoke Furniture and, on the reverse side, a concert at the university. The concert was entitled *Out of their Comfort Zone*, and the son of the Sanderson family, Andrew, would be performing a piece by Grieg. A poet from the maths department was doing a reading, while a lab assistant attached to the School of Tropical Medicine was executing stand-up comedy with a zither. It would be sit-down comedy because of the zither, and the girls remarked about that. Proceeds were earmarked for a children's charity, and refreshments would be purchasable in the interval.

They went through a lengthy list of names of all who

would perform sketches and the like, but Mary had left her red biro mark under one name, and that name was Andrew Sanderson. What did they think? What about John? was what they thought. Engaged to her childhood sweetheart from the age of sixteen, Miss Goody Two Shoes seemed to be wandering several pages off the book of true love. And she'd changed the goody shoes to high heels, so something was afoot. The girl who made that remark laughed at her own pun, but nobody noticed. There was nothing funny about their missing friend's apparent faithlessness.

While Mary was on her way back from yet another shopping expedition, four fellow nurses sat in a row prepared to challenge her. What about John? As a seafarer, he was away for several months of the year, and it looked as if his little mouse was planning to play in his absence. 'He could have a girl in every port,' said one of the nurses. 'They're famous for it.'

'Or a boy. He could have a boy. Some sailors are quite versatile.'

'Shut up, Joan,' ordered the other three in perfect harmony.

The door opened. In trotted little Nurse Mary Collins with her purchases and a brilliant smile. The smile faded in the face of so much gloom. She glanced at the leaflet and realized what they wanted. 'Don't start,' she said, 'it just happened, and I can't help it.'

Pam, who was closest in every way to Mary, followed her up the stairs.

She closed the door of Mary's room quietly. 'I'm guessing this is the one who saved you from certain death outside the Cavern. Mary, what about John? Have you thought about him?'

Mary collapsed on her bed. 'Shut up, Pam.'

These two girls had known each other forever. Born

in flats above Scotland Road shops, they had attended school together, ridden trams together, had pinched molasses from carts, learned tables, eaten in each other's homes, helped in both shops, played truant, taken dangerous dips in the 'scaldy' behind the sugar factory, thereby risking life and limb together in warm, deep water. Whatever it was, they had done it as a pair. And now, they were engaged to two brothers, so life was supposed to continue in the same vein. 'Mary, we had it all planned out.'

'I know.'

'We've never been apart.'

'I know, I know.'

'We even work together. How could you let this happen?'

'I didn't. It was nothing to do with me. It was nothing to do with him, either. Something happened in the space between us. It was like that film where they bump into one another on a railway station, and every time I see it, I always wish the end will be different. I have to meet him again. If I see him, I might realize how daft it was.'

'And you bought a book about Grieg, so you're going to talk to this bloke cos he's playing Greig at the concert.'

'Something like that, yes.'

Pam shook her head. 'I thought . . . I just thought and hoped we'd always be together, you and John, me and Mike, living in the same street, our kids playing together like we did.'

'I'm sorry, Pam. Whatever happens, don't fall out with me.'

'Don't talk daft. I just wanted us to be real sisters-in-law.'

'We will. We might. Oh, I don't know.' Mary felt as if she'd been struck by lightning or a double-decker bus or a crowd of soft girls baying for the Beatles.

She hadn't been herself since the day outside the Cavern. He'd carried her to safety, and she'd heard the pace of his heart above all the hysterical shouting. His fingers, long and slender, had buried themselves in the side of her right breast, and she had wanted him. Yes, he had the hands of a pianist or a surgeon. And he was so handsome, he'd give Gregory Peck a run for his money any day of the week. She didn't know him, shouldn't care about him, didn't want to live without him. She was probably mad. At nearly nineteen, she should have more sense.

'Shall I make some tea?' Pam asked. 'Two sugars and a biscuit, keep your strength up?'

Mary nodded. 'Don't talk about me. Tell the other three to concentrate on obstetrics for the exam instead of gossiping. I'll let people know what's happening when I know what's happening.'

When Pam had left, Mary allowed Andrew into her head. He didn't arrive quietly, though she had no reason to think of him as a loud person. He wanted dinner for two, but that wasn't all. His eyes sparkled. Strong arms, square jaw, open face. He could have any girl he wanted, but he wanted her. And it wasn't just sex. What was it, then? Sex with friendship, sex with shared interests, sex with fish, chips and peas? Oh, life was so bloody complicated. Her lot had been laid out before her; she would marry John, Pam would marry Mike, and they would live in the same street, have children, grow old.

This was daft. A bloke in Mathew Street had helped her. What if he'd been ugly or ancient – would she have felt the same? She hadn't been looking for attention or love; she'd gone to see the Beatles. She'd seen them as The Quarry Men, but not since they'd changed their name. Strong rumour forecast that they were about to change the face of music worldwide, and she'd decided to have a look at this phenomenon. Instead, she would be listening to Grieg.

Of late, she'd noticed Andrew Sanderson lingering, probably waiting for her outside the Women's, so she'd slipped out of a back door of the hospital. Why? Because she couldn't be alone with him, couldn't take the risk. If they kissed, they would probably need surgical separation. Given half a chance and some privacy, they would make love. At a concert, all should be OK, because other people would be there. 'I don't trust me,' she told a wall.

Pam ran in without the promised cup of tea. 'Erm,' she began.

'Erm what?'

'There's somebody to see you.' The poor girl swallowed audibly. 'Oh, God help you, queen. He's bloody gorgeous. Cary Grant.'

'Gregory Peck,' said Mary without hesitation. She sat bolt upright. 'How did he get our address, Pam? Because I never told him. Stick him in the kitchen.' There was something dependable about kitchens. Everybody needed one, but they were mundane and, in the case of this particular kitchen, rather small and uncomfortable.

'Are you going to do your hair?' Pam asked.

'No, I'm not. I'm going to tell him to bugger off.'

Pam leaned against the door, her arms spread wide so that her friend couldn't leave the room easily. 'He's gorgeous,' she repeated.

'I know. And when he picked me up and carried me, I was at home, as if I'd always been there in his arms. I'm scared, Pam. I'm scared of me.'

'It's called love at first sight, babe.'

'You disapproved till he turned up. You were all worried about John. What's changed?'

'He's beautiful, charming and standing behind a dozen long-stemmed red roses is what's changed. I know we had

282

plans, but I was being selfish. Calm down. If you tell him to bugger off, he might just do that, and you could well live to regret it.'

Mary's little alarm clock poured its disparately loud ticks into a heavy silence. 'Tell him I'm not well. No, that won't do, because he's halfway to being a doctor and he'll come up and take half my temperature.' He'd take anything he liked if he got up here, but she kept that suspicion to herself.

Pam went down to put him in the kitchen.

After a decent interval during which she did change her clothes and tidy her hair, Mary sauntered down the stairs. Three people looked at her with daggers in their eyes, but Pam nodded in the direction of the kitchen. 'Go on,' she mouthed before shooing the other girls out of the living room.

Pam was right; he was gorgeous. He rose from a rickety chair at the rickety table as soon as she entered the kitchen. 'Roses for a rose,' he said.

Right. So he was one of those, was he? All flowers and flowery words, but no substance. Well, this could be dealt with quite easily. Although engaged, Mary had not kept herself completely to herself during her fiancé's long absences. This would just be sex, then finished.

He placed the roses among debris on the table.

'Thank you, they're lovely,' she said, 'but how did you find my address?'

'I have friends at the Women's.'

She glared at him. 'Then I shall complain to personnel. Your friends shouldn't give out personal information to any Tom, Dick or Harry.'

'I'm Andrew.'

'Don't get clever with me, sunshine. I may be just a nurse, but I've a full set of teeth and nice long nails. Oh, and there are no slates missing from my roof, so back off.'

The bloody man was smiling at her. 'What's funny?' she asked.

'You are. You're a perfect if somewhat miniature pot of anger. Beautiful, too. Meeting you altered me. I've started to avoid women, and my arms have felt empty since the moment I set you down on terra firma. So I've come to claim my prize.'

'Which is?'

'You.'

He was so direct, so damned bold that she found no answer.

'Just a meal one evening?' he begged.

'I'm not sure.'

'Are you afraid of me?'

Mary shrugged. 'I'm not the sort to be afraid of anyone. People as small as I am have to stand their ground.'

'Unless they're being scraped along a wall in Mathew Street. Mary, when I picked you up, something happened, and not just to me.'

She concentrated on the roses. 'It's called sexual attraction.'

'Which always comes first,' he said. 'And it's more than that. You know it as well as I do. Look at me. Look at me, Mary.'

She obeyed reluctantly.

'We have nothing to lose.'

'Except my fiancé out there on a merchant ship in all kinds of weather.'

Andrew wanted to tell her that she wouldn't be needing her sailor, that she was his, and had been his since long before they'd met, but he knew how daft that would sound. He was like his mother. Emily seemed to know what was what even in areas as grey as this one. 'I won't give up,' was all he managed in the moment.

Mary looked straight into his eyes. 'I did want to see

284

you again,' she admitted. 'But in circumstances of my choosing. Sanderson's Kitchens advertised your concert, and I plan to attend.'

'Right. I suppose that must suffice. As long as you wait for me at the end of the concert. Oh, one more thing. The orchestra will not be playing for you and only for you, but the soloist will. Music was my alternative subject. I'm good at it. I'm good at several things.' He winked, just about managing not to be crude.

'So am I. I sing.'

'You see?' He stood up. 'A perfect match.'

Mary rose to her feet and walked to the door, but he caught her up in his arms, just as he had at the Cavern. But this time, he kissed her gently, tenderly. When he pulled away, his eyes questioned hers and seemed satisfied with the answer, as he repeated the action, this time with urgency.

And that was that. When their mouths were finally separated, each did a brief but fair imitation of a hyperventilating patient during a panic attack.

'Oh, my God,' Mary whispered.

'No,' he answered. 'Just Andrew, but Drew will suffice – I am not quite a deity. Drew's the abbreviation I saved for my wife.' He put her down and left.

Pam found her friend on the brink of collapse and on the edge of an unreliable kitchen chair. 'What the bloody hell happened, Mary?'

Mary shook her head. He seemed to have sucked all the words out of her.

'Mary?'

'Shut up a minute.'

Pam busied herself with roses and a vase. She found a card among the blooms. *This is it. You know it and I know it. Semper Fidelis. Drew.* 'He's left his phone number, Mary.'

'Shut up.'

Pam closed her mouth in a grim line and shoved Andrew's note under her friend's clenched fist. *'Semper fidelis,'* she muttered between gritted teeth. Then she stopped gritting her teeth. 'Please your bloody self, Mary, but like I said before, he's gorgeous. And that *semper fidelis* bit translates to always faithful, which means he's slowed down, cos he's had a few nurses according to Joan. That would be part of his training, I suppose, part of getting ready for the real thing. You.' She left the room, vase of roses held at arm's length.

Mary blinked stupidly. These things didn't happen except in films, daft books or women's magazines. Nobody real met somebody real for the second time and declared undying love with an implicit proposal of marriage mixed in with other unstable ingredients like foolhardiness and hot-headedness. Her mouth felt bruised and lonely. Well, the lips had each other, so they'd have to be satisfied. He was a brilliant kisser, not invasive, not yet.

She jumped up. Not yet? Not yet implied a future, and there couldn't be a future. She felt dizzy. Postural hypotension, shock, idiocy? Or a mixture of all the above? Fresh air. She let herself out via the back door and strolled up the side of the house. Hell's bells and buckets of blood, there he sat in his car, head resting on the upper curve of the steering wheel. She stepped back into shade, peering through a balding part of the privet hedge. The man was one hundred per cent incredible. He was mad, absolutely crackers.

Was he intending to spend the night here? Oh, heck. Was he preparing to become a liability? She strode out to the pavement and knocked on his windscreen. His hair was tousled. He looked like a gigantic five-year-old who'd just tumbled out of bed.

He opened the passenger door. 'Sit,' he said.

'Woof,' she replied before climbing in beside him. 'You must go,' she advised him. 'A few ladies of the night have started to pick up trade along here, and you might be mistaken for a kerb-crawler.'

'And you might be mistaken for one of those ladies.'

They sat in silence for a few beats of time. Then he picked up her hand and began to kiss it. Mary tried to ignore the shivers that crept up her arm. 'Please try to behave yourself, Andrew. How old are you?'

'Twenty-two.'

'Stop acting like a teenager.'

'And a half.'

'What?'

'Twenty-two and a half. So I'm almost grown up. I'll go home now so that Mummy can put me to bed. I live in Rodney Street, by the way. And I want you to have my babies. Off you go, sweetest girl. I'll see you tomorrow.'

She climbed out of the car and watched him drive away. He was funny, intelligent, mercurial, as mad as a hatter and absolutely adorable. He was also in reverse. 'Come home with me,' he begged after slewing to a halt. 'My kitchen's better than yours.'

'So it should be, Mr Sanderson.'

'I have dolly mixtures.'

'Tempting.'

'Custard creams? Oh, and a friend named George. Rather thin, and not much to say, but he knows his place. We won't be disturbed.'

'Go home, Andrew.'

'Or he can join in if you'd prefer.'

'Bugger off, you mad clown.'

'Can I press you to a jelly? With custard?'

It was in this, the silliest of instants, that she felt truly alive. She had met her other half, and she would never escape him. What was more, she didn't want to escape, because he was her heart's home.

'What on earth are you doing?' Emily asked. Her son with a cylinder vacuum cleaner made an unusual picture.

'I'm cleaning my flat,' he answered. 'I've done the one in Dad's house.'

She was stunned. For years, he'd changed his address every time his rooms got out of order, since he had no time for cleaning. 'Why?' she asked.

'I'm bringing a visitor. Her name's Mary Collins, and I have plans for her.'

Emily folded her arms. 'You're about to seduce a young woman under my roof?'

He put down his burden. 'Something like that, though my intentions in the long term are honourable. She's the most beautiful girl ever, so you have been shifted, *sine* prejudice, to second place.'

She blinked. 'Isn't all this rather sudden, darling?'

'Compared to what?'

Emily shook her head. 'Don't nitpick, Andrew. When is she coming?'

He sat on the stairs. 'I don't know. I haven't told her yet that she's coming.'

'Shouldn't that be asked, or invited?'

'No. I'm training her to do as she's told. I believe in starting the way I mean to go on. She'll walk in my shadow, have too many children, make excellent meals, and be decorative at all times.' He glared at his mother. She was doubled over in laughter. No one took him seriously. Ever.

'But first,' he continued determinedly, 'I have to strip her of one dark sapphire and two diamonds.'

'She's engaged?'

'A detail,' he said. 'It's like . . . well, I think it's a bit like you and Geoff. It overrides every sensible cell in my skull, Mother. You and he should understand what I mean.'

Emily sat next to her son on the wide staircase. 'Tell me about her.'

'I warn you, this is my best subject pro tem. She's tiny, probably a couple of inches over five feet in height, shapely, with dark hair and eyes the colour of mine. Good skin, perfect bone structure, excellent legs, amazing ankles, straight teeth, full lips, beautiful smile and a—'

'Tell me about the contents, not the box.'

'Ah. Well I picked her up – literally – outside the Cavern to prevent her death by stampede. We went for coffee and stared at each other while pretending not to. And we just knew. She's a nurse at the Women's, where she's much appreciated. Top marks in all her exams, cheeky, opinion-ated and has a tendency to tell me to bugger off.'

'I like her already,' Emily said.

'Thought you might. Where are you going?'

'To clean your rooms. I can't have my daughter-in-law seeing the flat in its current state. Oh, and one more thing.'

'Yes, Mother?'

'When you clean a room, it's not just about the floor.'

'Yes, Mother.'

'Are you mocking me, Andrew?'

'Ye— I mean no, Mother.' He went off to practise the Grieg in A Minor, a particularly difficult piece for piano. He was to be backed by music students, plus several members of the Liverpool Philharmonic, one of the oldest orchestras on earth. But that didn't account for his nerves. She did. Little Miss Bugger-off with her cheeky grin and lustrous hair.

*

The day flew, as is the way when a person is nervous about evening. He hoped he could cover his mistakes, hoped she wouldn't laugh at him in his black tie and tails, hoped she would come, wished she wasn't coming. As the final performer, he took advantage and left his silly suit in the dressing room. After placing his three parents in the front row, he slammed a Reserved sign between Dad and Mother. 'I'll bring her to you,' he said.

'Bring who?' Joe asked, but his son had disappeared, so Joe got the story from Emily.

Andrew stood outside the door of the Philharmonic Hall. The charitable arrived in their droves, and he decided that everyone was far too tall. She could be lost somewhere in the middle, and he might have to do another Mathew Street job so that she wouldn't get trampled.

But no. Here she came, taller in high-heeled shoes and more beautiful than ever. Under a brown jacket, she wore a simple linen dress in a warm, creamy shade. He went to meet her. 'Come with me, miss. I've reserved your place.' And he led her by the hand to the front, where he reclaimed his sign before introducing her to his three parents and leaving Mother to explain.

His nightmare began. He heard laughter, cheering and applause, and began to doubt his ability because he didn't practise regularly. Was he good enough to provide a decent finale? Why hadn't he chosen something simpler? Why hadn't Grieg made the piece easier to play?

The orchestra clattered into place before beginning their tune-up. They needn't have bothered, because he felt completely out of tune with himself. The MC delivered his two penn'orth, introducing a young man who had refused a place at the Royal School in order to attend Liverpool University's Faculty of Medicine.

Then some evil swine pushed him, and he was on

stage, black tie and tails, with a monstrous full grand staring at him. Ebony and ivory; he felt sick. He sat, flicking out the appendages on his coat, trying to look professional, since he had no chance of sounding in the least way adept.

The conductor raised his baton. When Andrew struck those early, dramatic chords, Mary grabbed Emily's hand. This beautiful, clever creature at the piano was hers for the taking. The music hurt, but she didn't know she was weeping, didn't realize that she was squeezing the life out of his mother's fingers.

Emily looked down at the tiny, powerful left hand. The ring had gone, though a line of white flesh betrayed its existence. Of course, Mary had arrived not knowing that this splendid boy could have been a concert pianist rather than a doctor. She noticed that during his pauses when the orchestra played, Andrew was gazing in Mary's direction. The auditorium was dark, and he was spotlit, so his chances of noticing details like tears were few, thank goodness.

Edvard Grieg's final triumph poured its majesty into the hall. As one man, the audience rose to its feet, applause threatening to shatter the whole place. The small orchestra took a bow, Andrew took another and another before urging his colleagues to stand once more.

The wags were in from medical school. 'Go, Andy,' and 'Encore, encore.'

So he sat and played for *her* the most beautiful piece he knew, one he had played since childhood. The orchestra sat back, as they were not needed. His delivery of 'Für Elise' was faultless and moving. Again, they rose and shouted for more, but he bowed, left the stage, and returned with two bunches of red roses. 'For the two women in my life.'

The lights went up. Emily collected the flowers, as Mary

was now in floods. 'You made her cry,' she told her son, mouthing the words over yet more applause.

The auditorium began to empty. Small groups of friends and relatives waited for performers to appear, but the majority of the audience left. Andrew dashed in, still dressed à la penguin, as he described his attire. He picked Mary up and carried her to the outer door. 'I must break this habit,' he told her. 'If you gain weight, I shall get a hernia. Tears now. From how many more situations must I rescue you? Where are your roses?'

'Your mother has them.'

'Good. That's a bit less weight for me to carry.'

He was lovely. She kissed him on the cheek.

'Right.' He placed her in the passenger seat of his car. 'We're going for a light supper. At my mother's house. And I didn't mean to make you cry. As a matter of fact, Grieg and Beethoven did it. I was just their carrier pigeon.'

'You're good.'

'I know.' He winked. She remembered the wink. It meant he wanted sex. Well, she thought it might mean he wanted sex. She didn't know him, but if he was as good at sex as he was at the piano . . .

He climbed in and started the car.

'Andrew?'

'What?'

'You should be a concert pianist.'

'Are you saying I'll be a poor doctor?'

'No.'

He explained that concert pianists travelled all over the world, and he didn't want that. He wanted a wife, children, a nice house and a good job. 'I like bones,' he explained. 'The human skeleton beats the Sistine Chapel as a work of art. I shall probably be a sawbones because of my history in carpentry.'

'Is there anything you can't do?'

He thought about that one. 'Fly,' he said. 'I can't fly.'

Mary laughed. Where had he been all her life? And she was so happy to have missed seeing the Beatles. John Lennon, Paul McCartney – who the hell were they? She should write and thank them for having fans insane enough to perform in a rodeo without wild animals. 'Have you always played the piano?'

'Well, never while asleep. But I think I played every day until I left school. These days, I don't practise enough.'

'You were wonderful.'

'Thank you. I must give you a sample of my other talents. But I was terrified, mostly because you would be there. I wanted you to come, and wanted you to stay away in case I made a mess of the music.'

'You didn't.'

'I know, but I was still scared.'

He wasn't the type to make a mess, Mary thought. The man probably knew his limits and would leave alone things that didn't suit or interest him. Rugby, soccer and motorbikes were unlikely to be his scene – too many broken bones. 'I took the ring off.'

'I noticed.'

'Do you ever miss anything?'

'Meals,' was his swift reply. 'And when my glucose level plummets, I'm a monster.' He pulled up outside his mother's house. 'Gladstone was born over the road there. Queen Victoria hated him, said he talked to her as if addressing a public meeting. The Stanley who said, "Dr Livingstone, I presume?" was from Rodney Street. But shall we save the education and questions and answers until later? I have a comfortable double bed.'

But Mary had decided that this was going to be a serious relationship, and should be treated as such. 'I have to tell John first. And he won't be home till next month. I'm sorry, but that's the way I am.'

Andrew already knew the way she was. Decent, honourable, amusing, beautiful and his. He could wait. It wouldn't be easy, but he'd do it.

The light supper was very civilized for such an eccentric household. Mrs Sanderson fed both her husbands while they chatted together about kitchens and infantile diabetes. Andrew, sitting opposite her, was not civilized. He removed a shoe and ran his foot up and down her legs. 'Stop it,' she said.

'What's he doing?' Joe asked.

'He's getting familiar under the table.'

Joe clouted his son rather gently across his head. 'Can't hit him any harder, love,' he said. 'Brain's scrambled enough as it is.'

Geoff studied his stepson. 'You always have to push it too far, don't you, Andrew?' He turned to Mary. 'His skeleton, George, gets put to bed every night. Andrew says standing up all the time is too stressful for the joints.'

Mary tried not to choke on her sandwich. No wonder her beloved-in-waiting was mad. The whole crowd was mad.

Emily sighed. 'All I wanted was the ordinary life.'

Mary laughed. 'Be grateful. The ordinary life can be tedious.' He was doing the foot-on-the-leg thing again. She awarded him one of her collection of dirty looks, but it didn't work. Nothing worked. Nothing would ever work, though there would be no inequality, not with this man. Underneath the brashness, a gentle soul resided.

The phone rang, and Emily went to answer it. When she returned, her face was grey, and she held out her arms to Joseph, the rejected husband turned best friend. He stood and walked into the offered embrace.

'I'm sorry, sweetheart,' Emily said. 'That was Betsy's sister. Betsy had a stroke while out shopping. She didn't make it, Joseph.'

Geoff joined them, and all three clung together.

'Daisy,' Joe sobbed. 'What will happen to her now, Em?'

'I don't care what we have to do,' Geoff said. 'We'll see she's catered for, Joe. Daisy belongs to all of us now.'

The foot-on-the-leg business stopped. A lone tear crawled down Andrew's cheek. 'My half-sister,' he explained to Mary. 'She needs constant care.'

So Mary and Andrew were left alone in the huge house while the others went to St Helens. He told her about Dad and how he had hated him. He told her about Marty Liptrott's suicide and the part he felt he had played in it. 'I was so damned rude and arrogant, Mary. He hanged himself, and the house set on fire because he'd left the chip pan bubbling away. Drunk, of course, but still a grieving human being.'

'So your mother found someone else because of your dad playing away?'

He shook his head sadly. 'No, nothing like that. Mother was assistant almoner at Bolton Royal. She and Geoff were like you and me – an accident. It was hard for me to understand the dynamics of their situation, because at first Dad was angry with Geoff. But it's impossible to stay angry with Geoff; he's such a genuine, decent bloke. And Mother never stopped loving Dad, but their relationship had shifted towards brother and sister before Geoff appeared. Now, they're a family.' He shrugged. 'I have two dads. I also have a handicapped half-sister who must be looked after. God, life can be hard.'

She took his hand. 'I'm here for you, Andrew.'

He told her about Mother's history, the marrying for land plan, her escape, her swift marriage to Dad, who had no land and no family. This ran into the plot he had concocted, his meeting with the grandparents, their joy at being reconciled with their daughter. 'And they all lived happily ever after,' he concluded. 'But it's no fairy tale,

Mary. Life still happens, as does death. Poor Betsy, poor Daisy. She is the most incredibly beautiful girl who walks and grunts, but she can't look after herself, of course. Betsy dedicated her whole life to her daughter, and I'm not surprised about the stroke, because she had a difficult time of it. Dad always took care of them financially, which was all he could do, really.'

'And I thought life down Scotland Road was stressful. Mam and Dad won a few bob on the pools and buggered off to Cornwall last year. They'd moved to Kirkby, and they were all right, but they love Cornwall. It's a tiny stone cottage in the countryside, just a few miles from the sea. They're happy, though they miss their kids. Six of us in a two-bedroom flat above the shop. Mam and Dad slept in the living room so that the girls could have one bedroom, while the boys had the other. Pam lived a few doors along in the flat above another shop. She's the one who put you in the kitchen. My best friend, is Pam.'

He offered to take her home, but she insisted on staying. 'I'm not leaving you to fret on your own, only I'm not sleeping with you.'

But they did sleep together. He buried his head in her upper body and, in darkness, told her all about Daisy, about his early assessment of Betsy having been wrong, about Dad and his genius with wood, about Stuart, about grandparents, about a house known as New Moon. He told her he loved her too much to break her rule about John, that she was his future and he would wait.

When he finally slept, a few more sobs made their escape, and she cradled his poor head, trying to stroke away the unhappiness. It was then that she realized that she had collected her first child, that this doctor and brilliant pianist, older than she was, more vulnerable than she had imagined, was about to become her much-loved responsibility. Mary remembered a lecture on psychology, where the tutor had said, 'When I see a young man with his girl, I see someone who has found his next mother. Much more than a mother, of course, but there to nurse the pain and bind the wounds.' It had sounded so daft at the time, but now the message seemed real and true.

She released him gently, made sure he remained asleep, and went to the bathroom. In the mirror, she saw an unkempt girl wearing a pyjama top that hung like a collapsed tent round her tiny frame. She also saw a fabulous bathroom. Earlier, she'd viewed his Sanderson kitchen, his massive living room, a spare room, a gigantic bedroom. 'We can live here,' she told the mirror before returning to look after him.

He woke. 'Where were you?'

'Bathroom. Go to sleep. I'll be here in the morning.'

And she was.

They separated the next day. Andrew drove Mary to Sefton Park, where she picked up her belongings, Pam, and Pam's belongings. He installed the two girls in his flat at Mother's house, while he went to live with Dad. Dad needed looking after. While Joe would be fed across the road at Emily's house, he drew the line at sleeping there, a decision of which Andrew approved. Joe had his pride, and he owned every right to that pride in whichever form he decided to exercise it.

Pam couldn't believe her luck. 'No rent?'

'No rent,' Mary repeated. 'We just have to feed ourselves and be supportive if we're needed.'

'It's lovely here, isn't it?'

'It is. We have a bedroom each, both bigger than the ones we had in Seffy Park.'

'You could both live here.'

'We might do that.'

Pam paused and gazed round the room. 'When?'

'When I say so,' Mary replied. 'Though I'll let him think it was his decision, of course. John first, Pam. I admit to sleeping with Andrew last night, but nothing happened. I have to tell John before anything does happen.'

'And I'll have to go back to Sefton Park and the three witches if you get married and live here.'

But Mary had plans for her friend, too, though this was not the time to illustrate the details. 'Put your stuff away, babe, then come and look at this Sanderson kitchen. He's left food for us, proper food, not beans on toast, and we have apple crumble for afters, made by his mum.'

That evening, Andrew dined with the two girls while his dad ate downstairs with Mother and Geoff. His list of 'good at' grew longer, as it now housed lamb with rosemary and real gravy laced with rum, as well as roast potatoes and crisp vegetables, all followed by crème caramel. The apple crumble would do for tomorrow, he advised them, as he had wanted to demonstrate his ability with a bain-marie, whatever that was.

They played Monopoly, and he changed the rules every five minutes, in his own favour, of course. His behaviour in the company of two lively Liverpool lasses was not appreciated, and he finished up on the floor, bestridden by two females who beat him mercilessly with cushions. He had needed some fun, because life with Dad promised to be grim until after the funeral and the settling of poor Daisy.

'Who's with her now?' Pam asked.

'Augustinian sisters, God bless them,' he said. 'In so far as we can tell, Daisy knows them, though she keeps looking round and making an extra-loud grunt. We think she's calling for her mother.'

'Heartbreaking,' Mary said.

'And she sits there playing with the same toys she's

had for about seven years. Not playing, not really. Just holding them. I feel so bloody useless. We all do.'

Pam leapt up and gave him a kiss on the cheek. 'You'll do for our Mary,' she said. 'You're a good lad. I'm off to bed now. Night-night.' And away she went.

Andrew and Mary sat on the sofa holding hands. Nothing needed saying. She leaned her head on his shoulder, and he stroked her hair. It was yet another of those forever moments she was beginning to treasure. Time lost meaning. They had always been here together, would always be like this, no beginning, no end, no clocks, no calendars. It was just as Andrew had said; it had been designed before their births, and they must embrace the gift.

'I have to go and look after him, darling. He won't sleep here. It's the only rule he has where Mother and Geoff are concerned.'

'OK.'

'Are you sure you'll be all right?' he asked.

'I'm a big girl, Drew.'

'That's it – that's my name. And you're not a big girl. I could eat you in two bites.'

'I sting.'

'So do I,' he promised. 'But I always kiss it better.'

The family went as a whole to support Joe through poor Betsy's funeral. Mary was working as usual, but Andrew was determined to be with Dad, as were Emily and Geoff. Betsy's sister Elsie accompanied them, though her husband, not the most sociable of folk, stayed behind to run their business. With paying guests staying at the pub, someone had to keep the place ticking over.

So just one funeral car followed the hearse to Bolton. As they neared their destination, Emily and Andrew inhaled sharply at the first sight of their beloved moors. Joe hardly noticed, as he was too busy going through his list of should-haves. He should have employed people to relieve Betsy for at least a few hours each day, could have sent more money, ought to have been more supportive and more frequently involved on a personal basis.

His gratitude to the Augustinian sisterhood knew no bounds, and he had already made a sizeable contribution to their coffers. At this very moment, two nuns were with Daisy, while two more were trekking about to find a decent place for the child.

Emily hung on to his hand. 'She'll be taken care of, sweetheart.'

'We'll all make sure of that,' Geoff added.

It occurred to Andrew yet again that this unconventional family worked better than many ordinary marriages. Since their arrival in Mother's Rodney Street properties, Dad and Geoff had grown close, and the latter never turned a hair when Emily fussed over her very best friend, the man to whom she remained legally wed. They were courageous people leaving their mark on a brave new world that wasn't quite ready for their eccentricity, and Andrew felt that they were making no small contribution towards a more tolerant society.

Betsy had left a letter for her sister.

Dear Elsie

I know that my Daisy is not expected to live till she's grown up, but I wonder what will happen to her if I pop my clogs first. If I do, go straight to Joe. I want to be buried at home with Marty. I know he was handy when it came to a fight, but he died as my husband, and I registered Daisy as his, born after his death. There'll be room for Daisy in the same grave when the time comes.

*The sisters will mind her till Joe finds a place good
enough for her. All she needs is kindness, her soft toys
and the music I collected for her. On telly, she likes
the children's programmes and cartoons. She doesn't
always look at the screen, but she listens. She wants
things repetitive and familiar. If one of her records
gets scratched, it has to be replaced or she has a
tantrum.*

*I tried my best, Elsie. I got her walking, but that
was it. Apart from a special noise when she wants
me, it's just that grunting business all the time. She'll
want to keep her wooden jigsaws with the big pieces.
Sometimes, not very often, she picks a piece and sticks
it near the right place, and that's the closest I got to
making her concentrate.*

*Joe and Andrew will visit her, and I hope you will.
But she doesn't have to stay in St Helens, because
Liverpool's not far and Joe's there. She needs sedating
to go on a car journey, or she might take another fit,
and she needs help with walking after a fit. Tell them
not to let her hair get knotted, because she screams
when it's brushed. She likes a bath. She'd live in the
bath if she could, like a little mermaid.*

*Well, our Else, if you're reading this, I've gone.
I've gone to make sure heaven's good enough for my
angel. Joe, when Elsie reads you this letter, please
remember I haven't regretted for one minute having
our Daisy. It's been hard work and I've been tired,
but she's my life and I love her to bits.*

*Daisy, I'll see you when Peter opens the gate to let
you in.*

Joe dried his eyes. Betsy, once upon a time a scruffy
mare, had turned out to be a perfect mother. 'I wish I'd
done more, Em.'

'We all feel like that when someone dies, Joseph. Here we are, St Augustine's. This has to be done.' She squeezed his hand. 'Come on.'

'I'm coming, I'm coming.'

Stuart Abbot, who was managing to make his name without a degree, was there with his parents, and they completed the tiny congregation. The vicar, who had never met Betsy, had taken the trouble to speak to those who had known her, so there was enough said to remind the assembled few about Betsy's virtues as a mother and a carer.

She was interred in her husband's grave at Heaton Cemetery, which was nicer than Tonge, as it was further from the centre of town. Andrew, Joe, Geoff and Emily, who had discussed the terminus of life, had all chosen cremation for themselves. Seeing Betsy's wooden box being lowered into a subterranean cavern served only to strengthen their determination not to become part of the earth's crust.

They repaired to the Abbot house behind their shop, which was about to be sold. With one novel and several radio plays under his belt, Stuart's first priority was to get his parents out of town to somewhere fresher in the shape of a brand new bungalow in Harwood. He lived at New Moon, which property belonged to Andrew. Instead of paying rent, he had financed upgrading work, always consulting his lifelong friend before instigating a project.

Andrew cornered him as soon as he found the opportunity. 'I'm getting married,' he said. 'And you have to be my best man.'

'Who is she?'

'The love of my life, Stuart.'

A few seconds passed. 'So when did you meet her?'

Andrew grinned. 'Before I was born and after I died.

About four or five weeks ago. I've been celibate ever since, because she has to rid herself of a fiancé.'

'Can't you ever do anything normally?'

'No. I don't do normal, and neither does she.'

Stuart tried not to laugh. Laughing among sausage rolls and curling sandwiches at a funeral tea seemed inappropriate. 'Are you sure about her?'

'Oh, yes. Absolutely.'

'And she's sure?'

'Naturally.'

'So . . . when?'

'Whenever, so get writing a speech. Mary and I will live in my flat at Mother's house, and Pam can live across the road above Dad. She'll have somebody with her. Mary and Pam are like us, friends since childhood, now engaged to a pair of brothers in the Merchant Navy. It was all planned until I happened along. Their ship docks soon, so I'll let you know when the coast is clear. Or should I say when the coast isn't clear?'

'You're mad.'

'Yes, and happily so.'

'Describe her.'

'No. You come and meet her, judge for yourself. She has a pretty friend if you're interested.'

'Sorry. I'm still a queer.'

'Don't use that word. You're one of the least queer folk I know. Medical students beat you into a cocked hat. Some were sent down for having a party in the morgue. The attendant got the sack, too. *That's* queer. I never in my life met so many weird people gathered together in one place.'

'Not even at school?'

Andrew thought about that. 'Some of the teachers were odd.'

'And at university?'

'Oh, they're all peculiar. Clever-peculiar, but none the less . . .' He shrugged. 'Come to think, doctors are rather unpredictable.'

'There you go, then. You're nearly one of them.'

'But the daftest of all are writers, Stu.'

They were five years old again. And the sandwiches continued to curl.

Thirteen

Some people refused to accept defeat gracefully, as Andrew found out to his cost when John and Michael Webster, home from their travels, tried to beat the living daylights out of him. Having never been attacked before, he was more frightened by his own automatic reaction than he was by this pair of ocean-toughened thugs.

Andrew had never trained or boxed or played team games. There'd been the compulsory stuff at school, but he hadn't done much since apart from a bit of cycling and the occasional lengthy walk. His next piece of heart-quickening activity would probably take place in bed with Mary, and that would be no marathon, would it? Oh, no, loving her would never be a chore...

He was strolling homeward up Rodney Street after a modern jazz session in student digs off Mount Pleasant, when he was accosted from behind, sworn at, spat upon, and kicked in the ribs, the nose and the skull. While the two maritime heroes took a break from their labours, Andrew decided to play comatose. Blood poured from his nose, forming a large pool blackened by moonlight. They possibly thought he was dead, and he was more than happy to allow them to continue mistaken. His ribs hurt like hell and his nose imitated Niagara, but his skull seemed to have survived the onslaught without too much damage.

'Look at all that blood. We've cracked his skull,' said

one of the charmers, panic lifting his tone. 'You shouldn't kick people in the head. If they have a thin bit of bone, it goes into their brain and kills them. You could get done for murder, and I'm telling you now, you can swing on your own because I never done that.'

'Calm down, Mike. He'll live, worse luck. Where the bloody hell do you think you're going?' The rejected fiancé stood and watched helplessly while his brother abandoned him. 'Come back now, you rotten coward. Tell you what, you keep going in that direction, and I'll give you a clout later. I'm serious, lad. Come here this minute.'

But brother Mike continued to flee the scene at speed.

John Webster turned away from his escaping sibling to find a vertical, bloodied, tall and well-built man facing him. He curled and raised his fists, but was too slow for Andrew Sanderson. The student doctor who had stolen Mary smashed him in the face, and as he fell he felt a weighty size ten shoe banging forcefully against his genitals. Too winded to call again for his brother, the sailor rolled into a fetal position in an effort to preserve what, if anything, remained of his manhood. He retched and brought up several pints of ale that had tasted a lot better on their way down.

Andrew stood back and frowned. For the first time ever, he had hit someone deliberately. The realization did not please him, because he seemed to remember feeling momentary triumph about what he'd done. There was absolutely no excuse for such behaviour, though what other course of action might he have taken? He flexed his fingers to convince himself that there were no breaks in the digits. The man on the ground groaned. This curled-up wreck was Mary's ex–intended. What a mess.

With blood still dripping from his nose, Andrew looked down at his handiwork. He wasn't designed for such behaviour, but when push came to shove it was every man for himself. The two lunatics could have killed him, and Andrew had too much to live for. She was worth the pain. To him, she was more valuable than anything or anyone on earth.

Alerted by the noise Mary and Pam arrived, both breathless. They'd been enjoying a game of dominoes with Joseph, helping to keep his mind occupied by something other than poor Daisy while his son played jazz down the road. 'Oh, God,' Mary said quietly. 'I think we need an ambulance.'

'I'll be all right,' John groaned. 'Just give me a few minutes and I'll be on me feet.'

'The ambulance won't be for you,' Pam snapped. 'I wouldn't stop a bloody muck cart for you. The ambulance is for Dr Sanderson.' She awarded John another kick, this time on his arm. 'I saw what happened. We both saw, me and Mary. So you can tell your Mike to take his sodding aquamarine and shove it up his arse. I'm not marrying him, and she's not marrying you.'

Mary was holding on to her man. 'Sorry about that, Drew. Pam has a wonderful way with words, very Beatrix Potter. It's what comes of mixing with riff-raff like this. Come on, let's get you sorted, baby. You look like the wreck of the *Hesperus*. I'm sorry, so sorry.'

'Just a minute.' Andrew bent over his assailant. 'Only as a matter of interest, what made you believe that kicking shit out of me would persuade Mary to take you back? Are you so devoid of intellect that you still fight like rabid dogs? She doesn't want you, doesn't need you, doesn't love you, and now she doesn't even care what happens to you. My solicitor will be in touch with both you and your brother.' He glanced round; several doors had opened. 'Look at all the witnesses, bird brain. Set one foot in Rodney Street again, and you'll be looking at life through bars. And I don't mean these railings.'

Joe arrived in shirtsleeves, best tartan braces on show. 'Did this bugger bust your nose, Andrew? Let me at him, damned animal. He'll be sorry he was born when I've done with—'

'I've dealt with him, Dad, so don't panic. Just drive me to get checked out, will you? My nose isn't broken, but I need looking at for ribs and perhaps for concussion, though I think I'm OK. Mary, don't cry. I can't carry you this time. Take her in to Mother, Pam. This object can crawl away under its own steam. Fortunately, it's in dark clothing. With any luck, it'll be run over.' These words had the desired effect, as John Webster edged his way through vomit to the safety of the pavement.

'I'm coming with you,' Mary said in a tone that would brook no argument.

After making sure that Pam was safely inside Emily's house, Joe helped his son and Mary into the rear seat of his car. Andrew's nose seemed to have slowed down, so that was a small blessing. Joe was pleased for little Mary. She was better off, because Andrew knew how to behave properly, which was more than might be said for her previous boyfriend.

As they made their way to the hospital, Andrew whispered innocently to his inamorata, 'I take it that you are no longer engaged to be married to that . . . that fragrant gentleman?'

'If your ribs weren't hurt, they'd get my elbow.'

He nodded, a serious expression on his face. 'Did you give back the ring? Because we could save some money if we used it again to—'

'No, I'm not wearing it ever.'

'So I have to—'

'Yes, you do.'

He laughed, but pain in the ribs soon put a stop to that.

Andrew was X-rayed, poked, prodded, questioned and irritated. So this was the receiving end? He decided that he did not have concussion, was not prepared to discuss further the possibility of concussion, nor did he want the police, a bed, another X-ray or a cup of the dishwater that was passed off as hospital tea. 'You shouldn't be offering that muck to somebody who may be concussed. Make your mind up.'

He thanked them for strapping him up, though he was of the opinion that ribs should be left alone unless a lung was pierced, thanked them for stopping the nosebleed, for winning the war, for inventing penicillin and for allowing him to go home at last.

'We didn't say you could go home,' said the amused ward sister. 'We always keep a head injury for a few hours. It's hospital policy, Dr Sanderson. You surely know that after all your training.'

'They're often the worst patients,' Mary commented. 'I never yet came across a doctor with the ability to be patient or to be *a* patient. I'll accept responsibility for the child. Because that's what he is under all this bluster.'

Andrew awarded Mary a withering glance, though she withered not at all.

'Take him away, then,' said the ward sister. 'Because I've had enough of him – how on God's good earth do you cope? He's a very argumentative young man.'

'I don't cope. I'm still serving my apprenticeship. Come on, you.'

Joseph giggled to himself on the way home. These two in the back of his car would never be short of work, because they could go on the halls as a comedy duo if medicine didn't suit. There was something so right about them. 'Mary?' he asked. 'How did you come to be engaged to such a wally?'

'I was young and foolish,' she replied. 'And John was never violent; neither of them was. Now I'm the foolish one again.'

'She's marrying me, so that's how foolish she is,' Andrew said. 'As soon as she can get her family together, we'll be wed. Her parents emigrated to Cornwall, you see.' He touched Mary's hand. 'Wait till you see the ring. You may not come across another like it ever, because it's a one-off, very different. You'll be the talk of Liverpool, believe me.'

Oh, heck. What had he done now? 'What have you done, Drew? Is it a skull and crossbones or a dragon's head?'

'Wait and see. I'm too busy feeling pain.'

'Get used to it if you're marrying me.'

'Promises, promises,' he replied.

An anxious Emily stood on her doorstep. How was he, why hadn't she been told, why had she been forced to wait till Pam arrived? 'I came out, and you'd gone – I could see your car disappearing round the corner. We've been worried sick. Are you all right, Andrew?'

'As long as nobody touches me, I'll be fine. Mary's ex managed to walk away, I see.' He looked at his soon-to-be fiancée. 'Come upstairs and soothe my fevered brow, woman.'

Emily led Joe inside. 'I'll make you a toddy. How's Daisy, Joseph?'

'Exactly as she always was, Em. I don't think she has much of a memory. She's got Bunny and Teddy and all the others, and the home staff look after her very well. The nuns are keeping an eye on her, too.' He followed his wife into the morning room where Geoff was setting up the chessboard. 'That's me in for another hammering,' Joe said before sitting across the table from his opponent.

They were all so good to him, all concerned for his welfare and for Daisy.

Upstairs, Andrew led Mary into his bedroom, which was currently hers. He asked her to peel back a beautiful Hamadan rug and take up a floorboard. She complied, and lifted out a box.

'Right,' he said. 'First, what the hell were you doing engaged to that twit when there were brilliant men like me in the world?'

'Ooh, get you, Mr Perfect. They saved our lives down the scaldy when we were about ten.' She had to explain the scaldy, the sugar works and its warm effluent. 'I started to drown through cramp, and Pam nearly drowned trying to save me. John and Mike dragged us out and looked after us for years after that. We drifted into it when we were sixteen. It was just the next step so that Pam and I could be together for always.'

'So you're lesbian?'

She bared her teeth. 'Do you want another thump?'

'Er . . . may I take your kind offer under consideration? Give me the box.'

She handed it to him, her heart in overdrive, because she knew what was in it, but continued to wonder what the heck he'd done to ensure that her ring would be different from anything else in the world. Ah, here came the dramatics. He was such a ham at times like this.

'Don't hug me,' he said.

'I won't hug you.'

'Don't kiss me. My nose is sore.'

'I won't.'

Like a man of at least seventy, he steadied his feeble person by placing a hand on his bed while lowering himself on to one knee. He opened the box with his teeth. 'And don't laugh.'

'I won't laugh.' Hysterical, she turned her back on him.

'You're laughing.'

'I'm not.'

'Your back's shaking. And I am not proposing to your bum.'

Mary managed to calm down, but she couldn't look at him.

'On this solemn and important occasion,' he began, 'I must say before we go any further—'

She ran into the bathroom and slammed the door while her almost-fiancé banged the box lid closed.

Andrew stood up with no difficulty and sat on the bed. They had just made another time to remember, a gem that would shine forever like Great-gran's jewellery. He opened the box again. The engagement ring was an ellipse crammed with small, perfect white diamonds. A wedding ring in a second slot was shaped to cradle the ellipse. Mary was going to love this because it was not only beautiful, it was also unusual and quirky, as was she.

Mary emerged, still dabbing at her face with a flannel. 'Well? Get on with it. I've rearranged myself and altered my attitude.'

'You have done no such thing. Here I am, mortally wounded, and you think it's hilarious. So I'm sulking. I'm good at sulking.'

'Ah, yet another talent. Shall I go home, then?'

'This is your home. Pam can move across the street over Dad's house once we're married. Is there someone she'd share with?'

'I suppose so. Still sulking?'

'Oh, yes. I forgot.' He folded his arms, cringed, and unfolded them. 'I was hoping to bed you tonight, young lady. However, under the circumstances, I have to allow you to tether me blind. While mixing metaphors, I might as well say we're jumping in without testing the water, aren't we?'

She nodded. 'You may be no good at it.'

'I love you, Miss Collins.'

'And I love you, Dr Sanderson.'

He offered the box and watched her face while she became a delighted child. The jewellery, recently cleaned, was splendid without being garish. 'This wedding ring's made to fit round the shape of the engagement one,' she cried, clapping her hands. 'No one else will have anything like this, you're right.'

'It's an heirloom. *Semper fidelis* is engraved in the wedding band.'

'Thank you, thank you.' She stopped jigging about. 'Oh, you missed a bit out. The marrying bit.'

'Will you?' he asked.

She considered the question. 'OK. Just this once, though.'

And that was it. In the interest of ribs and nose, no hugging, no kissing, no cuddles. Sometimes, a moment became special and memorable because it was wrong, because it didn't live up to expectations. For many years, the picture of Mary delighting over Great-grandmother's rings was set in a frame in Andrew's memory. Occasionally, he would take it out, rub it clean with his mind's eye and relive the joy of that precious time.

So, in the space of a few hours, Andrew had been battered, fought back, sorted out a hospital department's attitude to suspected concussion, had his ribs strapped, become engaged to a beautiful woman and learned to play the piano in modern jazz tempo. It was one of the best nights of his life. And Mary was top of the bill. Always.

*

Andrew went back to Dad's to nurse his wounds. He visited Mary and Pam every day, but grew determined to save lovemaking until the wedding night. Why? He had no bloody idea, but he'd hung on this far and could manage the extra mile. There was stuff going on behind his back – dresses, hair ornaments, shoes – all the items he wasn't allowed to see because of bad luck. Bad luck? He'd had his share already with the Webster boys.

He knocked on the door of his own flat in Mother's house, unable to walk in, since the bolts were on. It should be easy to get annoyed, yet he couldn't, no matter how hard he tried. There was something lovable about Pam, too. She was another good nurse, a pleasant girl with humour and no boyfriend, but Andrew had plans for her. Stuart was going to be best man, of course, but a few young doctors would be attending, including one shy lad who needed a Pam to bring him out of himself.

The door opened a few inches, and a green face inserted itself in the gap. 'You can't come in. We're green.'

He pressed a hand to his chest. 'Thank God for that; I thought I was haunted. Are you my Mary or Mary's Pam?'

'No, I'm the ghost of quarter to twelve.'

He had to ask, couldn't resist. 'Why quarter to?'

'Cos I'm not all there. I mustn't be all there, letting Mary spread this mess all over me gob.'

Andrew felt he deserved that reply for taking the bait. 'May I come in, Pam? It's a bit of a bugger when a man can't get into his own place.'

Pam shouted over her shoulder. 'It's him. Can he come in?'

'Not while I'm green.'

'She says not while–' She suddenly found herself pushed to one side.

Andrew strode in, determined to be bold. He said a quick hello to George, then sat in his own living room on

314

his own favourite chair after tossing aside a bridal magazine that was nothing at all to do with him. Women, in his opinion, made far too much fuss about this sort of thing. A second green-faced woman passed through. 'Hello, love of my life,' he said. 'May I have the ring back? I didn't know I was marrying a Martian.'

'Shut up, you,' was all he got in return.

He'd show her who was boss. In a few days, she would be chained to the sink or to a bed, no choice in the matter. Mary had bought new sheets, silk ones. They'd probably need to stick together just to stay warm in those slippery, shiny things. He wondered idly why the girls had turned green, but guessed it was something to do with beauty. 'How often do you go green?' he shouted. 'And can you give me adequate warning in future then I can take my pleasure elsewhere?'

She reappeared, back in the pink, but bearing weapons. She waved a loofah and a brush for scrubbing backs. 'Where would you like me to shove these?' she asked sweetly. 'Think carefully before naming an orifice.'

'In my bathroom.'

'Come on, then.' She led him by the hand, locked the bathroom door and undressed him. She studied his fading bruises, said he'd live and told him to get in the bath. 'Fine figure of a man,' she said before beginning his ablutions. 'Yes, very promising, Dr Sanderson. Though so far, a promise is the best I've been given. No action whatsoever.'

He hadn't been bathed by a woman since childhood. 'I believe I couldn't live without you, Mary.'

'You could. You might have to one day.'

He shivered. Did someone just walk on his grave? Or hers? *Dear God, let it be mine.* He stood and allowed her to dry him. She was meticulous but gentle, so tender, so loving. 'I'm a lucky man,' he whispered.

'From my point of view, I'm the fortunate one,' she

replied. 'You're just about perfect except for the bruises. They've nearly gone, but I was responsible for those.'

'No, you weren't. Life at sea seems to change some people, though they must have allowed the change to happen. Where's Pam?'

'In her room. I told her to go away. Still want to wait till Saturday, then?'

'No. But I shall. It will be special.'

'Dr Romantic. I'll make a drink, then you can go back to Joe's.'

'Oh no. I'm sleeping with you. Dad's OK. I'll see you in bed.'

It wasn't easy this time. Compromises were reached, possibilities explored, while sighs and giggles abounded. 'We are the forever children,' he told her. 'We go hand in hand. I forget the name of the poet.'

'Get your toenails cut,' she ordered.

'No, that wasn't his name. I think it was Wilfred Owen.'

'Will we be happy, Drew?'

'We have to be. Go to sleep.'

Morning brought a different story altogether. Mary didn't want to wait. As far as she was concerned, people should have a few trial runs before embarking on the marathon named marriage. Practical as ever, she took charge. 'Don't worry about this,' she told him sweetly when he opened an eye. 'I won't hurt you. Just lie back, close your eyes and think of England.'

The words 'role' and 'reversal' shot through his sleepy brain. It was already too late; she was taking advantage of him, and she was doing a fair job. Fair became good, good became excellent, excellent became amazing. This small, naked woman was a force he would never tame. Not once did she lose eye contact with him. Oh yes, she meant what she was doing, all right.

'There,' she said when the deed was done. 'I can cross that off my "to do" list. Your mother's icing the cake, Pam's going to see the florist and Stuart will mind my wedding ring, the sex was OK—' She burst out laughing. 'That was lovely, baby.'

'Yes, it was,' he agreed. 'But I thought you were a lady.'

The laughter stopped and became a frown. 'No. I'm a woman. I was born in a cruddy little flat over a chandlery shop on Scottie Road. I have three brothers and two sisters, and nobody knows where they are, because they buggered off down south when I was young. My mam and dad were tired, so when they won the pools I sent them off to live somewhere a bit warmer. The others don't know about the win, or they'd have hung around like bad smells till they got their hands on that bit of money. We never had much, Mam, Dad and I, but they looked after me, Drew. They're so proud of their little girl going in for nursing. But the word "lady" actually annoys me. I'm a woman. A lady's a boring bugger in a hat.'

'You certainly are a woman. Shall we try for an encore?'

'Yes, please. But get those bloody toenails cut before Saturday.' She stood up and pulled on a robe. 'Tea and toast first, have to keep your strength up. Where are your clippers?'

'Top drawer.'

'I'll cut them myself in a minute. I don't fancy scratches on my legs.'

Andrew lay with hands clasped behind his head and stared at the ceiling. She was incredible. He'd had sex before, but he'd never made love. Love made the difference, then, just as he'd expected. Did he regret what had happened this morning? No. She had wanted closeness, so she had instigated it. One of the most lovable qualities in Mary was honesty; another was her refusal to be shy, and she didn't mind taking the lead. He looked forward to living under her dictatorship. As for her parents, they were right to be proud of her.

She came back with toast, tea, honey and marmalade. 'Eat,' she ordered. 'Why are you staring at me?'

He smiled. 'I suspected that you were wonderful, and I do love to be right. Ouch! That's no way to treat the *Daily Telegraph*, or my head.'

They ate, did his pedicure, made love, washed, dressed, and went to work. It was a brilliant day. Mary discovered that she'd come out top in the exams and that she was to receive an award, a medal of some kind left by a long-dead hospital matron. Andrew was approached by Mr Compton-Gore, who was just about the best orthopaedic surgeon for many a mile. At last, he was on the team and on his way to making George's existence more meaningful. Bones. He was going to be a mender, a reshaper, a carpenter.

Andrew fell in love immediately with his precious girl's parents. The first thing they asked of him was a run to Scotland Road where they clung together while staring at their old shop. They had raised six children here and, because of the business, they'd been too worn out to keep track of the five older ones. Mary, their little afterthought, was the only one who had turned out to be decent. 'We had more time for her, you see,' they said, speaking in turn like a well-rehearsed act. 'We got help in the shop. Mary was one on her own, always bright and clever, though she was a little monkey when she had a cob on. We just feel we should have made time for the rest of the kids when they were young.'

'It's not easy,' Andrew said.

'No,' they chimed together.

'You did your best,' Andrew told them. 'With six stomachs to fill, you had to work long hours.' But he could tell that Enid and Bert Collins would always blame themselves, and that saddened him.

He left them there to explore the old neighbourhood, because he wanted to get to a lecture. There was more planning going on. Groups of colleagues stopped talking whenever he was within earshot, so he knew that a plot was being concocted. There was to be no stag night, as half were working or on call, and they were probably targeting the wedding day, when most would be available. Fortunately, the bride had a sense of humour, as did her bridesmaid, though Andrew wouldn't be surprised if Pam clouted a few heads.

He found out no more. Even Tim, often called Timid, was giving away little or nothing. 'I want you to look after Pam, Mary's bridesmaid. She recently separated from her boyfriend, so she'll value your company.'

Tim blushed.

Andrew hoped the poor lad wouldn't go in for obs and gynae, as he would probably be permanently pink if he did. Pam was exactly what Timid needed, though she might just frighten him to death long before any relationship got the chance to develop. Oh well, never mind. Andrew was a bit oversized to play Cupid anyway.

This was his last night as a free man. He and Stuart were to stay at Dad's, while Mary, Mary's parents, Andrew's grandparents and Pam were across the road at Mother's. It gave the two younger men the chance to catch up, as Andrew was too busy in hospitals to visit Bolton, while Stuart led the life of a typical writer, shut away for most of the time, buried in his work, unaware of life outside his narrow sphere. 'So, you stood still long enough for a woman to catch you, eh?'

'I caught her.' And he reminded his friend and best

man of the saga of the Beatles, the odd courtship, the attack by the ousted sailor.

'Serious, then.'

'Of course it's serious. I wouldn't be marrying her if it wasn't. Though I suppose some people would view the relationship as lightweight, because we laugh a lot and pull each other to bits. But I haven't wanted or needed anyone except her since that day in Mathew Street.' He raised his glass. 'To the Beatles.'

'The Beatles and all who queue to scream and don't listen to them.'

'And how's life with you?' Andrew asked.

Stuart shrugged. 'I don't really have a life. I live vicariously through my characters. I mean, where do I go to meet people? Am I supposed to stand outside the Swan Inn with a notice round my neck – *I'm queer, anybody interested?*'

'Oh, Stuart, use your loaf. Get to Manchester or Liverpool, do a pub crawl without getting blotto, and talk to people. You'll know him when you meet him.'

'Just stop it. All that gets you is a quick grope – might as well go cottaging and be arrested. The law will change – it has to – but I could be fifty by then. How far did Wolfenden get?'

'Far enough to make intelligent people think. It's brains, not knee-jerk reaction, that will bring a bit of sanity into the arena. Anyway, you're supposed to be keeping me cheerful.' A thought occurred. 'When they make your film, you'll meet all kinds of creative people.'

'Oh, shut up and get the bloody dominoes out, Andy. It's your big day tomorrow, and I'm happy for you. You know what I really envy? That you get to be a dad one day.'

Andrew scattered dominoes. 'I've scarcely thought about that. I suppose we will have kids at some stage, but for now she's all I want. Can't imagine life without her. Within an hour of meeting her, I knew. And that's how it'll be for you, mate. The only difference is gender, no kids, and don't get caught while the bloody government's still out at lunch.'

Joe entered. 'Dominoes? Hutch up and make room for an expert. You amateurs might as well lie down and play dead.'

Joe was right. He beat them time after time, and was accused of cheating. During the fifth game, Joe responded to a knock at the door.

'Hello,' the two men heard him saying. 'This way.'

And in they came. Immediately, Andrew could tell that Dad and Stuart knew about the deadly plot, since they helped to hold him down while the incomers, all in white coats, bandaged him to the point of mummification. He was strapped to a stretcher and bundled into an ancient ambulance. The curtains in his other living room over Mother's house twitched. Mary was in on it. They were all in on it. Somebody would pay for this.

The pubs, too, must have been made aware. In each one, the medical perpetrators, all bedecked with stethoscopes, placed a coffin in a corner and stood Andrew in it. He was fed drinks via a plastic straw poked through bandages and, as he spat out most of the alcohol, the face, neck and chest areas were soon saturated.

Eventually, he was released. Dad and Stuart unravelled him while the white-coated cowards picked up their coffin, dashed outside and drove off in the ambulance. 'Dad, you will suffer for this,' Andrew promised.

Stuart smiled broadly. 'I got Tim's phone number,' he said.

Andrew, feeling foolish, blinked. It was supposed to be Pam and Tim, not Stuart and Tim. Mind, they all deserved to be confused after what they'd put the groom through, so he kept his mouth shut. Whatever happened tomorrow, they all bloody well deserved it. Yet he suddenly realized that he'd quite enjoyed being a mummy. A mummy got to observe life through a gap in bandages; a mummy didn't need to do much. Stuart wanted to be a daddy, but— Inwardly, he told himself to shut up, because Stuart's situation wasn't funny.

A thought occurred to Andrew. 'Where the hell are we?'

'Your carriage awaits,' Joe said.

It did. Two funereal black horses with plumes waited outside the pub. Regulars, definitely under instruction, covered Andrew, Stuart and Joe in confetti. The black-hatted driver took no notice whatsoever while his three multi-coloured passengers climbed aboard. Passers-by laughed. There was more to this than met the three men's eyes. Andrew asked the driver to wait, climbed down, and walked to the rear of the vehicle. *CONDEMNED MAN ON WAY TO WEDLOCK* the sign said.

'Oh well, true enough,' he said before returning to his seat.

Wherever they'd been abandoned was some distance from Rodney Street. They were driven past the Liver Building and right through Liverpool's centre while crowds of Friday-night revellers pointed and laughed. Andrew, who had decided to be regal, waved a hand at his various audiences. Faculty of Medicine? It was more like a training ground for clowns.

At last, they arrived in Rodney Street. Curtains at all levels moved in Mother's house. He imagined Mary and Pam in cahoots with the lunatics who had kidnapped him, the lot of them in a huddle in a canteen planning the stag night that wasn't supposed to happen. After climbing down, he made a Shakespearean bow in the middle of the road. Now she would know that he'd guessed who was at the back of this plot. How would he punish her? Bandages? No. He'd bide his time and get her when she felt safe.

Joe put away the dominoes. 'Well, lad, they got you good and proper.'

'They did. But I'm the one attached to a consultant already. They'll be lucky if they get to wash pots in the canteen. Anyone for brandy?'

Joe went to bed, leaving the two old pals together.

'We call him Timid,' Andrew said.

'He's not. I've invited him to New Moon, if that's all right with you.'

'Of course.' He said nothing about Pam and the plan he'd arranged for her and Tim to be thrown together at the wedding party.

'He's a decent bloke,' Stuart said.

'He is. Very shy, though. As far as I know, he's going to train for general practice. Is he the one?'

Stuart doubted it, and said so. 'Like you so-called normal folk, we have to kiss a few frogs before we meet our prince. You made a lovely mummy, by the way.'

'So pleased.' The groom drained his brandy globe. 'Right, time for bed, old chap. You're in the spare room up in the gods.'

Stuart stood up. 'Are you nervous?'

'No. Tomorrow's the first day of my real life. But she'll be punished. If I have to wait a month, I'll make her pay. She was at the back of tonight.'

'Are you sure?'

'Oh yes. It definitely had her golden touch.'

The golden touch was very clearly in evidence on the wedding day. Mary's dress, as simple and unadorned as most of her wardrobe, was pale gold, while her hair was bound close to her head in a plait encircling her skull, with the same pale gold material threaded through to form the edge of this Juliet cap-style of hairdo. Escaping tendrils made her look angelic. She was not angelic, Andrew reminded himself.

Pam, blonde and in a much darker gold, was also stunning. All flowers were white with green foliage, and everyone in the register office inhaled sharply when they saw Mary on her father's arm, Pam close behind. No one could deny that these two young women looked beautiful despite the absence of buttons, bows and lace.

'She has good taste,' Emily whispered to Geoff.

Enid, on the bride's side of the room, wiped away a tear. Her little girl was gorgeous, and she was marrying a lovely man, a doctor who was going to be a surgeon. Enid's cup ran over, so Bert passed her his handkerchief. 'Here, love, don't spoil your make-up.'

Andrew reached out his hand. 'Hello, beautiful,' he whispered.

The registrar went through the rigmarole, the happy couple said their bit, and it was over. They walked out to a guard of honour consisting of last night's miscreants, who made a corridor of plastic femurs under which man and wife had to walk. As they stepped forward, the femur-bearers sang, 'Dem bones, dem bones, dem dry bones.'

Once all the photographs were done and Mary had thrown her bouquet, the party repaired to Rodney Street, since they had two houses to choose from, and the wedding had been kept small. Andrew noticed Pam hanging round near Tim, who was hanging round near Stuart, but he said nothing.

'How was your stag night?' Mary asked, a layer of innocence coating the words.

'What?'

'I asked about your stag night.'

He pondered. 'I didn't have one. You knew I wasn't having one.'

She looked at her feet. 'Oh. I thought I saw you going out.'

'And you saw me coming back. I even bowed to the gallery.'

'So you did have a stag night?'

'No. I was kidnapped, mummified, manhandled, half drowned in beer, placed in a coffin and brought home in the nearest thing to a hearse I ever saw. For all of the above, you will be punished.'

The best man rattled a spoon in an empty glass. 'Order in court,' he shouted.

Finger foods were put down or eaten hastily.

Stuart cleared his throat. 'Will the accused join me here? Andrew and Mary? Thank you.' He placed them in chairs and stood between them. 'I have known Andrew since we were three years old, and he's been a very good friend. He paid me to say that, but he didn't pay me enough. He was OK, I suppose.'

Andrew picked up his chair, walked round the best man and sat with Mary. 'I'm on her side,' he said.

Stuart shook his head sadly. 'After what she organized last night, I was opening divorce proceedings here. So you're standing by her?'

'Sitting, actually.'

Stuart made notes. 'Signs of mental impairment,' he quoted. 'There was a plan, so I am told, to put Andrew on the Isle of Man ferry and abandon him to the vagaries of the Irish Sea. Fortunately, the ferry was not in dock, though this young woman stands – sits – in dock accused of a heinous crime against the bridegroom, Andrew Winston Sanderson.'

'I am not Winston,' Andrew shouted.

'For the duration of this flaming speech, you are what I say you are. In so far as Mary Florence Nightingale Collins of no fixed abode did take it upon herself to have Andrew Winston Sanderson kidnapped, contained in a coffin and paraded through the streets of Liverpool, I put it to you, ladies and gentlemen, that she is unfit to be his wife.'

Mary stood up; Andrew pulled her back into the chair. 'Behave yourself,' he said.

'I have access to poisons,' she yelled.

Another note was made. Stuart read aloud, 'Threats against my bodily integrity have been made by the bride.'

It was all downhill from there. Whatever Stuart said, the bride or the groom topped it. Accusations and counter-accusations abounded, and the best man's speech ended when the groom shoved a large vol au vent in Stuart's mouth.

He spoke to the assembly. 'This has been my best wedding so far. I thank Pam for getting my wife to the register office sober, and Stuart for being the worst best man in history. To my colleagues I say wait till you need a bone mending, because you'll get no help from me.

'Mother and Dad, thanks for having me. Enid and Bert, thanks for having Mary, and does she come with instructions and a guarantee? Grandma and Grandpa, you know we all love you. I thank my wife for marrying me, my stepfather for helping me with my studies and being a good bloke, and I can't finish without warning you all about playing dominoes with Joe, my dad. He cheats.

'Mary and I are off to honeymoon in Cornwall while her parents stay here for a few days. Thank you all for coming; we're going.' He lifted Mary and carried her out of the room. 'You are in so much trouble,' he whispered. 'I'm going to put you over my knee and—'

She placed a forefinger on his lips. 'Don't get me excited. Not yet.'

It was dark when they reached Mary's parents' home between Padstow and Bodmin. Andrew parked the car, remarked unnecessarily that they were in the middle of nowhere and, after walking round the vehicle, picked up his girl yet again. He set her down, took a huge key from a pocket, and opened the door of Gamekeeper Cottage. Then he hoisted her up once more and carried her over the threshold. 'Are you gaining weight?' he asked.

'Are you losing strength, Drew?'

When their eyes had adjusted, Mary was dumped without ceremony on a sofa while Andrew lit candles and oil lamps. The whole downstairs was one large room, kitchen and sitting areas jumbled together. A wood-burning fireplace fuelled the oven, while a blackened kettle sat on a grill that straddled the grate. 'Cooking in the height of summer must be a chore,' Andrew commented.

'And there's a cesspit,' Mary informed him. 'They grow vegetables well away from that, and buy meat, flour and dairy produce from a farm on the edge of Bodmin Moor. See the bulgy bit with a door at the other side of the fire? That's the bread oven. They're so happy, Drew. They own a few acres, so Dad's going to get a couple of greenhouses for growing tomatoes and the like.'

'Will they sell the produce?'

'Oh yes. Once they have a horse and cart, they'll go to markets and make a few bob. My parents don't understand a life without work in it.' She stood up. 'In the morning, I'll show you Dad's answer to summer cooking. He's made a grill thing. They cook outdoors. Come on, wedding night things to do.'

Upstairs, there was just one bedroom and a very basic bathroom. Andrew wondered whether his Mary's parents ever missed the bustle of Paddy's Market and Scotland Road. He looked at photographs on the walls. 'Here you are, Mary. You were a beautiful child.'

'Yes, I was, but that's our Audrey. There's Shirley, and that's me.'

'The baby.'

'Yes. And over there are the boys, Bernard, Peter and Chris. God alone knows where they are now.'

They undressed and climbed into a high but comfortable bed. 'Do you know how much I love you, Mrs Sanderson?'

'No. But if it's half as much as I love you, it will be a pain.'

'*Semper fidelis*,' he said.

'Amen.'

Thus they began their married life in the middle of a wilderness, with primitive cooking facilities, no real bathroom, tinned food left by Mary's parents, foxes barking in the night, trees rustling all round, milk, cream, butter, bread, eggs and cheese left on their doorstep with a greetings card from the local farmer. Again, it was one of those glorious times made special because it was not running quite to plan. Always, they would value most the things that went wrong or didn't come up to scratch, since they needed only each other.

They were young, healthy and full of hope. They went to the sea, splashed about among rocks, found crabs, collected shells and pebbles, made love in woods while smaller mortals rustled in nearby foliage. They lay in inky blackness and stared up at a sky in which a million stars came out to look at them. They had candyfloss, ice cream, and other delights that took them back to childhood.

'We have to be grown-ups when we get home,' Mary said on their last night in Cornwall.

Andrew disagreed completely. 'No, no. At work, perhaps. But at home, we can go with Wilfred Owen, forever children, hand in hand. The sea is rising and the world is sand.'

'What does that mean, Drew?'

'No idea. I pinched it off Geoff; it's his mantra. But it sounds impressive. A bit soggy, what with the sea rising, but very clever. I'll look it up when we get home.'

Fourteen

The problem had been contained successfully for several years in the chaos room before spreading small tentacles across other parts of the house. Geoff was an untidy soul, and Emily had known that right from the very beginning when he'd taken her to his home and made love to her for the first time. She closed her eyes for a moment, saw his flat with the desk shoved against the window, nowhere to sit because books and papers occupied every bit of furniture. Not the bed, though. Oh, he'd known that she needed him . . . *Come back to me, please, my darling man.* Always, he'd been different, special and rather eccentric. But . . .

This was different, and she became disturbed, then tense, finally landing at the edge of panic and despair just before Andrew's marriage to the lovely Mary. But everything had to look right for Andrew and his bride, so she said nothing, simply returning to Geoff's messy room all the clutter he was spreading through communal areas. Keeping up with him was difficult, but she managed, more or less, to hide from other people the various overspills her man was creating.

Several hidden items began to turn up in very odd places. She found pages torn from medical books, certain words ringed by coloured inks. Childhood cancers in particular found space in his socks and pants drawer, while a three-page treatise on the subject of cerebral palsy appeared in a leather pouch right at the bottom of a dirty-linen hamper. And she stood there holding this in her hand, hearing him telling her that she would go to him willingly for sex. 'Come to me. I love you,' he had said. *Oh, Geoff, Geoff, where are you, where did you go? What's happening to us?* They'd been happy, so happy. Was this a punishment because she'd abandoned Joseph? 'Then punish me, not him,' she muttered.

Quite often, a saved column from a journal ended in a jagged tear halfway through a sentence, while his notes in margins made little sense. 'He's a doctor,' she told herself often. 'They can't write properly, since that seems to come with the territory. They take exams in how to write illegibly.' He couldn't be ill. Wouldn't someone at his work have noticed? But she knew only too well that the person closest to a patient usually saw symptoms first, and she was very close to her sweet, precious man. They still made love. He still read to her, wrote for her, made breakfast on Sundays, fed the cat. No, the cat had gone, had moved upstairs with Andrew. So many changes, some glaring, others so subtle as to be scarcely noticeable, except to Emily.

When Andrew and Mary were settled in the flat after their return from Cornwall, and when Mary's parents had left Liverpool, Emily asked her husband to come across and see her while Geoff was still at the children's hospital. For many years her closest and dearest friend, Joseph had been trusted with any information she chose to impart. While waiting for him to come, she hoped he wouldn't find her ridiculous, because her lover was still fine when it came to verbal expression. It was just . . . just things. And sometimes, an expression approaching confusion in his eyes.

'What's the matter?' Joe asked as soon as he arrived.

'You look worried halfway to hell.' She was pale, as white as a bleached sheet. 'Come on, kid, tell our Joe.'

And it poured. 'There's something very wrong with Geoff.' Just those few newborn words took a little of the dead weight from her shoulders. 'Toodles has moved upstairs to live in the flat with Andrew and Mary. Cats know things, Joseph, and she's a particularly clever old soul.' She then told Joseph about the bits of printed articles found in strange places, Geoff's tendency to shut himself in his messy room for hours on end, his new habit of examining carefully every forkful of food before allowing it to enter his mouth. 'He's not Geoff any more. I found his new socks in the bread bin. And he keeps buying pens. He must have at least fifty. Joseph, he's just odd.'

Joe took a sip of tea. 'At least they were new socks. Better than dirty ones in a bread bin, I suppose. But Em, what about his job if he's losing the plot? I mean, he carries a lot of responsibility, and he's accountable if anything goes wrong with his work.' Geoff loved his job, loved kids, too. If he lost his position, would the poor man cope?

'I know. Believe me, I've been worried sick. One mistake could cost a child's life. But I can't talk to his bosses about it. What if I'm wrong? He's always been a bit of an absent-minded professor. That's why he's had a special room for his books and his junk. He knows we don't want rubbish all over the house, especially when people come to look at the kitchens and the furniture you've made.'

Joe stood up and began to pace back and forth. 'I know some people think we're mad, the three of us, but I'm fond of the daft bugger. Still beats me at chess, so the intellect's right enough. What do we do, love? Where do we start? I mean, I'm just as lost as you are on this one. But we need help. Where from, though? Where do we go to talk about something as serious as this, Em?'

She started to cry. 'I think we probably pay a visit to our GP. Luckily, we're all with the same practice. But I shan't know how to deal with Geoff. What if it's a brain tumour, Joseph?'

'Oh, Emily.' He held her for the first time in years. She was weeping for another man, but Joe was her refuge. 'I'm here. I'll always be here for both of you. Tell you what, stick an extra plate on the table and I'll come back for my evening meal and see what I think.'

Emily dried her eyes. 'You can't tell there's anything wrong if you're talking or listening to him. It's just this putting bits and pieces in wrong places and buying stuff he doesn't need, like all the pens and lots of new socks. Will you be here while I tell him what he's doing? If I pluck up enough courage to tell him what he's doing, that is.'

'You know I will.' He waited until she was calmer before returning to his own house across the street. Geoff was still in his forties, and men in their forties didn't get senile dementia, did they? But there were cancers in his family, which fact had caused Geoff to render himself sterile . . . Bloody hell. Geoff, being a doctor, had little time for the breed. According to him, general practitioners made more mistakes than the government, and he seldom visited the surgery.

He wouldn't go to the doc, that was the problem. He would simply put his foot down and apply the brakes. The man was impossible when it came to his own health, and there was no shifting him. As far as Joe, Emily and Andrew were concerned, both Doctors Cawley were good folk. The father had lengthy experience, while the son was still close to his books and up to date with new developments. They were an ideal combination. But Geoff's opinion was very different from theirs.

What then? What about when Geoff refused to see a

333

doctor? Get him certified, have him dragged away to the asylum? Poor Emily. She was going to have her work cut out with the problem, that much was certain. He wondered whether Geoff had begun to move things about in the hospitals, but there was no way of finding out without endangering the man's position. The more Joe thought, the more confused he became, because he kept hitting brick walls.

He sat at the table and scratched his head. There was no set-in-stone method of telling a bloke that he might be going crackers. Emily would probably find a way of framing the message, because she was close to the man and very good with words. Even so, it would be no walk in the park. And if poor Geoff was losing the plot, he would need looking after, and who was free to do that job? Paid help would be needed, and Geoff would hate that, too.

Well, it was best to keep quiet for now, best if just he and Emily knew. There was no point in dragging Andrew and Mary into it at this juncture. Perhaps Geoff had an explanation for his behaviour. 'Don't jump the gun, Joe. Read your newspaper and play it cool, as the kids say.' He made a pot of tea, but he couldn't settle to read his paper, couldn't face the crossword. The custom-built dining table screamed for a bit of beeswax, yet Joe couldn't bestir himself. And he had some paperwork to do, but that, too, would have to wait.

He bathed, had a shave, and changed into clean but casual clothes. Going across for a meal in shirt and tie might seem a bit funereal. He allowed himself a tight smile. Andrew's stag night had been one to remember, all right. Mary was funny. She awaited the promised reprisal with dread, because they were both tinkers when it came to practical jokes. They were great together. Joe was glad that his son had found a good, happy, hard-working girl.

He sat down and sighed sadly. The tea was cool and

stewed, but he couldn't be bothered with a new brew. Hang on. That book of Andrew's was somewhere in the sideboard under tablecloths. He rooted about, dragged it out and looked for something he'd skimmed before. Ah, here it was. In 1906, Alois Alzheimer had treated a patient with ... No, it was further down underneath all the waffle. Only at autopsy was his patient's behaviour explained. Her brain had shrunk. It had bits missing, bits that governed memory, speech, coordination. Oh, bugger. It couldn't be that, mustn't be that.

He turned the page. The cause was a build-up of deposits on brain cells and some fibrous developments inside cells that eventually led to total dependence and death. He threw the book across the room. Research was being done, but there was, as yet, no sensible treatment for the condition. Poor Em. Poor Geoff. Was he aware of the changes in his own behaviour? One sentence in the thrown book stuck in Joe's mind. 'Alzheimer's cripples not just the sufferer, but whole families. A patient can live for many years . . .' He'd forgotten the rest, didn't want to bloody remember it.

In a way, a brain tumour might be preferable, because there could be a chance of surgery and improvement, but this other thing . . . Geoff would lose his job, and Em would need to give up hers. Andrew and Mary, in the flat above Em and Geoff, might well be dragged in for step-father-sitting duties. 'So will I,' he said aloud. 'If it's that bloody disease.'

Praying for somebody to have a brain tumour seemed strange, but Joe had a word with a god of whose existence he was not entirely sure. 'Let it be something mendable,' he begged, 'or she won't survive.' Emily would never bear the loss of Geoff. She bruised easily on the inside, so something as huge as Geoff's death could finish her off altogether.

335

He went across the road for his meal. Geoff greeted him in the usual way – 'Anyone for chess?' – while Emily carried on cooking in the kitchen. Joe knew that she was hanging on to every spoken word, because the rattling of utensils became quieter.

'We'll eat first, eh, Geoff?' Joe sat down. 'What's on the menu tonight?'

'Fish pie. Our missus does a grand fish pie.' Geoff placed himself in the chair opposite Joe's. 'And how are the kitchens coming along? Hardly a day passes without me seeing one of your trucks on the road.'

'Fine, thanks. Fleets of lorries all over the place, a lot of blokes with jobs, and that has to be a good thing. We're opening in the Midlands and the south soon.' He paused. 'What about all your sick kiddies?'

'Always a worry,' was the reply. 'We can only do our best, but we win some and lose some. Fortunately, we win more than we lose.'

Nothing in Geoff's verbal or body language betrayed him. Had the situation involved anyone other than Emily, Joe would be planning to question what had been said. The proof of the pudding was in the fish pie. She was right; the man did examine food before eating it.

Braver with Joseph at the table, Emily spoke up. 'Am I poisoning you, Geoff?'

He froze, fork halfway between plate and mouth. 'What?'

'You study your fork as if it's loaded with arsenic.'

'Oh, sorry. I'm testing my blood, trying to assess the effects of various quantities of various foods on my sodium and potassium levels. I write down what's in the meal, and try to judge the amount I've eaten, the weight of fish, potato, asparagus and so forth. Because I believe some severe illnesses are triggered by imbalance in the blood.'

'So you're a guinea pig?'

'I am. Well, I can hardly practise on my patients. A couple of my colleagues are testing themselves, too.'

'Are you endangering your health?' Emily asked.

Joe simply listened. So far, it all made perfect sense to him.

'No,' Geoff said, 'because we seem to stay pretty level whatever we eat. But it may teach us something when compared to the blood of our patients. It's a good idea to find the normal in order to treat the abnormal. I think it may be too broad a field, yet it's worth a go.'

Emily couldn't eat. 'Geoff, look at me.' She put down her cutlery.

He looked at her. 'What now?'

So she told him about the socks, the pens, the notes hidden all over the place, the mess spilling out from his chaos room. 'You've changed,' she concluded.

'But you know I've always been absent-minded. I lose pens all the time. I do research and hope to publish one day. I walk about with stuff in my hands, put it down and lose it. It's not intentional, and I'm sorry.'

She looked at Joe as if begging him to speak.

He spoke. 'Put her mind at rest, Geoff. Go and see the doctor, tell him you're more forgetful than you used to be, and just get yourself checked.'

Geoff looked from one to the other a few times. 'Have you two been discussing me?'

'She's worried,' said Joe in his wife's defence.

'About what?'

'About how you've changed. You got given your messy room, and your messy room's started walking all over the house. She's up and down the stairs like a scalded cat because she's a worrier. I don't know, do I? Em might be thinking anything from . . .' He left a deliberate pause. 'Well, from brain tumour to some kind of premature dementia.'

Geoff laughed. 'And you want me to go and see a man who's a quack? He doesn't know an eye infection from athlete's foot. There is nothing wrong with me except tiredness. I've been researching too hard.'

Emily felt foolish, but Joe didn't. While it was true that nearest and dearest often noticed first when something was wrong, a person who came and went had value, since he began to see the subtler differences that occurred during short absences. The man had altered, though Joe couldn't put his finger on the problem.

Geoff laughed again, but there was a hollow quality to the sound.

The other two occupants of the room would hear that laugh for the rest of their lives. Because just over a year later, Geoff was dead.

Andrew and Mary were living their dream. When not at work, they ate and studied, but continued their honeymoon period for what Mary declared to be 'a time of total self-indulgence'. But their euphoria was ended abruptly by the deaths of two children. The first was not developed, as it had existed for just a few weeks in Mary's womb and didn't have an identifiable gender, but the second was the fault of staff at Liverpool's children's hospital, and it was a four-year-old girl disabled by serious heart problems.

Immediately, Emily and Joe visited Dr Charles. His real name was Cawley, but as his father still worked at the practice the younger man used his given name. 'What can I do for you two?' he asked. 'Aren't you living with Dr Shaw, Mrs Sanderson?'

'Joseph and I are still legally married,' Emily said. 'It's an unusual situation. And Geoff . . .' She could say no more, as she began to sob. 'Forgive me.'

'A zero too many,' Joe said. His own voice was shaky.

He explained as best he could the arrangements in his wife's house, Geoff's untidy 'cave', his increasing forgetfulness, his deteriorating behaviour. 'It started off with the mess spreading a bit, and Em just shifted it back to the chaos room. He's always had a room like that, it's been part of who he is. Or was. Emily? Shall we come back later when you feel a bit better?'

She managed a degree of control. 'Then my daughter-in-law heard him talking to himself.'

Joe shook his head. 'No, love. She told you he was talking to somebody who wasn't there. When I'm drawing a piece of furniture, I talk to myself all the time. A lot of people do that – it's instead of making notes. It was a nurse who wasn't there. She's the one who followed Geoff's instructions, and she gave a hundred measurement of something or other instead of ten. The kiddy died. Everybody blamed the poor nurse till they saw Geoff's notes with the extra zero. See, up till now, Doc, it's just been like eccentricity and absent-mindedness. But it's changed lately. My son has had to sit with him while we came here, because we believe he soon won't be fit to be left. And my son's wife's just lost their first baby, as you already know.'

Dr Charles listened intently.

With each prompting the other, they placed the whole truth before him. Geoff was getting up in the middle of the night, making toast and tea, then setting off for work, sometimes in his pyjamas. He was easier when out of his mind, because each time he returned to his senses the fact that he was suspended from work crashed into his head.

'Does he talk sense to you?' the doctor asked.

'He says very little now,' was Emily's reply. 'He examines all his food before eating, something to do with research, and I'm thinking of labelling the cupboards. I found three cups in the oven yesterday.'

'Can you bring him here?'

'No,' they chorused.

'He hates doctors,' Joe added.

'Most doctors do,' Charles said. 'Then the mountain must move. Go home, and I'll be with you shortly. I know this is easy to say, but try not to worry.'

For the first time in four and a half decades of life, Geoff Shaw turned nasty. 'Bring my family,' he yelled at Joe. 'They live in West Derby.'

Emily spoke. 'They moved to Northampton, darling, to be near your nephew. Remember?'

Geoff blinked. 'Emily, don't let the doctor do this to me. I didn't write that extra zero.'

'I'm doing nothing,' Dr Charles said. He had already sent for a second medic and an ambulance. 'You aren't functioning properly, Geoff. You need your engine looking at, maybe your battery charged. No hospital, I promise you that.' This was the truth, because Joe was paying for a private facility between Liverpool and Southport. Technically it was a fully equipped medical centre, though it presented itself as a top-class hotel, especially in public areas. 'We're concerned for you and want to help you get better.'

'You can piss off,' was Geoff's answer. 'I don't mean you,' he said to Joe and Emily. 'I mean this bloody quack. Doesn't know his housemaid's knee from his tennis elbow. Waste of space.'

The quack moved closer to the patient. 'Calm down.'

'You calm down. What the hell are you doing here?'

Charles Cawley was probably keeping Geoff out of court, though he said nothing. The possibility of this paediatrician's being tried for negligence or even manslaughter was very real. The press had been told as little as possible, though the little girl's parents had not been gagged. 'I'm trying to help you,' he said. 'Believe it or not, this is all for your own good.' The Royal College of Nursing wasn't best pleased about one of its members being blamed, however briefly, for the death of a child. That weighty power might swing into action any day now, because the nurse in question was suffering from nervous exhaustion.

They came for him. Three big bruisers in white coats dragged him kicking and screaming into the private ambulance. Andrew and Mary, who had sat on the stairs through the whole palaver, held on to Emily while her lover was taken away under certification. Joe simply wept. He curled into Geoff's fireside chair in Emily's drawing room and cried like a newborn. He'd just found yet another pack of cheap ballpoint pens under the cushion. Oh, yes. There was something wrong with that poor lad.

Emily broke free from her son and watched the vehicle pulling away. She sat on the doorstep gazing into the near distance. But what she saw now was miles away from Liverpool. A bench facing a park, her bench, the one she'd chosen to occupy while eating her home-made lunch in warm weather. And he placed himself there with her, knowing she would love him, rock solid in his belief that this woman, ten years his senior, would be his forever. She felt the summer breeze on her neck, saw roses nodding in the infirmary garden. *Geoff, don't leave me. Without you, I am half of nothing.*

'Come in, Mother.'

And she was in the arms of both her son and his wife, all three of them sobbing noisily. Joe joined them, a handkerchief held to his eyes. 'Look at us,' he said. 'We should be praying, not skriking. I'll stop here tonight, Em, in that smaller back bedroom, if that's all right with you. I just feel a bit . . . a bit down.' Pam and her friend had moved out, and his house was enormous.

And they stayed together for days, advised by Dr

Charles not to visit Geoff just yet. While they waited, the dregs of humanity caught up with the story and began to haunt them. Representatives of presses local and national lived in the street, and no one said a word to them. It was like a circus with just clowns, except this lot wore two days' growth of beard rather than red noses, oversized shoes and gaudy make-up.

When the bigger picture emerged, the reporters had a new, more sympathetic attitude. Dr Geoff Shaw was ill, and the whole sad business had been a terrible accident. So would-be hunters oozed concern for the poor man, yet still no one spoke to them.

Geoff was not suffering from a brain tumour; nor did he have the dreaded Alzheimer's. Without realizing it, Geoff had experienced a series of small, cerebral accidents, commonly known as strokes. Undaunted and unaware, he had carried on like the stalwart he had always been, seldom complaining of headaches or other symptoms, as complaining was not in his nature.

It was then that Liverpool began to show her true nature. Once the sad truth was published, Rodney Street was occupied by bearers of little gifts, cards and flowers. These same people bulldozed reporters out of the area, attended the little girl's funeral, and finally brought the bereaved mother to see Emily. The two women cried and clung together, then sat and did the good old Lancashire thing involving cups, saucers and the brew that cheers.

'What can they do for him?' the child's mother asked.

'Well, they can thin his blood, but that might kill him if he has a bleed. He hasn't had bleeds yet, you see. It's something about oxygen starvation, and I don't really understand it properly, but at least you know little Alison's death wasn't his fault.'

'I do know. And she wasn't awake, so we hope she felt

nothing. But you have a hard time in front of you, Mrs Shaw.'

Emily was too tired for further explorations into the future. It was going to be about blood pressure, gentle exercise and a sensible diet. 'Thank you for coming to see me.'

'Tell him I know it was an accident, won't you?'

'I will.'

'It's not easy, Mrs Sanderson, but it's been explained to me that he had no idea that he was ill. And my Ally wasn't in the best of health – she had a couple of years left at best with the state of her heart. But it still hurts, and now I'm hurting for you and him. It's a mad bloody world, isn't it, love?'

'Oh, yes. Thank you for coming.'

Alone once more, Emily stared into an empty grate. The lack of flame and movement underlined yet again her absolute loneliness. As for Geoff, how would he cope without his work? She'd visited him twice, and he now seemed to be aware of the mini-strokes. Despite his relative youth, he had a degree of vascular dementia, though it might slow down. No one could make a real prognosis, as the disease took different forms in each patient.

Soon, she would bring him home. An unlikely mixture of joy and dread filled her chest. She loved him and wanted him back, but he was changing all the time, sometimes clear and amusing, sometimes withdrawn, brow furrowed, lips tight, no words, no laughter. Treatment remained unclear. There were drugs under development, but nothing thus far had been declared fit to use on humans. Patience and communication were mentioned in the home pack, and Emily was good at both.

'But must I watch him die? How do I know if he has another . . . what's the word? Ischaemic event?' That meant something about poor blood flow and a loss of oxygen to more areas of the brain. How would she recognize that? 'It should be me. I'm nearly ten years older.' But it was him. And the knowledge was a knife in her heart.

Phenobarbital. That was what the enemy gave him, and those tablets were for epileptics or very anxious patients. The staff kept him quiet by sedating him, and they probably thought he would carry on taking the bloody stuff so that their life might remain easy, but he wasn't here to please them. Here? Where was here? It was far too luxurious to be a hospital, so Emily and Joe must be in on it. Who could be trusted these days? The tablets piled up in his toiletries bag.

Geoff wanted to go home, but he wondered whether Emily would send him away again. Was there a plot afoot? Did she want to go back to Joe? So where was his home? West Derby. The family house was in West Derby. Yes, his parents had gone to be with his brother's son in Northampton, but the house remained theirs. He'd been having strokes. The strokes weren't bleeders, but they had reduced the supply of oxygen to parts of his brain. Where the hell was he?

Finding out wasn't difficult. Brain damage? He was well enough to defeat this lot any day of the week. He donned a dressing gown, left his room, discovered that he was at Elmswood, a facility of which he had heard, returned to his quarters and dressed himself. Many of the patients were dressed, so he mingled for a while in a sitting room, helping an old man put together a jigsaw, playing a too-easy game of chess and making sure he was seen by staff who would, no doubt, make notes about his being up, dressed and out of his room at last. This improvement would be written in

344

his notes, and they would take the credit and the money for having performed the miracle. Charlatans.

Behind a Staff Only door, he stole a few pounds from wallets and handbags, then left the establishment through a rear entrance. He was on the moss, an area of lanes and fields between Southport, Ormskirk and North Liverpool. At an isolated farmhouse, he told the occupant that his car had broken down, he was a doctor and he needed a taxi. And that was that. Less than an hour later, he was back on Rodney Street.

When Emily answered the door, he pushed her aside and strode in. 'Do that to me again, and I shall be angry,' he said.

Open-mouthed, Emily stood in the hall. 'Do what?' she shouted to his disappearing back.

Halfway up the stairs, he stopped. 'Lock me away in a place for rich, sick people.'

'But I didn't. It was the doctor's idea, not mine. We've been terribly worried.'

'Have you? So sorry. You and Joe plotting behind my back, eh? Are you two planning a reconciliation?'

She followed him. 'Geoff? Geoff, look at me.'

At the top of the stairs, he waited for her.

'A child died, darling,' she said. 'You've had ischaemic strokes—'

'I know. I'm a bloody doctor, after all. And I'm sorry, but I didn't know these things were happening. Anyway, I can't stay here. If I stay here, you'll be following me round in case one piece of paper escapes from my study.'

'Have you any idea of how lonely I've been?' she asked. 'And how I've wished that I could be the sick one? I love you enough to die for you, and look at me while I'm speaking. Joe is my best friend, no more than that. Don't leave me. Spread your mess everywhere, buy a thousand pens, keep socks in the refrigerator – we'll manage. We've always managed. There are hundreds of get well cards downstairs, and the little girl's mother came to see me, because she's worried about you. She asked me to tell you that she knows it was an accident.'

He sat in a chair on the vast, regal landing. 'Send money to that bloody Elmswood place,' he said. 'I stole from the staff cloakroom. It was about eight pounds, I think. But don't send me back.'

'I won't send you back.'

'Even if I go mad?'

She smiled. 'That would be a short journey for either or both of us.'

Geoff took her hand. 'Never a moment's regret have I had about you, about us. Sometimes, when I've looked at Joe, I've felt sad for him, because I stole his jewel.'

'He's a good man, Geoff. He loves you like a brother, like the family he never had.'

'Lie down with me,' he implored.

'But I don't want you to have another accident in your head.'

'What a way to go, though. But I mean just lie down. I can't sleep without you next to me.'

They lay together on the bed and, within minutes, he was in a deep sleep. Downstairs, the phone rang repeatedly, and Emily knew it was the private hospital trying to tell her that he'd disappeared, trying to ask if he'd arrived home, but she wouldn't leave him. With the possible exception of a house fire, nothing on earth would have persuaded her to drag her beloved out of that bedroom. He needed her. So she stayed. It was her precious duty.

The meeting was held about six weeks after Geoff's escape from the place he termed prison. He was calmer and seemed reasonably well; he was also fully aware of the subject intended for discussion at the meeting, since Emily allowed him few shocks.

Emily explained that she wanted to dispose of both Rodney Street houses. 'I shall transfer this house into Andrew's name, but I must tell you that interest has been shown by medical specialists seeking consulting rooms and so forth. Andrew, you and Mary will make enough to buy a big house further up the coast, or wherever you wish to live. The decision will be yours, though. Joseph, I have found two bungalows, one for you, the other for me and Geoff. There's a beach and a wooded area quite nearby. It's healthier than here. And the sale of your house here will pay for both bungalows.'

Joseph said he didn't mind as long as he could get to work.

'It's just a few miles,' Emily said reassuringly. 'About seven or eight.'

'Then I'll come,' Joe said. He trusted Emily implicitly. Her replacement at Sanderson's couldn't hold a candle to Em, because Em had been born with a good head for business.

Emily turned to her son. 'There's a marvellous house for sale nearby. It needs a bit of work, but I fell in love with it. And strangely, it's named Rosewood. There are wild roses in the gardens, the original flower with just one layer of petals. You remember your bookcase?'

'Well, we still have it upstairs in the flat, Mother.'

'Edged in rosewood.' Emily smiled. 'Quite a good omen. Come and see it. There's no one in it, but it's fit for habitation. You and your father could make it quite spectacular. Lots of doctors live up there in fresher air. But if you choose to stay here, that will be fine, too. If you sell, you'll have enough to make Rosewood the most beautiful house in Liverpool.'

347

'We should look at it,' Mary said. 'There's nothing to be lost by just looking at the place.'

So the five of them went together to view the house and the pair of two-bedroom bungalows. Andrew and Mary followed Emily's example, toppling head over heels immediately with a tired-looking house set in a huge plot. Joseph ran about, waxing excitedly about banisters, monks' benches, new doors, a kitchen, a four-poster bed.

At last, Andrew's Mary was smiling. She'd been pre-occupied of late, mostly because of the miscarriage, partly because she'd been tied up at work lately, since a friend of hers had a problem Mary refused to discuss. Andrew guessed it was probably an unwanted pregnancy and left her to it, hoping that the friend would act sensibly. But he was glad to see that his adored partner was at last regain-ing a little *joie de vivre*.

As both Emily and Joseph were downsizing, much of their bespoke furniture was earmarked for Andrew's new house, so the two young ones inherited a great deal of Joseph's work, plus beds, fridge, cooker, curtains and rugs. They had a project, and they sank their teeth into it cheerfully. It was a new beginning for all of them, a new life.

Joe's house went quickly. It was to be used by eight consultants in this, Liverpool's Harley Street. Joe placed his possessions in a storage unit before encamping tem-porarily in Emily's smaller back bedroom, which was now Andrew's property, since the deeds of the house had been signed over to him.

As an insider, Andrew got his colleagues to put out feelers and he was inundated by specialists wanting to use the house. To make things fair, an estate agent was employed to handle the sale, and Andrew gained enough to pay cash for Rosewood and to make some improve-ments. He kept an eye on his wife, who seemed to have recovered from the early failure of her first pregnancy, and was reassured by her that her friend's problem no longer existed. 'She's gone to London,' Mary said. 'The difficulty's been overcome, and she's working as a midwife in a large general hospital. She'll be fine.'

They all moved out to Blundellsands. Each house overlooked the river, and Toodles had a great time, because she began to move from house to house, and she pleaded hunger each time, gobbling up more food than was good for her. This old, wise cat made her peace with Geoff, because he no longer worried her, and he was particularly generous with leftovers.

People became used to an extremely unusual sight – a man walking his cat over the grass, down the erosion steps and across the sand. When Geoff sat on the concrete steps, Toodles sat next to him; when it rained, the cat was wrapped inside Geoff's coat, head peeping out at the collar, tail hanging below the hem of the short, waterproof jacket.

Although no one else noticed, Emily felt her man slipping away from her month by month, week by week, then day by day. Joe was on his travels all over the country, opening up offices, finding premises in which his kitchens could be made. The bespoke furniture was limited for the present to the north, since fitted kitchens had fast become the most desirable part of a house.

Emily could not talk to her son, because he was busily involved in his attachment to Compton-Gore's team of sawbones, while he and Mary were so happy that she hated the idea of heaping trouble on their heads. She watched Geoff with the cat, drove him to his hospital visits, made sure he took the various medicines that seemed not to help.

The second bedroom in the bungalow failed to contain his enormous collection of books and papers, and she simply gave up, devoting her life to him and hiding overspill in cupboards, the garden shed, even in the roof space. Now well into her fifties, she at last began to develop wrinkles and worry lines, especially when Geoff stopped cluttering the house.

He no longer went into the spare bedroom. Instead, he sat for hours on end, Toodles on his knee, eyes fixed to the sitting-room window through which he could see the river. Conversations became fractured. Sometimes, they were almost one-sided; occasionally, Geoff would jump headlong into a subject and deliver what almost amounted to a lecture.

'I'm a good swimmer,' he told her one day.

He hated water. She'd always known that. 'Would you like to go to the swimming baths?' she asked.

'No.' And that was the end of that particular discussion.

In the middle of one night, she found him having a bonfire in the rear garden. 'What are you burning?' she asked, trying hard to dampen rising panic.

'My rubbish,' he replied.

'Why, Geoff?'

'It's all out of date now. Someone else will start it all over again. I've had my day, and I completed nothing.'

Emily led him into the kitchen and made cocoa. 'I wonder when Andrew and Mary will try for another baby?' she said, trying to distract his attention from the fire outside.

'He's resting her body.' Geoff smiled. 'He's a good man, says he wants to leave her free of pregnancy for a few years. They use some form of contraception.'

'I see. You and I never needed that.'

He was suddenly grinning. 'I was terrified, you know. Frightened silly in case you wouldn't have me. But you did, and thank you. You have given me so much happiness, more than any man deserves.'

'We're still happy,' she said.

'Yes. Yes, we are. But you know I'm dying, don't you?'

Taken by surprise and shock, Emily dropped her cup. While she mopped and tidied, she answered him. 'We're all dying from the moment of birth, darling.'

'Yes, yes, I suppose we are.'

They returned to their bedroom, lay down and held each other close.

When Emily woke in the morning, she was alone.

She found the man who had made her life worthwhile dead at his desk in the clutter room. He was as cold as ice, though the fire he had made during the night still glowed outside the window. She stroked his hair and, through clouded eyes, read his final piece of work.

My darling Emily

This is too much for both of us, so I must bring it to a close. Yesterday is becoming a mystery to me, though I remember our lives together, our bench, the flat, Joe's anger, then his friendship. But more recent memories disappear, and it is clear that my brain deteriorates. Now, while I still have some control, I intend to end my suffering and yours.

More than anything, I think of our joy, our closeness, the laughter and the pleasure we gained from each other's company. You were and still are the love of my life, and I cannot become your burden. So I am going out for a walk, and I shall not return. Keep Toodles in. I do not want her following me into the river, nor do I wish to

And it ended there. There was a jagged line, and the pen remained next to his open hand. He had intended suicide by drowning, but a final stroke had taken him. The scream that tore its way past her throat was not a real scream; it was more the primeval howl of some antecedent of humankind, a creature recently ascended from the earth's slime. He could not be gone. The world should cease its turning, birds shouldn't sing, she should stop breathing.

'Phone.' She left him and entered the hall. 'Andrew?'

'Mother?'

'Come. Come now. He's dead.'

His fire still burned. It was half past seven, and he was dead, but his books remained curled in embers. At least half his collection had gone. He had been tidying up for the first and last time, had made an effort to render her life easier, and that effort had taken his life. *I didn't mind the mess any more, Geoff. You could have carpeted the place with your litter.*

People came and went. The police had to attend, as the death was unusual. That very private note was taken away, as was its author. A policewoman tried to remain with Emily, but she took the advice of Andrew and went away. Mary sat and waited with her mother-in-law, but the weeping did not begin. All that existed was this terrible, dry silence. Emily spoke from time to time, but she didn't grieve.

Andrew managed to track down his father, who said he would come home immediately. 'Stay with us tonight,' Mary suggested.

Emily refused politely. 'Joseph will look after me. Andrew's father and I have always taken good care of each other. Mary, make me some sweet tea, there's a good girl. I don't like sugar, but I'm light-headed.'

A post-mortem was ordered, and the whole family decided that this was the right thing. Geoff had been a great believer in research, and if anything could be gained from the examination of his brain, he would have agreed readily.

While her son and daughter tidied the bungalow, Emily sat with her sweet tea. She was a frightened, angry woman in Queen's Park, but he came for her. She caught shingles, and he fussed like an old woman, comforting her, babying her. When she sprained an ankle, he brought crutches and a borrowed wheelchair; when she cried, he wept with her.

Gone. In one or two breaths, the life-force quit his body, leaving him to chill and stiffen in his work chair. A dead man still owned a dozen pairs of brand new socks and enough pens to furnish a large office. His fire had gone out just after his body had left the bungalow. Memories now, just memories. And Toodles was searching for him.

Andrew came in. 'Everything he didn't burn is up in the loft in cardboard boxes. His clothes and so forth I'll leave alone for now.'

'The Salvation Army,' Emily said. 'When I'm ready.' Would she ever be ready? 'And his best suit goes with him.'

'All right.'

'Aren't you going to work?'

'No, Mother. We've phoned in. Don't worry about us.'

She stared intently at him. 'You were never a worry. You've always been the best son we could have hoped for. And Mary's so right for you.'

'Yes, she is.'

'I'm glad you're happy.'

'Yes, we're very happy.' But would Mother ever be happy again? She and Geoff had been so close. 'Anything you want, just ask, won't you?'

'Of course I will.'

Joe, Andrew and Mary carried Emily through a non-denominational cremation that was attended by so many people that dozens had to stay outside. The mother of the

353

child who had died came to pay her respects, but Emily seemed to see or hear nothing. Geoff's parents were there, but she looked through them while her son explained and apologized.

For days, she sat with the urn, clutching his ashes to her chest. She didn't eat. She didn't wash herself or change her clothes. Mary came in and forced her mother-in-law to take a bath. Something would have to be done, and Andrew called in help. Each time, Emily cooperated until the helpers left her alone, at which point she reverted to type.

A friend of Mary's was employed to force-feed Emily if necessary. This little woman, Eva Dawson, had more strength than her body advertised. She kept Emily clean, read the paper to her, gave her food and fluids, then went home to her own family. At weekends, Andrew, Mary or Joe took over.

But one Sunday morning, bolts were on front and back doors. When his mother didn't answer the bell or the knocking, Andrew ran home and phoned for real help. Mary sat on the stairs while he made the call. The police would find Emily dead, of that Mary felt quite sure.

Real help arrived to a locked door and closed curtains. Real help broke in and discovered another body with another note, this time for Joe. All she asked was for her ashes to be mixed with Geoff's. She had written the method of her suicide on the same sheet; she had saved and swallowed all the tranquillizers. Toodles was in Andrew's chaos room.

'We could have stopped her,' Andrew wailed.

A doctor in attendance yelled, 'A pulse. Faint, but a pulse.'

There wasn't time to travel to a hospital. Ambulance men carried in equipment, and Emily's stomach was forcibly emptied on the spot. She was injected, prodded, wrapped in blankets, and fluid was dripped into a vein. 'Hang on a bit longer,' the doctor begged. 'Just a few minutes, then we'll take her in.'

A sound like the death rattle emerged from Emily's throat, but this was a life rattle, caused by a sudden, huge intake of breath. Andrew, weeping, sank to the floor.

Mary sat down and hugged him. How was this to be managed? If Andrew's mother required twenty-four-hour care, would she end up in a home filled by old people?

'Two intended suicides,' he wept.

'She thought she couldn't live without him.'

Andrew dried his eyes. 'And he didn't want to be a burden. My father will be heartbroken, because he never stopped loving her. Where is he?'

'Dock Road doing paperwork. You'd better go and get him. I'll stay here with your poor cat.'

'I can't drive, Mary.'

'OK. I'll ask the police to go for him. I love you. I'll look after you.'

She would. As long as he had his Mary, Andrew would be all right.

Fifteen

It was a long, hard and unevenly paved road for all of them. Andrew visited repeatedly a shrunken, silent mother in a psychiatric facility that catered for all kinds of people wrecked by overwork, by society in general, or even by their own families. He talked to Emily in spite of the lack of response, steeling himself against screams and groans that travelled up corridors to invade all wards along the route. The place was a nightmare, yet she seemed settled. Well, she was quiet, and that was some improvement, because the sounds she had produced a couple of years earlier had been unearthly.

His lovely, once-fragrant mother did not belong here. She was ageing, and he hated that. The application of pine disinfectant and polish did little to cover the smell of dried urine and overcooked vegetable matter. Even curtains that hung round beds were limp, lifeless and depressed. Staff wandered about clanking like Scrooge's ghosts, great key chains hanging from their belts, as they had to unlock then lock every door as they made their way through an institution that contained some dangerous people.

Emily Sanderson was not dangerous; she was simply uncommunicative. 'We love you,' he told her repeatedly. 'You're going to be a grandma very soon.' But she remained in a state that was not quite catatonic, because she responded physically to commands from staff. Nevertheless, she made no effort to converse or to make eye contact. When touched, she flinched sharply and drew back. Mother had closed her shop and seemed to have no plans to reopen for business. Andrew, a doctor who knew many others from various disciplines, felt useless and guilty. This was his mother, and he should have been able to discover how to snap her out of the trance.

'Move her,' Mary suggested yet again when he got home. 'Put her somewhere better, but for God's sake shift her out of that graveyard. It's just not a good place, and she should be elsewhere, somewhere cleaner and brighter with gardens and so forth.'

'Where do I put her? She's used to that dump and hates change.'

'Move her to Elmswood, of course. They have a unit for people with mental or emotional problems. Between the two of you, it can be afforded, because I know Joe will chip in. Elmswood will try harder to get through to her. It's quieter and has more staff. She'll get used to it. It might be difficult at first, but she'd stand a better chance.'

Andrew considered the suggestion. 'Geoff was there. He hated the damned place. Remember how he stole money and buggered off home? He spent days in the Rodney Street house begging not to be sent back to prison.'

'Will she remember that, though? Does she remember anything?'

Again, he pondered. 'Well, it's hard to say, love. She goes to the dining table when told, swallows her medicines, gets to the bathroom several times a day, and there's no perceivable brain damage. Her kidneys have sorted themselves out, thank God, because they could have been ruined, as could her liver, when she took the overdose. But she's living behind a steel door. Somewhere deep in her brain, she's refusing to see or hear those who're close to her. And she loves me, Mary. I know she does. No matter what happened, she was always close to me.'

Mary agreed. 'We're all on the wrong side of her barricade. Sometimes, the people closest to a person are the least suited to giving help. Perhaps she's shut down in the area of all who knew Geoff. Who can say? Two years, though, Drew.' She sighed heavily. 'Oh well, I'll go and finish cooking.'

Andrew went into his study and had a word with George. Was talking to a skeleton symptomatic of mental illness? Perhaps he should book a room for himself in Elmswood, save everybody else the bother in a few years' time. But no. Mary was thirty weeks pregnant and looked as if she had stayed the course this time, thank goodness. He had plenty to live for. 'George, what the hell must I do? I'm all out of ideas, old chum.'

It was 1968 and the world was changing fast. The trouble was that Mother was not changing, and several extended visits home had not improved her. She'd simply stopped working. Emily Sanderson had become a grey person who, with other grey people, lived a colourless life in a place tinted only by fear, panic, anxiety and depression. 'And that's just the staff,' he mumbled before turning to his companion. 'I bet they have to drink or take pills themselves just to get through a working day.'

He walked back and forth for several seconds. 'George? What shall I do?' He thought of the grandparents who had bought George for him. 'Mother doesn't even know they're dead,' he told the arrangement of bones. 'She doesn't know how rich she is, how much they left me, because she doesn't bloody listen. This mess is into its third year now. Come on, George, give me an idea of some sort, damn it, be some use for a change.'

George, while a great thinker, was a man of few words, but he'd been an excellent teacher in his time. George's pupil, one Andrew Sanderson, was teetering on the brink of consultancy, since he had a way with bones and connective tissue. Spines were his forte, so he worked in tandem with neurologists, and he loved the job. Twenty-eight and already established, Andrew looked forward to an exciting career. But Mother . . . 'There has to be an answer. She's a wonderful, intelligent woman under the surface.'

He remembered being prepared to leap to her defence when he'd discovered Betsy and Dad, closed his eyes and 'saw' her in her apron bustling about in the dining room on Crompton Way, in the new kitchen on Mornington Road, where Thora Caldwell had entered her life like a tornado ripping through America. He remembered her love for Geoff, the trouble at the beginning, the way things had settled and become civilized.

Thora. 'Thank you, George. I knew you'd think of something.' He walked to the door, tapping the skeleton on its skull as he passed. 'Mary, darling? Are you busy?'

'What, O sweetness and light of my life?'

'Cut the sarcasm, Fatso. Will the food keep till tomorrow?'

Mary joined him in the hall. 'Why? And tell your dad to have another go at the newel post.' She pointed to the elegant banister. 'He missed a bit. I got a splinter in my thumb.'

Andrew laughed, just as he often did when his lovely wife put in an appearance. Mary was short. With only ten weeks to go till labour day, she looked like a bouncy little elf.

Her hands were placed on her hips. 'Listen, buster. I know how I look. Even my best friend calls me Butterball or Lard-arse. But that's Pam for you, and that husband of hers isn't much better. However, I would expect some appreciation from my adoring husband and father of my baby. Pregnant women are hormonal and sensitive, you know.'

'You're a terrific cuddle. It's like having my very own teddy bear in bed. Hot water bottle, too. You radiate heat. Oh yes, a very warm personality.'

'What did you mean about keeping the food till tomorrow?'

'Thora,' he said.

Mary parked herself on a monks' bench. 'Thora?'

He nodded. 'Our next door neighbour in Mornington Road. I'm going to phone her and ask her if we can go and fetch her here. My mother might just respond to her. She's as thin as a threepenny stamp, but she's noisy. And she owes us. We gave her our house. She's gone posh. Thora gone posh is a power to contend with. She puts her h-aitches where there h-are none.'

'Let me just . . .' She struggled to stand. 'Can your dad not do something about these floors? They're not near enough to my feet.' She returned to the kitchen to deal with food while Andrew phoned Thora. 'We're on,' he shouted. 'Come on, Pudding, lie on the floor, and I'll roll you out to the car.'

She was not amused. 'Do you have plans to live to see this child? I might be short and inclined towards the spherical just now, but I still pack a fair punch, and I am not afraid of you.'

He looked down at her. 'I suppose you could reach my knees if you stood on tiptoe.'

Mary glowered. 'Mark my words, ear'ole. When you're asleep, I can reach parts that don't even have a medical name. You will feel excruciating pain, depend on it.'

Andrew grinned. Mary stamped a small foot.

He picked her up in his arms. This was a habit he had never tried to break, because it continued to be a message without words. He'd saved her from the Beatles' mob, and he would protect her from all comers, no matter where or when. 'I think I'm getting a hernia, sweetheart.'

'Good.' She gave him a sloppy kiss. 'See, I'm small, yeah?'

'Yeah.'

'And you're huge, yeah?'

'Yeah.'

'So your baby weighs about three stone, and that ain't my fault. When this child invades an unsuspecting world, I'll be like an empty balloon, all stretched and wrinkled. And you're moaning about a flaming hernia. Where are we going?'

'Bolton.'

'Why?'

'Thora. She may be going to the psychiatric unit to kick-start Mother.'

'Jump leads?'

'Probably.' He deposited his precious burden in the car. 'She's as lean as a rake and more terrifying than the plague. Her husband died just to get away from her. One of her lads is Dad's right hand man, and Thora's recently retired from her job as an orderly at Bolton Royal. She hires herself out as a carer, and she's a damned good nurse in spite of the lack of qualifications. We can get Mother home. Between her and your friend – what's her name?'

'Eva. Eva Dawson.'

'Very similar type. They might just manage her.'

Mary had her doubts, though she kept her counsel. Her Drew's mother seemed to be drifting nearer and nearer to catatonia, but at least he was trying to find a solution. Emily needed to be moved; the place she was in, the ward to which she had been repeatedly returned after failed home visits, needed fumigating and possibly demolition. 'Come on, lad. Let's give it a go. Any port in a storm.'

Thora was waiting for them. She had moved from next door after the death of her husband who, according to her, had been no use at all.

'He fell off a roof,' she replied when questioned about the reason for his demise. 'In town. Brought half the guttering with him, but I refused to pay for it.'

'Was this in the course of his work?' Andrew asked.

'Don't talk so wet. He were trying to break into the Dog and Duck in the dark through a skylight, rolled off and broke his neck. He was h-inebriated at the time, so I suppose he didn't feel much.' She picked up a suitcase. 'I h-offered his body to medical science, but they couldn't take him anywhere near a place with Bunsen burners in it, being as he was ninety per cent alcohol, so I had to bury the bugger.'

Mary managed, just about, not to burst out laughing.

Thora continued. 'Emily's not getting over Dr Shaw? Ooh, when they told me mine had gone, I went for a pie and three pints. I would have thrown a party there and then, but I waited till after the funeral. Well, you have to, don't you? We had a smashing do.' She handed her case to Andrew and tied a scarf round rusty curls where silver threads had begun to show. 'Three-course sit-down meal with a glass of sparkling wine thrown in. Red letter day, that were. No more sweaty socks and mucky h-underpants? Magic.'

As they walked to the car, Thora motored on. 'My eldest's moving in here with wife and kids while I'm gone.' She rattled on about weather, food prices, and her from number nine with piles. 'A martyr, she is. I said to her, I said, "Bertha, put your name down for an operation," but she's scared. My, you're looking bonny, lass. When are you due?'

'Ten weeks,' Mary managed to say in the midst of Thora's barrage.

Thora tutted. 'How many have you got in there?'

'Just the one.'

'Hell's bells on a Monday, it'll be more like a launch than a birth. Have you got a bottle of champagne to smash on its bum? Is Princess Margaret coming?'

Andrew glanced at his wife. 'See? If anyone can bring Mother round, it's Thora.'

On their way homeward, the rear-seat passenger commented on everything she saw, from shops to unusual buildings. When they reached their destination, she was overawed. 'I never knew you lived at the seaside with sand and everything. Ooh, it's lovely here, it is. Grand.'

Andrew explained that this was the river, and that the bar was nearer to Formby.

'Is it open, this bar?'

He chuckled. 'The bar's invisible.'

'Right. Does it serve h-invisible Guinness?'

'Thora, the bar is where the river becomes the Irish Sea. It's just a word, not a pub on a boat.'

'Ooh, and there I were getting excited. Is . . . er . . . is this your house?'

'It is.'

'It's a bloody mansion. Get me in there.'

They allowed her to take herself on an unguided tour. Mary advised her husband that she was exhausted. 'A full day with her and I'll be joining your mother. Do her batteries ever run down?'

'No.'

'Why have you got so many bathrooms?' The dulcet tones floated downstairs like a pound of lead on a string. 'How many pees do you go for at once? There's only two of you. Ooh!'

'She's found our bedroom,' the couple chorused together.

'Four-poster,' she called. 'And some very passionate

colours. No wonder you're in that state, missus. A room like this means trouble.'

When Thora came down the staircase, she pretended to be a Hollywood star. 'Tomorrow is another day,' she announced just before reaching the hall. She curtseyed and looked round. 'Where is he?'

'Fish and chip shop. We haven't eaten.'

They sat in the drawing room eating supper straight from the paper, though Mary did supply forks.

'She's posh,' Thora commented on receipt of her cutlery. 'Is this one of them there h-inglenook fireplaces?'

Mary almost choked on a chip.

'Yes.' Andrew's face never flickered. 'It's a h-inglenook. The man who built the house a hundred or so years ago was a very wealthy Liverpool merchant. Most of these places have been made into flats or offices, but we managed to save this one.'

'It's grand.'

He agreed with her. 'Dad and I have done a lot to it. We spend almost every weekend messing about with wood – when he's at home, that is.'

Thora screwed up her paper and belched loudly. 'Better out than in,' she declared by way of apology. 'Now, Andy, tell me all about your mam, God love her.'

So they explained at length and in detail about Geoff's suicide note, his death during the writing of it, the illness that had caused him and all who loved him so much misery. Thora learned about the dead child, Geoff's suspension, his decline, his intention to drown himself in the Mersey.

'Bloody hell,' Thora breathed. 'He were a gradely doctor.'

'He was,' Mary agreed. 'Till he got ill.'

'My mother took an overdose,' Andrew said. 'Enough to kill, though we found her just in time. Before that, she'd lost interest. Mary and another woman used to give her a bath and change her clothes. And she almost needed force-feeding. It's over two years now.'

For once in her life, Thora was quiet.

'Cup of tea?' Andrew asked.

'Shush while I think about Emily.' Thora thought about Emily, a good mother, good worker, great housekeeper. But she'd always had a funny bone, a tendency to laugh when something amusing came up, like a dog tearing out of the butcher's with half a dead pig, or Thora's lads coming home covered in most of the mud from the bottom of the Croal.

Andrew crept out to make tea. 'There you go, Thora.'

'What? Oh, ta.' She took the cup. 'Emily were so kind. I weren't. Never been kind, me. And when she met Geoff, she blossomed like one of them apple trees in spring. She had her teenage years in her forties. But she lived for him, you see, and that's what's at the bottom of it, and I suppose you already know it. So if you can't drag her out of the full stop, how can I? The world without him in it is something she doesn't want. I can't bring him back, Andy.'

'I know that.'

'But I'll do me best with her.'

'I know that, too. And something else – you're a liar, because you're one of the kindest people I've met.'

Thora sniffed. 'She and Joe gave me that house. And you say she's been in and out of the loony bin for two years?'

Mary nodded. 'It's been hard on Joe and on Drew.'

'And there's been no improvement?'

'None at all,' Andrew said. 'She's like a puppet or a robot, sits on her bed, sits on her easy chair, sits at the table in the middle of the room, eats, goes to the bathroom, goes to bed.'

365

'Not much of a bloody life, that, Andy. Right. Get me to this here bungalow so I can see what's what.'

They showed her what was what and furnished her with the makings of breakfast. 'Joe lives next door,' Mary told her. 'But he's off in the Midlands again expanding his empire. He'll be back soon.'

Thora asked about Toodles, and was sad to hear that she'd gone to the big scratching post in the sky. 'Well, you get off now. I'll watch a bit of telly and get myself to bed. There's thinking to be done.'

She did her thinking aloud, of course. 'So Joe's thrown in the towel and said she can be plugged into the electrick-ery. She's not a bloody iron or a lamp, and I've never known that ECT to do anybody any good. I mean, look at her opposite with agora-wotsit. It never worked on her, did it? Mind, they had to drag her screaming through her front door.'

She made herself a jam sandwich and a pot of tea. Sweet stuff always helped when it came to thinking. 'I wonder what the hell I'm supposed to be? A miracle? No idea what difference I'll make just by turning up out of the blue. It's a nice bungalow, is this.'

There was a photograph of Emily with Joe and Geoff. It sat on the mantelpiece with a clock and a couple of ornaments. The relationship between Emily and her two men had been a rum do and no mistake. What a mess.

On a corner cupboard stood an ornate box with Geoff's name carved into its surface. 'So she brought you home, eh, lad? Eeh, she loved you. She walked different, with what they call a spring in her step. I knew it had to be the other – you know – sex and all that. But it were more than sex. Aye, she loved thee more than any man has a right to be loved, and it's damned near finished her. Can you help me, son? Can you show me what I must do to get her started up again?'

She slept fitfully. Geoff was in the dream. 'Don't forget the bourbons. Thora loves bourbons.' Then Emily was there making tea, bringing it to the table with biscuits on a plate, a little doily between the china and the food. 'Where's me bourbons?' Thora heard herself ask.

'She has to have bourbons,' Geoff shouted.

Thora woke. She could hear the second syllable of the word echoing through the bungalow. Perhaps she hadn't been quite awake, but she could almost feel a presence in the bedroom. This was daft. 'Who's there?' she asked quietly. Of course, there was no reply. 'Hello?'

She got out of bed and went to the kitchen for a drink of water. Having been in the room earlier, she knew exactly how she'd left it. What she saw in there she would never forget, nor would she speak of it, because people might think her mad. On a tray near the kettle she had used was an empty packet that advertised its used-up contents. Bourbon cream biscuits.

Thora Caldwell was not easily fazed. When it came to faith, she was of the live-and-let-live school, but she believed her own eyes and was confident where her memory was concerned. The power of love. Her eyes leaked saline not because she was afraid of spirits, but because she wondered at the trouble that had been taken tonight to show her how to begin breaking into Emily's locked mind.

She had her drink of water, picked up the empty packet and carried it to the living room. 'Thanks, Geoff,' she said to the urn. 'Just so you know I found it and I will do my best, I promise you. You know I won't let you down, lad. More to the point, I won't let Emily down.'

The windows were closed, and there was no wind, yet the curtains moved. In that moment, Thora decided to return to Catholicism. There was a God. There was another step taken after death, and Geoff had managed to come back for Emily's sake. So that was the power of love, a love Thora had never known.

She stayed where she was to keep Geoff company. Stretched out on the sofa, she slept dreamlessly, waking in the morning strangely calm and peaceful. She sat up, stretched, rubbed her eyes and looked round. The biscuit packet had gone.

Thora wrote the script and presented it to Mary and Andrew. 'It's like a play,' she explained. 'I were sat there all day writing it, and I'm no good at spelling, so put up with it. See? I've even done a title. The Case of the Bourbon Cream.'

Andrew stared hard at his ex-next door neighbour. 'What are you going on about, Thora? If you're Sherlock Holmes, who's Watson?'

She snatched back her work. 'Not you, for a kick-off. I'd sooner have somebody what takes me serious. I'll have to hire a proper h-actor.'

'You can have Mary, but she can only do Humpty Dumpty or Snow White's eighth dwarf, Fatty.'

Thora sat down and glared at her small audience. 'Bleeding pathetic,' she accused them. 'Is your mother certified at the moment? Or is she a voluntary patient?' These words were separated, as if spoken to someone with limited auditory comprehension.

'She's nominally voluntary, since she's not dangerous, but we do the volunteering, because she never says a word.'

Thora sniffed. Her sniffs were legendary, and they meant she was a long way from best pleased. 'Get her home. Stick her in that bungalow and I'll barge in, just like I used to do on Mornington Road. I'll supply the biscuits, plus a few tales about my dear departed what should have departed long before he got round to it. If I have to bloody sit on her, she'll listen to me, damn it all.'

Andrew explained that in his opinion, although Emily seemed to notice very little, she was completely institutionalized. She knew the rhythm of her day, of the ward, of the staff. She was told what to do, and she did it. At home, everything had to be done for her.

'Then let me be the doer. I'll shift the bugger.'

'She's not a bugger,' Andrew said.

'No, but her illness is. It wants shifting. And I'll bet you they've give her no exercise, which she will be needing to build herself up, like.'

He had to agree with that. Thora had clearly managed to separate Mother from the mental illness, and she was intending to kill the latter and save the former. 'What do I have to say?'

'It's not as if I've give you one of them monolog-yous. If you fetch her home, tell her Thora's waiting for a brew, then keep mentioning me on the way back in the car. Tell her Bertha's piles have come back. Tell her Margaret Wilson's got dry rot and her hair's falling out. Oh, and Margaret's Bernard got rid of all his teeth and had a new bathroom put in.'

Mary was in pain. 'Stop it, Thora. I don't want to give birth just now.'

'Suck it back in. That's what I had to do with one of mine. I sat on his head for half an hour, cos I'd paid to see *Gone with the Wind*, and I weren't missing the end.'

Mary wiped her eyes. 'Weren't you in pain?'

'Listen, love. There were more pain at conception than there were at birth. He were no good at owt. Four years we had the New Testament propping the table up till Andy's dad made us a new leg. Matthew's gospel has no chance at all, because there's a hole through his middle at the start, and he's a bit dented right through. My hubby were a drunken bastard son of an Irishman on his way to Appleby for the horse sale. They had a whirlwind romance, him and Harry's mam, and Harry were the result. Whirlwind? She birthed a tycoon.'

'Typhoon?' Andrew suggested.

'Yes, that and all. The only thing as made him quiet were drink. And the drink made him permanently quiet and all. Oh, I've a lot to be grateful for. I think them as makes Guinness should get a Blue Peter badge off that kiddies' programme. Any road, I'm going to give the bungalow a good seeing to, bit of weeding, polish her furniture, get the Hoover out. I'll leave you this.' She tossed her script onto the coffee table. 'I'm going.'

She went, but came back immediately. 'Andy?'

'What?'

'Did she cry when Geoff died?'

He thought about that. 'Not really. She howled like an angry wolf. At the funeral, she simply looked through people. Even his parents couldn't get a reaction from her. And she just retreated inside herself, didn't want anyone or anything. I know this is going to sound daft, but I sometimes think she's with him, but she left her body behind.'

It didn't sound daft to Thora. It was nowhere near as daft as what she'd been through last night, biscuit packet, curtains and talking to an urn full of ash and splinters of bone. But she kept that to herself. 'I think you might be right, Andy. They were inseparable.' She paused. 'You two are the same. No way would you manage apart,' she prophesied before leaving again.

Mary blinked back some unexpected tears. 'She's right, Drew.'

'I know. Goes a long way past sex and splintery banisters, doesn't it?'

She nodded. 'If Emily and Geoff had half of what we have in each other, the loss must have devastated her. And we knew that already, but Thora is so perceptive. How does she know all that?'

'A bad marriage. She managed to position herself on the outside of her own experience and watch other people. The jokes are part of her method. She could probably break through concrete with a sewing needle.'

'She'll need to, darling.'

'I know.' He sighed deeply. 'But if anyone can, it's Thora.'

The phone rang. Thora lifted the receiver. 'Yes? Who's that then?'

'It's me. Andrew. Something's happened, Thora.'

She pressed a hand against her chest. 'Where are you?'

'Hospital. Mother's hospital. She spoke, Thora. She spoke. I'm coming home, and she'll be home in a few days.'

'Well thanks for the near heart attack. But she's not coming today?'

'No. I'll tell you when I get back.'

Thora picked up two bourbons and ate them before replacing the rest in Emily's biscuit barrel. She'd got the place all nice, fresh flowers, a pretty little lamp to shine on Geoff's urn, a new rug, some cushions with fringes on the seams. 'Never mind, old lad,' she told Geoff's ashes. 'She'll be back soon.'

Andrew arrived.

'Well?' Thora thrust a cup of tea at him. 'What's going on?'

He explained that he couldn't stay long, as Mary needed driving home. 'She's at Pam's. I don't like to leave her for too long, because she lost our first about three years ago. Anyway, back to Mother. It all happened round midnight the night before last.'

'The night I arrived?'

'That's the one. According to the duty sister, Mother sat bolt upright and screamed Geoff's name.'

Thora swallowed hard. He'd been here at midnight, too, messing about with biscuit packaging and curtains, but she wasn't going to say anything. 'I wonder why?' she said. 'And did she talk to you?'

'She whispered. She sounds like a hinge wanting oil. I suppose her vocal cords have slackened off over the years. But she's had electro-convulsive therapy. If she comes home, she'll have to go back four times as a day patient to finish the course. It may be barbaric, but it seems to be working.'

'What did she whisper, Andy?'

'She told me Geoff had been to see her and she had a headache. The headache would be from the ECT. And her face is less lined. She looked more like her old self, thank goodness. So.' He looked at his watch. 'I'd better go and get Dumpling from Pam's. You will stay, won't you? The staff will be bringing her home.'

'You know I'll stay with her. Go on. Get your wife while I . . .' No, she couldn't tell him she was going to talk to an urn, could she? 'While I have a nice long bath. See you tomorrow, love. So glad she's on the mend.'

Andrew went off to retrieve his beloved.

Thora picked up Geoff and carried him to the table. She spread a tea towel, then took a baby's soft toothbrush to get any bits and pieces of dust out of the ornate carving of the outer container. 'You must look your best for Emily. Do you remember that navy skirt? Pencil, the style were called. A split up the back where you could see a bit of navy lace on her underskirt. And her hair, Geoff. Like satin. And there was I stuck with horrible ginger curls. Eeh, I wish I could have looked like her for a few days.'

She applied beeswax and rubbed it in. 'And she give me a fair ear'ole rattling when I talked about you and her. There were strength in her, but so gentle in her ways, you'd never have guessed. Thing is, lad, you and I know you're round and about looking after her, but we have to let folk think the electrickery worked. Cos I don't want to end up in a padded room, and you don't want to get yourself exorcised.'

Something feather-soft touched the nape of her neck, and she laughed. 'Don't play tricks on me, Geoff. And go easy on Emily, too, because we want her sane. If she starts telling everyone you're here, she'll be judged crackers all over again, and that's not what we want. You'll have to keep your distance.'

Joe would be home any day. There was something solid about Joe, something dependable. She grinned. 'Joe's solid, and you're not, Dr Shaw. Emily will lean on him, and he won't fall over. Go back, hon. Go where you should be and let us get on with mending Emily. She loves you. She'll be with you one day.'

After she'd said all that, she suddenly felt alone and abandoned. But she had done and said the right thing, because Emily was here and now in bodily form, and he wasn't. Thora didn't pretend to understand the hereafter, but she knew it was supposed to be a state, a condition rather than a place. There was no time, no today, no tomorrow, so how Geoff had managed to come back would always be a mystery. She would pray for him. She would get her priest to pray for him, once she found a priest.

Mary and Andrew arrived. 'Isn't it exciting?' Mary said, her face lit by a beautiful smile. 'She spoke, Thora.'

'She did, love. We'll get her back, Mary. I'm sure of that.

And when yon babby puts in an appearance, let her hold him.'

'Her,' Mary said. 'Katherine Mary, shortened to Katie. I'd know if it were a boy. This one might be a great lump, but she moves gracefully. I just wish she'd stop leaning on my bladder. I'll be the one in nappies soon. Three times, I've thought my waters had gone, but no, it's Katie stretching her limbs like an Olympic athlete. But Andrew, won't it be great if your mother's here in time for the birth?'

'It would be my idea of a good day, because she was an excellent mother, and I'm sure she'll be good with our child. Come on, small circular person, let's get you home.'

They walked the hundred yards that separated Rosewood from the bungalows. 'She has to come right, Mary. I didn't realize how badly affected I'd been until we got this ray of hope.'

'I know. She's your mum.'

'She's special, darling.'

'Oh yes, she must be. Because she had a special son.'

The miracle lay in the fact that Emily Sanderson, after years of withdrawal from society, recognized and acknowledged Thora immediately. 'Is this your new house?' she asked. There was confusion, but her eyes were alive at last.

Yet Thora insisted inwardly that the miracle had come from Geoff, though she had to admit that shock therapy might have had something to do with it. She sniffed back emotion and went into Bolton mode. 'Nay, lass, it's thine. Does tha not remember living here with Geoff? I can tell tha remembers owld Bowton talk, so look round. It's your bungalow, is this. Joe lives next door, only he's off somewhere being a millionaire, and your Andy lives a few strides that way.'

Andrew and Mary entered. 'Mother?' He held out his arms and she entered his embrace. 'Oh, son. What happened? Where've I been?'

Mary turned away, because her tears flowed too freely.

'Never mind all this mawping about,' said Thora. 'Get that kettle on, Emily Sanderson – I'm fair clemmed. I'll have a bourbon with my tea, ta.'

Emily went straight to the kitchen. She never faltered, didn't ask where anything was.

Mary mopped her cheeks. 'Will she be all right with a kettle?'

'She will,' Thora replied. 'Some memory goes with ECT, but old skills remain. I've seen this bloody game before.'

The nurse who had brought Emily home entered the house. 'Is it all right if we go? You know where we are if you need us.'

'That'll be a cold day in hell,' Thora muttered sotto voce, though Andrew heard her.

'Behave,' he chided.

Emily wandered in. 'Carry the tray, please. My arms don't work.'

'See?' Thora's hackles were up. 'They try to treat the illness, but they ignore the bloody patient what's fastened to it. Her muscles have wasted with all that sitting down. Don't worry, I'll sort her out.'

The nurse left the house quickly.

Emily wandered to the corner cupboard and placed her hand on the box. 'Geoff,' she said. 'He's dead, you know. But he came to see me and said I had to go home. So this must be home. I have a blue bedspread with matching curtains. A reading lamp with a cream-coloured shade. In there.' She pointed to her bedroom.

There were bourbons on the plate and there was a doily under the biscuits. Every cup had a saucer and a spoon, and there was an extra spoon in the sugar next to a jug of milk. Yes, this was all very Emily Sanderson.

'Where are we?' Emily asked her son.

'North Liverpool, Mother.'

'Ah. And Joseph?'

'Away on business. He lives next door.'

They drank tea. 'Bourbons for Thora. Don't forget the bourbons. Where's Joseph? Yes, business. Furniture and kitchens. They hurt my head, you know.'

'It's the treatment,' Andrew told her. 'You have to go back, but you won't sleep there. You'll be here with Thora and us. Four more headaches, that's all. After that, we'll see how you go.'

'You're a doctor,' Emily said.

'I am.'

'Geoff was a doctor.'

'He was, and a bloody good one, Mother.'

She looked up at the ceiling. 'A lot of papers in the roof. I'm tired.' Without another word, she went to bed.

Thora was quiet. She was seething. Mary sat next to her while Andrew perched on the arm of the Sanderson sofa. 'Thora?'

She shook her head angrily. 'I'm just thinking about all what they've took away from her. They try to treat the mental side, but the physical end of things goes to hell in a handcart with bells on. They should have flexed her legs and arms a few dozen times a day, but oh no, they're treating the illness, not the patient. She's just flesh and bone fastened to a problem. She's as weak as a newborn kitten. Oh, and get her one.'

'A kitten?'

'Yes. Something what she has responsibility for. I've ten weeks to get her right. When that babby comes, she needs

376

the strength to hold it and enjoy it. Go home. I'll walk her up later for her dinner or supper or whatever it gets called these days. Protein, veg still crunchy rather than drowned, hold back a bit on the dairy while we see what she's used to except for milk in her tea.'

Andrew patted his old friend's hand. 'I told Mary you were as good as any qualified nurse.'

'Better than that bloody lot what brought her back today. They should be shamed of theirselves. Nurses? They couldn't nurse a h-interesting thought.'

In that moment, Andrew realized yet again that Thora was a lot brighter than most people he knew. Given an education, she would have been a hospital matron by now. She talked sense, albeit delivered in flat, Lancashire tones. He knew many people like her, men and women shoved in factories at fourteen, no chance of further schooling, no chance of promotion. George had been right, then. Thora was the answer. Andrew planted a kiss on her cheek. 'See you later, sweetheart.' He left with Mary.

Thora blinked. Sweetheart? Why hadn't she met somebody like him instead of Harry? Well, she'd never looked like Mary, had she? Thin, flat-chested except when pregnant or feeding, dark, rusty-red curls that wouldn't behave like proper hair, a face only a mother could love. Whereas Mary, though rather distended at the moment, was a real looker. 'You play the cards you're dealt, Thora Caldwell,' she said aloud. 'And you got a bum hand. Still, never mind. You can come here for your holidays, bucket and spade, check on Mary, look after Emily, sit in the garden. Lovely.'

When evening came, Emily and Thora walked up to Rosewood. Emily's pace was slow, and she had developed what

Thora called 'the hospital stoop', with her shoulders rounded and her back curved as if promising to become a dowager's hump. Well, Thora would put a stop to that as well.

Still rather confused, Emily seemed to enjoy her food. 'Where's Joseph?' she asked several times. The response was always the same; he would be back very soon. She remembered the banisters, the monks' benches in the hall, an antique grandfather clock that had cost a fortune after being restored, the big garden, the huge Sanderson kitchen.

But she surprised them, too. 'My parents died within days of each other.'

'Who told you?' Andrew asked.

'You did, silly boy. Don't you remember?'

'Yes, of course,' he replied. 'They left you a lot of money, Mother.'

She remained consistent in that area, as she didn't ask how much and didn't seem impressed. 'They visited me, but I wasn't there. It's a shame.'

There wasn't one person at the table who didn't understand what she meant. Mary suddenly lost her appetite. This poor woman had just spent the best – or worst – part of three years in Purgatory, all through no fault of her own. She had loved too much, and that was no sin.

Andrew squeezed his wife's little hand. If he lost her ... it didn't bear thinking about. From that very first day outside the Cavern, he had recognized her as part of him, and he knew it had been the same between Mother and Geoff. Certain of Mary's love, secure in his happy bubble, Andrew needed only to look across the table at Mother to realize how fragile life was. Everyone was breakable.

With the possible exception of Thora. No, that wasn't the case. Difficult as life had been for her, Thora could never guard herself completely, since she had invested everything in her sons and her grandchildren. She never moved without her photos of little Matthew, our Eileen, who can read and she's only four, Sam Cheeky-face and Laughing Jimmy. So yes, most people were vulnerable.

The women went to the drawing room while Andrew made coffee. 'That's a h-inglenook fireplace,' Thora announced.

'There's no aitch in it,' Emily advised her.

'No h-aitch?'

'No aitch in aitch, either.'

'Course there is. Stands to reason there'd be a h-aitch in h-aitch.'

Emily started to giggle. The giggle caught hold, and she became breathless. 'No, no,' she moaned.

Thora held her friend's hands. 'Come on, let it out. Emily, for God's sake, set it loose.'

The full-blown hysteria that should have seen the light of day well over two years ago suddenly filled the room. Andrew stood in the doorway, a coffee mill in his hands. Thora knelt on the floor in front of Emily and took the blows, the temper, the frustration that had been locked away for so long. 'It's all right, hit me, I'm tough as old boots.'

A rhythm developed. 'He's dead, he's dead, he's dead.' With every 'dead', she slapped Thora's arms. 'Dead, dead, dead. Where's Joseph?'

'He's coming.'

'He's here,' said a voice from the hall doorway. Emily's husband opened his arms, and Emily staggered to him. 'All right, love,' he said. 'You cry all you like, all you need to. I'll look after you now. Thora will, too, and Andrew and Mary. You're not alone. We've been waiting for you.'

Joe was given cheese on toast, and everyone got coffee.

But the *pièce de résistance* was saved until it was time to go home. Andrew gave his mother a cardboard box with holes in the top. 'For you, Mother, from all of us.'

It was a tortoiseshell kitten with a lot to say for itself considering its size. Emily dried her eyes. 'Toodles,' she said. 'Is it a queen?'

'Oh yes, definitely female.' Joseph laughed. 'It hasn't shut up yet. Come on, girls, let's get home.'

Sixteen

'You look rather pale this morning, my darling circular person.' Andrew studied his very pregnant wife across the breakfast table. She wasn't eating. She had reached her due date almost a week ago, and he had booked time off work. If she didn't get into gear soon, she would need to have labour induced, because the weight was too much for her, and her blood pressure had taken a couple of walks on the wild side. 'Poor little Mary,' he said. 'That kid needs a calendar and an alarm clock.'

'Oh, shut up,' she snapped. 'You may be a doctor, but you're only a man, so you know nothing at all about this.'

Her skin was whiter than normal, and she seemed uncomfortable. In fact, she appeared to be in pain. But he had been warned. Should he panic and cast a shoe or sprain a fetlock when she went into labour, he would be downgraded immediately and put out to grass rather than to stud. Oh, and oats would be off his menu long-term.

'Pale? That will be a pigment of your imagination,' she went on through gritted teeth, a frown creasing her damp forehead. 'At this moment, O knight in once shining and now rusty armour, I feel a strange urge to kill the person who altered the shape of my destiny.' She inhaled deeply. 'As you qualify for that position, you should bugger off quickly and get your mother. My waters have gone. The chair on which I sit, the upholstered seat, is saturated with said waters. Don't start fussing.'

He gulped audibly, stood up and knocked over his own chair. 'Oh, God. Oh, God, God, God.'

She looked at him in despair. 'Bloody doctors? Just look at the state of you. I knew you'd fall to bits, you great lummox. Go before I find a use for this bread knife. And find me a change of knickers and the other pair of maternity trousers.'

He wasn't going anywhere. Mary sat and listened to him failing to make sense on the phone in the hall. 'She's ... Mary's waters ... yes, yes. I have to get her case for the ... yes ... for the ... will you come, Thora? Bring Mother. I have to ... yes. Thank you.' Mary heard him replacing the receiver and dashing upstairs. 'Damned wonderful damned fool,' she muttered. He was as much use as a chocolate kettle.

There was just one small but pressing problem. Stage one, with the backache, the waters, and the fingers of pain creeping gradually from spine to abdomen, lasted just a few moments before the real business began. This wasn't supposed to happen, not with a first labour, but Baby wanted out and Baby was breaking out.

She heard Drew running upstairs for her case. The urge to push was suddenly overwhelming. Though if she screamed, he would probably fall downstairs and break his neck. Not a good idea, even though he was the one who'd put her in this mess, God help him. She tried panting, but the urge to bear down was primeval and undeniable. The base of her spine was moving outward, so she knelt on the floor, as sitting was no longer the easy option.

Thora rushed in and dealt with everything while Emily watched. She removed Mary's undergarments. 'Yon babby's got black hair. Well, at least we know it's the right way up, eh? Or the right way down. That's it – lie on your side. You'll be all right now, flower, because I'm here.' What the hell was she saying? Had she ever done this before? No, she bloody well hadn't. 'Breathe easy, breathe easy. Just a minute; hold your horses, missus, this isn't the Grand bloody National. Pant for me, love. Emily – sharp scissors and something to clamp the cord. Andy? Get your backside in here this minute. Bring towels. Right, sweetie. Give us a big push. Andy?'

He rushed in clutching a case and a couple of towels, placing them on a sofa before staggering backwards against the wall. 'Erm...' He glanced at his poor wife and Thora. 'I ... er ...'

'Help your mother. Kitchen. Clamps. Something to cut the cord. Go before I clout you,' Thora snapped.

He left. 'I love you, Mary.' The words were thrown over his shoulder as he fled through the house.

Thora tutted. 'Now he tells you. They pick their bloody times, eh? Just let me wriggle this little shoulder round, sweetheart. Don't push. Pant for me again. Curse if you like. Here we go, one more push, Mary. That's it, that's it, keep it coming. Aw – lovely. It's a nice little lass. By, she's got some lungs on her. Emily? Come on, Grandma.'

Katherine Mary Sanderson was born on 1 June 1968 after just a few minutes of sharp, vicious labour. She was tiny, furious, and very vocal. Her mother, stretched out on a beautiful silk Persian rug, was in shock. On Mary's chest, a screaming bundle of birth-stained humanity emptied her anger into an unattractive, over-bright world. Andrew, dangerously close to tears, dealt with umbilicus and afterbirth.

'I hope you can see what you're doing,' Thora said. Then she joined in with a bit of weeping. She'd delivered a baby. She couldn't believe she'd delivered this healthy-sounding baby. Her knees didn't belong to her. She had thighs and shins, but nothing substantial in between.

'Jesus, we're a flaming quorum, all crying,' said the new mother. 'Cheer up, for goodness' sake; it's not a funeral.'

Emily was the only one who held herself together. 'Well done, Mary. Thora, will you do the tying off? Let's have a tidy navel, shall we? Andrew can't see properly.'

'Neither can I,' howled Thora.

The baby, once separated from her mother and wrapped in a towel, became the star turn in a game of pass the parcel. She managed to stop complaining while Thora, after rediscovering her knees, carried the newborn to the kitchen and put her through her paces, checking the reflexes, counting digits and making sure that Katherine could do a very strange thing that she would forget within minutes; yes, she stood, bore her own weight and 'walked' on tiptoes while Thora held her arms. 'I wouldn't care, I've only read about all this, but don't tell them, Katie. This is our secret, little one. Never let them know you were my first.'

Andrew, standing over his wife, stopped weeping. 'I'll get an ambulance,' he said. 'You should both be looked at in a maternity ward.'

Mary forbade it. She was going nowhere, since she had too much to do, as her daughter needed to learn breast-feeding. 'I've a big enough audience already, thanks. You should have sold tickets and given everybody a balloon and a slice of cake. If I'd wanted an ambulance, I would have said so. Thora's an excellent midwife, better than most trained in our hospitals. Stop panicking. I knew you'd fall apart at the seams, soft lad. All men are stupid when it comes to the birth of a child.'

Thora entered the room with Katie in her arms, opened her mouth to say she'd never done this before, thought

384

better of it again, and snapped her jaw into closed position. It was best to look professional even though she'd almost made it up as she went along. If the truth were to be told, she felt a bit queasy, so she sat down and shut up. Had the situation been less busy, someone would have remarked on this unusual phenomenon, because she was reputed to talk even when asleep.

Emily couldn't take her eyes off Katie. 'A little girl,' she said over and over again. 'He never had a sister, but he's got you instead, baby. And see there? That lady you're lying on? That's your mother. Lucky girl, you are. Geoff would have loved this, you know. He would have made such a fuss of you, young Katie, because he loved babies.'

Andrew helped his wife to sit up.

'Wash this little one,' she told him. 'Keep her navel dry, but get all the muck off her. She looks basted ready for the oven. There's some powder for the belly button, so use it.'

He blinked. 'That's not muck. That's the endometrium of the woman I love.' The colour had returned to her face; his wife was beautiful once more.

Emily accompanied him. They used cotton wool and the handbasin in the ground-floor bathroom. Katie liked the water. She remembered the water. She remembered the voices, too. She also discovered how to be hungry and started to scream again. Making noise was fun; she'd never made noises before.

Andrew sat at the piano while Mary put her daughter to the breast. He played the tunes he'd played right through the pregnancy, and Katie did what was required of her to bring in the milk. She remembered her mother and the music. This was the right place, though it was too bright and rather crowded for her liking. But she was warm, she was celebrated, and she was feeding.

Glad that he needed no sheet music, Andrew shed a

couple more tears. He thought about his grandparents who had left him enough money to see everyone through life without needing to do a hand's turn, and they had both died and missed the birth of Katie. Stuart, a man who would have made a brilliant father, could never have a child. But Geoff was the one who loomed largest. Emily, clearly pleased as Punch to be a grandma, remained sad to the core. She'd gained the skills to spread a layer of marzipan and icing over the devastation, but she didn't fool her son.

Geoff was missed by everyone. He'd been a blazing beacon of light and eccentricity. Andrew wanted him here now. Geoff would have written a poem, smoked a cigar and dished out some large servings of brandy, though not necessarily in that order. Dad was on his way back from Manchester. He would bring a teddy bear. Whenever anyone at all had a baby, Joe Sanderson bought a teddy bear.

As he played through his repertoire of Chopin's etudes, it dawned on Andrew that he was very like Emily. He and Mother weren't good at letting go. Geoff continued to be loved by his partner; should anything happen to Mary, Andrew would probably follow in his mother's footsteps. Like mother, like son. She'd fallen in love suddenly and deeply, as had he. They were both hopeless cases; there was no cure.

The new baby, dressed now in a cotton nightdress, was left with her father while Emily and Thora took Mary upstairs for a tepid shower.

He studied his daughter closely. She looked as if she'd arrived through the post, wrinkled, tousled, blotchy and a bit squashed. 'They should have written *Do not bend or fold* on your packaging. You're about seven pounds,' he informed her. 'Now, this new place is Earth. It hangs in space with lots of other bits and pieces, and we do what's called living. You eat, defecate, urinate and scream. It's your job. I mend bones, and that's my job. Your mother does whatever she likes, so that's her job.'

Katie opened one eye.

'Can you see me? I'm your father. Your mother's in the shower, and she's your feeding station. You are our first child, and if you don't stop giving me the evil eye, you'll be the last.'

Tiny fingers curled round his left thumb. She was perfect apart from the crumpled face. He couldn't see her toes, as her feet were encased in bootees. But he could see that she knew him, recognized his voice. 'I won't be able to call your mother Fatso any more soon, but at least I'll get her back. I've missed her, you see, because you borrowed her for a while.'

He droned on. Although she was asleep, Miss Katherine Sanderson maintained her grip on her father's thumb. She was her mother all over again. 'You're going to be trouble,' he said. 'Just like Mary.' He told her about Liverpool, the Mersey, a cathedral that was taking forever to build, how to deal with a fractured ulna; he gave her directions to Sniggery Woods and to the nearest library, and related how Christopher Robin went to the palace with Alice to see the changing of the guard. 'I'll find a bridge and we'll play Pooh sticks,' he promised. 'We'll leave Eeyore and Wol for now, because they have personality disorders and trouble with communication skills. Tigger's all right. You'll get on very well with Tigger.'

Mary sat on the stairs with Thora and Emily. They covered their mouths to prevent the escape of giggles.

Katie, lulled into contentment by her father's steady voice, snoozed happily. She definitely remembered him; he'd made noises at her before.

'I rescued your very ungrateful mother from the Beatles, you know. Not insects, just four boys with guitars, drums and a very large retinue of mentally unstable females. And I knew straight away that she was my wife.' He sighed heavily. 'Life's odd. I'm sure you'll discover that through your own mistakes. But she wasn't a mistake. She was magic, still is. So treat her well, or you'll answer to me.'

The same eye opened.

'Ah, you're back. Where do you go? What do you dream of? Warmth and darkness inside Mummy? Swimming about like a little tethered dolphin? Well, that's yesterday, pal. You've got responsibilities now. There are rules. First, don't allow your parents any sleep. Second, when you burp, bring back milk and spray it on anybody within a foot or two. Don't bother with the real projectile vomiting, or they'll stick you in hospital. Third, straighten your face – this is your father speaking.'

Andrew listened. He listened to them listening to him. A herd of elephants would have been quieter than the women on the stairs. 'About your mother. She's very short since I put her in a hot wash, but don't call her Titch. Her temper's a bit short, too. Thora's all wind and pi– urine, and your grandma is nice. What is Grandma? Say it with me, Grandma is nice.'

A giggle exploded, but he pretended not to hear it. 'Thora's in charge of everybody, and Grandpa is a millionaire, so be good to him, and he'll buy you a bike. You'll need stabilizers for a while, but we'll get you going. We've put your name down for a good school, and you'll be a doctor and a brilliant pianist like your dad.'

The women came in. They stood in a row and looked at him, such a tall man with so tiny a scrap in his arms. 'You look the part,' Mary said.

'Can we keep her?' he begged. 'I found her outside under the rhubarb. She says she doesn't like gooseberries.'

Joe, in the company of a toy bear bigger than the infant,

crashed in via the front door. 'By gum,' he said, a smile stretching across his face. 'I missed the main feature, then. And I did eighty up the East Lancs Road.' He thrust forward the inevitable gift. 'You were quick, Mary. Did the baby come by air mail?'

Mary nodded. 'A jet-propelled stork,' she answered, relieving her father-in-law of his furry burden. 'This is Katherine Mary Sanderson. She was born at nine fifteen this morning on a very good rug. Go on. Take her away from Drew; he's becoming too attached.'

Joe, the businessman who had built an empire from a shed in a back garden, spilled a tear of joy over his granddaughter. 'The most beautiful sight I ever clapped eyes on,' he said.

Mary and Andrew exchanged glances. 'Have you been to the optician for an eye test lately, Dad?'

Joe grinned through saline at his cheeky son. 'Give over. She'll grow into her face. Perfect babies seem to lose their prettiness as they get bigger. But Katherine will be the belle of the ball.'

Emily joined her husband. He turned to her. 'Em, remember our Andrew's first nappy? The nurses thought we were mad when we screamed like that. It was a sight I'll never forget. There were colours in there that don't exist in real life.'

Mary tutted. 'Stop picking on my poor husband. He's just given birth, remember. We don't want him going all postnatal, do we?'

Thora was in a heap on the floor, and even Emily smiled. No matter what, her Andrew always maintained his dignity. 'Joseph, give Katherine back to her father before he starts to fret. Then go down the road and bring that hotpot up here. It's in my fridge next to the cheese. With some pickled beetroot and crusty bread, it should be sufficient for everyone's lunch. And you must tell Daisy she's an aunt. Whether or not she understands isn't important. I'll go with you to St Helens.'

Thora hauled herself up and sat in a chair. Witnessing the development of this group of people, albeit by proxy for much of the time, had opened her eyes. She knew now how true love worked, how men could cry without ceasing to be men, how relationships changed while remaining strong. Joe, who had never stopped loving Emily, had stepped back for a force known as Geoff. Father to a daughter with special needs, he soldiered on. Andrew, raised through his teens by three parents, was a normal, decent man. And as for Mary, she was just wonderful. Without this family, Thora's life would be very dull.

'You'll be going home soon, then?' Andrew asked.

'Aye, I will. But first, I have to hand over to this Eva you've been telling me about. You're a lot stronger, Emily, but housework gets a bit much. If you'd stopped any longer in that bloody place, you'd have lost the use of your legs. I've written to the government about it. They want talking about, them mental doctors and nurses. You could have finished up in a bloody wheelchair.'

Andrew stood up. 'Thora, you swore twice. My child isn't used to that sort of language.'

Thora delivered a raspberry. 'They listen through their mother's bodies, you daft bugger. How many times has Mary threatened to deck you with one of her copper bottoms? More fights in this house than in a boxing club.' She folded her arms.

He grinned. So far, paternity seemed not to have affected his ability to torment women. Life without the taunting of the superior sex would have been dull indeed. Although he shared no genes with Geoff, he had learned much by watching a master at work. Mary stood her corner every time, of course.

'Ignore him,' was Emily's advice.

'I will,' promised Thora.

'I do,' Mary told them. 'In fact, I've no idea how Katie happened, because I've been sleeping in the summer-house for a year.'

'Osmosis,' Andrew told her. 'Look it up.'

The banter continued until Katie called time. She was taken upstairs by her parents while Emily and Thora began to prepare the table for lunch. Joe brought the hotpot and it was placed in the oven. The grandparents nodded off in chairs. Joe and Emily, opposite each other, dozed near the fireplace while Thora, midwife and grandma-by-proxy, stretched out on the sofa. She had never before felt so thoroughly at home anywhere. She didn't want to go back to Bolton, though she needed to see her real grandchildren; she wanted to stay with Emily. She could visit her family whenever she wished, but she was so happy and settled here.

Upstairs, Katie was feeding.

'The real milk should be in soon,' her mother said. 'If she gets the colostrum, she collects my immunities. After that, I may bottle-feed. Well, I don't want to end up shaped like a failed barrage balloon. Don't laugh at me, Andrew Sanderson. She's only a couple of hours old, and I already feel drained.'

'Shall we call her Draculina?' he asked.

'She's Katherine Mary. Do you think I should try press-ing her face with a cool iron? She's very crumpled. Looks like she got screwed up, thrown in a bin, then rescued by a passing Samaritan.'

'You're a cruel woman, Mary.'

She nodded her agreement. 'Caesareans are the best. They come out ironed, happy, completely dressed and potty trained, full set of teeth, table manners – the lot.'

'She's lovely,' he insisted. 'Different, but lovely.'

'She's ours, Drew.'

'We made a person,' he said.

The weight of his statement hit home for both of them. Katie was them. 'I've seen this so many times, Drew, and I've wondered about the expressions on parents' faces. They've made a person. Even when the wife's bigger than a bus, the baby's still no more than an idea. Then, whoosh, and it's so flaming real.'

He sighed. 'Three hours old, and she already rules the roost.'

'It's not that, love. It's her needs and her wants and her disposition. It's nature and nurture and where will we go wrong? It's understanding the crying before she learns to talk. They say nurses, doctors and teachers make the worst parents.'

'Rubbish.'

'Quite. No good at it, you see.'

'She'll be fine.'

'Will she? She's Gemini. They can be all over the place. My belly hasn't gone down much, so I'll be all over the place as well, because there's too much of me. And with her being a Gemini, so naughty they are, I shall be too fat to catch up with her. And with me being fat, you won't love me any more.'

'True.'

'I'll kill you.'

'I know. And you'll get away with it, post-partum blues and all that. Now, there's a song title. Louis Armstrong might be interested. I don't wanna be in yo shoes, yo woman got the post-partum blues, I think I'm gonna go away, try to live another day.'

'You are sick.'

'Yup.'

'Tell me some more.'

'She killed the chickens in the yard, hit you on the

head so hard, shot yo momma and yo dad, got them blues so very bad.'

'It's crap.'

He summoned his broad, slow-to-arrive smile, one he preserved just for her. '*Semper fidelis*, Mary.'

'Right. Plenty of vinegar with mine.'

They had survived.

They survived twice more, and Mary regained her figure within six weeks every time. By 1972, they had two daughters and one son. Helen joined Katie in 1970, and she was born after nine hours of labour, uncreased, unblemished, unruffled and stunningly beautiful. Katie, who had ironed out her face by growing, was pretty, dynamic and naughty. The second little girl was so perfect that her parents thought she might be a Katie in reverse, but she didn't deteriorate.

Katie was very pleased with her new doll. She called Helen Len, as she wasn't ready for anything duosyllabic, and she dragged the tiny baby from her crib more than once, cuddled her rather roughly, sang to her in nonsense and was eventually confined to prison at certain times, which pleased her not at all. Her hatred for the playpen grew daily, and she screamed magnificently. 'Bad,' she yelled, 'bad, bad, bad.'

Helen didn't cry. She yelped like a puppy when hungry, purred like a kitten when picked up even by her older sister, wore a smile at all times, and was heart-touchingly gorgeous. It occurred to Mary on several occasions that Helen might be thick, but she was proved wrong when, at nine months, having never crawled, the child stood up and walked. She took four steps to the playpen, stared at her mother, and stood gripping the bars until lifted and placed inside the holding cell with Katie. This baby girl had a quiet power that must surely have come from intellect, so she wasn't thick, then.

The bond was clearly unbreakable. The older child, well into her third year, became a second mother to little Helen. Mary, feeling redundant, brought Eva back into the recipe. A nursery was created, and the children spent much of their time with Eva, who needed the money. Her own children were handed over to her sister, who lived in Eva's house, and Eva found herself becoming a nanny to the Sanderson children when Mary took part-time work at the Women's.

Ian's birth wasn't so much an event as a slight interruption. Like Katie, he arrived suddenly and without fanfare, but in the medical corner of the Picton Library's reference section in the cultural sector of Liverpool. Although this caused something of a hullabaloo, Mary and the baby remained unfazed. They were scooped up, manhandled, and placed in an ambulance.

Andrew arrived at the Women's bearing gifts and a strong resemblance to an unmade bed. His stethoscope hung down his back, his hair stuck up in all directions, and he was wearing odd shoes. Mary knew all over again why she loved this man so much. He was a generous, adorable, unpredictable fool. 'It's a boy,' she said, 'so we can give up now.'

He picked up his son. 'In the reference library, eh? That's a good sign. He'll be a great reader. Give up what?' he asked.

'Only my tubes, you daft swine. Who got you ready? You look like something out of a hospital pantomime.'

'I did it all by myself.'

'Oh, God.'

Eight weeks later, Mary was back at work full-time as a

ward sister. Eva Dawson acquired another charge, a solemn little lad who followed her with his eyes right from the start. Katie, now four years old, displayed little interest in the new arrival. When questioned, she put her hands on her hips in the manner of an old woman, and shook her head at Eva. 'I got a-nuff,' she said. 'I got her. She missed potty and did it on floor.' Training her little sister was enough of a trial without sitting and singing to a baby who was so determinedly unimpressed.

'Her' smiled sweetly. Whatever happened, Helen remained calm and beautiful.

'He's your brother,' Eva snapped.

Katie wasn't 'bovvered', and she said so. 'I got Helen,' she said, proud of her pronunciation. 'Get anovver Katie for him.'

'That's us told, then,' Eva whispered to Ian when she lifted him for his bottle.

Emily arrived. 'I can see a small deposit in the bathroom,' she called through the doorway. 'I'll clean it up, Eva.'

'Thanks.'

Emily's situation had altered. The pair of bungalows had become one with four bedrooms, a large Sanderson Intelligent Kitchen, a dining room, a reading room and a double garage. Joe no longer went away regularly; he sent others to look after his widespread business, while he travelled no further than Staffordshire and West Yorkshire, as he would not leave his wife overnight unless Thora was visiting. During weekdays, Emily spent time with Eva and the grandchildren, and weekends were devoted to her amusement. She was taken to Southport, the Lake District, the Dales, Derbyshire, and even London.

She entered the room. 'Eva?' she whispered.

'What? Why are we whispering?'

'She can read. Katie can read.'

'Course she can. I made sure she can. She's going to a preparing school, so I had to get her ready.'

'Preparatory school, Eva.'

'Yeah, that as well. Mary did some words with her, but she's tired when she gets home, so I learned her – I mean taught her.'

'Well done. That opens a lot of portals for her. But . . .' She closed the door. 'They're having their nap,' she explained. 'Getting her to school, separating her from Helen, it's not going to be easy. And it will probably be down to us.'

Eva nodded sagely. 'It's nice to see a married couple so wrapped up in each other, but . . . I hope you don't mind me speaking out, Emily, only they've got three kiddies, young kiddies. They'll never grab these years back.'

'Neither will you, Eva.'

'I know. But I need to work for the money, don't I? Mary doesn't. My feller's a gardener, but Doc's a consultant. These little girls eat in the nursery except at weekends, and your son and daughter-in-law don't seem to put their kiddies first. I know they take them out Saturdays and Sundays, but look what they're missing.'

Emily nodded. 'I've tried to tell them as gently as possible that they should spend more time with the children, but they're both career-minded.'

Eva sighed. Had it not been for the money, she would have been at home with her own family, because this job was a bugger. Mary and Doc didn't always work set hours, and Eva often got home after her own children had gone to bed. 'Well, I don't want to lose me job, babe. They look after me well, money-wise. But I miss me kids. Don't say anything.'

'Wouldn't dream of it. Look. They wouldn't know if you went home for a couple of hours, would they? I can manage. Once young madam's at school, I can look after the two littlies.'

Eva didn't know what to say.

'And I can drive. We can take these three to your house and start a riot.'

Eva maintained her silence.

'It was a breakdown, Eva. I'm fine now. It's true – whatever doesn't kill you serves to make you stronger. I've no intention of being plugged into electric sockets again. They weren't so much headaches as earthquakes.'

Nanny Eva burst out laughing. 'He got his way with words from you, didn't he? You know Mary's had her tubes tied?'

Emily nodded.

'He chased her round this house last night with a puncture kit and a bike pump. Threatened to reinflate her equipment and take her for a ride. But she has the measure of him. If looks could kill . . .' She shrugged.

'To go forever children, hand in hand. The sea is rising, and the world is sand,' Emily said.

'You what?'

'Geoff's philosophy. Andrew borrowed it, too. It's Wilfred Owen, a war poet. It's about accepting love, yet battling it in case it takes over. Something like that, anyway. Children running, playing, love joining them, life going so fast, too fast.' She paused. 'Oh, Eva, I miss Geoff. Sometimes it seems like a hundred years since I saw him; at other times, it feels like yesterday.' She forced a smile. 'I don't seem to keep pace with real clocks and calendars. There was Geoff time, and no-Geoff time. I'm a silly old woman.'

Eva blinked rapidly. 'Well, if we were all as silly as you, we'd be OK. And you're not old. Sixty isn't old, not these days.'

Emily glanced in the mirror. She had aged since his

death. Joe had shown his true, mellower colours, had made a beautiful home for them to share, but there remained in her chest only a flicker of a heart that had once burned so bright a flame that it had shown in her face and in her stance. Sixty wasn't old for some, but it was for her. Was needing to die a sin? Could a person love another so much that a good son and wonderful grand-children were not enough? Still, at least the suicidal thoughts had dissipated. She could wait. And for a reason she didn't need to understand, she suspected that the wait would not be a lengthy one.

'Emily? World of your own again?'

'Sorry.'

'No need to apologize to me, queen. We all loved him. I didn't know him well, but I liked what I saw. Thanks to Mary, he signed the adoption papers for our Lucy, you know, and gave us a reference. So did Doc.'

Emily smiled. 'Put the kettle on. As Thora would say, I'm fair clemmed.'

'Gob like the bottom of a bird cage?'

'That's the one.' As Eva clattered in the kitchen, Emily sat and folded her arms while the next slice of time peeled away. *Soon. Make it soon, Geoff.*

As in life, Emily Sanderson was calm and dignified in death. She simply slipped away in the night, a gentle smile of acceptance on her face, a curl of Geoff's hair wound round her ring finger.

Yet her death was far from quiet. Three o'clock in the morning found Joseph seated on her bed, an arm across the body of his beloved and wonderful wife. They did not share a bedroom, yet he knew the moment of her passing, as he had woken suddenly and thoroughly, no yawning, no stretching, no cursing the sound of an alarm clock's raucous bell. He sobbed, and he didn't hold back. Into Emily's pretty bedroom he poured years of grief, self-loathing and frustration.

What happened tonight had been real, as real as his love for Emily, as real as every day spent in the design shop, in warehouses, in the knowledge that he would see her and eat with her at the end of a working day. And now he felt the drift of a light hand across his shoulder. Geoff was here, in this house, in this bedroom.

'Sorry, Joe,' he had said earlier, just as Joe had opened his eyes. 'It's her time. I've come for her.'

'Thanks for waking me and telling me, lad,' Joe said now. 'Look after our angel. I'll put her ashes with yours. Let heaven know how good she is.'

A floorboard creaked the message that they had gone. 'Forever children, hand in hand.' Geoff and Andrew both loved that piece. Joseph wept.

She wasn't here any more. Her body was just the building that had housed her, and she had vacated it, no lights on, no fire burning, no cups of tea, no buttered scones. Joe kissed her forehead, which still retained the warmth of life. There was a void in his chest, a space where his heart had lived, where she had lived. He had to get Andrew, as Andrew would never forgive him if he waited until sunrise.

Those poor children. Katie, now five and at school, came home every day and taught Helen all she had learned. Helen, at three, was reading. Ian, one year old and of a serious disposition, listened to all that was said. They would miss Grandma. Emily had been the only one who could calm Katie's occasional tantrums. Ian, young as he was, had adored the quiet lady who'd rocked him to sleep. Poor Eva would be bereft. And Thora. Oh yes, Thora would be here later today once Joe had phoned her.

Andrew. The boy, now a man, had always adored his

mother. He had been her life's work, her treasure and her pride. Overture to an Overture. Andrew had written that while still a child after questioning his mother about childbirth. 'Oh, Emily,' Joe whispered. There were words to it now, and Andrew had named a section of it 'A Liverpool Song' – it was about Mary, of course.

'I'll have to shift myself,' he advised his dead wife. 'Phone the doctor, get Andrew, start learning to live without you.' He blew his nose, stood up, and a chest of drawers caught his eye. A scarf of Thora's hung out of the top section. Had that been there earlier? Did he care?

After phoning Andrew and the doctor, Joe sat on the stairs, Toodles the second in his arms. He'd made a room in the roof with a large dormer window that overlooked the bay. A powerful telescope enabled him to look at the stars and to map their placement by reading books on astronomy. Emily had loved all that. He'd explained to her that light from those faraway suns took so long to reach the earth that some of them weren't there any more. 'Light years away,' he whispered to an empty house. 'Like you are now, my lovely girl.'

Where had she gone? Was it all mixed up with the space–time continuum? Was she still a part of the universe? Geoff certainly was, because he'd been here, he'd spoken and . . . and he'd pulled Thora's scarf out of that drawer. Emily would never have left the scarf hanging from a drawer. Geoff would, though. Given half a chance, Geoff could mess up a room in ten seconds.

Andrew fell in at the door. 'Dad? Is she in her room?'

Joe nodded. The cat ran out through the front door.

'I can check her, but I can't issue a certificate. Is the doctor coming?'

'Yes.'

She was dead, of course. Andrew held the hands that had soothed his brow during measles, painted him with

400

calamine when he'd had chickenpox, tied his laces when he'd been at nursery. She had never lost her temper, never reached the rim of patience.

He couldn't have stood up if he'd tried. There was no strength in him; he felt like someone suffering from a severe neurological problem. Mother had always been there. Even since his marriage, Andrew had seen her almost every day. Dad. How would he cope? After Geoff's death, Joe had stepped up to the plate, not as a lover, but as a friend, carer and brother. Perhaps he would bury himself in work? Ah. Joe was on the phone. He was speaking to Thora at four o'clock in the morning. Yes, Thora had been close to Mother.

'If Andrew will stay with Emily, I'll come now,' Joseph said. 'It'll give me something to do apart from skriking my eyes out. All right, love. About an hour, yes. Go and pack a bag.'

Andrew agreed to stay while Joe went to Bolton.

The doctor arrived, moccasin slippers on his feet, pyjama bottoms peeping out from the hems of his trousers, a cardigan thrown over the pyjama jacket. 'They'll want a post-mortem, Andrew.'

'I know.'

'Your dad found her?'

'Yes.'

'Did she call out for him? I know they didn't share a room.'

The cat was scratching at the front door. Andrew delivered a look designed to rivet his fellow medic to the wall. 'They shared a bond of deep friendship and love. If she'd had toothache, he would have felt it before she did. Do your bloody PM. The root is grief caused by the loss of her lover. It isn't suicide, and it isn't murder.'

'I'm sorry.'

'I know. Doing your job and all that rubbish. Get

Mother taken away, please. Dad's gone to fetch her best friend from back home. I don't want Thora any more upset than she needs to be.'

Half an hour later, Mother was gone. Her warmth, kindness, beauty and generosity were now confined to the pages of a history book that would never be written. Long, slender fingers flying over piano keys, the expression on her face whenever Geoff had entered a room, their warmish arguments about the meaning of Wilfred Owen's poetry, her gentleness, that sweet smile, her love. He would miss her love. Yes, he adored Mary with all his heart and soul, but his history with Mother was lifelong. It was as if every drop of his blood had descended to his feet.

He managed to get to the hall and phoned Mary. He knew she'd be awake and waiting. 'Post-mortem,' he told her. 'Dad knew the minute she'd died. He's gone for Thora. Thora's been a good friend to both of them.'

'Come home, Drew. I'll put all the lights on so that your dad will come here.'

He explained that he needed to sit for a while, but he'd be home soon. Back in Mother's bedroom, he noticed the shape of her head on the pillow. On the back of the door hung her dressing gown, deep pink with a hood. Matching slippers stood side by side beneath her dressing table. A stray hair remained in the nacre-backed brush. 'Oh, Mother, I love you.' There was a photograph of a beautiful young woman with a baby son in her arms. 'We freeze bits of it and stick it in pretty frames, but where does the rest of it go?' He picked up the article. 'You and I, Mother. You and I. And fixed moments behind cold glass are all I have left. What's Dad going to do without you?'

There was a list somewhere of aunts and uncles he had met briefly at his grandparents' house and at funerals. He would need to phone them all. Stuart would come, of course, as would Thora and people from Dad's work. There was something else, but he couldn't remember what. The something else swamped him when he picked up a photograph of Geoff. Yes, he had to cry. It was important to grieve immediately instead of saving it up until it became too large to handle. Bereavement unreleased could cause damage, and he allowed his heartbreak full rein, because the child in him needed to scream for his mother. It was nature's plan. Toodles was wailing.

'Stop the car, Joe.'

He pulled in at the next lay-by.

'Are you sure?' Thora asked.

He nodded thoughtfully. 'See, I can tell somebody like you, Thora. The young ones these days would laugh me out of court, so keep my secret. He woke me, said it was her time and that he'd come to get her. Only I might have heard that in a dream, but . . . But no. It was real. It happened.' He dried his eyes yet again.

Thora released a relieving sigh. 'You're not wrong and you're not going daft. And no, she would never have left her room untidy. A scarf sticking out of a drawer would have offended her sense of order. She was a very particular woman. My scarf would be Geoff's doing, and I'm telling you now, it's not his first offence. He was telling you to come and get me.' She paused and remembered what had happened before Emily's release from hell.

Joe waited patiently for the rest of it.

She told him about the bourbon packaging, the sound of his voice when he woke her, movement in the curtains. 'He helped me to deal with her. He helped us to get her out of that terrible place, Joe. I told him to go away,

403

because she would have talked to him, and she might have got herself in trouble again. I felt him leave. He must have stayed away till now.'

'Aye. I reckon you're right. A floorboard creaked, and I knew then I was on my own. Funny thing is, there are no creaky floorboards in the whole house. I replaced them, and a lot of joists, too, when I made the two bungalows into one. It means . . . I suppose it means there's life after death.'

'It does. Now, Joe, I'll keep your secret and you keep mine.' She placed a finger on her lips for a second. 'That way, we'll both stay out of the mental hospital.'

They continued their journey in silence and at speed, since the roads remained empty. Life was empty. She'd been a quiet woman, but Emily, constant, true and honest, had affected and improved the world for all who had known her. Thora couldn't imagine Joe without her.

They reached the coastal road. 'Thora?'

'What?'

'Can you stay a while, like for a few weeks till I learn to live by myself?'

'Course I will. I'll have to nip back for a birthday party, but you can come with me if you like. Look, the lights are on in Andrew's house. Let's call in, shall we?'

They found the couple clinging together on a sofa in the drawing room.

'Is your mother on her own?' Joe asked.

'They took her,' Mary answered for her husband. 'There has to be a coroner's inquest because it was a sudden death. Drew can't stop shaking. He's swallowed a tablet that should calm him down soon. Hello, Thora. Take over while I make some cocoa.'

So Thora held her best friend's son while he shivered his way through shock and grief. She wished she could tell him about Geoff, but, having made a pact with Joe, she had to stand by her word. 'Come on, lad. You know how she loved you. You were her world.'

'Geoff was her world,' Andrew managed. 'But he had to accept me, and I him, or they'd never have got together. So yes, I was important to her. So was Dad.'

'That's all so true,' Thora said.

'If there's any justice, they're together now,' Joe said. 'Thora's going to stay with me and help with arrangements.'

The sad foursome drank their cocoa. No one wanted toast or a biscuit. The soft, gentle heartbeat behind all their lives had been stilled. But the sun rose, birds fussed and children woke. As the old adage had it, life went on, though the sun, temporarily ashamed of his splendour, had the grace to hide his glory behind a cloud.

Seventeen

The dressings applied by time mended much of the pain, though scars didn't disappear completely. The sense of loss remained, as Emily had been loved and appreciated by all who had known her. That such a quiet, tender person could leave so huge a fissure in the geology of their planet was a lesson; she had been strong and powerful behind that serene facade.

Emily had died of a coronary occlusion caused by advanced arterial disease, so no one went to prison. Andrew was slowest to heal, because the loss of his mother cut a huge swathe through his history, slashing into an area in which he had been rooted, since Mother had always been there. Letting go of the past and facing life without Mother was hard, so he threw himself headlong into his work and was quiet at home for a while.

When Mary finally got through to him, he told her the lot; not just the facts, the dates, the sequence of events, but also the mutual love that had sustained him and Emily through difficult times. 'I'll be all right now,' he said to her after some months of mourning. And he was all right. As long as he had Mary, he would be fine. Every man needed scaffolding at some stage, and Andrew's outer support was a feisty little woman with attitude and enough guts for a whole army of soldiers.

Time ticked on regardless of circumstance. By 1980,

Katie was completing her first year of secondary education, Helen was studying for her entrance exam, and Ian, at eight years of age, was also at the prep school. Like Katie, he scarcely needed school, as he seemed to have been born crammed with knowledge. The trio appeared to have arrived ambitious and hard-working. Andrew and Mary were truly blessed.

Toodles Two changed gear and became a movable feast. Her territory covered the hundred or so yards that stretched between the bungalow and Rosewood, and it embraced several houses en route, the coastal green and, in better weather, the top step of the erosion barrier. Picnics could be tasty, as could the pickings from residences as select as these. She knew how to manipulate people; a straight tail quivering slightly at the end, the sideways approach, two or three little feed-me mews, a lengthy purr. Life was good for a cat in the summer of her life.

Eva Dawson, still opinionated and loyal, kept her job at Rosewood, though as housekeeper she came and went more or less as she pleased. The only unbreakable rule was that she had to be there when the children arrived home from school, and she covered school holidays, though Thora, when available, became a voluntary second lieutenant, director of games, first aid administrator and occasional cook.

The two women also enjoyed the closest of friendships, as both had treasured Emily, both had mourned her, and they found comfort in each other. With one speaking cotton territory Lancashire and the other galloping along in Scouse, some hilarious misunderstandings occurred, and they laughed at and with each other. For these occasions, they both thanked Emily, who had instigated their relationship.

There was just one major change on this stretch of the

Mersey's coastal road. Thora Caldwell, taking her cue from Emily, ignored convention and moved in with Joe Sanderson. She had her eye straightened by surgery, while her hair altered of its own accord. Although it remained coarse, the colour changed over time until it managed a reasonable shade that was close to platinum, and the owner of the new look began to take care of her person. To see a woman rebirth herself in her sixties was wonderful. Her skin was good, and her features looked less sharp without the glasses on which she had always depended to pull the lazy eye into its rightful position.

Joe enjoyed her company greatly, because Thora was enormous fun. As with Emily, he kept to his own bedroom while Thora stayed in hers. But they were content during shared meals or TV programmes, happy at weekends when they repaired to Bolton so that Thora could check that her son and his family were taking care of her house. The couple visited the rest of her family, and Joe dropped in at the factory where most of his furniture was made. Now situated on the road to St Helens, it was housed in a massive mill in which cotton had been spun, and it employed over two hundred people. Thora was proud of him; somewhere among the stars, Emily would also be pleased.

On the way home, they invariably went to see Daisy who, having survived childhood against all odds, showed every sign of outliving most people. She had her own pretty room filled with soft toys and brightly coloured pictures. The first teddy, now almost bald, remained her favourite, with the first toy rabbit coming a close second. Somewhere behind a silence punctuated only by grunts, she was capable of making a choice, usually First Ted or First Bun, as Betsy had named the popular pair. Daisy, now in her twenty-eighth year, stared at cartoons for hours, walked about with her toys, never spoke, and seemed as happy as she was capable of being. To an observer, this was no life at all; to Daisy, it was safety and routine.

For Joe, the saddest thing about his beautiful blonde baby daughter was that she'd turned into an overweight and shapeless young woman with lank brown hair and a face whose expression betrayed her condition immediately. But he loved her. She hadn't deserved any of this, and neither had her long-suffering mother. Daisy was the unfortunate personification of Joe's weakness, stupidity and guilt.

'Come on, Joe,' Thora would urge. 'You've seen her, but I doubt that she's seen us, God love her.'

'Poor Betsy,' he sometimes said. She'd turned out to be a good woman, one of the best, but she'd had no life beyond her bit of bingo. The burden weighed heavily; he could have, should have done so much more for Betsy and Daisy.

At seventy-three, Joe Sanderson retained the energy of a man half his age. He didn't believe in retirement. Retirement was for cowards, weaklings and lazy people who took no pride in their work. 'Numbers don't mean a thing,' he told his son as they reclined in the sun-bathed rear garden of Rosewood. 'We should work for as long as we like. What's the point of saying it's over when it's not? It's like throwing the towel into the ring before the fight's properly under way, isn't it? What do you think?'

No reply was delivered.

'Andrew?'

'No idea,' Andrew replied, his voice muffled by *The Times*, which he was using to cover his face while he dozed. He was supposed to be relaxing under the apple tree, but Joe clearly didn't believe in relaxation, either.

'If a man wants to work, he should work.'

'Quite.'

'And if he wants to stop, he should stop, stay out of the

409

road of gradely folk, pick up his pension and go crown green bowling.'

'Yes.'

'Might as well talk to meself,' Joe grumbled. 'At least I get an audience and a bit of feedback with Thora. She's gone shopping for a new frock, going to wear it at the opening of your events suite. That must have cost a pretty penny, what with the bar, toilets and what have you.'

'It did. I nearly had to sell the wife.'

Joe laughed. 'What's it for again, Andrew?'

The younger man gave up and pulled the newspaper off his face. 'It's for cancer. Mary's working with some terminally ill women under forty, and it's got her back up. You know what she's like, Dad. Once she gets her teeth into something, she's like a bulldog with a bone. She's beyond my control.'

'So her back's up and her gob's full. At least she'll be quiet. Once she gets on her high horse ...'

'We're mixing enough metaphors to make a cake here, Father. My lovely wife is watching little kids' mothers dying of cancer and leaving orphans behind. She wants to help all she can. So the suite's my contribution. It's going to take millions for all the research that's needed. God alone knows whether or when the monster will be defeated, but it won't be for lack of trying in this house.'

'Oh, right. OK, son, my contribution will be ten grand. First prize in your raffle after your inaugural ball will be a Sanderson kitchen, real wood, none of your plastic.'

'As well as the ten thousand?'

'Aye.'

Andrew kissed his dad on the cheek and went in to look for Mary. He found her fighting again, this time with the decorator. So far, she had alienated two lots of plumbers, one electrician, a builder and a whole wallpaper company. She went through workmen the way other women went through nylon tights. 'Mary? What the hell's wrong now? Can you not leave well alone for a change?'

She swung round. 'I don't like that colour, do you? Look at it. It's insipid.'

Andrew folded his arms and tried to glare at her, which was almost impossible because she was funny. When riled, she allowed carefully honed vowels to broaden; she became a little guttersnipe once more. 'Mary, you didn't like the apple green, the primrose yellow, the Wedgwood or the lilac. About the lilac, I agree completely. So buttermilk will have to do. Any more paint and I might as well buy shares in the company.' He turned to the beleaguered tradesman. 'Carry on, Charlie. Very good of you to give up a weekend for charity.'

'I don't like it,' Mary repeated. 'It looks like something heaved up by a week-old baby.'

'Mathew Street,' Andrew threatened quietly. 'You are ten seconds from Mathew Street, madam.'

'You wouldn't dare, Drew. Not in front of . . . people.'

He folded his arms. 'After all these years, small angry person, you above all should realize that I make no empty threats. If you don't start behaving yourself, it's Mathew Street. Just be glad we don't live in my home town, else it might very well be Vernon Street.'

Mary raised a quizzical eyebrow.

'Vernon Street was where they put animals down.'

Charlie was up a ladder, and his back was shaking with laughter. Andrew worried for the man's safety until Mary stalked past both men into the hall. He followed her, picked her up and 'Mathew Streeted' her into the drawing room where he dumped her on a chair. 'Stay,' he ordered, a finger wagging dangerously close to her face.

'But I have to—'

411

'Stay. And no biting. You have to stay, otherwise I'll tan your bum till it glows, and you know where that always leads.'

'You should be so lucky.'

'I am quite ready to pick you up again and carry you upstairs.'

Little daggers glinted in her eyes. 'You are a bully, Drew Sanderson. I'm going to run away and live with Mam and Dad out in the wilds, and you will never see me again. I shall grow my own tomatoes and have a go at orchids in the greenhouse.'

'Right. Don't forget your broomstick and the book of spells. But you'll lose ten grand and a Sanderson kitchen. Dad's donating the money, and the kitchen will be first prize in one of your raffles. Where are you—' She'd gone. She would be in the garden jumping all over a man in his eighth decade. Andrew grinned. The magic remained. He had friends and colleagues whose marriages were stale, but he and Mary continued to shine. Successful wedlock required work, dedication, fun, communication and sex.

A hesitant bit of Mozart floated through from the breakfast room. He stood in the hall and listened carefully in order to identify the executioner. It was Helen. Helen was the most stunning and brilliant ten-year-old for miles, and she was assassinating his beloved Wolfgang Amadeus. Her true gift lay in the area of languages, and the prep school had the sense to start early. She was ripping her way through Katie's French homework, and it was becoming clear that Helen's future lay in words, not in music.

Katie was another kettle of kippers. She was a people person. School was the place in which she pursued her hobbies – maths and science. Her natural naughtiness had gained an edge; at twelve, she was sassy, determined, secretive underneath all the chat, and bright as a button. She had a list of possible careers that included acting, politics, writing, medicine, law and teaching. Her more immediate ambition was to become a deliverer of newspapers, since she wanted to earn her own money. A determined character, she had declared her independence at a very early age. With Katie around, men would need to fight to gain liberation, as she was a bossy little besom.

The playing stopped abruptly. After a few minutes, Andrew returned to the drawing room and saw all three of his children walking past the front of the house. They had a wheelbarrow filled with unidentifiable objects, and they were up to something. The something to which they were up would be Katie's idea, and Katie's ideas were capable of starting a war in an empty telephone box.

He went to warn Mary. She was in the kitchen preparing a light Sunday tea. At weekends, they had a brunch at about ten o'clock, tea mid-afternoon, and a supper in the evening. 'They've gone,' he told her.

'Who or what have gone?'

'The children.'

'Well, they've had their sandwiches and fruit, so they'll be fine until supper unless they've got tapeworms.'

'What they do have is a wheelbarrow.'

Mary stopped slicing cucumber. 'Have they left home? Is my catering substandard? What was in the barrow?'

'How the hell would I know? It wasn't Dad – he's still out at the back, so they're not guilty of grandfathercide. Ian looked serious.'

'When does he look anything else? You'd better go and follow them.'

'Only if you promise to leave Charlie alone. The buttermilk stays. OK?'

'Yes, sir.'

He found them on the erosion where many people had brought their children to play in the sunshine. Ian was doing what he did best; he stood solemn-faced holding a

413

placard. 'Cancer research' was inscribed on its surface. Katie was doing what she did best; she was showing off her little sister, the little sister who would probably be the taller of the two girls quite soon. And they were selling their toys to families on the beach.

He swallowed his emotions and left them to it. They had no permission, no licence, and they were disturbing the peace, he supposed. But something in his throat made him gulp suddenly. How many kids would part with treasured playthings in order to help mothers to survive? They were special; they had a special mother.

He told Mary. 'I wouldn't swap them for the Crown Jewels.'

'Katie will be at the back of it,' Mary said. 'Helen could charm fledglings out of nests, and Ian likes to do good deeds, but Katie's the ideas man. God, don't they make you want to weep when they do something like this? They're wonderful. So different from each other, too.'

He agreed. 'Katie's you all over again, and Helen's my mother. Ian's studious, serious and determined. There's a bit of Dad in him.'

'They're themselves, Drew. They don't seem to need us, do they?'

Andrew sighed. 'Could be our fault. Perhaps marriage is designed to cool off after a few years. Maybe those who keep a distance from each other are doing right by living for their children. I know several marriages where the kids are the glue. We're pretty selfish, aren't we?'

'Our closeness makes them secure,' Mary insisted. 'They don't fall asleep worrying about us getting a divorce, don't fail at school because there's trouble at home. Ian bothers me a bit. But I've heard him laughing when he's reading the *Beano*. He's just a private person with a high IQ, I hope.'

'He's not unhappy, Mary. He's just Ian.'

'Quite. I still don't like that paint.'

'Oh shut up and butter your bread.'

She shut up and buttered her bread.

'You can't keep on with that, Helen.' Kate dropped her books onto a huge desk they shared in the spare bedroom. 'You might be doing yourself damage. Apart from that, you'll be needing a psychologist if this carries on. You're not handling life properly. I'm going to talk to Mum about it, and this time I mean it. Because I've had enough, and I'm damned sure you have, too.'

'Please don't,' Helen begged. 'I'll take it off now and put a bra on.'

Kate studied her 'little' sister. Helen was inches taller than Kate, and she had a figure most grown women would kill for. 'Look at me,' Kate moaned. 'Two years older and a thirty-four B on a good day. You're like a film star.'

'Shut up.'

'Your hair's beautiful, your skin's perfect, your waist's tiny, your legs are wolf-whistle gorgeous – it would be easy to hate you, Helen.'

'Don't say that. I get enough of the evil eye from girls in my class.'

'I'll say this. You can't keep binding yourself flat with crêpe bandage. For games and PE, you have to unwind yourself anyway and wear a bra. Across in the boys', their eyes are out on stalks every time you leap for the ball. It's something you have to live with, I'm afraid.'

Helen burst into tears and sank into a chair.

'Right,' Kate said. 'I'm going for help. You sit there and howl while I do the talking, as per bloody usual.'

Mary was in the kitchen. She had done enough extra shifts to gain a day off in lieu, and was using the opportunity to do some cooking and baking for the freezer. 'Ah,

Kate,' she said. 'I can tell by your face that something's going on. Is it school?'

'Sort of.' Kate perched on a stool. 'My sister, who as you know looks twenty-five and gorgeous, is winding half a mile of crêpe bandage round her bust to flatten it. She's in pain, Mum. When it's PE or games, she goes in the toilet and unwinds, puts a cotton bra on, then tries not to look at the boys' windows because they're all staring at her and drooling like hungry dogs. She can't keep the bandage on through sport, because it shows through those horrible perforated or aerated or whatever stupid tops we have to wear.'

Mary sat. 'Poor kid. Where is she?'

'In our study crying and hiding her assets. Even lads in Ian's class are asking will she go on a date – thirteen, they are. Some in the sixth are running a book on who will get to second base first with Helen Sanderson.'

'Second base?'

'Breasts. First base is kissing, second is bust, third is girl touching boy, fourth is God help us.'

'Oh dear.' Mary swallowed a chuckle. She remembered similar trouble, though she had never been as wonderfully statuesque as her younger daughter.

'Then there are men in the street, grown men who practically knock themselves out on lamp posts staring at her.' She paused. 'Mum, I don't want to frighten anyone, but I worry about her getting attacked.'

'Rape?'

Kate nodded. 'I never let her walk home alone. Ian's started to come with us, because he hears smutty talk in the boys' school. Her name's written all over walls in the showers and loos. Like Helen, Ian's tall, so he's quite a good bodyguard. Mum, why are boys so gross?'

Mary sighed. 'It's a phase.'

Kate blew a raspberry. 'A phase? Then why do adult

men lose all sense of direction when they see her? We can't do anything any more, can't go anywhere. Do men ever grow up? Do they?'

'Well, your father didn't, thank goodness, but he's not predatory. And men always look at women, sweetheart. Even the best of them will stop and stare when they see someone as beautiful as Helen. I'll go and speak to her, and your father will have a word with your headteacher. Don't tell her about your father going to the school. But I won't have Helen upset just because she's a stunner.'

'Stay cool, Mum. She's fragile.'

Mary washed and dried her hands. 'Trust me. I'm a nurse.'

Upstairs, Helen's mother stood on the galleried landing and listened while her baby girl wept. The baby girl was fifteen, Ian was thirteen, and the senior daughter was seventeen going on forty. Kate was as pretty as a picture, but she was tiny, gamine and lively. Helen possessed the stillness that men loved, the gentleness, the softness of body into which a male longed to immerse himself, the placid facial features seen in many a valuable oil painting. She seemed biddable, innocent and perfect. She was what most stupid men wanted, so she was vulnerable.

A man of character would choose Kate. No. That was wrong, because the reverse was more likely to be the truth; Kate would do the choosing and would achieve partnership, whereas Helen was likely to become a decorative item picked out and adorned to illustrate a man's success. Yet she was an academic, a linguist, and a very capable student.

Mary knocked and opened the door. 'Helen?'

'Mum.'

'Kate told me. Now, look at me. Look at me, sweetheart.'

Helen looked.

'I want the roundness to disappear from your shoulders

417

before you develop a hump on your back. I want you tall and straight in a well-fitted bra that shows off your figure. You are what you are, so embrace it with pride.'

'I hate it.'

'Tough. I hated being small, but I didn't buy stilts. I got on with it, love. Let them look, but don't let them touch. Walk tall. Show off your figure and let them see what they can't have. I have a police whistle downstairs, and don't be afraid to use it. If anyone gets too close, you can perforate his eardrum with one blast.'

'Mum!'

'You need to borrow a bit of your sister's cheek and a lot of your brother's nonchalance. To hell with them, Helen. Listen, now. There's a very good corsetiere in Knotty Ash. She could make you some bras. We'll get a couple of strong cotton ones that stop your breasts leaping about, and some pretty ones, too. You have to learn to celebrate what you are and who you are.'

'Like Uncle Stuart?'

'Exactly like that. Accept yourself and love yourself. No two people are the same. He was a bit older than you are now when he told your dad about his difference. Details, Helen, mere details and happenstance. You could have been born with an enormous birthmark on your face or with one leg shorter than the other. Your details happen to be a beautiful body and a perfect face. Women will be jealous and men will be roughly of two types – those who would set you on a pedestal and those who will want to get into your knickers–'

'Mum!'

'Helen! There's nothing wrong with plain speaking, and do remember my origins. Where I come from, a spade's an effing shovel. Your dad's from a cotton town where toughness is bred in the bone, and I survived Scotland Road.' She paused. 'That's not true. I survived it and I loved every minute of it. And they destroyed it, bloody government.'

Helen dried her eyes. 'I'll be good.'

'You're always good, too good. Start biting back, Helen. There's nothing wrong with finishing a war, though there's plenty wrong with starting one.'

'I'll try. I promise I'll try. We'll do the bras in the long holidays, Mum. You're right; I should be grateful. Thank you.'

This was the day on which Helen Andrea Sanderson learned how to cope. She practised putting her hair up. It suited her, but was less enticing than the free-flowing dark silk that usually hung down halfway between head and waist. A slackened belt made her less shapely, and she found some clumpy shoes in the bottom of her wardrobe.

She found something else, too. Deep down in her core, she discovered a place she had never sought before now. Helen Sanderson was a strong girl. Because of archery, an option chosen for its lack of quick movement, she had muscles. But beyond the muscles, there was something easily as useful; there was self-respect and a deeply buried and furious resistance. If any man touched her, she would break his neck. 'You can do it,' she told her reflection. If ever a male stepped one inch too far, she would deal with him. Kate, like Mum, had a quick temper that dispersed within minutes. Helen was more calculating than that. And these horrible shoes might inflict a lot of damage ...

What neither girl realized was that each was already under surveillance.

Richard Rutherford met his Waterloo when a ball flew over the wire fence between boys' and girls' playing fields. A tiny, dark-haired female approached the divide. 'Oi,' she shouted. 'You with the hair; can we have our ball back?'

419

He sauntered towards her. 'Are you talking to me, Shorthouse?'

Dark blue eyes glistened. 'No, I'm talking to myself; I've already been locked up for it three times, padded cell, back-to-front coat and all that. But I have failed so far to meet a conversationalist as accomplished as I am.' She looked him up and down. The up and the down were well separated by a substantial body. 'What happened to your head, long person?'

'Cricket,' he answered.

'Then leave insects alone, because I think it's made a nest in your thatch.'

He grinned. Even in the horrible chocolate-brown divided skirt and yellow top, she had style. 'You're Kate Sanderson.'

'Thanks. To remember who I am, I usually have to look inside my PE kit to read the name tapes. Well?'

'Well what?'

'Tennis ball. We're playing rounders, and I slogged it.'

He thought about that. 'In cricket, that would be a six.'

'Ah, but look what cricket does to your hair. Ball, please.'

'Helen's sister?'

Oh, heck, another one. 'Yes, and she's not for sale. We've decided we're keeping her because she matches the drawing-room curtains.'

He wasn't interested in Helen, though he said nothing on the subject. This one was another matter altogether. She answered back. Kate had what Helen lacked – chutz-pah. Fighting with this little minx would be fun, he decided.

'Ball,' she repeated, eyes glaring, foot tapping.

'How much is it worth?'

Kate shrugged. 'Not much. We have a spare.' And she ran away.

Richard remained where he was, watching her. She had a Leslie Caron haircut with irregular spiky bits framing her face. Her little body was perfectly proportioned, her wit was quick and clever, and he wanted to know her. Yes, Helen was beautiful, but this cheeky monkey was his cup of tea or arsenic or whatever else she wanted to give him.

He was a late scholar, because a long fight with glandular fever followed by meningitis had stolen a huge chunk of childhood, so Richard was a man in a boys' world. Tomorrow, his schooldays would finally end and, if he got good grades, he would be reading law at Oxford. Rumour had it that Helen was aiming for modern languages, while her older little sister intended to read something like politics. 'Come to Oxford with me, Kate,' he whispered.

She was having an argument with a girl twice her size.

'You're out,' she screamed.

She would win. He knew without a shadow of a doubt that she would always win. What a waste; she would have made a brilliant lawyer.

There'd been a long lecture after a recent assembly. Boys were forbidden to leer at, salivate over, follow or make lewd comments to or about their counterparts in the girls' school. Anybody touching a female pupil would be summarily expelled from this fee-paying school for young gentlemen. Richard guessed that the real subject was Helen Sanderson, a girl who was probably at the core of many damp and untidy dreams. She was lovely, almost perfect, but her sister was probably the golden girl in that household.

He retrieved the tennis ball and pocketed it. The three Sandersons always walked home together, probably because the younger girl needed guarding. Since he lived fairly close to them, he would return the ball after school and accompany them. If Kate would allow it, that was.

In the school library, he thumbed his way through a precedent set during the Crown versus Edwin Taylor, a case of suspected fraud. Even her hair seemed alive. Edwin Taylor was a prat, but his case had been compromised by a sergeant from CID. Entrapment. He'd like to entrap little madam in a nice, soft bed. She would be feisty. The law was an ass, indeed. Three grand, Taylor had filched from a deaf old lady.

He gave up. Edwin bloody Taylor should have got seven years, but bad handling of evidence had set him free.

She's not for sale. We're keeping her because she matches the curtains. It was possible that Kate was unused to being admired. Everybody wanted Helen; few noticed the little firecracker by her side. It seemed that Ian and Kate acted as minders for the family's treasure, an item that was most people's idol. He found himself hoping that his newly discovered prize really had no more admirers. But he might be wrong. Why on earth should he be the only one who'd noticed and desired little Katie? 'And why would she look at me?'

The tennis ball remained in his pocket for the rest of the day. He would travel homeward in her company. Tomorrow, a barrier would come down for the sixth form summer ball. Lowers and uppers from both schools attended, and he could only hope that she would come. Teachers' corporate vigilance would not be aimed at Helen and her flock of admirers, since she was too young to attend. Kate would be free of her sister. But she wouldn't be free of him. Richard intended to fill Kate's dance card for many moons to come. If she would allow it, that was.

Daniel Pope opened Pope's of Waterloo in 1984. The shop was the first of the chain to be established in Liverpool

North, and Mother was pleased with him. It was best to stay on the right side of Beatrice Pope, as she could be toxic when displeased. His father, obviously under the thumb of old Beatie, as she was known to all who hated her, was Victorian by nature, though he did not rule the roost. Their son wondered how they'd managed to create him, since he had never met people colder than his parents.

Daniel lived two lives. There was the obedient, lovable and grateful son; then there was the alter ego. The latter had been manufactured due to necessity, as without it he would have had no life at all while still at home. Secrecy became paramount when he was a child, and he honed his skills as he reached maturity. A handsome man, he navigated his way through dozens of women, bought second-hand jewellery about which his family knew nothing, kept two sets of books and opened a very private and increasingly healthy bank account.

Then Helen Sanderson drifted into his life. She came into the shop to buy a locket as a birthday gift for her sister. She was the most stunning girl he'd ever seen, so he allowed her a decent discount on an antique piece acquired from the estate of a recently deceased woman. He told Helen nothing of its provenance, though he emphasized its age and the embedded hallmark. Her uniform he recognized immediately. 'I see you attend my alma mater,' he said.

Helen made no reply. She had discovered that reply led to conversation, which in turn led to a request to which she had to reply in the negative. Yes, fifteen was old enough for a girl to have a boyfriend, but this was a man of the world, a good-looking jeweller with the usual hunger in his eyes.

'Shall I gift-wrap it?'

'I'll do that myself, but thank you.'

'Would you like her name engraved on the back?'

She thought about that. 'Her birthday's next week.'

'Plenty of time.'

'All right. Sister Kate, please.'

'Older than you?'

'Lower sixth.'

'And you are?'

'Helen Sanderson.'

Daniel asked for her telephone number.

'No need,' was her answer. 'My father's a doctor, so we must keep the line as clear as possible.' There was a second number for the family, but she wasn't about to give him that one, either. 'I'll come back in a few days,' she added.

'I'm sure Kate will love your gift. See you soon.'

As she closed the shop door, a thought struck him. Next month, the school would close for the summer. His parents were school governors, and they had received invitations to the sixth form ball. They wouldn't use the tickets. A ball was not their scene, so he would go in their place. He would go alone, too. Kate. The sister must be found. '*Cherchez la femme*,' he whispered. The loss he'd sustained on the silver locket was of no significance, because Kate's sister was worth every penny and more.

He stood in the window and watched Helen crossing the road. She was clearly aware of herself, ugly shoes, slackened belt, hair scraped away from a classically perfect face. Well, she didn't fool him, not for one minute. The girl was jail bait, far too young for tampering with.

Helen could feel his eyes burning into her back. He was a very handsome man, and he knew it. Dad had explained this kind of stuff. 'Chemistry,' he had told her, 'is a word used for the basic attraction between male and female. It starts in the brain. Without being aware of it, we

424

search for a match, someone to have or to father our babies. Almost invariably, the chemistry happens between two people who would measure as equals if looks were quantifiable. A beautiful woman picks a handsome man and vice versa. The moderately attractive mate with each other, as do pairs considered ugly. It's an animal thing.'

Had it just happened? Why was she tightening her belt? She was too young for this type of thing, and he was ... older. And he was gorgeous.

Dad had also explained that teenage years were difficult. 'As with all animals, we reproduce best when young. A girl who menstruates is ready, in the physical sense, to breed. Her body is supple, yet not fixed, not hardened by time. A teenage birth can be as easy as shelling peas. But civilization has altered our code. Caveman bred early and died early. So remember that any feelings you have for a boy must be put aside until your education is over.'

It all made sense. The education of women was of prime importance, because there might be widowhood, abandonment, divorce, and many women these days were responsible for fatherless children. But none of these thoughts rendered the jeweller less attractive. This was probably just the first of many such encounters she would experience before reaching the magical age of twenty-one. She glanced across the road. He waved. She waved back. But he was surely a man who wanted to get into her knickers. At his age, he wouldn't want to put anybody on a pedestal.

She couldn't have been more wrong. He already had her on hoardings rather than on a plinth. In something diaphanous, diamonds on her earlobes, diamonds and a sapphire at her throat, a sapphire chosen to agree with those dark blue eyes, three carats on the engagement finger, hair severe, hair free and flowing, a very slight smile, a pout, a profile, full face, looking over her shoulder, taut buttocks pushing against pale voile . . . oh hell, he would need a woman tonight.

Mary and Andrew Sanderson, also governors of Grange College, attended the end-of-year ball. For half the young people here, this evening marked the completion of their schooldays. Kate, with a year to go, was with Lower Sixth pupils. She looked amazing in a plain silver shift, silver shoes, silver bangle, and the locket bought by her younger sister. 'She has wonderful skin,' Mary whispered to her husband. 'And her hair's glorious among all that metallic garb. When she stands away from Helen, she's a real corker.'

Andrew smiled. 'And Helen's not here, so Kate can position herself in her own limelight.'

Governors and teachers were here as chaperons. People could dance together, of course, but kissing and wandering hands were strictly out of bounds.

'That tall fellow keeps staring at her,' Mary said.

'Oh, it's young Rutherford. We saved his legs and his life years ago, and there's not a mark on him. Meningitis, a bad dose of it. He was away from school for more than a year what with one thing and another, so he's older than his classmates.'

'How did you save him? Was it blood poisoning?'

'Yes. And never tell him, but we used maggots and leeches. Building him up again took the longest time once he left hospital. Three nights, I sat with him. He was talking some of the finest rubbish I ever heard. Yes, he's fixed on our girl, all right. But so is that other one, older still, I think.'

'Jeweller from St Johns Road,' Mary pronounced. 'He'll be here because his parents are governors – you know them. Popes. He's got a face like a busted gusset, and she has a bloodhound's jowls. So much for your idea of ugly people having ugly children – look at him. Anyway, he's too old for Kate.'

He was talking to Kate. He was touching her locket. 'Helen must have bought that from him,' Mary said. 'I can't see his parents, so he's probably here in their place, like a deputy governor. They wouldn't fit in here. Joy's a word missing from their dictionary.'

Andrew noticed that the Rutherford boy was scowling at Pope. A part of him wished they would fight over Kate, give her a sense of her worth, but fights were not listed on the curriculum at the Grange. Pope walked away and was intercepted by Richard Rutherford.

'I wish I could hear what they're saying, Drew.'

She would have been disappointed.

'What's that girl's name?' Richard asked, just to open the conversation.

'Oh, it's Kate. Kate Sanderson. I sold that locket to her sister, Helen. It was for Kate's birthday last month. Have you seen Helen?'

'Not here; she's in the fifth come September, so she's too young.'

'I didn't mean tonight. Have you seen her?'

'Yes, I sometimes walk them home. Helen's continually persecuted by men and boys.'

'Oh, right.'

The light dawned. 'If you're interested in Helen, there's a very long queue.'

Daniel straightened his tie. 'I don't mind competition.'

'She's fifteen.'

'She won't stay fifteen, though, will she?' He walked away.

Richard Rutherford inhaled deeply, crossed the room and invited Kate to dance. 'May I have the pleasure?' he asked.

She pulled him away from her group. For a reason she failed to understand, no badinage could take place within the hearing of others. 'What pleasure would that be? I mean, do what you like for your own amusement, but not in a public place.'

'The pleasure of dancing with you, of course.'

She scarcely knew what to say. 'Listen, Rich. Thanks for walking us home and all that, but she's not interested.'

He frowned thoughtfully. 'Neither am I.' It was a modern waltz, and he was holding her. She proved light on her feet and a good dancer. 'Helen's not my type. You are.'

Kate stumbled slightly.

'If we were elsewhere, your head would tuck nicely under my chin. You smell wonderful. And you shine like a little silver star in that outfit.'

She stopped moving so suddenly that he, too, was forced to stand still. 'Are you on tablets?' she asked.

'No.'

'Well get some, then. Because you're talking twaddle. Mind, your hair's in better shape than it was. Did you get rid of the cricket?'

'Yes. Very sad. It croaked.'

'Was it a cricket or a frog?'

'Both. The frog ate the cricket.'

'So they both croaked?'

He nodded. 'It was a terrible day. As a nature lover, I was forced to wear a black armband. You've no idea how beautiful you are, have you? May I ask for a date?'

'Not till Christmas. Mum buys a couple of boxes then.'

'Give me a chance, Kate. I enjoy your company. I shall disappear soon into the bowels of ancient Oxford, and I want you to miss me.'

Kate was seldom stumped for words. She opened her mouth, but nothing emerged. It was all so surreal, almost like history repeating itself. Mum had gone out to see the

Beatles at the Cavern, but she'd accidentally collected Dad instead. They'd tried to explain to her and Helen that it sometimes happened that way, but that it was rare and often just a passing fancy.

'Lost for words, little one?'

He made her feel special. Thus far, she'd felt special only in maths classes, where she left the rest of her fellows standing. 'I'm not used to this sort of thing,' she replied eventually. 'This is Helen's department. My brother and I try to keep her many admirers at bay.'

'I know.'

'And I suppose you did return the tennis ball.'

'I did.'

Only then did they realize that the waltz had finished, that the DJ was playing pop, and that they stood out like a pair of statues among all the writhing bodies. 'Shall we sit down?' she mouthed over the cacophony.

They sat at a safeish distance from the speakers. He continued to hold her hand, and she made no attempt to retrieve it. There was no one else in the room; everything melted away like snow in strong sunlight.

'Your father and grandfather saved my life many years ago.'

'Did you need a wooden leg?'

It was Richard's turn to be silent.

'Granddad makes furniture and kitchens from wood, Rich. Your saviours were my dad and my grandmother's lover.'

'Whoa! How modern is your family?'

'Very. I have an aunt in St Helens born out of wedlock. She's my real grandfather's illegitimate daughter. He now lives with a woman called Thora, though they don't share a bed, or so I'm told. But my parents are monogamous.'

'Good.'

'You're an old-fashioned boy, then?'

'Not a boy.'

'You cross-dress?'

'No. I'm a man, twenty next birthday. But the glandular fever, meningitis and recovery took a total of eighteen months all told. I lost time, forgot a lot of the stuff I'd known since infancy. I was a blank page. Catching up took a while, and my parents worried about brain damage.'

'Yes.'

'What does that mean?'

'If you've chosen me, it could be a symptom. You clearly can't tell the difference between gold and iron pyrites.'

'But I know my little silver girl.'

She blushed. Kate Sanderson never blushed.

'Kate—'

'I hope you're not going to be a nuisance,' she said before he managed to say anything more. 'As things are, we may have to auction Helen to the highest bidder, because it's all becoming tiresome.'

Richard grinned. 'What about the curtains?'

'They're not for sale.' She looked into his eyes. 'Neither is my virginity.'

His reply almost floored her. 'I've no intention of paying for it.'

Goose pimples covered her arms; every tiny hair seemed to be standing to attention. So this was it, then. This was chemistry. But she didn't remain fazed for long. 'About that ball, Richard. 'You can have it back and stick it where—'

A speaker above their table suddenly came to life, belting out Michael Jackson at a level that was almost deafening. But he read her lips. She didn't mince her ancient English, then . . .

Eighteen

Andrew Sanderson, sixty-one years of age and in several minds, stared hard and critically at his image in the cheval mirror. He was a man. He was a man well past his prime, but in spite of that fact he continued an adult human male. He had a full set of chisels, two pianos, four valuable cars, a macho-looking dog, enough spanners to service a fleet of taxis, two daughters, one son, six grandchildren, one headache and a few problems. He was being managed. Never since his years as apprentice to Compton-Gore had he felt so mithered. They were all watching him and no, this was not paranoia; he'd smoked no skunk since 1962 when a student known as Steve the Weed had been sent down for growing his own.

Tired and worn down by the will and supposed wisdom of others, he had finally conceded and agreed to do their bidding. Strangely, all he had needed to do was nothing, because his superiors took silence to mean total submission. Females, self-elected presidents of the whole world, were drawing detailed maps and listing ingredients necessary to make his life enjoyable and fulfilling. Well, he was OK, and he wanted no changes for better or worse, yet here he stood like a shop-window dummy, because this was expected of him. Being in several minds was not suiting him in the slightest way. This, he supposed, was the definition of real confusion.

He'd done hip replacements and knee surgery, mended countless numbers of limbs, invented a special fixing agent that most human bones found acceptable; he had met Her Majesty, had waded through blood and tissue after major road accidents, had even revived the dead, but he couldn't deal with his own family. Perhaps he should invest in a gun or start slipping tranquillizers into their drinks.

All dressed up in a good suit and crisp white shirt, he wondered what the hell he was up to. He knew very well what he was up to. No, he didn't. Yes, he did. But why? Helen had pushed him along with a determination he'd never noticed before. Yes, he had. She'd been pretty stubborn while leaving Daniel Pope, and she was at it again, wasn't she? Was she? Oh, what wouldn't he give for a bit of quiet, the ability to finish a crossword, read a book, stand on his head in a corner should the need arise.

Sarah, now in her third year, was a questioner. Why didn't the sun fall out of the sky, did it hang on a string, how did birds fly, when would Cassie walk? Two-and-three-quarter-year-olds were supposed not to be so verbose, but she had to be the exception, of course. Cassie was a crawler. She got under everything, behind everything and inside a lot of things not suited to occupation by a quadruped child who was desperate to become a biped. As for their mother, well . . .

Bloody interfering, meddlesome women. They rendered him perplexed, and made life unnecessarily complicated. Was he eating enough, shouldn't he wear a heavier coat while walking on the beach, when was he due for a prostate examination, were his bowels behaving normally? They'd be checking his teeth next and making sure he wore a vest.

Well, they'd gone too far this time. Should the revolution begin now, at this very moment? Where was Napoleon bloody Bonaparte when he was needed? Even Oliver Cromwell would have been a diversion, and he'd had warts and no discernible sense of humour whatsoever. Anyway, Andrew rather liked Queen Lilibet. He'd noticed how, while giving out medals and awards to total strangers, she kept alive the twinkle in her eyes, bless her.

'Nope. Republicanism's not my idea of the way forward. I'd better write to Buck House and Number Ten, get some help. The Duke of Edinburgh's probably my best bet.'

He sat on the bed. Kate was in on the plot, of that fact there could be no doubt. Anything out of flunter was usually connected to her, Chief Busybody and Chairperson of Organizers Unanimous. She was probably down the road with the second victim of the latest scheme. 'I am allowing my daughters to orchestrate my life,' he said aloud. 'They've no sense of rhythm – and why am I doing as I'm told? For the sake of a bit of peace? Because there'll be none. In the words of Bamber Gascoigne, they've started, so they'll finish. They should be prosecuted for trespassing on me. I'd be better off like Stuart, two blokes in a house, no oestrogen, no unsynchronized premenstrual tension, no tantrums, no moaning or yackety-yack.'

Through the window, he looked across the green and beyond the erosion fortifications. The river was picking up. Earlier in the day, it had been as calm as an abandoned boating lake or a sheet of greyish glass, but it was now changing its mind. Andrew knew how it felt. Like the Mersey, he didn't know whether he was coming or going. He was going. No, he wasn't. Er . . . he might be going. 'God help me, and God help them if I finally lose my rag.' He knew he was balancing on the very edge of his patience, and that he would push someone else rather than launching himself into space.

Storm moved the door ajar just far enough to allow the front end of his lofty, muscular body to enter. For a few seconds, he waited to assess the boss's mood, because he'd seemed a bit out of sorts just lately. When Andrew nodded, the rest of the dog came in, turned, and pushed the door into its closed position. Storm was in need of male company, which element was in short supply round here.

He was a fed-up dog. Looking after two mobile little girls was taking its toll. The younger one, who walked on four legs, had some terrible habits, so he placed himself for the moment next to the pack leader, who would guard him. He was sick to death of fingers poking about in his ears, his eyes and his mouth, and tired of chubby little hands pulling his tail. Like Andrew, he was a bit fraught and fragile. Life was tough.

'Hello, Storm. Very clever, these females, what? But I really miss Thora. I even miss the Bolton accent. Thora might have been on my side, but . . .' But Thora was back in the home town, where her oldest son and his family took care of her. She'd started to age quite suddenly, and the whole business had broken Eva's heart. 'I knew she was older than me, like, but I never thought she'd end up like that, all arthritic and frail, God love her,' Andrew's housekeeper had wailed.

'None of us knows,' Andrew told the dog. 'And Thora's with loved ones, which is what really matters.'

Loved ones? 'I've four lads,' Thora used to say, 'three training to be hooligans like their father, and one nearly normal.' Eventually, she'd changed hooligans to fooligans and they'd all turned out fine. The nearly normal one was now managing director of Sanderson's Intelligent Kitchens, and he was making a fine job of walking in the footprints of Joseph Sanderson.

'I miss Dad,' Andrew told his dog. 'And Mother. Until they're gone, we've no idea of their true value. By the time we appreciate what we've had all our lives, it's simply too late.'

Mary. Oh, Mary. When he watched his daughter Kate with Richard, he saw an echo of his own brilliant marriage, an institution built on humour and communication at all levels. But Mary was dead, had been buried in the back garden for eleven years, and he'd been ordered to get his act together. 'Pull yourself up, Dad. You've just the one life like the rest of us, and you must make the best you can of it.' He was outnumbered and overruled; when or why had he allowed this to happen?

Get his act together? He had five piano pupils, four of whom were good; he'd played yet again for Cancer Research his oft-adapted Overture to an Overture, his own nocturnes, and a polonaise he'd recently finished for Anya. Then the song. 'A Liverpool Song' had since been purchased for a quartet of tenors and was to be released as a single next Christmas. His act was very together.

'Surgeon, carpenter, composer, lyricist, pianist, teacher, father, granddad, OBE,' he said, counting on his fingers. 'What more do they want of me, Storm? If I'm number one at the end of the year, we'll buy an island, lad. We'll come back from time to time to visit the old homestead and Mary, but just imagine the peace if we go all Outer Hebridean. Think of the fishing, eh? And the walks with no one watching us from a window. I know what happens. They spy on me and Anya. I know they go on about us sharing a rug and a cup.'

Storm grunted; he had come to understand when an intelligent answer was required of him.

Helen tapped at the door. 'You decent in there, Dad?'
'No.'

She came in anyway. 'You look wonderful,' she whispered. Dressed up, her dad was extraordinarily handsome.

'Prince Charming,' she added. 'Any woman would be proud to be seen with you.'

'I don't feel like Prince Charming. Migraine, lots of zig-zag lines tracking across my eyes, and a slight throb in the left temple,' he lied. Mendacity was becoming essential in this household. 'I'm fit for nothing,' he said in order to emphasize his statement.

'Never mind. You don't need to drive, because you're going in a taxi.'

'Am I? Can't I curl up in a chair with a good book instead?'

'You can't read with a migraine. You're going.'

Oh, she was quick. 'Why?'

'Because I say so, Kate says so, even Ian says so.' She folded her arms; this action underlined the fact that she was in no mood for a change of mind.

He gazed at her for several seconds. When had their positions been reversed? Was this some over-repeated sitcom rejected by the Beeb and put out by one of the inferior commercial stations? 'And Eva?' he asked sharply. 'What about Madame Parquet?'

'Eva started it.'

He tried to look surprised, but failed completely. Eva had been in charge of everything for as long as Andrew could remember. The sun rose because she ordered it, rain fell when she needed it, buses ran on time because she wrote the schedule, the tide ebbed and flowed in accordance with her timetable.

'I feel henpecked,' he grumbled.

'We learned from our mother. And from Eva, of course.'

Astounded, he bent his head and gave her the under-the-eyebrows look, which was his version of folded arms. 'Your mother did not henpeck me.'

'That's how clever she was. She kept your machinery

436

so well oiled that you didn't know she was in charge of your gearbox.'

Andrew blinked a few times before turning his head and staring into the depths of an increasingly agitated river. Anger bubbled in his throat like heartburn. 'Go away,' he said. 'I am about to change my clothes and take Storm for a walk. You and the rest of your coven can bugger off and tell everyone concerned that I have changed my mind and will not be eating out tonight.'

'But what about all the—'

'Out. Get out. It's time you found somewhere to live, too. I want my life back, my own bloody life. I am sick of women. Even the dog wants a bit of peace and quiet.'

Helen slammed the door in her wake and ran down the stairs. He heard her talking on the phone. Everything would grind to a halt within minutes, though the women's tongues would carry on clacking, no doubt. Kate and Helen, encouraged by Eva, would sulk. Anya might be slightly hurt, and Sofia could well come out in sympathy, but he'd had enough. Like water on a stone, they had dripped on him, wearing him down with looks, words and heavy sighs. Knowing Anya as well as he did, he guessed that she wouldn't have enjoyed being dragged from pillar to post by younger people. 'She'll be on my side,' he said quietly. 'She has to be, since she's the only sensible person I know apart from you, Storm.'

Helen finished on the phone. He heard her walking across Eva's famous parquet and into the dining room, where she and her daughters had lived for many moons. Never before had he spoken so harshly to her or to his other children. But they were planning his existence, cajoling, suggesting, pulling, pushing, and he'd reached the end of his rope. And he needed his rope in case he decided to strangle somebody.

He changed his clothes before picking up his mobile phone. 'Anya?'

'Yes?'

'Is Kate there?'

'Upstairs with Sofia, yes. Angry, both of them, but Kate is being loud. I cover my ears before.'

'Right. You bring the rug, I'll bring the coffee. We do this our way.'

'Good,' she replied. 'I can wear clothe not so tight. There is no room for food in this cockertail dress.'

'Cocktail.'

'Yes. I am come in taxi, you are wait.'

'Indeed. I are wait.'

She paused. 'You talk wrong, making fun to me – of me.'

'Yes.' Anya understood. In spite of some small language difficulties, she never failed to get what he really meant. She was a treasure. Sometimes, she altered his heartbeat. Sometimes, things needed to be left alone to develop at their own pace, with or without arrhythmia.

'OK, Andrew.'

He sighed. 'It isn't that I don't want to take you for a meal; it's just the kids pulling on our reins all the time as if we're a couple of horses. I can't escape Helen, you see. My house is no longer mine.'

'This, Andrew, I am know. I suffer, too. The dress tight under arms and kills me.'

He grinned. 'Don't die on me, Anya. You're my sole ally in a field full of landmines.'

'Ally is?'

'Friend.'

'This I am be. You wrote for me polonaise, yes.'

He cut the connection and sat in the window on Mary's chaise longue. Dad had re-covered it for her. 'I'm not good at letting go, Storm. Mother was the same, and Dad

438

seemed to have caught the infection. Thora, Dad, Mother, grandparents . . . Mary. I'm an intelligent man, wouldn't you say?'

'Woof.'

'Gifted, too.'

'Arf.'

'And modest with it. But I'm stubborn. I won't be told, refuse to be pushed, and they learned none of this orchestration from Mary. With Mary, it was tit for tat. I'd get one over on her, and she'd return the favour. I tarred and feathered her once, you know. And she let me, because she'd abandoned me in ladies' underwear at George Henry Lee's, took the car and left me to get home by train. Mind, I used black treacle instead of tar, and we were finding pillow feathers in here for months afterwards.' He paused. 'I even found a couple in her wardrobe after she'd . . . died. They're over there in that little cloisonné pot with a snip of her hair. She had hair like dark silk until the second lot of chemo. It came through as white silk after that.'

Storm laid his head on the master's knee. He was a dog who always looked sad, so his morose demeanour was eminently suitable for this occasion.

'Come on, boy, let's get back to what's laughingly called normal. Coffee, the steps and Anya.' He donned a sweater, picked up his Sunday best and hurled it onto the four-poster where it settled in a creased, uncared-for heap.

Storm led the way. He knew where his lead was kept; he also knew he didn't need it, but the master always wanted it these days in case something went wrong. Oh well, the boss was the best judge, Storm supposed, although everyone was aware that Andrew's dog never bit a human, never fought with another animal. Even the wilful Toodles Two slept in Storm's bed, usually alongside the dog, sometimes instead of him.

Helen was in the kitchen. 'Sorry, Dad,' she said quietly. 'We should have left you alone – Anya, too.'

'I'm sorry, too. My temper seems to shorten with age, though I must insist on being left alone to make my way through the wilderness. Yes, I like Anya and yes, she likes me. But you shouldn't be putting ice under our feet and forcing us to move so fast that we lose purchase on terra firma. You're doing more harm than good, because Anya and I appreciate the simple life.'

'Sorry,' she said again.

'But the rest of it – I'm not throwing you out. That was my vicious side – thank goodness I don't drive down that road too often. This was and is your home, your place of safety.' He filled the kettle. 'Pass the cafetière, please. I'm on coffee, Anya's on the rug.'

Helen burst out laughing. 'That sounded terrible.'

'And it was completely intentional. I am still alive, dear, and my dotage is many years in the future. You, Kate, Eva and Sofia must stop being my mothers. I don't need a mother. There is a possibility that I shall, in time, require a wife, but that's all down to me and some poor woman, who may be Anya. But consider this. We can all fight and defeat or negotiate with humans we see and hear, but who can win against a ghost? This is still Mary's house, and she's buried in the garden. I won't leave Rosewood. How can anyone argue with and overcome a dead woman?'

'I don't know.'

'Exactly. Read *Rebecca*. And don't pursue a cause until you've worked out all possible repercussions. Anya and I are good friends. We shall continue at our own pace. Because it's no one's business, just hers and mine.'

Andrew left the house with the dog, an unnecessary lead and his flask. Anya hadn't yet arrived, so he threw driftwood for Storm while sitting on the steps. Like him,

Anya was stubborn. She would have gone for the meal, but she hadn't wanted to. He'd given her the key, and she was out of a prison created by his two daughters and her own girl, Sofia. And Eva; he must never forget Eva, because her input had probably been substantial.

The little Polish woman arrived with her rug and a small basket of food. She wore an ageing navy-blue jogging suit and a pair of disgraceful trainers. 'For my face, I am sorry. Kate made me a painted lady. And she coming for your blood this minute, because you don't do what she is saying. I explain. I tell her we are sit on rug drink coffee people, but she angry. Sometimes, they just do not listen. They talk, and we must listen, but . . .' She shrugged. Anya performed very expressive shrugs.

'You look pretty, Anya.'

'I look Max Factor,' was her swift reply. 'Face feels tight, like cement stuck to it. To speak is difficulty. And I not like taste of lipstick.'

'You have food?'

'Yes, because things happen. We move, yes?'

'Where to?'

'Further down where we never sit. Here, she will look and find.'

'That's true. But she'll see us further down as well.'

'We must be armed for combat, and army march on stomach, so I have sandwiches. This time, is not Germans walking into Poland, is Kate driving into here. I ran out of house, jumped in taxi and come. She come soon, also.'

Quick thought was required, as was quicker movement. 'Come with me. Storm, come.' Man and best friend ran back to the house with Anya and jumped into the Merc. Andrew burned some rubber as he reversed out of the drive and set off towards the coastguard station. When he rounded the corner, he spoke to his colleague in crime. 'We're still not out of the woods.'

She looked round. 'Is some trees, but not enough for woods.'

'It's a saying. It means we could still be in trouble if the level crossing's against us.'

'Ah. Train.'

'That's the one.'

The barrier was down and the red light glowed its warning. Oh, heck. This stretch was famous for being a two-trainer, as the Southport- and Liverpool-bound trains passed each other not too far from here. Anya looked in her wing mirror. 'Kate comes. I see her further back.'

'Right.' He applied all door and window locks. 'Don't look at her, don't try to open your window, as I can override your decision from here.'

She reacted immediately. 'Then you as bad as she. I do what she tell me or what you tell me. Why? If I want open window you should allow. Always you moan about they telling you what to do. Do not tell me what about anything.'

And the words fell out of his mouth of their own accord. 'Mathew Street.'

'Beatles,' she answered. 'About Liverpool, I am knowing things.'

He swallowed a sob. She could never be Mary. She should never be Mary. After so many years, why had Mathew Street raised its head again? There was no way of repeating what he'd had with his wonderful wife. Anya was Anya. 'That was where I met her,' he said.

'I know. I open window now, let your daughter lose some steam.'

Kate's head entered the car. 'What the blood and sand are you two up to?' she demanded. 'After all the trouble we went to and the money we spent, I just—'

'Living,' was Anya's swift interruption. 'Sorry about restaurant, but I not eat Italian food, not pasta, not pastry for

442

the pizza – is for me too heavy. So we do as we always do, rug, coffee, and this time is sandwiches with good Polish sausage and salad. Your father and me are being us. This is what we do. Also, Storm likes sandwiches, so he is come.'

'Dad?'

'Go away. The Liverpool-bound train will be here shortly, because Southport's already gone through, and we shall be holding up the traffic. Here it comes now. Get back in your car and organize your own life for a change.'

'Where are you going?'

'To hell in a handcart. Move your head out of the car, or we'll be taking it with us, and I can assure you that hell is where you'll feel quite at home.' He revved the engine, and Kate backed off. The lights were green, and drivers behind Kate's stationary vehicle started to lean on their horns.

'What a thankless task is the raising of an ungrateful parent,' she shouted before running back to her car.

'She will follow?'

'She may. Kate isn't known for her patience.'

'Good. This is to be fun.'

'Glad you think so, madam.' She was small enough to need rescuing from a crowd, but he hadn't lifted a female since 1990. He liked a feisty one. He liked small women, as they were usually difficult. He liked Anya. 'They want us married,' he said bluntly. 'That's their aim and the reason for all this palaver.'

'And you want, Andrew?'

'No idea.'

Anya engrossed herself in thought for a few minutes. What she needed to convey was delicate, and her knowledge of the language was far from perfect. 'I not marry never,' she said finally. 'But when I find good man like you are, I live sometime with him, sometime not with.'

443

She sighed. 'Your Elena, she is right. This English one bloody stupid language. She say like climb Everest on skateboard.'

He exploded with laughter. 'So you're going to be a loose woman?'

Anya nodded vigorously. 'Since coming out of cocktail dress, I am loose. Was very tight clothe. No like tight clothe on me.' She turned her head and stared at him. 'Always laughing to me. Is no my fault I come from sensible country with sensible words. Where we going?'

'Swan lake.'

'Ballet?

'No, I forgot my tights. We're going to look at water with swans on it.'

'OK.'

'See if they like Polish sausage.'

'Too good for birds,' she snapped.

'These are Queen Elizabeth's birds. She owns them.'

'Then let her feeding them.'

'She's two hundred miles away.'

'Helicopterers. She can drop it to them from above.'

There was something about Anya, something rare. She didn't want to dress up, didn't want to marry, yet she seemed ready for a relationship not unlike the one enjoyed by Mother and Geoff. Was he ready for anything? How preciously clean he had kept himself since Mary's passing. But if he was going to fail in the bedroom, Anya would never mock him; mockery was not in her nature. And while the feelings he nursed for this woman were different from his love for Mary, she did occupy space in his heart.

Andrew was no longer a maker of quick decisions. Way back down the years, he had found an adorable little munchkin outside the Cavern. He'd looked at her, picked her up and recognized her from the future. But that was a

444

young man's game and, at the start of his seventh decade, he was no youth. 'We're all right as we are for now, Anya.'

'Yes.'

'We make our own way. Let Eva, Helen, Kate and Sofia live their lives while we live ours.'

'Exactly.'

'We do as we like, you see.'

'I am agreeable. We make mess without help. And when do they listen to us? Never. I saying to Sofia, "Look, he no good, he have tattoo on arms and ring through one ear," so she go out with him. Another one with pin through eyebrow, also ring through nose like pig. I tell her not take him near magnets, he get stuck, but she not care. Is like talk to wall, as you English say.'

He parked the car. 'I am putting a stop to Kate,' he said. 'She's still behind us. I've had enough, you've had enough, and the dog doesn't care one way or the other.'

She grabbed his arm. 'But if she stay with us, we both fight her near swan lake. This will be fun.'

He removed his hand from the car door. 'You're a terrible woman, Anya Jasinski, but my Kate is worse. She was born on an expensive silk carpet and has felt superior ever since. Without suits of armour, we are no match for her.'

'Hmmmph.'

Hmmmph was the same the world over, Andrew decided. It cleared every language barrier, and was usually the property of females. 'On your head be it.'

'I do not like hats.'

'That was a perfect English sentence,' he told her. 'Well done. And Kate has turned back. We won.'

Anya had not won. Now, with no audience to release her, she had to perform a task in order to save Eva an unpalatable duty that had haunted her since young woman-hood. Why had Anya taken it on? Because she had played no part, because she had been a child in Poland when certain events had taken place? Her detachment was supposed to make it easier, but things had changed, and she was growing fonder of Andrew.

Would she lose the man she valued? Was the bearer of bad tidings ever welcome? And she couldn't tell him while he was driving, so she would be forced to tell him at swan lake, and that would spoil the outing. Andrew loved birds. He seemed to have a fondness for most animals. She could tell Eva she'd failed, that she'd been unable to force herself to do it, but that wouldn't mend anything, would it? The idea was to save Eva from stress, from the weight of knowledge she had carried for well over thirty years.

'You've gone quiet.'

'Yes, this I do when I have nothing to say.'

She made sense. Her English was broken, but her mind was intact, and he had no doubt that he could live with her. She would not marry, though, and Andrew remained a conventional soul. Although not particularly religious, he believed that society's rules were there for a reason, but why? Stuart, his closest friend, had been forced to walk a different route because of his nature, so why the shock now? Why couldn't he and Anya be different? And there was a lot to be said for Anya's way, since it precluded divorce and made its own kind of sense. He wasn't ready – was that it?

'You thinking hard, yes?'

'All the time. Sometimes, I wish I had a switch to turn myself off.'

'Sleep does that.'

'Depends on the dreams, Anya.'

She sighed heavily. 'Mary never come back. My man never come back. This we both know, yet we dream of them, yes? We dream about young days, happy days all

446

gone now. So we drink coffee, sit on rug, comforting us both. The dead loved ones will not like us be unhappy.'

'I know.'

'Then in time we know what to do, Andrew. Our girls not say what we do; we say. If Sofia marry, I may go home, as I have some family and friends there.'

That idea hurt him. She had never before mentioned the idea of returning to Poland, and he realized at that moment that life without her would be less bearable. Was it love? Was love in later life quieter, gentler? What he'd had with Mary could never be repeated, but he needed to feel something stronger than this, surely? Living in several minds was not easy. 'I'd miss you,' he said.

'Yes. I miss you, too, if I go back. But I am not sure that I will go. Sofia must be settled before I am to decide about it. But now, we look at swan lake.'

Storm, unhappy on his lead, walked with them to the park pond. The birds were huge. He behaved himself.

Kate Rutherford was not in the best of moods. She'd booked the restaurant, paid for the meal, ordered flowers and a string quartet, organized taxis – oh, Dad was such an infuriating man. She slewed her car onto Rosewood's drive, parking it in a position that was rather less than tidy. 'We were only trying to help,' she said between gritted teeth. 'Months they've sat on concrete drinking coffee; we just wanted to chivvy them on a bit.'

She left the car and marched to the front door. Having forgotten her key, she rang the bell and waited, a foot tapping on the step. After all the trouble Kate had gone to, Anya had set off in a raggy old jogging suit and trainers that looked as if they needed fumigating. So much for preparation, then. What was a person supposed to do with

447

delinquent parents? Shove them in a Borstal while they sorted themselves out? Did they have Borstals for the almost geriatric? There was Help the Aged, of course, but she doubted that such a charity would provide counselling for Dad.

A flustered Helen opened the door. 'Sorry, Kate. Sofia and I were bathing the girls. She says Anya shot off in a taxi.'

'She did. I dropped Sofia here before following them. They were in Dad's Merc, but I got fed up and turned back. Aren't they infuriating? You go to all this trouble, and they bugger off without a word. And I have to get home early, because Richard's bringing a case against a lawyer tomorrow – tricky.'

'Suing one of his own?'

'Defending the solicitor's victim, but it amounts to the same thing. Very few firms are good enough to have that questionable privilege, and Richard's is one of them. He always says a bent lawyer is a very talented crook, so he's working hard to trip the chap up. And I worked hard to get Dad and Anya a good night out, all to no avail.'

They sat in Andrew's drawing room. 'No gratitude,' Kate snapped.

'Worse than that,' Helen said. 'Anger. Real fury.'

'Oh? Why?'

Helen told her sister that their father had reached the end of his tether. In her opinion, retirement had disempowered him slightly, and he was building a new career in music. 'I backed you up as best I could, sis, but he's sick of what he sees as our interference, says he's had enough of women.'

'But we were only trying to help.'

Helen swallowed. 'I went along with you, Kate, as did Ian. And all the time, we should have remembered how

448

ordinary Dad is. He doesn't want frills and string quartets in some overpriced restaurant.'

'But—'

'And he hates us treating him as if we're parents and he's the child.'

Kate sat back in the armchair. If Richard died, would she want people pushing her towards someone else? If Richard died, would she want to live? Of course she would, because she had young children. Dad's children were grown, had been adults when Mum died, so . . . 'Whoops,' she said softly. 'I've jumped the gun again, haven't I?'

'Ian and I could have stopped you, but he's too busy and I've got other matters on my mind. Our brother's been brilliant. Daniel jumps out of planes all the time, goes on digs and . . . well, he's left Pope's.'

'What?'

'Opening his own shop. The Lion's Den.'

'Weird name.'

'Well, he is Daniel, so he's in the lion's den.'

'Right. And you're going back to him?'

Helen made no reply. Having taken the lecture from Dad, she was ill-prepared for a second assault.

'Helen?'

'I am undecided except for one thing. I want no advice and no manipulation. Push Dad too far, and he pushes back. Push me, and I destroy clothes and wine. There will be no discussion on the subject, because it's my life and my decision when I reach it. Go back to your perfect marriage—'

'Helen, I—'

'And leave me to mend or end mine. OK?'

Kate shrugged. 'OK.' Some people never learned, it seemed. Helen had gone berserk, had destroyed her husband's property, yet she was continuing to consider a move back to the Wirral. Daniel Pope would never change.

449

If he stopped travelling, the evidence of his philandering might well sit right on Helen's doorstep, but Kate had to keep her mouth shut.

'Cup of tea or coffee?' Helen asked.

'No, I'd better go. I've left poor Richard to put the kids to bed, and he needs to rest before tomorrow. See you anon.' She swept out of the house. Kate wasn't good at sweeping out of the house, because she didn't have her sister's height, but she did her best.

As she drove home, she found herself in pensive mode. Although she had no memory of it, she'd been told by Mum that Helen had stood up and walked early just to get to her sister in the playpen. They'd been inseparable. Kate, being the elder, made all the decisions. She chose what they would do, where they would go, what they would wear. 'And it's time I resigned,' she told herself. Helen had outgrown her sister, and not just in height. Kate needed to back off.

Now, having perceived a gap in Dad's life, she'd decided to close it. He was a grown man. Anya, though fifteen or so years younger than Dad, was a mature woman. 'I am a busybody, a nosy parker, an interfering menace. The one I need to organize is me.'

She pulled into her driveway. On entering the house, she found her man literally knee-deep in paperwork on the living-room floor, so she waved at him and carried on upstairs. The children were asleep and beautiful. 'Heal thyself,' she ordered the bathroom mirror. 'And look after your own husband.'

She bathed, dried herself and put on a beautiful night-gown. He was working hard and would need her, as lovemaking helped him sleep well.

In bed, she read some letters from work, recorded answers into a voice-activated machine, then lay back and waited for him.

When he eventually came in, he awarded her a broad grin. 'Just what the doctor ordered,' he said before going for a shower.

'My perfect marriage,' she whispered to herself. 'And I'll hang on to it till my last breath.' She had to, because when all came to all, it was what really mattered. Richard was half of something, while she was the other half. It hadn't worked out for Helen because her man was a fool. Poor Dad had lost his excellent partner to cancer, and he'd been a pitiable wreck ever since. But if Kate put too much energy into their situations, she might have very little time for her own beloved man.

So Helen was right after all; Kate should literally mind her own business, because marriage was a business. It required balancing, supervising, care and attention. Oh, heck. He was back in the room in a curly blonde wig she'd worn for a vicars and tarts party months earlier. He, of course, had gone as an archbishop. She shook her head in mock despair.

'Don't worry, love,' he said, his tone high-pitched. 'I'm a lesbian.'

'I'm not. I have a wonderful husband.'

'Him?' he cried. 'That idiot downstairs with all the paperwork? I can show you a much better time. Move over while I shave my legs.'

So Kate lay in her bed while the comedian she'd married started to denude his lower limbs with a small battery shaver. He'd be proselytizing tomorrow, upholding laws legal and moral, standing tall in his court clothes. But just now he was complaining because the shaving hurt.

'I do that every fortnight at least,' she told him. 'But I don't have legs covered in coconut matting. Give up, or you'll be sore tomorrow.'

He turned, an evil grin on his face. 'Can I do your moustache?' he asked.

'I don't have one.'

'Let me pretend you have one.'

'No. Shaving encourages the growth of hair.'

Richard thought about that. 'I shall grow a beard,' he pronounced finally. 'It will come through grey to match my real wig. And I shall blame you.'

'For what?'

'For the grey. My beard and wig will be the same colour, so they won't see the join, and I can be Santa in Lewis's at Christmas, make a few bob extra.' He looked at her. 'Kate? Kate? What's the matter? Oh, baby, don't cry.' The blonde wig was tossed to the floor.

'I'm stupid,' she wailed.

'You're not. A man of my calibre wouldn't have a stupid wife.'

She delivered a fractured account of her day, ending with her opinion that her father and her sister both hated her. 'And I'm so lucky to have you, Richard. Why can't I be nice? Why do I always have to dip my pen in other people's ink every five minutes? I have a job, a family to care for, so why do I need to go about interfering?'

'It's an extension of your job. The company's there to intervene for people – and you've always been like that. Who looked after Helen? You and Eva. Who taught her to read? You and Eva. You were there when she found out about Pope's antics, and you've supported her ever since.'

'While you, Dad and Ian have supported Daniel.'

'No. We've tried to get him rebuilt, because she needs him, Kate. She's a one-man woman, like you.'

She dried her eyes on the sheet. 'Don't be so sure, buster. The Cunninghams across the avenue have a new gardener – very easy on the eye.'

'Slut.'

Kate sniffed. 'Do you look at other women?'

'Yes.'

'Do you fancy them?'

'Yes.'

'Do you imagine them in bed with you?'

'Er . . . no. There aren't a lot of beds in Crown Court or Chambers. So it would be up against a wall or in an empty office.'

'Bastard.'

'Trust me – I'm a lawyer.'

She dug him in the ribs with a very hard elbow. 'Would you?'

'That hurt. I swear you sharpen your joints.'

'Would you, though?'

'No.'

'Why?'

He kissed her. 'One, you would kill me. Two, guilt would preclude any pleasure. Three, I love you.'

'In that order?'

'Yes. I'm an honest man, and that's a beautiful night-gown. Take it off and stop weeping before you drown both of us.'

And that was when the telephone rang.

Anya decided to tell Andrew the truth tomorrow while they drank coffee on the erosion steps. He'd been so happy with the birds. Although swans could break a human leg with the sweep of a wing, he had gone amongst them, no fear in his demeanour. And Queen Elizabeth's birds had eaten almost the whole picnic, leaving just coffee for the two humans. Storm had stayed near the bench with Anya while his master associated with the killer birds. From time to time, the dog's boss displayed symptoms of lunacy.

On the way home, Andrew stopped and bought petrol and some chocolate. Storm got the remnants of the swans' feast while his human companions ate Fry's Chocolate Cream. They sat in the car near Formby beach and watched the sun setting over the sea. It was a peaceful, pleasant few minutes, though Anya wished she could feel less guilty about having failed in her mission. But tomorrow would do, she supposed.

He held her hand. She giggled like a girl, touched his face, then kissed him. A man sometimes didn't realize how hungry he was till he took his first bite, she thought. And she wasn't thinking of Fry's Chocolate Cream. Yes, he was needful, as was she.

He was realizing that the lipstick didn't taste unpleasant, that the thought of dalliance with Anya was suddenly delightful, and that he was still very much alive in mind and body.

Then his phone rang.

Helen sat in Dad's chair in the drawing room. She read his *Times*, completed the crossword and tidied away some of Storm's toys. Solitude was a rare privilege in this house, and she relished it. Her days were punctured by some chores, part-time work at the university, and the older of her two girls, little Sarah, Infanta of the Spanish Inquisition. Sofia was upstairs in her room, but downstairs was all Helen's for an hour or two.

She found herself grinning. Not yet three, Sarah had a reading age of seven years, plus a demanding nature that was very much in the style of Auntie Kate. Did God wear shoes was one of the newer questions, probably put there by Eva as an explanation for thunder. Then there was the honey thing. How did the bees get out of the pot after donating the sweet, sticky stuff? Oh, and pigs were stupid. Only a stupid type would build a house from straw while there was a wolf on the prowl.

Sarah conceptualized. She was going to be brilliant at school. Fortunately, she looked upon her younger sister as something not quite oven-ready, and Cassie was left alone to organize her own development. Cassie was quiet, but deadly. She emptied drawers and climbed into them, stole small items and hoarded them in unlikely places, taunted the dog without mercy, and 'talked' to someone who wasn't there. So far, she was something of a mystery, though she did watch people. Both girls were heart-touchingly beautiful, and Helen adored them, as did Sofia and Anya.

Daniel wanted his family back. He had 'divorced' his mother, had persuaded Helen to put the real divorce on hold, and was opening a new business on the Wirral. The Lion's Den was two large premises made into one. Its upper floor was about to become a school in which arts and crafts would be taught and learned. Painters, potters, needleworkers and sculptors were to be given a chance to sell the best of their work in the shop below.

Helen sighed. Was this all a ruse to tempt her back, and would he revert to type in time? He was definitely different, calmer, less controlling, but was he putting on an act? Only time would tell, and was she willing to risk it? Sarah was certainly old enough and bright enough to be affected by a second separation. With Cassie, it was hard to tell.

The shop was going to sell costume jewellery that equalled anything put out by Butler & Wilson, artefacts from locals and from the third world, works from Britain's less celebrated artists, good china and light fittings, plus decent coffee and tea with snacks. Every October, a Christmas corner would stock superior items for the season, and he was exploring further avenues.

She still loved him, though the love was no longer unconditional. Helen's main problem was indecision. Her thoughts moved in a continuous circuit like a toy train stuck on one track, round and round, no points on which to peel off in a different direction, no shunting yard where she might rest.

The phone didn't ring.

Nineteen

Richard replaced the receiver and stood still for a few seconds. His side of the conversation had been a yes and no affair, so Kate had no idea about what he had just been told. Oh, what a mess. With the fingers of one hand raking through his hair, he spoke to his wife. 'Has Angela gone home?' he asked. 'Or is she in her room?'

Kate knew he was agitated – fingers in the hair betrayed his state of mind. He'd been quite harassed years ago, when she'd first met him and asked for her rounders ball back at school. 'Richard?'

'What?'

'Are you all right? Of course Angela's at home with her boyfriend – it's Thursday. She'll be back in the morning. Why? What's happened? You're as white as a sheet, darling, and I think you've got crickets in your hair again.' There was wetness in his eyes – Richard had never been too proud to cry. Sometimes, he wept when she did and said he was keeping her company. This was one male creature who had no fear of his feminine side.

He sat on the bed and took her hands in his. 'You'll have to stay here, Kate, if we've no babysitter in the house. I need to go down to the Countess of Chester – Daniel's been admitted into A and E. That was a nurse on the phone informing me, because it seems he's put me down as next of kin since the trouble with Helen and the discussion with his parents. He's been in a crash just outside Chester, and I have to go, since I'm named on the paperwork he carries.'

Kate swallowed hard. 'Oh, God help us. He does drive like a madman sometimes. Is he in a bad way? Is he going to die? Because my poor sister—'

Richard's finger on her lips cut her off. 'No details except he's in resuscitation. But I have to get hold of your dad. He's probably the best person to tell Helen. Don't phone her. Whatever happens and however you feel, this has to be left to your father. Sofia's there, isn't she? At the house with Helen, I mean.'

Kate nodded. 'Yes, I dropped her off earlier. She can look after the girls. But if you want me with you, I'll ask one of the neighbours. Doesn't resus mean they're having to shock him or something?'

'I'm not sure. But you stay here. There'll be four of us already, because your dad will probably bring Anya. As soon as I have news, I'll let you know.' He picked up his mobile, kissed his wife, grabbed a pile of clothes, and went downstairs to phone his father-in-law. There were some details, but he didn't want his little missus upset while he was away being next of kin to a man who had just been cut out of his car by fire officers. There was blood loss and there were broken bones. Not all the blood loss was external, so . . . Daniel Pope had travelled a mile too far and too quickly this time. And another driver was dead.

But he'd been doing so well, damn it all. 'Jesus, let him live. Helen will blame herself if he dies.'

Andrew was occupied. Like his son-in-law, he was with a woman who excited him, who was excited by him, but he, unlike Richard, was thinking about making love after a very long drought. Nothing had been further from his mind, but Anya had started the process, and he was far from sorry about that. She had soft skin, kind hazel eyes and beautiful hair. Anya Jasinski was small, lively and lovable; she was also a giggler, and he loved silly women with humour. 'I don't think we should continue in the car,' he said between kisses. 'This is hardly adult behaviour.'

She agreed. 'In sandhills, then?'

He declined. 'At my age, the knees and the back are not what they once were. Sand flows gently through the fingers, but it's hard to lie on. Trust me, I'm a retired medic.'

Anya sighed like a ham actor. 'This is trouble with old men.'

'I'm not old.'

'I have forty-six years, you have sixty-one. You are old.'

'And you are cheeky.'

'This I am knowing. I think something, I say it.'

He chuckled. 'Am I the man with whom you will live sometimes?'

'Yes, very much that man.'

'I have a big bed.' He would buy a new mattress. This was a fresh start, and several things needed to change. 'Plenty of space and very comfortable.'

'Then I may live with you all of the time. You would not mind this?'

'I'd be pleased.'

'And we still have coffee on concrete steps just the same?'

'Absolutely.' Their teenage behaviour amused him. Fumbling about in a car was hardly appropriate for a pensioner with a Mercedes and with a dog as witness, yet it was hilarious. And the relief he felt was almost overwhelming, because he could function again, should be capable of living a fuller life with a lovable, amusing

459

woman. She was delightfully different, yet very down to earth and normal.

'They all know we right with each other, Andrew. This is why they push to send us to restaurant. They do not understand it is different second time. We jump when young; older, we move slower.'

'Woof.'

'He's agreeing with you,' Andrew said.

'He like Polish sausage. This is why he agree, as dog thinks with stomach. I like him much. I never before saw a dog like this one.'

'Nobody did. He's definitely different.'

'Yes. Storm ugly but beautiful, nice person.'

'He's not ugly; he's a fine figure of a dog, according to Keith. He's thinking of buying a Labrador and a French mastiff and inventing the Mastador. Or the Labrastiff.'

'Keith is funny. I am meeting him at funeral of your father. Says the most dangerous animals are human females in teenage. He has horses and four wolfhound, but daughters worse.'

'His wife's far more of a threat. She thinks she's a cook, but he uses a lot of indigestion remedies. The girls have gone on diets. I see them stuffing their faces with crisps and burgers or pizza near the shops on South Road. Then they go home and eat salad. Michelle can't do much damage with salad.'

Anya laughed. He loved the sound of her laughter. 'One more kiss,' he begged.

'Is difficult to stop the kissing, yes?'

'After long abstinence, it's very difficult,' he replied.

'Yes.' His hands wandered, and she didn't stop him. But the phone did.

'Richard? What is it? Is everyone all right?' He paused. 'Yes, I see. What?' Again, he listened. 'I'll drive home. Don't

460

phone Helen, because it's best I deal with her face to face. Yes. Yes, she's been through a lot lately. Bye, Richard.'

Anya stared at his profile. 'Andrew? Something bad happening?'

'Daniel's been in a nasty accident just outside Chester. He must have gone for an extra session with one of his therapists.' Andrew turned and looked at his companion. 'We must go now, Anya. I have to tell Helen.'

'Yes, of course. Will he die?'

'No idea. But there's a lot of damage. He's losing blood and he has broken bones.'

'You can mend the bones. Was your job, the mending bones, yes?'

He shook his head sadly. 'No, I can't treat my daughter's husband – it would be unethical and against the law. But I can be there in theatre if I act pushy and lean on my OBE. They know me, anyway. Fasten your seatbelt, because we have to get back.'

Helen would blame herself. As he drove homeward, Andrew imagined her reaction to the news. Had she forced herself to forgive, had she persevered with mediation, this terrible thing would never have happened. If God could forgive, why couldn't she? Helen was often too hard on herself. If one of her children became ill, it would be her fault; if a house set on fire, if a meal were spoilt, if furniture got scratched, it would be down to her.

Anya was quiet throughout the journey. She had always thought of Daniel Pope as a bad man, since he had tried to interfere with Sofia, but she wished this kind of ill on nobody. Why had this happened? According to Daniel and his lovely wife, one failed breath test should mean a lifetime ban, though he had possibly forgotten his rules once the stress of probable divorce had kicked in. But what had he been doing in Chester?

'Are you praying?' Andrew asked, watching her twisting a rosary on her lap.

'Yes. You don't mind?'

'No, I don't mind. Say one for Helen, because she'll need God on her side to help her through.'

'And for you. For all of us I am asking.'

He pulled into the drive and sat still for several seconds. He was almost sure that his younger daughter would fall apart when she heard the news. There was a fragility in Helen, a sensitivity that put Andrew in mind of his own mother. 'I hope she doesn't get destroyed by this, Anya.'

'There is strength in her, Andrew. From what Eva is tell me, Helen has power in her soul, deep down where we not see. He will not die. He must not die. Come. I am with you now.'

As they walked into the house, it occurred to Andrew that Mary hadn't entered his mind for a couple of hours. And he didn't feel guilty. Yet.

Richard took absolutely no notice of anyone. He marched through A and E with certainty in his stride, because as a lawyer he had to appear confident. But in aged jeans, a creased shirt and trainers, he didn't look exactly ready for court. He found the coloured line on the floor that led to resus and walked straight into a small anteroom.

A policeman at the other side of the door stopped him. 'And who might you be, sir? You can't go through the inner doors, sorry.'

'Richard Rutherford, barrister. Next of kin to Daniel Pope. Is that him in there?' He peered through scarred plastic in the upper half of the second pair of doors.

'Come outside, please,' the constable said.

Back in the main thoroughfare, the officer spoke in low tones. 'The lad who caused this was as drunk as a lord and in a stolen car. According to witnesses, the collision was virtually head-on. He paid for it with his life, and his two friends are suffering from all kinds of injuries and alcohol poisoning. If Mr Pope dies, it will be manslaughter, but there's no one we can charge.'

Richard's legs suddenly weakened.

'Whoa.' The uniformed man held him and called for a chair. 'And some sweet tea,' he ordered.

'Is he in a bad way?' Richard managed.

'Well, his heart stopped twice for lack of blood, but they managed to jump-start him. Broken legs, broken arm and ribs, suspected damage to his spine. I'm told they had to drain his chest. But he's strong. His pupils are the same size as each other, so his head seems OK. We can only leave them to it. They're pumping all kinds of fluid into him.'

Alone on the hard chair, Richard drank his tea and waited for Helen to arrive. He hated sugar, but this was medicine, and he needed to be in one piece for Kate's sister's sake. Behind him in resus, they were clearly still working on Daniel to hold him together until he became stable enough for surgery.

The constable returned. 'You all right, sir?'

'How's he doing?' Richard asked.

'Well, I'm no expert, but the monitor sounds steady enough. They've not needed to put the jump leads on him a third time. Is he a jewellery Pope?'

Richard nodded.

'Isn't it a family business? What about his mam and dad?'

'No idea. There's a rift, a big one. I understand that Daniel's left the firm and is starting his own business over the water.'

'Wirral?'

'Yes. I suppose they should be told, but when this

fellow regains consciousness, he won't want them here. And if they come, they might set him back. Daniel's wife's on her way now, and he'll definitely want to see her. They've been separated for months, but I haven't told you that. He's made me next of kin, though I'm not a blood relative. He and I married sisters, you see.'

The policeman tutted. 'Bit of a bloody mess in more ways than one, then.'

'Yes.'

'Well, they're doing their best; four are with him now, and others keep coming and going. I heard them say his heartbeat was picking up and his blood pressure's crawling towards normal, so fingers crossed.'

Richard was left alone once more to wait.

There was advice tacked on the walls: how to deal with strokes, the dates and locations of baby clinics, pleas for organ donors and a staff noticeboard advertising accommodation to let and cars for sale. But there was nothing up there about making Daniel live.

And in a few hours, Richard had to be wigged, gowned, briefed and in court. Oh, it was a grand life, especially for poor Daniel Pope.

Helen surprised both Andrew and Anya. Clearly shocked, she braced herself against the wall and nodded. 'Right. We must go to him. Anya, will you stay with Sofia and the children? And ask Sofia to phone Professor Brooks before ten in the morning. My lectures must be cancelled.' She walked upstairs.

'She not running,' Anya said. 'Very quiet.'

Andrew kissed his companion on the top of her head. 'Stay here till we get back, please. It will probably be tomorrow. Look after Sofia and my granddaughters, and

I'll let you know as soon as I find out what's happening. And . . . thank you for this evening.'

'You welcome. You easy man to love.'

His heart lurched, but he had no time to examine personal feelings. Helen was descending the staircase. 'Come along, Dad. Let's see what he's been up to this time.'

They left the house and sat in the car. 'My problem will be solved if he dies,' Helen said, almost in a whisper.

'But you don't want that.'

'No.' She fastened her seatbelt. 'No matter what, I still love the fool. It's not unconditional love, but it's still a big part of who I am. Will he die?'

Andrew offered no answer.

'Dad, will Daniel die?'

'I don't know. He had to be cut out of his car, but that's just about the extent of my knowledge. There are broken bones, and he will have lost blood. Beyond that, I'm in the dark.'

She clutched her handbag tightly. He glanced down and saw white knuckles pressing hard against skin. His poor daughter was holding herself together by sheer willpower. 'We'll soon be there,' he said.

'Through the old tunnel?'

'Yes, that's right. Try to relax, Helen. I know it's not easy, but by fair means or foul, I'll get into that theatre and make sure they do their best. Trust me; I'm your father.'

When they reached the Countess of Chester, Helen escaped while her dad was looking for a parking space. Like Richard, she ignored everybody and found the right department. A physically powerful woman, she passed her brother-in-law, fought off the constable and opened the inner doors. 'Daniel!' she screamed. 'Don't you dare die on me, you damned lunatic. I love you, Pope. I love you.'

465

The policeman dragged her out. She should have been one of those female wrestlers, because she was as strong as a horse. He handed her over to Richard, who was now upright and full of sugar. 'Sit on this woman, sir. If she does that again, some very ugly security men will deal with her. Most of them are ex-coppers, so they're bad buggers.'

A nurse emerged. 'Mrs Pope?'

'What do you want?' Helen was in no mood for politeness.

'He heard you and opened his eyes, managed to say he loves you too.'

Helen slid down the wall and sat on the floor. Richard brought a chair and helped her into it. This was the stronger of the two sisters, and he had wondered about that for long enough. Madam Helen was a powerhouse. Kate was quick-tempered, quick to love, quick to anger. This tall little sister of his wife's had a core of steel covered by a thick coating of gentleness.

She looked at the nurse. 'Will he live?'

'Er . . .'

'WILL HE LIVE?' Helen screamed. A sudden, short-lived stillness hit the whole area.

'He has a good chance, Mrs Pope. We're going to put him in the lift from resus straight up to theatres. Would you like to come in again? You can lean on me. Ah.' The nurse looked at a newer incomer. 'Mr Sanderson? I remember you from the Royal. Orthopaedics?'

'Yes. Helen's my daughter.'

'Then you help her. Follow me.'

Father and daughter stood one each side of the trolley. She held Daniel's undamaged hand as he was pushed towards the lift. His eyes were on her and only her. Then, just as he went into the lift, he begged his father-in-law to

466

stay with him. So Andrew Sanderson, retired orthopaedic surgeon, ascended with his least favourite son-in-law up to theatres. 'Go back to Richard,' he urged Helen before the automatic doors closed.

The nurse remained with Helen.

'That's my husband's blood on the floor, isn't it?'

'Yes, but spilt blood always looks more than it is – you lose a pint and it lands like a gallon. Come on. Sit with Mr Rutherford.'

Helen allowed herself to be led and deposited next to her sister's husband.

'I've signed some papers,' he told her. 'For the surgical procedures. I'm down as next of kin since he divorced his mother. His legs are broken, and he'll need metal plates and what have you.' He didn't need to give her the full picture; splinters of Daniel's bones together with some flesh were probably still attached to his car. 'It wasn't his fault, Helen. A drunken kid pinched a car and died in the almost head-on collision. Daniel's alive due to the fact that he drives an Audi – good protection. Even so, he's taken some punishment, because the lad was doing about seventy miles an hour and most damage was done to the driver's side of Daniel's car.'

Helen stared at the floor. 'Is his spine affected?' she asked in a whisper.

'Not sure. Look, I'm going outside to phone Kate. Can I get you anything? Tea, glass of water?'

She shook her head.

'I'll be as quick as I can.'

He phoned Kate. 'Sweetie, find somebody – anybody – from Chambers. Let them know what's happened and tell them someone will have to take over, or the case must be postponed. It should be a short session tomorrow, I im-agine, just details and come back Monday. Daniel's bad, baby. As far as I can work out, there are bits of him in the car, and his right foot's almost severed. But your dad's in theatre supervising.'

'Oh, my God. And Helen? How is she?'

'Strangely quiet after her outburst.' He told her about Helen's little adventure. 'She woke him. They'd failed to do that. In fact, they had to electrocute him twice before we got here. But he's in the best hands with your hawk-eyed father watching over him. I can't leave her, darling.'

'I know that. Get back to her. I'll phone Sofia and try to reassure her.'

'And Anya, too, Kate. She isn't here.' He paused. 'Look, if she's with Sofia and if she agrees, send a taxi to bring her, then she can stay with Helen, and I can do my job in the morning. I want to face that creepy lawyer from day one, if possible. Try to get Anya, and I'll pay the fare, and you won't need to contact anyone from the office. OK? Text me. I'll keep the phone on silent in my hand, so I'll feel the vibration if you send a message.'

He returned to Helen, who remained in a world of her own. She didn't want coffee, tea, water or words of comfort. When he asked if there was anything at all he might do, her answer surprised him.

She turned and looked directly at him for the first time. 'All I want is my mother,' she said, 'and even a clever lawyer like you can't bring her back. But at times like this, only my mother could help. She was . . . she was so knowing, you see.' And Helen withdrew once more into her trance-like state.

His phone buzzed. Anya was on her way. A huge clock advised him that if the little Polish lady arrived soon, he could get six or seven hours of sleep before the alarm sounded. It had been a long day. He'd wrapped up a case in the morning before immersing himself in the huge brief for tomorrow, which would soon be today.

One of the items he hated most in the world was a bent lawyer, especially a crook who thought himself clever enough to turn the tables on an innocent client. Richard would bury the solicitor and pour concrete on the grave. *Be all right, Pope. Andrew, show them how best to pin him back together.*

Upstairs, Andrew wondered how much more Daniel's poor body could take. A collapsed lung and a ruined spleen had been dealt with, and the time had arrived when the putting together of smashed limbs was being undertaken. It was like doing a jigsaw with some bits missing, so the gel-like, hard-setting substance for which Andrew had received his OBE was very much in demand.

Together with the main surgeon and his team, he could only advise, as this patient was related to him. Using magnification, pieces of a shattered and useless rib together with bone stolen from a femur, Tom Howard, a very good bone man, began the process of reconstruction. Andrew acted as a second pair of eyes and, over a period of more than five hours, he watched and guided his fellows through several intricate and delicate processes.

'Thanks,' Tom Howard said more than once.

'There'll be scarring, but his spine's looking good,' was Andrew's opinion.

The foot was repositioned in its proper place of residence. This was the most threatened part of the body, since blood supply to the extremity had been compromised for several hours despite early reinstatement of some flow. 'He'll limp,' Andrew said.

'He'll live,' was Tom's answer. 'Problem was, according to police, that the dead boy came head-on, but slightly over to the driver's side, and this poor bugger was the driver. But he's fit, I'll give him that. His legs took some knocks.'

They stood back and surveyed their handiwork. Daniel's arm and legs looked like patchwork quilts, stitches everywhere and their surfaces displaying many shades from black through purple and red with the odd patch of Caucasian skin colour doing its best to shine among all the devastation.

A nurse wiped Howard's damp forehead.

'Take him down to ICU,' Tom Howard said. 'Keep him wired, of course, and get one nurse to sit full-time with him. And well done, you lot. Andrew, I can't thank you enough.'

'Yes, you can. You used what I call my double-glazing putty, and that's thanks enough.'

When his scrubs were discarded and after a shower, Andrew felt his age for the first time ever. Anya was right; he was old. He saw more grey in his hair and two dark patches under his eyes. That was when he looked away from the mirror and at his watch. He'd counted five hours, but another three had passed during the patching up of bone and blood vessels. 'You were right to quit, me owld fruit. You've had enough of that flaming malarkey.'

He took the lift down to A and E, where Anya squealed when she saw him. 'You did it,' she cried. 'Elena gone to look at him through window of ICU, I think she say. Now, no worry about colly-sterole, because—'

'Cholesterol.'

'Yes. One time, you need protein and fat. This is the one time.'

She supervised him while he ate his way through a full English breakfast. 'I had mine before,' she told him. 'But your Helen – my Elena – she eat nothing. One cup of tea, one bite of toast, and her face grey. We take her home, Andrew.'

'Will she come?'

Anya shrugged. 'No idea in my head. But she talk to me about needing her mother, so I said I pretend be her mother, and she pour her feelings. She has been mixed up, poor girl, loving him, needing him, hating him, divorcing him.'

'She stayed away because of the children,' he said. 'If the marriage folded again in a few years, they would be old enough to suffer. Always, she puts Sarah and Cassie first.'

'She does right thing, Andrew. But I think all children should know their father even if marriage ends.'

'Absolutely.'

This was not the time. And Anya had decided that she would not, could not do alone what needed to be done. She would be there with Eva, but neither woman should take the full weight of what must happen. Andrew looked so tired, too exhausted to face further shocks. 'Now, go and get Elena. We take her home, she has bath, changes clothes, comes back with Sofia if she wishes. You, Eva and I will care for the children. My daughter is very close with your daughter. But Elena must come home and eat. Helen, I mean. I say Elena because I have friend in Warsaw with that name.'

Helen put up no resistance. She wanted to see her children, to hold their warm, whole bodies next to her, because she could not yet comfort Daniel, who remained sedated, post-operative and full of painkillers. Just now, she could do little for him, but she needed Sarah and Cassie; she also needed sleep.

The drive homeward was silent until they reached Rosewood, when Helen spoke. 'Dad, when he's well enough, I want him to recuperate here in the function suite. We'll need a hospital bed, equipment to help him move, physiotherapy and round-the-clock nursing. I can pay for all that. When he's mended, I'll take him home.'

Andrew simply nodded. If Daniel's career as a woman-izer ended due to disability, it would have no real mean-ing. When he'd promised to quit travelling for the family business, that idea had not been acceptable. But he had made some giant strides, Andrew reminded himself. And this final stride had almost killed him through no fault of his own.

Helen went upstairs to see her girls and Sofia. Andrew fell asleep on the sofa with his head on Anya's lap. For some unfathomable reason, he felt at ease with her, as if he'd known her all his life. She leaned back and dozed, because she, too, had suffered a long and wakeful night.

And this was just the beginning. For weeks, every member of the family, including Ian and Eliza, visited the stricken Daniel. At first, his recovery was painfully slow, but he eventually regained some use of his arm, though his lower limbs remained plastered. Two further minor surgeries were required, but after six weeks he was dis-charged into the care of his wife and father-in-law. Two nurses and a physiotherapist were employed, and all necessary equipment was hired. It was time for Daniel to get better.

Andrew's house was fuller than ever. The only respite he enjoyed was on the beach with Storm or on the steps with Anya. Things had to improve soon, surely?

'All will be good,' Anya reassured him.

But first, something else had to be faced . . .

Helen nursed her husband from six every morning until two o'clock in the afternoon, so just two nurses were needed to fill in the remaining sixteen hours. She kept him fed, watered, clean and medicated.

For both of them, this was a strangely romantic time. A new intimacy developed, since Daniel was forced to allow

Helen access to a body over which, at the beginning, he had little control. As his reconstructed arm healed, the exercises began. He learned to squeeze a soft ball of sponge, to hold a spoon, to feed himself.

More importantly, he learned how to talk to his wife, who had given up her career in order to care for him and their children. 'Any regrets?' he asked.

She served up a delicious smile. 'This is my number one job, just as it always was. I regret what I did to your clothes and your wine, and I regret baulking at mediation. It took a dreadful accident for me to bury my pride. I never stopped missing you.'

'I'm a fool,' he told her.

'Yes, you are. Or you were. As for my position at the university, I'm sure something will come up eventually. Meanwhile, I shall have a shop to run until you're properly up and about.'

'If I walk again.'

'You will. I'll make sure you do, even if I have to take a whip to you.'

'Promises.'

'Shut up, Danny-boy. You will walk. Tomorrow, your legs will be free of encumbrance. Then we work hard to build up muscle.'

'If I have any left.'

'You do. Dad said so.'

'Then I suppose it must be true.'

She left him for a while. If Daniel needed her, he would text her on his mobile. Standing at the drawing-room window, Helen watched her dad kissing Anya. They were sitting close to each other on the erosion steps while Storm renewed his argument with the Mersey. 'Poor Dad's waiting for us all to leave,' she whispered.

The Eyes and Ears of the World entered. 'You're right,' Eva said. 'But she won't marry him. You know how . . .

metickerlous he is, wants everything right and proper. But Helen, isn't it great that he's taken to Anya? Mary was a lovely, special woman, but he couldn't carry on mourning like that.'

'He loves Anya,' was Helen's reply. 'And the sooner we're out of his way, the better.'

'Doc won't see it like that. He's very prag— what's the word?'

'Pragmatic. But they need their space, Eva.'

The older woman nodded. 'They do, and they'll get it. She loves him too, you know.'

Helen smiled broadly. 'So she should. He's wonderful.'

Eva retreated into the kitchen muttering, not quite under her breath, about that bloody dog, another towel and her best roasting tin, and people who had so little sense that they took in stray animals.

Helen giggled. Nothing changed with Eva.

Then she continued to watch her father. As soon as Daniel's legs lost their coverings and gained some strength, she would take him, Sofia and the girls back to the Wirral. The couple out there looked so right together, and Anya was a kind woman who knew her own mind. In fact, she was a bit like Mum . . .

Eva, quieter now, was having a think. She left the house by the back door and crossed the road.

'What's she up to now?' Helen wondered aloud. It was time for Daniel's snack, so she left Eva to her fate. Dad wouldn't like being interrupted. No one welcomed interruption during courtship. Now, Daniel also needed his heels rubbed, so where was that new bottle of surgical spirit?

'I need to borrow Anya for five minutes, Doc.' Eva backed off. That flaming dog, seeing her out of context, decided

474

to throw himself at her. He was wet, sandy and over-enthusiastic. 'Go away,' she shrieked. 'I've had enough.'

Andrew diverted the dog while Eva and Anya went into a huddle on the green. 'I'm asking you about that Russian beetroot soup,' Eva began.

'Ah, you will need fresh—'

'No. If Doc asks, we were talking soup. Right? Not that I'll ever make it, because I don't want beetroot on me tablecloths.'

'If you say. So what is this?'

'The other business that I asked you to help me with. Leave it. Things are different now, love. I didn't realize you and he would end up a lot more than friends. Let me be the messenger. I don't want to spoil what's between you and Doc. I mean it. Just keep your mouth shut and let me deal with it. OK?'

'OK. When will this happen?'

Eva shrugged. 'When the house is empty except for me and him. When that bloody dog's out of sight and I can concentrate.' She turned and walked back to the house. It had been one of Mary's last requests, so it had to be dealt with. And Eva would have to do it alone.

Anya watched her man as he threw a ball for the canine rascal. Mary had lived a lie, she supposed, but she'd done it for Andrew's sake as well as her own. Man and dog were being chased in by the turning flow. 'Like Mersey, life has tides,' she muttered softly. 'And poor Eva must make big tsunami wave.' Although they were closer, Anya and Andrew had not yet made love. What he was about to learn might put him off women forever. She walked back to him.

'What did News of the World want?' he asked.

'Recipe for borsch.'

'God help us,' he said. 'Come on, dog. Let's go home.'

*

Eva's mobile rang. Up here, in Doc's house, she always got a good signal. It was something to do with the river and the open sky, no buses in the way, no motorbikes, few aeroplanes and just the odd ship. 'Hello?' she screamed. 'Are you receiving me?'

'Eva, I may have lost an eardrum.'

'You what? Say again.'

'It's Ian. Lower your voice. The results are through.'

She gulped. 'Eh? Is your satellite playing up, love?'

'You were right.'

She sat down abruptly. Fortunately, she landed on the sofa. It was a weird feeling, because she'd always known the truth, but scientific proof underlined everything, didn't it? 'Well,' she breathed. 'I knew I was right, but this is really right, isn't it? This is *right* right.'

'Have they all gone?'

'Yes, he's on crutches now and doing well. His ankle will always be trouble, but he reckons he's sexy with a limp. Yes, they've gone home, and I sent Anya off, too.'

'And Dad?'

'On the beach again with that bloody hound. It's ate me best handbag. Doc bought me a new one. I think it's designer, cos I can't read the name.' She rattled on just to keep her mind busy. This was the day, the big day.

'I'll be there in half an hour. Keep my dad there. Tell him I'm on my way. And thanks for coming to me, Eva. You did the right thing, because I'm less emotional than my sisters.' He ended the call.

'Less emotional? He's as much fun as last week's cabbage, but at least he has sense.' She stood up. Over eleven years she'd waited for this, and Doc was finally as ready as he ever would be. The letter was in her new bag with the unpronounceable name. Oh, God. 'Help me, Jesus.' She walked to the window. Soon, Anya might be living here, and this had to be done first, as it might take Doc time to recover. He was walking back towards the house. Coffee. A shot of caffeine and a chunk of carrot cake might help him out a bit. Not that she was worrying about him; oh no, she didn't care, did she?

The tests were final proof. They were an undeniable medical conclusion, and Ian had been so helpful. 'Sound as a pound behind that smacked bum of a gob,' she said as she ground the beans.

When Doc was parked with his cake, his coffee and *The Times*, Eva began the business of waiting. For her, waiting was not a passive thing; she walked. Back and forth she went, a bit of a wipe of the hob, swill the sink again, go out and sweep Mary's grave. She looked down at the words on the stone, realized that her eyes were full of tears. 'You should have told him, babe. He'd never have left you, no matter what.'

'So you're talking to her now.'

Eva clutched her chest. 'That's right. Give me a bloody heart attack on top of everything else.' He hadn't heard the words she'd spoken. Had he heard her, he would have had more to say. Much more.

'Sorry. What's bothering you?' Andrew asked.

She couldn't take any more. She should wait for Ian. It needed to be done properly. 'Ian's coming,' she managed finally. Panic bubbled in her throat, and she felt sick.

'And?'

'And nothing.' She turned her back on him and began to walk away. Her legs were jelly, and her heart was certainly contemplating an excursion on the wild side.

'Eva?'

She stopped dead and waited for him. She was suddenly ill and frightened for him.

He caught up in a few strides. 'What's eating away at you?' he asked.

And in that moment, just before Ian was due to arrive,

she snapped. After eleven long years of near-patience, her rope finally ran out in these final few minutes. It was stupid, because Doc's son was coming and . . . and she hissed at her employer. 'Look in the mirror, you damned fool. Then look in the top drawer in the kitchen. For once, really examine something outside your own precious bloody misery. Be your own doctor. I'm going home. Let Ian deal with it, because I've had enough of it all. I resign.'

On her way out of her job, she almost collided with Ian. 'Sorry, lad,' she said. 'I blew up in his face. I've resigned.' She ran.

Ian found his dad in the kitchen. The top drawer was open, and he was staring into it. 'Dad?'

'I always felt that I'd seen this face before. And I had. She's the image of me. Who is she, Ian? Who is she?'

'Come and sit down. She's your granddaughter. Hang on, please.' Dad never fainted, but Ian caught him just in time. 'Come on.' He held his dad firmly. 'I don't think I ever told you, but I love and admire you so much – you've been my inspiration.' Ian helped his hero into the drawing room. After placing Andrew in an armchair, he occupied its twin at the other side of the fireplace. 'Feeling better?'

Andrew nodded.

'Glass of water?'

'No. Does she know?'

'Yes. Since she was about thirteen. Eva adopted her mother. She died when very young giving birth in Eva's kitchen. Natalie was premature, yet she survived. Lucy was my sister, and Natalie is my niece. Lucy's mother was Judith Henshaw. She went home to Nottingham and gave birth. When she eventually returned to Liverpool, you and Mum were an item. So she confided in Mum.'

Slowly, Andrew raised his head. 'Mary knew? She knew I had a daughter?' Absolute disbelief coloured his words.

'Yes.'

'But why—'

'Why didn't she say anything? Several reasons. First, she knew your nature. She realized that you would feel compelled to marry the mother of your child. Second, Judith was ambitious. She rose to dizzying heights in a London hospital, then married an American and went to live in Boston. Eva adopted Lucy. Eva knows the whole story.'

Andrew closed his eyes. The woman he had worshipped had kept this from him. He remembered her being busy with a friend in difficulty . . . And Eva had carried the weight of it alone since Mary's death. 'I was no better than my father,' he whispered. 'He had Daisy, I had Lucy. Are we absolutely sure?'

'I have the DNA. Your strands are clear. So you have seven grandchildren. My mother adored you, Dad. She could not have borne to lose you or to have you split in two. Judith didn't want you, but Mum knew you would have taken Lucy into your heart and into your home. We all have a weakness, and this was my mother's. According to Eva, Mum intended to tell you before she died, but her end arrived too early.'

Knowing he didn't dare stand, Andrew held on to the arms of his chair. 'So Judith is about my age?'

'Yes. And Lucy would have been older than Kate, but she bled to death in her teens. Natalie's something of a miracle. Eva has a letter for you from Mum written many years ago. It was written in case Mum died by accident while still relatively young. For years after Mum died, Eva tried to tell you, but she knew you would have been devastated. So she kept quiet, then approached me for the DNA testing. We decided that you were ready to move on with your life, and here I am, and here Eva isn't. Though I notice she's resigned only as far as the erosion.'

In spite of the gravity of the situation, Andrew managed

a wry smile. 'She'll never leave me. We're the best of frenemies. Under all the banter, we're brother and sister. Thank you, Ian. Glad it was you. May I ask you to leave it a few days before telling the girls?'

'Of course. I think I'd better get Eva; it's starting to rain.' He left.

Andrew still felt stunned, as if someone had punched him in the solar plexus. Why hadn't he noticed Natalie properly? Why had Mary, who was supposed to have been honest and open with him, allowed this to develop? He should have known, should have supported Judith, Lucy and Natalie. Natalie. She was standing in the doorway. 'Come in,' he said.

'I'm here to be interviewed for the position of grand-daughter,' she said, no flicker of emotion on her face. 'Gran phoned me. She's out there with your son.'

'Your uncle.'

Her mouth twitched. 'Oh, goody.'

'I'd stand up, but my legs are on strike.'

'Shall I form a picket line?'

He could even hear himself, though her voice was differently pitched, of course. She placed herself on the floor at his feet, and he looked into her eyes, his eyes. 'Do you have a CV?' he asked.

'I come highly recommended by Gran.'

'References?'

'Ten GCSEs, four A levels and a blister.'

'Too much walking?'

'Wrong shoes.'

He smiled. 'Right candidate, though. The job's yours. You'll push me round in my wheelchair when I'm old, visit me even when I'm boring, and love my dog.'

'OK.'

So simple. So easy. So bloody heartbreaking. And suddenly Eva was on top of him, hugging him and crying like

480

a child. Natalie joined in, and he, for the sake of solidarity, found himself weeping, too. Through tears and over the heads of Eva and Natalie, he saw his son in the doorway.

'I'm going, Dad. I've a suspected pneumonia in Netherton, so I'll leave you buried under women again. It seems to suit you.'

Andrew heard himself once more. Beneath the glacier, Ian had humour.

They had lunch together, grandfather and new granddaughter, though she was not really new. Eva served them, dashing the odd tear from her cheek. She was happy, because it was finally done, but she didn't want to lose her Nat. A small flame of jealousy burned in her breast, and she pushed it away. Doc would put Natalie through medical school, would guide her and help her, so—

'Eva?'

'Yes, Doc?'

'You did a grand job on this young woman. Thank you.'

It would be all right. Gran went to make the coffee.

Andrew's waiting time was similar to Eva's, though it lasted many days. He walked. He walked until he felt he couldn't take another step; even Storm was exhausted.

The letter written by a very young Mary contained few words. It told him that she loved him, that Lucy was his daughter, that Judith was going to London, that Eva would be adopting Lucy. A *post scriptum* added years later informed him of Lucy's death and Natalie's birth; it also advised him that Judith had emigrated. *I did all this because I can't lose you. It's selfish, but I want your children to be mine. Forgive me, darling.*

'We're all flawed,' he told the dog. 'She loved me too much, and I felt the same about her. She loved me enough to hide the truth for her own sake.'

Eva had done her best to comfort and reassure him. 'Judith never loved you, Doc. Very calculating girl, married real money at the finish. I hope she didn't have more kids, cos I heard she never even looked back when she handed our Lucy over. But as for Natalie – well – you'll not find a better girl anywhere.'

That was true enough. She was bright, funny, pretty and a good student. So why was he doing all this walking? Perhaps a grandchild newborn at the age of nineteen was a lot to take on board. Or perhaps Mary's long silence had cut into his soul. She hadn't trusted him completely, hadn't been perfect.

He found himself laughing. Perfect? She'd alienated plumbers, decorators and electricians by the score, while her relationship with many local shops often hung in the balance. If the milkman left yogurt of the wrong flavour, he got a flea in his ear. At work, she terrified obstetricians, clerical workers and cleaners, because she always knew best. To be fair, she usually had known best, but . . .

But he'd walked far enough. Tomorrow, Natalie's welcome into the Sanderson family would be celebrated. It was time to move on; it was time to rest his feet.

Chaos ruled, of course.

Anya, wearing a cream suit, a winning smile and with a little devil in her eyes, brought a veritable cauldron of borsch. Cries of 'What about me tablecloths?' and 'What if it goes on me parquet?' flew from Eva's mouth and out through the kitchen door.

Helen brought her children, crudités and dips, plus a husband with a ball and chain attached to one of his crutches. The chain was plastic, the ball was sponge, but the message SPOKEN FOR affixed to his chest confirmed her ownership of the poor man. The same poor man looked extraordinarily happy, which fact pleased Andrew no end.

Storm, on the other hand, was not best pleased. The quadruped young female was no more; Cassie now staggered about on two feet, but she retained the urge to poke about where she wasn't wanted. He didn't need her prodding at him, so he hid under the table in the hope that the Popes wouldn't be living here again. With tablecloths that touched the floor, he felt quite safe under cover. He was wrong.

Eliza came with Ian, their boys and a huge cake with Natalie's name iced on the top. Eva provided cooked meats, bread, small cakes and a steady flow of complaints.

Kate and Richard donated the entertainment by accident, as their trifle had not quite set, and half of it was deposited in the car, so a bit of swearing and a lot of cleaning materials accompanied their noisy comings and goings. Pam, Mary's friend of many years, dragged in two grandchildren, one son, one husband and a box of Satterthwaite's fancies. 'I hadn't time to bake,' she said.

Stuart and Colin turned up bearing Lancashire hotpot and fruit pies, while Keith warned people in whispers about his wife's moussaka. 'Too much paprika,' he mouthed.

Natalie brought just herself, and she arrived last.

As Andrew delivered a short speech, his arm round the shoulders of his new granddaughter, Cassie found Storm and the tablecloths were dragged to the floor, along with all the food. Eva screamed, 'Me parquet, me parquet!' while Andrew and Natalie sank to the floor in hysterics. Because of the borsch, it looked like a bloodbath.

Sofia stood with her back to the fire, placed two fingers in her mouth and delivered a whistle of which any Saturday afternoon Koppite at Anfield might have been proud. 'Dogs and children out in the garden with my mother.

Daniel, sit, or you may slip. The rest – get cleaning, but not Natalie. Natalie, this family of yours is crazy.'

'I already knew that,' said Natalie as she cuddled her grandfather.

He stood up. 'Come on, you. We'll buy out every chip shop within reach.'

So they ended up with fish, chips and peas followed by what was left of Eliza's cake. Andrew promised Eva that 'her' parquet would be professionally cleaned within days, and she had to be satisfied with that. Not used to satisfaction, she muttered darkly to herself for the rest of the afternoon.

There was a sing-song, of course. Anya delivered a few Polish folk tunes while Sofia tried to dance with the children. Andrew played a medley of nursery rhymes, then his 'Liverpool Song', which was to be released within weeks. Part of his Overture to an Overture, it celebrated the calibre of Liverpool life, Liverpool love, and the river that brought everyone home.

Despite the food disaster, it was the greatest party, and Natalie felt very much at home. Yes, it was a madhouse and yes, she was used to that, since Gran's home was very similar, though rather emptier. She kissed everyone goodbye and dragged her complaining adoptive grandmother out of the house. The last words Andrew heard were Natalie's. 'Will you ever learn to behave yourself, Gran?'

'No,' chorused all who remained.

At last, Anya and Andrew were alone. Natalie had gone home with Gran to prepare for her move. The bungalow, usually occupied by tenants but now uninhabited, was to be Natalie's home. She would share it with another student, one who was feeling the pinch in these grey days when education was no longer free.

Anya sighed. 'So. Just the two of us at last, Mr Sanderson.'

He nodded gravely. 'I noticed.'

'What do we do now, Andrew?'

He winked at her before lifting her in his arms. 'Do you mind?' he asked.

'No.'

He carried her upstairs and placed her on his brand new mattress. 'Anya?'

'What?'

'I think it's time I invaded Warsaw.'

extracts reading groups

competitions books new

discounts extracts extracts

competitions

books new books

events books reading groups

extracts new titles reading groups

interviews

discounts events extracts extracts events

new books events

events new interviews new books extracts

discounts extracts discounts

www.panmacmillan.com

extracts events reading groups

competitions books extracts new